Beyond Twilight

A thriller with backlash of policies

Frans Welman

Originals
(an imprint of Low Price Publications)
Delhi-110052

Published by
Originals
(an imprint of Low Price Publications)
A-6, Nimri Commercial Centre,
Near Ashok Vihar Phase-IV, Delhi-110052
Phones: 27302453
e-mail: lpp@nde.vsnl.net.in
visit us at: www.lppindia.com

First Published 2007

ISBN 978-81-88629-64-0

Printed at
D K Fine Art Press P. Ltd.
Delhi-110052

PRINTED IN INDIA

This is a fictitious story, a story that could have happened for the Nagas are real and the conflict which has been raging since the inception of India is as real as it continues; due to Great Britain which leaders then, without consulting the people, handed their Nagaland over to India.

This story that could have been and just twist in time and person could lead to irreversible change.

This book is a tribute to the resilient Naga Peoples of Nagaland, both in India and in Burma.

Though in itself the story is not real, the people are. With the people the story goes real to venture far Beyond Twilight.

Contents

Chapter 1

Prologue

"What darkness," she murmured to herself, humming the word darkness with the emphasis on dark, "what is it in me that darkness has such irresistible attraction on me?" It was not the first time she asked herself this question. When thinking time arrived to take possession of her, recurrently this question ha popped up in her mind. She called it thinking time for to her it meant that she was going into some kind of recluse. I was like going into herself and though she called it thinking it actually was more like going into hibernation. Her thinking seemed to have frozen or when still active the thoughts would take possession of her, surround her, enveloping her. Yet, the darkness she felt was nothing else but her fear, fear of dying and she sought to confront it frontally. By doing this she hoped the confrontation would set her free.

"I don't feel free, yet I am," she repeated to herself, "this is my darkness; to feel like being lost in a forest at night, hearing creepy sounds and no one there to come to my rescue. Oh God in heaven, I feel so bound. Teach me how to be free?", she said in deep prayer, praying aloud to herself while seeking the connection.

The crying Lisa had surrendered to self pity, knowing her tears would set her free, freer than her icy ways of thinking. Irrespective of what she thought she sensed it was her ritualistic way of thinking that bound her. And, she knew very well that through this ritual she felt the pattern of at least familiarity, like a route she could follow. It was not a road she wanted to wander on and, though negative in outset perhaps, it was a route she felt safe on, familiar and bad it was may be, but safe:

"I should be so more adventurous," she said out loud as she realized she was talking to herself. And, hearing her own voice, she felt like it was a stranger talking to her. Startled she shot up and giggled till tears ran over her cheeks. Astounded at first and gradually aware of her tears, she drifted off to a slumber then was sound asleep.

"For the love of Ivy," Marius exclaimed, "how can anyone tolerate this?"

"Simple," Jeanie answered dryly, "through planning followed by executing on the basis of motivation of the desire to control."

"But to this extent?", he exclaimed further, "it is like people have no conscience."

"Right," Jeanie agreed, "but then what do you think? To use people for one's own end one can only do that when one has no conscience, Marius."

"Yeah, indeed," Marius replied more inwardly like he was speaking to himself only, "you know what do these people do when they have achieved that end?", he asked.

"There is no end to get to. There is always more to achieve and to control, it does not stop at their first goal. Once the appetite is wet, those people go further and further. Only when they are stopped, it will end."

"So that is the inner motivation of a dictator?", Marius asked sternly now looking Jeanie into her eyes almost menacingly.

"Expanding motivation, feeding on itself yes," Jeanie answered, a little startled now about the way Marius changed his posture.

"Yet these small time third world dictators can only act like that when they are supported by their so called democratic counterparts of the first world," he retorted.

"No dictator can stand alone," Jeanie remarked, "they all depend on something; fear brutality meted out of their subjects is one. Another kind of motivation is the dominant relations a male or female dictator has with those operating in the background. They prop up to execute. Those people know their advantages and they maintain the status quo. It is profitable for them to keep these dictators going. For their friends in more powerful countries it is all a matter of cheap labor and cheap resources. Use the tested divide and rule method and you can get rich over the backs of others," Jeanie said and concluded, "to be rich is not the goal itself but an exponential benefit in which control is expressed self evidently. If the dictator is like a queen or king, they may even have the luster of their people paying them tributes. But then when exploitation becomes too apparent people become defiant and rise. A real dictator will be inspired by this and, using any means, will force his people into submission."

"Yes," Marius agreed, "it is obvious when you see how the people are being kept ignorant. Yet there are always rebellious sections of society, they come out to fight against their leeching suppressor, they stand up for their rights, right?", he asked.

"Right," Jeanie answered curtly.

"This is Africa, this is the Cameroons, this is the scorned people and this is the people who will fight for their rights indeed. What shall we do?", he asked.

"Stand by them?" Jeanie asked suggestively.

"That means when the going gets tough, the tough get going," he answered.

"What else is new?", she replied.

"We will leave the mopping up to our capable friends and allies Jeanie," Marius said, "I am going to have a meeting in Paris in a few days, with a representative of the Forbidden Land. Care to join me?"

"Paris?", she asked.

"Yes, Paris then Amsterdam with one of the leaders," he answered.

"I will have to see if it fits my bill, but I would like to. Are you going to see Lisa in Europe?", she asked.

"I would love to," Marius said thoughtfully, "but after that assault she witnessed, she is very unstable now. I should like to help her getting out of the doldrums. It is after all the woman I love, provided that, in our line of work, love is possible, we have long way to cover still Jeanie, a long way indeed."

"Yes, I know, I this, she is a remarkable woman my friend. So we are going to leave the Cameroons then after the meeting this afternoon? I am sick and tired of both Yaoundé and Douala man!", she added and sighed, " I am ready for some real adventure."

"I am going, that's for sure. You better take it up with your boss big mama," Marius smiled at her now.

"All right," she answered, "consider it done!!!"

"Then we will do it and there is no one who can stop me, not even my superiors, who will no doubt come up with some sort of assignment in place of what I want to do, should I be so stupid to tell them that!"

"You will take that risk?", she asked, "you might be condemned a renegade."

"What do you do for loving a woman and the case of her people but to support?", he asked rhetorically, "especially when it is a neglected case of people crying out for justice and who have been prepared to fight for their rights for over 50 years?"

"You must be right and if I am not mistaken right out of your mind," Jeanie smiled, "what is so important there?", she continued.

"To find out the truth about killings and what can be done when it is revealed who did what concerning the consequences," he answered enigmatically.

"Well, that puzzling," she laughed, "you are a handsome man and you need not be nebulous with me at all!", she said.

"The Indians suppress all kinds of information. They have been successful in keeping things out of the public eye. They have done what they liked. Under a different identity I will go and investigate about who the culprits are that killed some crucial people. This partially will determine the fate of these people aspiring the right to self determination!"

"Sounds noble, but then why should you be you doing that? You are ready to sacrifice your life and freedom for that?", she asked when looking at a nervous and serious Marius. More than just asking he definitively had suggested it to her in a way she could hardly say no, "we will go as a married couple. That way we can get into Nagaland State, Manipur or Arunachal Pradesh. We will do that," he stressed.

Jeanie had only one rebuff on that and brought it on:

"But you love that other woman, this Lisa!"

"That's right," Marius was quick to reply but smiling all over, "we go as a married couple, so I can see her!"

"I do not get it," Jeanie answered quizzically.

"Think Jeanie," Marius said then waited for her to come up with something. She did not immediately and he went on to explain: "you see Jeanie, we work together. I am invited by the Nagas to come. Who are the Indians to restrict me? So, when they create stumbling blocks, let's be clever enough to circumvent them. As a couple we can get in, so we get in. I do not see why not. Only when you find the idea repulsive to –on paper- be married to me, I understand. On the other hand what I envisage is about much more than just purpose of meeting a dear friend. And, you know that too."Well of course, I am just teasing you and also because I am jealous," Jeanie laughed out loud now.

Marius and Jeanie had known each other for years, they worked closely together and had felt favorable suspense between them, yet had never had laid a hand on each other, much less a kiss. Though it was said playfully, there was a tinge pity, in the tone of her voice. Secretly Jeanie knew she had grown closer to Marius, until that fateful day when he had excitedly told her that he had fallen in love with a girl from a far away and from a very unknown place. It was the girl called Lisa. For not showing her disappointment till she could taste her won blood, Jeanie had bitten her lip; Obviously Marius had been quite oblivious of her attraction to him. She knew that for he had never made advances to her. It was not that Jeanie had been unattractive to him, on the contrary, but Marius was a professional and would not think of mixing work with personal matters. And she represented that, especially when potential intimacy was concerned. So, he had kept his distance but she knew she did not leave him cold. She could feel that, sense that. Marius, a responsible but playful person, after all had a very serious job. Likewise Jeanie was a very well trained agent and so just for Marius to tell Jeanie he was in love could really have an impact on their mission. Should their respective governments come to know then what? Being in love meant Marius and Jeanie would be vulnerable, others could capitalize on that knowledge and certainly if they knew who the person was Marius loved. So, when Marius broke that news there were really three things that shot through her: one was that he was now lost to her, second that he would be vulnerable and third the girl he had fallen for too could become a target. These three things would have effect on their relationship, she thought. Jeanie being a very independent lady thought she would never tolerate any man ruling over her. Yet, the idea to travel as couple in itself was not a bad thing to experience either. And not even Marius, whom she held high, could dream of landing himself in that kind of a position. But now, when she agreed to go with him to that darned Forbidden Land, she would both jeopardize her job as well as her friendship. She would become a renegade from her team too, the team that deployed her on dangerous missions. Marius meanwhile was thinking too. He wanted to be with Lisa but not just because of her but because she would too be a jumping board to get close to the leaders who with their fierce and convinced resistance had been able to keep an entire army of 200.000 soldiers in check. That, in itself, he found to be an achievement of the highest order. And, since they would never be commissioned there, simply because of the disinterest lodged by their countries, who in turn acknowledged India as having a domestic problem to be solved domestically and thus without any interference from outsiders, it was out of their focus. And Marius, who was a faithful follower of his nation's policies, even tough he knew politics were played with at times, this time disagreed for he wanted to find out what really went on in this land that was shielded from onlookers, observers.

"This must have some reason,' he said to Jeanie and I am compelled to find out what makes the people not just stand up for what they think is right, but also how they have been able keep a whole army at bay. Here is much to be discovered Jeanie and as my partner now, I want you to do this with me. The best thing is to take leave. We do not have to do it right away, but surely we can plan to take leave together?"

"Okay, that should be possible. That way we should minimize the potential conflict when we do it outside the extent of our missions. It will be our own incentive then!"

"Good and agreed," Marius answered her in a tone and gave her a wink and a smile as if he had been conspiring with her and had come up with a final conclusion plus a plan to execute. Then he added daringly, "I am ready to go right now, Jeanie!

Marius rapidly finished his work that day and left his office thereafter. He knew what to do and how to prepare. The problem now was only how to get in. Booking a flight and getting visas was no problem also, but for Jeanie he could only get the same day visa if she had returned with her passport. She should get one in London he thought and would take care of it he thought while at home in his flat in Buitenveldert, near Amstelveen, and thus close to Schiphol airport, while he was getting ready he put on the news. Only listening with half an ear up and occasionally briefly glancing, he suddenly heard something strange. The newscast finished already he switched on his laptop to follow up on the internet about the news which caught his attention. He found it in one of the local dailies as suggested by teletext on TV, not as a news article about the Philippines:

News Paper report page seven local dailies:

Unknown man, non Philippino, in broad daylight shot dead in busy Manila suburb

Today in broad daylight during rush hour a well dressed gentleman was shot dead in Cubao. The older man while trying to catch a taxi at the frantically busy junction of Cubao's Quezon City on Epificio de los Santos Avenue received multiple gunshots in head and body. He was fired at from a passing vehicle and died on the spot. The killers fled the scene in a car from which they had opened fire. The police, within minutes on location could not apprehend the killers yet.

Chapter 1: Preparation: This news cast appeared in the local dailies but failed to attract sufficient attention. No wonder really that was for in Manila many such murders take place in all formats and in all venues. Though it was rather odd this kind of news reached the Netherlands nobody actually paid any attention. The same was true for the local police at first, but then the idea to find the body in such an odd situation gave room for thought. Here was an older gentleman, obviously not Philippino, well dressed, who had only a few thousand pesos on him but plenty of dollars. After they had frisked him to find some identification papers on him a check on his strange name learned he had a residence permit and had lived in the vicinity of Cubao for years. According to his papers A Baptist minister he appeared to be. So the question rose: Why would anyone want to kill a foreign protestant minister? This was what the police of Cubao were toying with:

"What is his name again?", Efren, superintendent of the Quezon City police force asked the men who had found the victim and had questioned the people who had reported the shooting. They had taken the trouble too to talk to some of the people at the shops on Epificio de Los Santos or Edsa in short, just opposite where the assault had taken place.

"A strange name Sir, not Indian at all, but he is an Indian national," Eddie, head of the Cubao police answered, his pot bellied crew beside him, "Isak Chishi Swu."

"Good heaven, what name is that? Find out everything about this man, perhaps he has been leading some terrorist drive in the South on Mindanao and helps out Abu Sayyaf under another pretense. Get onto it now," Efren looking irritated ordered the Cubao team.

"Yes Sir," Eddie said showing a surprised face as he thought that this would be rather far fetched an idea. He knew very well he was talking to a superior much higher in rank, he thought for a moment before gathering enough courage he asked Efren:

"I hope you do not mind Sir Efren, but why so much interest in this murder? We still have more than ten to solve and we are overloaded as it is?"

"Í cannot imagine you people did not come up with the same idea Eddie. You have so many strange leads already. I want to know who this man is, what he does and what he was doing here and most of all why he was killed, Eddie? Just because you have a lot of easy murders does not mean you cannot appreciate a mysterious one man!", Efren smiled ironically, clearly showing how little he thought of his local counterparts. Eddie felt the sneer of course, but did not twitch. Rather than acting against it he had learned it wiser not to go against a superior of name and fame, but to comply. Yet this time he could not help to be show interest too and reacted:

"I am glad you see the mystery of this too Efren Sir. I am highly intrigued too about why this man was murdered and in broad daylight so for everyone to see. This is no ordinary pay back or the result of gangster war. This I feel has deeper ground and when we investigate this it might lead to very unusual findings?"

"Aaahhhhhh," Efren sneered again, "so you do other things here than drinking beer and get the women who you arrest? I am glad you people are capable of thinking too," he said as he scanned Eddie's men. Pot-bellied they were indeed. The Philippino police was well known for a kind of casual behavior and had quite a bad name concerning law enforcement. Grinding his teeth over that cynical remark with his men looking on sheepishly Eddie answered:

"Oh yes Efren, as you well know we do some tricky investigative work too. How else did you think we could find the man's family? We are ready to interrogate his wife and children as we speak."

"Good, do that and keep me posted," Efren smiled, "I feel we will be quite occupied with this case for quite some time Eddie. Let's work together on this and get committed. This is an order all right?"

"Right," Eddie agreed squeezing his toes being quite elated, for he felt that this cynical way of approaching Eddie had just gotten what he wanted, a clearance to devote his time to get to the bottom if this.

"Get on to it and report to me personally every evening," Efren ordered him further more concretely.

"Without fail," Eddie smiled as he saw Efren leaving his office. Eddie directed his team to resume the investigation, but first called in the three men who had answered on the emergency call. He then ordered them to minutely report what had actually transpired on the scene:

Leave nothing out of it, not even when you think it is insignificant," Eddie said.

"We got a call and we were warned a shooting was in progress, so we jumped into the jeep to ride to Edsa/Cubao, Sir," said Juan, quite a young police officer and the only one without a belly.

"Yeah," Franco his teammate added, "when we arrived a lot of people were around shouting and gesticulating. We came there and saw this man in a three piece suit stretched out on the pavement, covered in blood. I counted 16 shots Sir," he said.

"We began to examine the body while Juan asked some questions," said the older policeman by the name of Alphonse.

"Yeah I asked what happened and excited bystanders said that a Ford Fiera had stopped in front of this man and while going down for cover because of the machinegun shooting at him, just at him, they could not see who was in the Ford. The man was with these people here and he pointed to two young men who looked shattered. They said their father was shot and the shots were directed only at him. This way it was easy to get his name. The young men are no Philippinos either but they study here. The victim is 72 years old. He originally is from India somewhere, but strangely enough he has a Bangladeshi passport."

"No sign of the Ford Fiera?", Eddie asked.

"No sign but someone could take down the number plate and here is the number," Alphonse grinned.

"That is good, ask our men to run it through our system. Has the body been sent to the morgue for an autopsy?"

"Yes already," Juan nodded, "the results will be here tomorrow."

"Okay men, I will go and check on the body. Do we have any other lead? Remember head office will be on our tail. Get our detective on it rapido," Eddie commanded, "we are not equipped for that. We need a man who can interpret the leads. Let's first find out who this man really is. Let's get to his house and speak with his family, alright? You and you go," Eddie said to Juan and Alphonse as he readied himself to come along with them.

Moments later they were on their way to the suburb where the family of the murdered person lived. They took the two young men with them. They came to one of the so called villages in Greater Manila where the houses and neighborhoods by gates with guards are shielded from direct exposure. In this case the village had two gates, one on the main through road and one on the street of the centre of the small town, a suburb. It was a busy road which led them there. After they passed the Santa Lucia intersection with its two large department stores, called shopping malls, they reached the main gate and stopped to show their credentials to the guards. Since this was a rather large village those who lived there and visitors without transport of their own could either walk or could take an available tricycles. For a small fee of course a number of men were waiting in line to take passengers to the required address. Instead the policemen asked directions and drove off to the house. When they found it, they landed right into quite a commotion there as at least some twenty people had gathered outside. Undeterred they introduced themselves and told the family the purpose of their visit. A middle aged man then took the policemen aside and said cautiously and with tears in his eyes:

"We are all shocked and in mourning here now you know. Ask me what you want to know, I can probably answer most questions," he explained.

"This is not going to be easy," Jose one of the two policemen began, "let us first condole you and your family with your loss."

"Oh thank you very much," the man answered, "we need that now. His demise is a terrible loss indeed."

"Please tell us more about that," Jose prompted him.

"Well, he was a leader, our leader and one that has led us for so long. Not only when we were resisting the invasions of the Indian Army but also now that we experience some peace because of the cease fire, he leads the peace negotiations with the Indian Government too. And now he is gone," the man softly said, his head down in remorse.

"We know you are not Philippino, bur then where are you actually from? I do not understand what you are talking about. Resisting invasion?", a bewildered Jose asked with Eddie listening intently.

"I am sorry, you could not know of course. We are Nagas and we live in what is now India and Burma. The Indians and Burmese want us to be part of their countries, but since the British colonialists left and those two nations were formed, our people did not want to be part of those nations. The Indians then invaded and since then we defended. You can call it war since 1954 and now our leader has been shot dead here in Manila. What do you think of this?", he asked Jose and looked at him.

"It is too early to tell, but if what you say is true the finger points into a direction. I am sure our bosses will call on the Indian Ambassador here, but let me tell you this. I have never heard about a people called the Nagas and certainly not about a war which lasted for so long. Your people are here and you are a Naga, how come you chose to live here and not in Nagaland?"

"It is a long story and we are quite willing to disclose all if it does not jeopardize our residence permit. There is so much to tell to put you on the track of the prospective assassins," the Naga man said.

"We will report all you said to our superiors and we will let them handle it. This is much bigger than an open and shut case," Jose concluded and soon after the two left. Eddie let them go to report to Efren, but stayed behind to get to know some more. He was hooked on the puzzle in front of him and felt the urge to unravel this enigma. When he left the family to their mourning he hurriedly left to go to the morgue. He wanted to see the slain man. When he arrived the coroner called him and mumbled something he did not understand. Only when the man had calmed down something began to dawn on him and a plan took shape in his mind. He had an idea how to get to the culprits. But, in order to get things straightened out properly, both the coroner and Eddie would have to be tightlipped for a while. Eddie and the coroner talked lengthily and came to an agreement. Then only an excited Eddie left the morgue.

Away from Quezon City, in fact in Mabini so downtown Manila Bailung had an ice-cold beer in his hand and a woman next to him. Here, enjoying himself in the remnants of what once was a tourist trap called the tourist belt and under the smoke of Intramuros, the old walled city of the Spaniards, he smiled. He smiled but it was a sour smile. He had done what he was required to do and no one would be able to get him. He could not be traced and he was pretty sure of that, he thought. Now looking just like an ordinary man, one who could hardly speak tagalong and was easily seen as a foreigner when speaking with an accent of an Indian foreigner, he kept quiet but acted like a tourist with a strong zest for women who were rampantly on offer here..

"Hi man, do you like chicks?", the barkeeper asked him smiling a significant smile, "very cheap for you my friend."

"Yeah sure," Bailung answered and felt it was time for a nice reward.

"You look schmuck. Do you see that girl there? She has been eyeing you already and you can get her for the night. She is good man, if I had the money I would take her myself," he joked and winked at Bailung. Bai, as his friends called him, was not worried about the money. He got paid handsomely and could afford anything quite easily now. The reason why he could not be caught was, he thought, because no one had actually had seen him. It was Jackie, her nickname, the assassin who had actually done the precise shooting. Bailung had been her planner, her guard and her get away. Bai was once an Indian covert agent but years ago because of an very unfortunate mistake had left the service and gone drifting. Born in the Philippines it was because of this unfortunate happening in Rwanda that he could not refuse to be commissioned to guide Jackie to the place where they should eliminate the required man. Bailung had been working for weeks to get it organized before Jackie flown in to do the job. Bai had had paved the way for her and when he had planned it all he had signaled Sean. Now in this Mabini bar and surrounded by women who smelled his money he thought of Jacky who, he was certain, was about to board a plane to wherever she wanted to go. He also knew that Jacky would disappear to never been seen again. That was the plan. Bailung was here only to wrap things up and to see to it the police would not get to nosy. He knew this was the weakest point in the plan for, should the police indeed decide to investigate then of course they would find out the deceased man was no other than Isak Chishi Swu the president in exile of the Government of Nagaland, president over a people that since the inception of India has been fighting for its own independence.

Bailung did not work for any government but for what could be called an organization of assassins. This operation was involved in meeting the needs of those who, for fear of being discovered, wanted to eliminate their adversaries. Jacky and Bailung were hired by Sean for the sole purpose of actually assassinating Swu. Neither Bailung not Jacky had any idea who Swu was. At that point in time they had no knowledge of his importance. But when Bai was on the prowl to find out about this man and is routines he soon learned about Nagaland and the fight for freedom

Swu people were engaged in. As the mission was accomplished now it was his task to check on the aftermath. Because this murder had to be concealed no trace of who were involved should be left for the police to go on about. By those who had given him this contract, Sean in fact, this was as important as the murder itself, he was assured. So, here he was now, unwinding and with some gorgeous girls around him to play with and to entertain him. Yet he was not quite at ease, there were a few disturbing things on his mind. One of them was that he was not entirely certain if the man was dead or not. Sure, when Jacky shot him he had fallen and he also had seen the bullets riddling Swu's body, but was he dead?

As she read a newspaper which on page seven had a small report on what she had just done a few hours ago, Jackie's flight was called.

Very efficiently done indeed, she said to herself and smiled; a piece of cake it was. Well prepared Bailung, she complimented him. Jacky, a very good looking woman of Latin background, but of Dutch nationality, could easily pass for a Philippina but in this case she had not needed that for the glass in the Ford Fiera had been darkened so anything bystanders could see was the nuzzle of the machine gun she had used. She had painstakingly avoided killing anyone but her target and she had done that efficiently. To elude all suitors Bailung and Jacky had fled but for only a mile ahead where they had switched cars and again switched with another near Quiapo, the heart of old Manila. From there they had gone to the Manila Hotel where they, as a couple, had shared a room and where she had shown herself as a classy lady. But then after the deed was done and they had checked out they had taken a taxi to the airport. Passing Intramuros Bai was dropped at Roxas Boulevard to check into a hotel there and sent Jacky on her way to the airport alone now. Just a small kiss among professionals and no strings attached after payment and she was off, leaving Bailung to wrap up. On the plane Jacky smiled to speed off to Bangkok for a debriefing, then straight to Amsterdam after that, she rehearsed in her mind and thought: I will get back to being a call girl for a while.

That is a good cover indeed! The flight to Bangkok on Thai Airways took less than three hours and Jacky smiled all the way. I love it when things are dangerous, she thought. I am sure I will be caught eventually, she laughed. Then a serious thought enveloped her: 'this should be my last time and if I do not stop this, I will end up dead.

Bai meanwhile tasted the Forbidden fruit of the Philippines he knew so well. Not looking for possible trouble, he was in for a messy encounter with on of the women on offer. Messy only of course because of his likes and dislikes no woman dared to say no to when he was in a mood, not in the Philippines they dared to object. Should there be any doubt just raising the price would settle it for practically no woman would actually say no to the extra income. In fact Jacky was the only professional woman who had ever said no to him. Bai had known Jacky for quite some time. In comparison to him she was quite a remarkable lady. Jacky, a woman working for a high class on call bordello but always in command, had made it known to him from day one that he could forget about anything. Jacky was clear on this for she would do not for money or not as a reward for a job well done. She even went as far as threatening to kill him if he would ever try anything on her. Though Bailung was a well trained man, agile and versatile in almost every environment, he knew he should try to match Jacky. He knew her capabilities and did not dream of doing something with her. Oh, the desire was there, but over the years it had become dormant, almost like it did not exist. Yet, every time they had contact, his feelings flared. Especially so this was when she dressed up in her assault outfit. She actually changed from a classy woman in business suit into a cat like creature capable of doing anything she felt like. While a few girls were physically seeking his attention he remembered he had seen her changing and did recollect how fiery he felt and when Jacky casually had taken off her suit. Seeing her in just bra and panty as she discarded her heels then her nylons and garter, she had only laughed at him then smiled while saying these memorable words to him: 'Yes Bailung you can glimpse, but you will never touch. You are on my team, so we will never be close personally. You will be professional at all times. If you can't do that I will report to Sean, your good friend, and he will see to it that you are fired as my partner!' Oh, Bai knew he could not bear that, the thought alone made him shiver. So he had pleaded with her and in the process she had practically made him her slave. But now, in Jacky's image he was among women, gorgeous Philippina's and the thoughts of Jacky faded into how he was going to ride one of them, perhaps in the way like he imagined to ride Jacky. Finishing his beer after having made up his mind Bai paid the bartender and winked at a young woman next to him. Elated, she reacted as he took her to his room in a not so classy hotel in Mabini. The woman, a girl perhaps still for she could not have been more than twenty to twenty two, showed herself to be quite willing. She had reassured Bai that she could and would give him a splendid time. And, if he so desired, she would be at his disposal all day and all night. Before they left she had winked as she teased him saying she would much easier wear him out that he her. As they walked to his hotel Bai imagined it was actually Jacky on his arm but he had kept. It was not her clothes that gave Bai the idea of being with Jacky, but her face and features and he decided to buy her some mantle piece, a garter belt and some nylons too. The girl giggled for he not just suggested that but commanded her to do so. But he did not have to do that and he knew for she instantly realized that whatever he bought for her she could keep. Happily surprised she saw Bai looking approvingly in the fitting room as he saw her new outfit to realize it close to he image of Jacky he had in mind.

"You are mine girl," he had said and she had answered him with a laugh as she, before putting on the business suit, showed him the new lingerie:

"But of course!", she reacted, "you hired me to be yours so I will do everything to make you feel good."

"Okay, this looks quite good on you, now let's go and celebrate," Bai said and brought her to a liquor store where he bought a few bottles to enhance the celebration.

Jacky on her approach to Bangkok thought back on the successful job. Her job as a high class escort was a perfect cover for these important assignments. She was good in slipping in and out of roles at will. She would not be missed at the agency she worked for there would always be someone who could act as a stand in, not just in time but also in appearance. She received here orders through the manager and owner of Bangkok-London-Amsterdam Girls, pleasure agency, it's Amsterdam name was The Bordello.

In Bangkok Sean, the owner of the international agency was ready to fetch Jacky from the airport and her heart jumped when she thought of him. Sean after all was her lover, her man, and really the only person who could assign her to commit herself to the work they had set out to do. Though successful in most of what he had done, there was something about him now which made both of them think that things should change. Together, Jacky and Sean were a perfect but quite an odd couple. Quite complementary to each other out in the open, nobody could have pictured them as being in love. And in fact nobody actually knew they had much more than a working relationship. At the agency she did her tricks on a regular basis and Sean, while there, was not seen to treat her any different from any other girl. The success of the international agency Sean knew was based on mutual trust regarding the appointments for the women, the dependability of the women and the high ethics of all had regarding their privacy. Consequently, the women and the personnel of the Bordello could talk about anything but their privacy. That was the unwritten rule. So, while on the job and quite openly talking about the dynamics, no one would attempt to pry into the private life of any of the girls or the managers. This made it possible for Jacky and Sean to be together whenever they wanted. But what was all this secrecy for? Most women would be proud of having a sound relationship and loved to share details with their friends. Not so in the case of Sean and Jacky. Oh, this was not because Jacky was a high class prostitute, one who would escort the top brass of the commercial circuits, or the politicians and celebrities. No, it was purely because of the covert work both of them were involved in. Thinking back on her latest assignment Jacky wondered why Sean had taken it on. Since she had to come out from Amsterdam then there had not been time but she was certain she would talk to him about it in full. When he had come up with it, he had only given her details to consider her motivation to work with Bailung. And he had assured her it was to be done as fast as possible. Because Jacky had faith in Sean she had not questioned anything. But now with Bangkok in sight, she wanted get into this. No more secrecy, she said to herself, this time I want to know all about it. And on top of that this work, in more ways than one, was very dangerous too. It is time Sean and I will take on a different role. This time, and she beamed thinking of that, the role of two people in love, Sean and I two people attached to each other, with nothing to be ashamed about. I am getting on in age. I want a more regular life. Sean should commit himself too, she murmured as the plane commenced its descent into Bangkok Airport.

And there he was, she had just picked up her luggage from the conveyor belt and cleared customs when she saw him standing there and smiling at the left side of the arrival hall of terminal one.

"Hello darling," Sean greeted her with a broad smile on his face and moved forward to embrace her in full, "all went well?"

"Without a glitch, Sean, I am sure the news did not reach here?"

"Only what has been sent to me from the local papers, good work my love," he said and winked, "you did an excellent job. I would not have expected anything else by the way," he said and laughed, but Jacky did not. Not reacting to his laughing they way he did and expected, she said:

"Let's go sit and talk Sean, I have been thinking!"

"Okay, I like a woman who thinks," he reacted, still in good mood, "here at the airport or later in town when you have freshened up?"

"Now," Jacky answered to his surprise.

"Sounds serious darling," Sean answered arching a brow.

"It is and it is not, depends how you look at it man," Jacky smiled.

"Okay, let's go to the restaurant and have a drink there, all right?", Sean suggested.

“Fine,” she answered as Sean took her by the arm and pushed the cart which had her suitcases on it to the elevator, “lots of places between terminal one and two on the departure level,” he said.

“I know that Sean,” Jacky said as they walked over to a Japanese joint where Sean ordered sake. Once they were seated and relaxed, Jacky felt nervous. They could really talk about everything, she knew, but for some reason they had never actually talked about the assignments; neither about the ones she had been commissioned to do nor his’. Now she wanted to know but was aware that Sean could see this as a breech of trust, like it was something to question him on.

“Why is it that this old man had to be killed, Sean? I am pretty sure I should like to know this time. Was he an important person? Why did he have to die? Who are behind this? We are so close so I think I am entitled to know. We should not have any secrets for each other anymore man!”

“What happened to you my woman, my Jacky,” Sean reacted, eyebrows raised in surprise and looking at her like he saw a new Jacky, “these are a lot of questions!”

“Yeah, but I like you to answer them. Take your time. I have come to a point that knowing we are so close, I want to see a future with you, so I want to know it all.”

“Of course darling, but I cannot tell you all just yet. This man had to die to create a situation, one that will change things for a specific people and might lead to a big change for others too. Much more I cannot say yet. But, indeed let’s talk about us now.”

“Not so fast Sean,” Jacky cut in, “since there is only that very short report in a local daily, how can you say this murder will lead to a big change? In Manila there are homicides every day. I am sure the police have no time to investigate them all and this being a foreigner to them would not only grab their interest slightly more. To them this murder would only be a nuisance for a lot of work has to be done like finding out who this man is. I don’t think they really want that unless they get some info from abroad to oblige them to get active. Sean my man, I did not question the assignment, I trust you, but do realize that I hate to pull the trigger on innocent people. I did not have the feeling this man was guilty of anything. I took great pain in being precise and to hit only him, his family sons I think were with him. Considering I was your tool in this, I felt taken aback with the feeling of hitting on an innocent man. This dawned on me when I pulled when I fired at him. Now tell me man, what is this all about?”

"Hmmmmmm," Sean reacted, hand on his chin, "you have been thinking indeed. Let me first tell you that I wanted to talk to you too. We have made enough money to live peacefully and in relative wealth, so I was thinking to leave this trade for good and sell the business. It was an energetic way of doing things and get connected too but I am tired of buying and selling and I love you too much to let things go out of hand. You are talking about a future together and it is what I want too."

"What?", Jacky exclaimed, "you are going to sell?"

"It is ours Jacky," he said, "so I like you to be with me in this. I do not like you to do tricks anymore. This was good to get to know things and as a cover up, but now I think we should not jeopardize anything anymore. We should come to a stage where we secure what we have together, all right?"

"Well Sean, it is what I want too of course and I am glad you mentioned that, but do not evade what I asked you. Who is behind this possibly senseless killing?", she asked.

"No, no, no, I did not mean to evade. You may know but not everything for if we ever get caught on this, then I do not want you to be implicated. I will take fuli responsibility for all actions then."

"My God man, this sounds serious. So, there is much more behind this?"

"There is," Sean confirmed.

"Then tell me," she demanded.

"Oh, I will," he smiled, "but not here. I will say now only that it is quite a story, one I think you will like. I think you will approve of my decisions. Come, let's go, not to the agency here, but let's check into a hotel. There we can talk. First though I have to call the agency and see to it all is running like clockwork. I do not want anyone to think I am not available," he concluded.

"Okay do that and them I will be all ears!"

"Alright," Jeanie said, "I will do it. I will come with you. I have to arrange it though. Mind you, only in public we will act like husband and wife."

"I will get the passports made," Marius smiled.

"You do just that then," Jeanie smiled back at him, knowing he would be the fine gentleman who would unfortunately play his part well.

How he could organize passports? Simple that was for Marius. He had access to all official and unofficial information. In his capacity could easily get papers when he needed to go under cover. Since it was his aim to do just that, this is what he had in mind.

Marius was captivated by the predicament of the Nagas and with Lisa as a person. He felt compelled to act, though he knew very well too that he had to implicitly turn against the Government of India and thus would jeopardize the existing relationship between his country and that country. 'That was primarily a trade relationship,' he thought. Since the Netherlands was such a small country with a good track record on human rights, it would not be able to intervene into the conflict on that premise alone. Regarding this its dependence Marius knew it surely could not act on its own either. To encourage India in earnest to seek peace, there would be quite a number of other nations needed; this included the Indian civilians themselves too. Marius did wonder thought how the Indians had been so successful in keeping each and everyone out of the Naga Homeland.

"How it is possible India could keep this long war from being noticed, is beyond me Jeanie," he mentioned aloud to her, "the whole world should have known about it and considering the graveness should have done something. If only to press India to live by the human rights principles it had agreed on through the United Nations, sooner or later it would concede."

"I have been reading up," Jeanie answered, "and I cannot understand that this grotesque war cannot be won by the Indians. I am not saying they should, the Nagas have every right to determine their own future, but just to think that the Indians cannot crush them is incomprehensible, don't you think?"

"I think the Nagas really have invented guerilla warfare you know," Marius said, "most of these 200.000 or so Indian soldiers have no training or motivation to fight against the Nagas. They are, I am told, outwitted and outmaneuvered. The Nagas can fight and disappear, while the Indians occupy and defend what they control, but cannot really engage. They then take it out on civilians and so the Nagas are furious because the Indians apply the low intensity conflict measures, LIC, like the Americans call it. This means they punish civilians for the achievements of the Naga army. Many were killed because the Indians burned villages and fields, so crops and no food and the people had to flee into the forests. They tortured villagers and killed a few here and there to force the villagers so they talked about the hide outs of their Naga soldiers. However, whatever the Indian Army tried, they could not crush the Naga Army and this led to frustration of both the ordinary soldiers but the leadership too. Eventually, around, 1995 the generals of the Army advised their Government to change their tactics and so to come to the negotiating table. They said: 'this is not a law and order problem, it is a political problem and should be handled politically.' One of them even is quoted to have said: 'we can only win this war against the Nagas, if we annihilate them all.'"

"This is really a grave situation. The Naga people have been living with 200.000 Indian soldiers, did you say?" Jeanie asked in a tone she thought she might have misunderstood.

"Right," Marius replied, "indeed, from around 1954 some 200.000 soldiers have been there since the war began in earnest."

"So, more that 50 years now?", Jeanie asked.

"Yes sure," Marius replied, "it may be the longest war of our time and with so few people knowing about it, right or wrong, I admire these Nagas for their perseverance. I admire them for being able to hold their ground against an, in comparison, incredibly powerful nation called India."

"Yeah, and they are tribal people, people who until recently had only weapons like spears and knives and no fire power?", Jeanie smirked.

"That's right," Marius laughed, "incredible don't you think? They learned from the British fast enough. They saw the light when they were sent by British to the trenches of France during the First World War against the Germans. Later they also participated in the second world war."

"Well to hold out for over 50 years earns my admiration too," Jeanie smiled, "and I am all for it now to go and see what we can do," she said quite convinced now.

"Yeah, Jeanie," Marius nodded.

"I have to go to Paris and London. You will make the arrangements for next week then I will make sure I can go. You are sure we can go as a married couple?", Jeanie asked.

"Sure thing," he answered, "I have been talking to some experts. We will not apply for any remote area permit, for that might only wake up the sleeping dogs. Some people in Nagaland and of the Naga International Support Center in Amsterdam assured me that this is possible now. They gave me contacts of their friends who will receive us in Guwahati, Assam. From there we will get access to these permits I am told, so. tt should be fine," Marius said.

"You want to go and be with the Naga Army too?", Jeanie asked.

"Of course, but I am sure there will be a program lined up. I can make it so that it is absolutely necessary for our intelligence to know what goes on there. It is about Burma too you know and for that country a lot of attention is raised. Aung San Su Kye won the Nobel Peace Price yet still the world turns a blind eye on the terrible suppression leading to untold misery. I feel we have to do something to shake that unfavorable balance," Marius informed some more.

"Right then, I am off. I will see you next week. Take care of the preparations," she said and turned away from him to leave. Marius blew her a hand kiss when he saw her looking back for a moment when she passed through the door. They both smiled knowing that things would work out wonderfully well.. This was going to be a fine opportunity to do something worth while for a change, Marius thought and smiled. All this defensive behavior to savor the status quo is boring at times. Not that he was out of suspense, on the contrary, but to Marius it seemed that there was lack of purpose. There was no progress in anything he did and he was no youngster anymore. In his late thirties he wanted some prospects, yet felt he was cleaning up on things other people had messed up on. And then those politicians with the hunger for power were destabilizing things to make some profit themselves, of course under the pretense it would be for the common good. Marius was loyal to the policies of his country but he knew he could not always be. More often nowadays he was so with grinding his teeth. So to him it was no surprise he wanted to jump at this fine opportunity so as to strike a difference. He felt good in trying to destabilize with the aim of breaking through the deadlock the status quo. So, with something of his own making Marius wanted to go and do something significant. Here he was wrapping things up in Yaoundé, the capital of the Cameroons and Jeanie had just left to return to London. Oh how he loved Africa, the continent which felt like the original heartbeat. On his way to Douala soon, he would spent a last night in that harbor city to catch a few people and to experience a fiery night out, one like he remembered from ages ago when he had set foot on African soil for the first time and had been seduced by a slippery African maiden. In a way this continent, which many nations considered a lost continent, vibrated with life. Rough edges there were of course, as the people were not as refined as in Asia and other like some European countries, where in contrast to the coarse way of expressing prominent in the USA the intrinsic courtesy and regard for life was what had really hit him. This was true in Africa, Asia and South America for the courtesy of the indigenous peoples he had felt bubbling here, he felt good with. True of course this was not to be found in the cities that much, but when the varnish of modern and perhaps imitated western life was uncovered, the truly sensitive and sensual human being was there. This sensual human being he dearly admired. People like that were straight, honest and did not have double or triple agenda's. Deception was mostly absent, unthought-of of, and when there was a reason for anything faulty it had an embedded cultural background and could be explained. The lovely Jeanie had gone, his partner whom he loved as a friend, and now alone and on the last leg of his long African journey, Marius had finally time to think back on his encounter with Lisa.

In his spare time Marius had been studying this long term but unknown conflict and had come to the conclusion that it was rather incomprehensible the Indians had been so successful to keep it from the public eye. 'Was it because human rights were only important to those who knew how to pursue them?', he wondered. This was mostly applicable to countries where people had the knowledge and the access to sources, where they actually could handle their affairs in such manner that attention would be drawn to them, he knew. Those people in fact could materialize these rights because they could stand up for them and were recognized. Yet in many other countries this was futile, he knew that very well too. And, for these peoples in the northeast of India there was no way they could do that, they were not recognized as being part of the international community. They were acknowledged as rebels against their government and so a domestic affair. And, their plight was not spectacular, not fashionable and perhaps not sexy enough to get involved in. This is going to drastically change you know, he thought, and I will personally see to it this is going to happen. He was alone now and with his mission in the Cameroons almost over, he had time to think. Lisa, not her real name of course, shot into his mind again. Her real name was concealed, not just because it was difficult to pronounce for Westerners like Marius, but also and really primarily because with a different name she was less easy to trace. He recalled how he met her in Amsterdam that spring on a day when the sun had been shining unusually bright, just like on a midsummer's day. Lisa had been there for a purpose. Her purpose was to connect with agencies that had knowledge and interest to offer her people advice and possibly help on matters of drug addiction. Next to their long term occupation the Indians had unleashed psychological warfare on to the people and there were many casualties already, victims of aids and drugs. So, on the premise of seeking assistance to help those who had fallen for the dreams projected on to their minds, which had ruined them mentally and physically, she was here for to get expertise. It was not the only thing she was doing in the Netherlands. She also took the opportunity to take out a few words on the plight of her unknown people by contributing examples of how the Indians had been treating her people, how they were wearing them out mentally and physically.

Thought she did get some attention, it was a pity than none of her stories had any bearing on impartial validation which, in the end, could not be organized. Other than the distorted reports in the Indian press, a press which had little eye for the history of this raging conflict, there was not much to go on for those who listened to her. Yet at home every day she had to face the young people, who felt they had no hope to a future so commonly experienced and expected by her hosts. Though the people she had met were understanding and friendly they could not quite relate to her stories. But Marius was captivated when he listened to Lisa, whose real name she revealed to him was Shilu.

"You know, Marius," she had said, "when your whole life has been one of occupation, you do not know anything else. You see soldiers who treat you like dirt practically every day and you see our fighters who are among us enjoying a cease fire with peace talks which do not seem to lead to any kind of agreement. Then you do not know what to think or do. You have no real prospect. Many of the young people, our youth, they are teenagers really, feel hopeless. They try to get some sense into their lives. They dream away but drugs are readily available and are cleverly distributed by ruthless people who are also connected to the authorities. This is the world we live in, Marius. It is hard to describe what it feels like when you can be picked up and tortured for no reason at all. Out future is bleak. We do not know how or when we can begin to function normally. When here I sense, no I feel the freedom we are fighting for. But here it is taken for granted, it is not cherished. Please realize Marius, we do not want to be Indians. We do not want to be part of an oppressive regime."

That the regime oppressed was something Marius wanted to find out personally, both emotionally and physically. Marius listened and looked at her. She was quite an attractive woman, not so much because she looked good, but because of the way she laughed, talked, exclaimed and yet behaved like a lady, a true lady in but in jeans and very much her own person as well. He remembered how he had liked her instantly. A flirt she was at times, at least he thought. He had intended to ask her about it, but she had been reluctant. Reluctant, he thought, for it could be part of her culture to be open and communicative. Perhaps what he felt as flirting had nothing to do with it. So, with this on his mind, he thought it better to remain reserved. When after a meeting they had ended up on a terrace outside a modern type café in the old sector of town near the Jodenbreestraat, opposite the Rembrandt Huis, Marius had smiled. He could not help to do this as he looked at her when she had suggested having a beer to unwind a little. Marius had only nodded, but had felt her zest for life. Vibrantly, with a golden smile, she talked and could talk about matters on every level. Deflecting the chit chat and possible flirting he wanted to know about the negotiations between the Government of India and the Nagas and he had asked her rather suddenly:

"To me it looks like that little country of yours does not make much headway. The Indians are stalling for time? Who are these negotiators of yours that they do not demand the Armed Forces to be withdrawn from their lands?"

"First a toast," she had said after the beers arrived, "this is to you Marius. I toast to you and your naughty smile, a smile that is laced with serious undertones!"

"Hmmmmm," Marius reacted, "I do not think you can appease me with that flattery. Tell me all about it. I feel I should like to come to your place," he said, smiling now too.

"Most of it you won't believe," Lisa began teasing him some more. You cannot reliably check anything I say."

"Oh, and why is that?", Marius asked.

"What I will tell you cannot be verified. Oh, the historical facts can of course, but even those too are disputed. My point is, when people live in isolation and the invading nation prohibits anyone from coming in, nothing can be checked. Since the invading nation is a respected member of the United Nations, the data of that nation are not checked but are taken for granted. Whatever we say is held against those official data, is to be proved or we are not believed, but tell me Marius, how to prove it?"

"Oh, are your data than much different from theirs?", Marius asked.

"Officially our data don't exist. What we put forward does not become official. What to do?", she asked as she looked at him.

Marius could hardly believe what she actually said. In this world there is a country which prohibits people from entering, a democratic country and a country where, according to Lisa, atrocious things happened and are happening:

"Those casualties, those events are not documented?", Marius asked.

"Of course they are, but by us, but no journalist can check them. This is a militarized country. You can only listen to the people if you get in or talk to them outside Nagaland," Lisa answered, looking as she sat opposite him, quite relaxed and talking in matter of fact manner

"I will go in," he heard himself saying, "if you tell me all about it, okay?"

"It will be my pleasure to do so. Now?", she asked and mockingly smiled at him as she was not quite certain if he had been serious about it.

"Why not," Marius replied.

"Okay," she said thoughtfully, thinking for a moment where to begin, "to understand what happened and what compelled the Indians, we have to go back in time. We do not have much time right now and it is a long story. You will not remember everything, so make some notes," she suggested.

"That goes without saying," he smiled recognizing Lisa's orderly attitude.

"First let me tell you Nagas are a free people, we feel free. We are friendly but we do not like to be told by anyone what we should do or how we should live. When we talk about why Nagas resist, this is the essence of the conflict. It really boils down to that. The Nagas will not bow down just to be led into submission. In fact we grow strong when being pushed and suppressed. If you care to understand you must learn about our culture and our history?", she asked.

"Are you saying you cannot tell me in an hour or so?", Marius asked.

"Only as an introduction, a brief introduction," Lisa answered nodding.

"Of course when you give me a long lecture I will be overfed. I will not be able to take in all this new information, I will fall overboard," Marius smiled.

"Okay, a brief history and cultural intro then," she smiled.

"Catch my attention and try to hold it," Marius tempted her.

"The British called us headhunters you know," she began, smiling but negating his challenge, "the British were the first people to subdue us, colonize us. Other peoples before them were not successful. After some sixty years of fighting some Naga tribes gave in. The majority never did and the British called them Free Nagas."

"Headhunters?", Marius remarked frowning.

"We don't think so, but the British called us that," she laughed.

"You were actually taking heads?", Marius went on.

"Yes we did," Shilu said, "tell me Marius what do you people do with enemies that you killed for reasons of your own justification?", Lisa retorted.

"Hhhmmmmm," Marius replied while thinking.

"You bury them and honor your own warriors, but discard the slain enemies, right?"

"I am afraid so, yes," Marius replied.

"For the Nagas the soul as matter is in the head. Slain enemies would contribute to the soul matter of the village. Oh yes it was primarily villages which battle it out with each other. The point is, it was a rather local and it was not like what the Nagas experienced later from the British. The British killed, captured, sentenced and executed, their enemies killed and buried after they fought. The Nagas did not understand the British did not honor their enemies. The British in turn did not grasp the Nagas either. They were abhorred with our practices and called us headhunters. We never thought of ourselves as people who hunted heads though."

"Well I would not know," Marius answered truthfully for he knew little about indigenous peoples. This was because he, as an agent, moved in all circles, but hardly related to or operated among indigenous peoples. This Lisa intrigued him very much though.

"The Nagas are a very cultural people, you know Marius," Lisa said proudly while Marius watched her getting excited. Though he was all ears, he also felt attracted. She radiated, yet was in command. While talking she studied his face primarily to check if he kept attention.

"Let me tell you something about the Naga history and with that, the culture!", she said. "Please do," Marius replied sitting up.

"From our oral history it is known we came centuries, millennia ago, from around Tibet to eventually settle in the Naga Hills. We were all together then, but in two waves the first one from what is now called Burma or Myanmar and the second in India's Manipur, our people dispersed. From there they settled in villages on hilltops and developed their own subcultures. All of them expressed themselves in stone and wood. They made menhirs to demarcate the gate of a village or to commemorate important events. The dispersal stone at Makhel in northern Manipur bears witness to that Marius. This was a thousand years or so ago. So, no wonder eventually some forty tribes were formed. Tribes they are though we are all interconnected through history and through common norms and values, yet they developed their own identities. This you can see in their colorful attires and ornaments," Lisa said.

"I see," was all Marius could say as he sat on the tip of his chair. Though noisy traffic and people were passing by, Marius did not hear it. Lisa quite relaxed continued:

"Most tribes, villages really, have a kind of democratic government. The people, through tribal councils, decide what they would do and how to do it. We have private and communal lands and because of this system no one could go hungry or was poor. A system of feasts, called feasts of merit, saw to that. From a cultural economical and political point of view these were important elements in the fabric of our societies. Feasts of merit were thrown by those who could afford it, by the so called rich," she smiled.

"In a democratic society you had rich people too?", Marius asked.

"Oh yes, some people are more clever, have skills others do not have, use their lands better, or are better traders. In short they accumulated wealth, but they did not do so to hoard or scrooge. They did so to share, for that brought prestige. Prestige is the actual currency. A feast of merit is shared by all, all in a village participated."

"You mean that all food and drink would be supplied by those who throw that feast?"

"Precisely," Lisa laughed her attractive but teasing laugh, "it was an opportunity to prepare for the finest of all, both in looks like attires and jewelry and in showing skills in dancing and music. A feast like that was a big cultural happening Oh, I am sure you would be intrigued by it."

"Though I cannot imagine, I am sure there would be a lot of merrymaking," Marius laughed as Lisa said:

"Oh yes, and the rice beer would flow as well." She took a zip from her glass, "rice beer also was much more than a substance for mood enhancing or to get a little drunk on. It was a food as well. The men, women too, when on a journey, on foot of course, would bring it for energy so they could keep on going energetically up and down the mountains. The Nagas do not only grow rice and vegetables and keep pigs, but the forest is their domain for hunting too. We Nagas say," and she laughed out loud now, "we will eat anything that moves. Nagas know the forest is very important. It is nature and we guard the balance between agricultural and pristine nature. Nagas hunt in the forests and harvest what we need: medicinal plants, roots, and insects. The Nagas are a self sufficient people and don't need to rely on the outside world. Perhaps now we do when we talk of industrials products. In the past they made foraged in the plains and either peacefully or forcibly traded with the people there. We were feared for that, but no people ever conquered us. Until the British came Nagas have always been free. We fought the British for sixty years and indeed they colonized us; correction, partially only, because the Nagas living in the greater part of Nagaland were called Free Nagas by the British and the land they lived in were called by them un-administered areas. You tell me, who gave India the right to rule over us? Considering we were never actually conquered by the British and were asked to join, but refused, to Union of India, how can anyone think Indians have the right to our land and rule over us?"

"Do you mean the Indians just took it for granted that Nagaland should be part of India?", Marius asked.

"It looks like that, Marius, for already in the twenties the Nagas, through the emerging Naga organization the Naga Club, told the British Simon Commission which came to learn from the people how they felt and to prepare for decolonization and so to find. The Nagas said unequivocally stated they wanted to be left alone. They wanted to be in the situation before the British had come, they wanted to rule themselves. When the

British left, the Nagas thought the situation would be restored. After all, they had nothing to do with the Indians, not historically, not religiously, and not ethnically."

"Why did the British not allow this then?", Marius asked trying to grasp what actually happened, on what basis these decisions with far fetching repercussions, were made.

"As far as I can see there were two reasons for that. The first one was when independence came and as you know this was just after the Second World War, the British had their hands full with the decolonization process. I am sure they were not at their political best after the devastating world war. The Nagas were a detail in that process. The old paternalistic idea of the British, primarily in London but also in Nagaland itself, was that the Nagas could not govern themselves in this modern world. In London, though some of the old British district officers warned that this would lead to a lot of turmoil, it was decided no provisions would be made for the people of Nagaland. Then the Indians thought that all parts of their emerging country that were left and not settled by the British like Burma, Pakistan or Sri Lanka, was thus theirs."

"I heard Mahatma Gandhi had something to do with this?", Marius recalled.

"You are right," Lisa smiled, "indeed the Nagas came to see Gandhi for they knew things could turn ugly. Gandhi reassured the Naga delegation that they surely could determine their own future."

"But then something must have gone terribly wrong?", Marius remarked

"Indeed, Gandhi was murdered and when we put the details aside, you can read all about those, it was Jawarhlal Nehru India's first prime Minister, who felt offended when the Nagas walked out on him at Kohima. U Nu of Burma and Nehru had come together there to talk, among other things of course, about the border between Burma and India. The Nagas, the border was on our land, wanted to talk to Nehru, but he refused and wanted to address the crowd at Kohima ground. Nehru felt insulted when the Nagas walked out on him. So angry he was that, when back in Delhi, he is quoted to have said: 'When heaven falls and India goes to pieces and the rivers will run red with blood, I will never let the Nagas become independent.' Not long after that he unleashed the war and sent his troops to occupy our land. As we sit here Marius, after all these years these troops are still there. Peace talks or not, they are on our land."

"This is not known much outside Nagaland. I think not a lot of Indians know about this?"

"The democratic Indians do not demand their government's accountability on a severe matter like this. Cost and loss of life, in my opinion, must be motivated and the policies to be known by the public. India shows nothing like that to its people. It does not tell its own people why it occupied Nagaland, what it costs, how many people died in the conflict, or on what legal basis Nagaland is occupied. The government represents the people, but the people know nothing. The way I assess it is that the Indian high brow politicians who, haughty as they are, consider us as low life outcasts. We do not honor their self-proclaimed superiority and they feel offended that we dare to defend ourselves. The Nagas do not want to be part of that Hindu society in which the Brahmans call all the shots. People who feel superior do not feel accountable about anything they do. This is one reason why the Indians keep on doing what they do against us."

"There are other reasons too then?" Marius asked.

"Most likely India's sense of secure borders is at stake here," Lisa continued, "Indira Gandhi once said that she could talk about ending the conflict, provided the borders would be secured. She is quoted to have said to a Naga who had come to her with that proposition: 'I don't care about the Nagas. I care about the security of India.'"

"Considering how India lost Tibet, this is not too surprising?", Marius remarked.

"True, but then there is lot more too. India is afraid that, when the Nagas become independent, many other peoples aspiring self determination, will follow suit. This, they fear, will break up the now large and powerful nation India," Lisa answered.

"I think this might be quite enough for an introduction," Marius smiled, "I fear I will mix up things if you continue to throw more at me!"

"Okay, let's go and have a drink elsewhere," Lisa laughed, "I have hardly seen Amsterdam, this great colonial city of yours," she said sporting her teasing smile.

Thinking back on this encounter with here and getting ready to leave Africa, Marius laughed. Now back in Nagaland Lisa had occasionally corresponded with him through emails and though she had remained quite ironical, Marius was convinced she would be overjoyed when he would break the news of his prospective arrival in Nagaland to her. Would she be able to show him the ins and outs, he wondered.

Chapter 2

It begins

Lisa/Shilu had returned to Nagaland. For the moment stationed in Dimapur just inside the state and on the border of Assam, she was waiting to be sent back to one of the rehabilitation clinics for drug addicts. Regarding her work her visit to Amsterdam had been partially successful and she remembered it well. What struck her personally most was that she could not put this Marius out of her head. She had met him in one of the offices of the non governmental agencies, but she knew he did not work there. An enigmatic man with dry humor, he had kept her in the dark as to what he really did. The people she had met from the agencies also could not tell her much more than she knew from Marius himself, but that his work was government related. Strangely she had felt good with him and felt rather happy that he had taken such interest in the situation her people, the Nagas, were in. Would he really try and come to Nagaland? Or, had he just talked her up to see how far he could get with her? These were some of the questions that played in her mind as she was preparing to spend some months among the casualties of what she saw as the youth with no future, some of them had fled into drugs, into oblivion. How to motivate them, she felt, was one of the tasks ahead of her. Though convinced and committed, she recalled too how she was taken by Marius and in her moments alone she wondered how it would be if she would team up with him in a more personal way, yes sensually, romantically of course, she smiled to herself. But, as duty called, she had to remove these thoughts from her mind, for she was going into the countryside to work on a rehab set up organized by the National Socialist Council of Nagalim, NSCN. She was going off now to meet one of their leaders. Shilu knew the history of the deep routed conflict very well of course. She, after all, had only known Nagaland, her homeland as the occupied land and only her grandparents could tell her how it was when the British were there. She fully agreed with the NSCN and other Naga organizations that to be free of India essentially was what the Nagas should pursue. But since she was a practical thinker too and she was convinced that the long time suffering this resistance had caused would evidently disrupt the Naga Society. Already there were now three major players who were fighting each other. Money was thrown in by India deliberately to make people fight over it and divide and rule plots had been quite successfully introduced. First of all there was the 16th point agreement which in 1963 had led to the carving out of Nagaland State from Assam and which had divided the homeland of the Nagas. Originally led by the Naga National Council, NNC, which was up to 1975 the sole Naga resistance organization which its own Naga Federal Army, sadly the Shillong Accord between the NNC and the Government of India resulted in dividing the Nagas to the core. A minority stayed loyal to the NNC which denied there was an Accord but did disarm its Federal Army. And so when it became obvious the decision was not to be revoked the leaders in its ranks, who did not want that to happen, eventually formed their own organization. From 1980, the launching year of the NSCN, to 1988 all went well till vice president Khaplang, responsible for Eastern (Burmese) Nagaland sponsored by key people in the Nagaland Government and the Assam Rifles, staged a coup to try and overthrow leaders of the NSCN like Thuingalang Muivah and Isak Chishi Swu, secretary general and Chairman respectively. These me were nearly killed in the surprise attack Kaphlang launched, which took the lives of at least some fifty NSCN men. This was another schism in the Naga forces. Yet, seven years later the Indian Government had to come to the conclusion, its generals recommending that a military solution was not possible unless all Nagas were to be annihilated, a cease fire followed by peace talks had to be negotiated. When in 1997 this cease fire was signed and announced, things looked good for the Naga peoples. Finally they could embrace and experience a relative peace. Though no doubt the Indian Government was sincere in its approach to seek peace, there were many hawks with vested interests who tried to intervene in that process for peace. This is short was the history of events which led up to the current standings of the peace process in 2006, nine years and many rounds of talks after the signing of the cease fire in 1997.

Shilu knew all these facts and knew where she stood as well. She had the capacity to see things from within and from a distance, so from a geopolitical level, from a historical level but also from a domestic level. It was this domestic level that had her interest now. Though the Naga society knew some peace now, the forces to disrupt it were very active. One of the consequences of these activities was that Naga youths had the easy access to hard drugs. Those hooked and with nothing to do, do end up as drop outs. And, in this capacity Shilu worked with the addicts in the rehabilitation center. Now on her way to a meeting with NSCN members, she walked through Dimapur the commercial centre of Nagaland, but thought of Marius. Yes, I would like to see him here, show him what actually happens behind the scenes, the reality of an occupied land with the social consequences. Perhaps he could do something was one thought on her mind, another one was more private and warm. She had to admit to herself that she actually liked him much more than she had anticipated. She admitted too and smiled when she thought that indeed absence could make the heart grow fonder. 'I should not hope for anything', she reminded herself. Being realistic she entered the building where the meeting was held now sure he felt similar to what she tried not to think of, but could not set aside. So, with the thought of Marius she blushed as Shilu met the NSCN organizers to fully report on her journey to Europe and to talk shop about the rehabilitation centre.

Jeanie was wrapping up things with her African counterparts in Nairobi, Harare, Lusaka, Lumbumbashi and needed a week to straighten things out before returning to her London base. She felt inspired by Marius' sense of adventure' and in her spare time was reading up on what she agreed to do with him. She realized that she had agreed with Marius, after he talked her in to it, to go to Nagaland with him. Being an adventurous woman herself she was not just apprehensive but full of anticipation. Because she had accumulated quite a few weeks of holiday, Jeanie was lucky to take a break from work. On her way to Lusaka in Zambia then via Stanley ville and the Victoria Falls later to Maun and Gabarone in Botswana whenever she had time she gathered background information on Nagaland. On an overnight layover near Victoria Falls on the Zimbabwean side of the border, she had just settled into a hotel when her mobile phone rang:

"Yes Philip?", Jeanie asked when she recognized the voice of the man at the other end.

"The deed is done!", Sean announced.

"Already?", Jeanie asked not believing what Sean just had said, "you are quick man! No traces left, none that can lead to you or me?"

"None whatsoever, they cannot get to me very easily and how would they be able to get to you? There is no connection between you and me Jeanie. Just deposit the money in the account we agreed on all right?", Sean said.

"Of course, I will do that. I would not want you to send your assassin to me," Jeanie earnestly, "and the Baptist is the one who put up the contract, right. He is the one and we share the expenses!", Jeanie answered rather softly.

"You are right and within two days you will have the full amount."

"Good," Sean answered, "if not things will happen, you know, please remember that," Sean stressed before he terminated the call. Jeanie thought for a moment. Knowing she was wedged in and had to play the game now. She felt down for a moment. She was part of this scam now. She knew she could not get out of it and because all was covert, covert from her already covert work, she felt strained, unhappy and used. Most of all she did not have sense how to get out of this dreadful situation she had landed herself in. Only too late she realized there was no way out of it. It had been one reason why she had wanted to come closer to Marius. When on a journey together she thought that would be the venue to tell him all hoping she could help her. Later, she thought, for now I have to relay the news she heard from Sean the organizer of the assignment. When the phone was picked up she heard a voice saying:

"Yes?"

"The deed is done," Jeanie said recognizing the man only by voice. A recognizable voice, a voice Jeanie knew. Being a trained linguistic and suitable to detect accents and dialects, especially when acted and copied, Jeanie was certain about the man's origin. He was a go between, one who relayed messages and orders by higher up decision makers. As she remembered she had an established connection with this contact to use when things would go bad, she would get through to those who operated him. Listening now, she waited for him to follow up on what had to be done. The man hesitated to speak, Jeanie felt; wondering if that was deliberate, she did not prod him but waited for him instead:

"The funds will be transferred in the next few hours. See to it they land in the right hands. Failure cannot be tolerated. Be accurate," he said.

"You don't fail either," Jeanie said with a bite feeling a rage building in her. Mellowing the tone of his voice when he heard Jeanie the man continued:

"Both of us cannot fail, remember that. Our part is done as we speak, you do yours!"

"Of course, who do you think I am," she said defiantly.

"We know who you are. That is why you do it. Your motivation is correct, our motivation too. You are deployed for a reason, don't forget that!"

"When you do not disclose the reason, your superiors just used me," Jeanie answered bitterly.

"Not here, not now, we will talk about this. It will be revealed and you will be proud," he laughed mockingly. But, Jeanie felt anger rising for she knew she had been coerced. This was going to be too much for her, this is not they way to live. This strain could make her snap, she felt. The man at the other end did sense that and again mellowed but in another way. He began to praise her now:

"You did well and you will be rewarded. This is for a good thing," he said, "don't you worry, we are proud of you and you will be paid handsomely!", he said and immediately disconnected after that. Jeanie felt stunned, unreal. She knew very well she was in it and had no way to return or retreat from it. She felt horrible, especially now that she had agreed to this trip with Marius. Things were loose in her mind already. What did she put herself into, she thought again and she hoped, practically against better knowledge, things would come back together again. But then how she wondered? Things had been set in motion and under severe pressure she had agreed to do what was required of her. Now, remembering the words the deed is done, she knew there was no way back and she felt the suspense sweeping through her body. She trembled and to get hold of herself and went outside and walked the path leading to a bridge over the river to experience a splendid view of the magnificent Victoria Falls. There she stood and looked into the hundred odd meters wave of water thundering down into the river below, the spray rising high above the rim of the fall where the water kept on coming and thundering. Lost in time and space but thinking about how to get out of this doldrums, she had managed to get herself into, she stared for what must have been half and hour then went back in time to feel ashamed.

Sean had called her. The deed was done. There was really no way back now and the more she thought about going off on a journey with Marius, the more ashamed she felt. Jeanie had known Sean for a long time. Sean had been a covert operative once too, but he started his business, his own shop as she called it. Sean had to leave the service in disgrace and was running a bordello circuit, several high class joints in key cities of the world. The bordellos, according to Sean dello's, Sean used as fronts for his other still more covert operations. And, Jeanie, because he proved to be successful in both had to credit him for this, both for his on the ground and underground operations.

For both had debts to pay because of a shameful thing in their past both Sean and Jeanie was approached and subsequently coerced to plan and execute the assassination. Jeanie knew that one way or other she would have to pay and she was glad she was not alone in this. She could rely on Sean for keeping his mouth shut.

They had had a friendly talk before he had accepted the contract for the then prospected assassination, a contract she in turn had had to accept too. The plotter had been cleverly avoiding contact and Jeanie, perhaps Sean too were the only ones who could be connected to that person. Jeanie knew she knew him. Now for delivering the 'goods' off the hook forever to deliver this kind of service elation en horror traveled through her. It aggravated her sense of feeling guilty about this knowing Marius had practically forced her to come along with him to Nagaland. And, of all places why Nagaland, she thought, upon hearing Marius pleading to her not so long ago. Under normal circumstances she would not have hesitated twice of course. On the contrary because this was what she liked to do? This was an adventure and Jeanie was certain that this kind journey would be intriguing and still relatively safe. On the other hand, these were not at all normal circumstances. She recalled how extremely reluctant she had been, something of which Marius had no knowledge of, in accepting to act as a go between a suitable assassin and the plotter. And neither had she known anything of the target nor of Nagaland. In fact not until Marius had vigorously introduced her had she focused on that unknown and isolated land of the Nagas. The person plus the picture of the person to taken out she had received had shown the man to be a Naga. Curious and inquisitive as she was this had raised her attention and she studied all the information she could lay her hands on. She read about the place where the assassination was to be carried out, Manila, and the routine of the prospected victim. According to the assignment then it was up to her to organize things properly for an infallible result. But then when Marius began talking of these people at peril who had been at war with India for five decades, she was shocked to learn that it was one of the leaders who was targeted.

The inner conflict of Jeanie then had become even more prominent when Marius announced he wanted to go on a peace mission and also said he had fallen in love. Well, may be not yet completely but he had had the firm idea of wanting to meet this woman again. Her heart torn Jeanie secretly felt this Lisa could be a formidable rival and did not know what to do. Overcome by guilt and loss of love too alone on this bridge over the river she stared at the wall of water, Victoria Falls is an enormously breathtaking waterfall. It extends from the city named after it, Victoria Falls, the city in Zimbabwe to Stanleyville in Zambia on the other side of the bridge and Zambia already.

What to do, what to do, she kept asking herself in the midst of which she felt a touch on her shoulder. As she moved catlike sensing somebody had sneaked up on, she reacted like a lioness ready for the kill.

"Don't ever do that to me again," Jeanie shouted and wielded the blade of a knife against the throat of Muga, her guide and guard in Zimbabwe. Sensing mortal danger he yelled:

"Oh, ohhhhhhhhh, don't kill me. It is only me Muga."

Seeing and hearing him Jeanie's tensed muscles relaxed and adrenaline already shooting through her veins, the blade still on his throat, she calmed down and said:

"I am sorry man, it's my survival instinct. Never sneak up on me like that, please!"

"Yes ma'am, but I must ask you one thing?", he said allowing his smile to return when Jeanie took the blade away from his throat:

"Yes of course," Jeanie answered with some shame and embarrassment on her face.

"You could hear me coming from a long distance. I can hardly sneak up on you when the sound on the bridge alone should have alerted you. The wood and my shoes, but also your sense, normal sense, of feeling someone approaching did not alarm you. It is strange. I saw you were completely mesmerized. I could have killed you had I not spoken, you know Miss Jeanie," he said and smiled to comfort her. Jeanie knew very well he was right. She had drifted off and was not aware of her surroundings anymore. Taken in by this thundering waterfall and its vapors of water, its sound, she had gone into a world of her own and had to admit to Muga he had been right, for her reaction had been outrageous, it was a reaction reflective of her survival instinct. Agreeing with him Jeanie looked at Muga and acknowledged he had been right in the assessment of her behavior:

"Yes of course Muga," she said, " I am sorry I did not see you or hear you coming. I should have felt it. I think I must have been far out of it man," Jeanie said and laughed, "Come let's go back?" she asked him, all smiles now.

"Okay," he smiled back at her and stressed, "no questions asked."

"Oh Muga, I am just troubled, nothing to do with you or even Zimbabwe or Africa, but me only. Don't worry about it. It is far more important to focus on the things at hand here. What you are facing is no child play either," Jeanie continued, referring to the bitter aftermath of the colonial times of former Rhodesia after the Britisher Rhodes. Zimbabwe was re-baptized Zimbabwe but the people o this land realized their land had its own heritage and named it after the people who had built Great Zimbabwe. It was named after Great Zimbabwe, the brick designs of the Kingdom in Zimbabwe of which the British believed it could not have been built by Africans but by people of a higher sort than expected by them. The bloody war of independence eventually won and the leading British Masters had been driven out then only by renaming the land the

Zimbabweans could feel the Masters of their own destiny. However the British settlers, those with the large farms on prime land, had become target and many had either been literally assaulted and had left or their farms were taken over by Zimbabweans. With respect to the native Zimbabweans this sounds good for them, but what was not fully realized was that, because the Zimbabweans could not run the farms vacated by the British, the economy at large came tumbling down due to the lack of expertise, Now that the leaders of Zimbabwe turned against their own as the opposition in the land grew to large numbers, for many the country is in dire straits. The present government decided to demolish slum areas of the towns, but without organizing provisions for those without alternatives. Consequently hundreds of thousands were left without homes. This was the atmosphere in which Muga and Jeanie were operating. Both knew something was in the making and both knew also it was too early to know what this would lead to. Back in the hotel of Victoria Falls both of them, along with a few others of the service, had been discussing matters related to these current affairs of the land juxtaposed against the colonial aftermath of Africa at large as well. This was to be her last day here and though the men and women of the Zimbabwean service related well, because of what happened elsewhere she felt down. Muga who had seen a glimpse of that showed worry and announced:

"How about cultural show tonight Jeanie? There is a spectacle on this evening and I want to take you there. This is how Africa was before the colonialists came. Tomorrow before you go, I have arranged a short flight over Victoria Falls so that you can experience the falls from above. That should be the highlight of your visit," he said to encourage her.

"Okay, okay," she answered, "that is a fine idea. But let's wrap up and review our findings. We will make no mistakes in future. Then I can be entertained," Jeanie laughed.

"But of course Jeanie," Muga said with the others in the office looking on approvingly, "we were about to embark on that. It is essential we have our communications in order."

Jeanie had a wonderful evening and in fact got a little drunk on the locally brewed maisbeer. Though it was a little sour she had come to like it very much. The graciousness of the dances and songs of the people performing their traditional cultures in the open space of the cultural village in town astounded her. The songs encouraged many in the audience to get up and dance to the ravishing dancers in front of them. And, because Africans in general and perhaps Zimbabweans in particular were straightforward in the approaches to the other gender, she had many men trying to get her to get her to dance with them. The men communicated through the dances and Jeanie felt they truly tried to make a lasting impression on her. But, Jeanie could not get into that. Practically because she was shielded by her covert counterparts, but also because, even though attracted to some of the virile Zimbabwean men she would take on a man for just the night and, certainly not when she was in this mentally deranged state. So, she settled for the fun and teasing they created, but knew she would not indulge. Then one of the ladies among them, one who was extravagantly beautiful and well proportioned, noticed she not get the attention she normally received said to Jeanie within earshot of the men:

"This is rather funny Jeanie. Look how the men are after you and primarily because you are white and let's face it attractive, they come after you. They do not see any one of us anymore, ironically so because we ridded ourselves of exploiters. Yet now you see how shameless our men are. They want you Jeanie."

"Yeah Bria," Jeanie agreed and smiled at the member of her team, "but then don't forget they only want to taste me for I am alien and because of that attractive. They want the feel of a white woman and then move on to you or on any of the women of our team. Indeed ironic it is!"

"Right," Bria giggled, the other women overhearing their conversation laughing with her. The men around them heard and realizing they had been caught in their act looked sheepish now. It was all done being good natured. So after the show, the dancing and drinking Jeanie when finally alone in her room and about to go to sleep, she found herself full of the attractions of that evening but also felt the turmoil she had face. It was this returning mental disturbance which took possession of her before she drifted off to sleep.

The next morning Muga woke her up excitedly to fetch her for the short scenic flight over the falls. Just the two of them went over to the small airfield not too far away from the hotel. On their way by car Muga suddenly asked:

"Are you going to the Bulawayo station? If possible I like you to see where Rhodes explored and where a monument to his honor was made in the magnificent environment there. It is so beautiful Jeanie," he said.

"Should I go? Is it necessary?", she asked in her mind already preparing for things to do elsewhere.

"It is not, but for a better understanding, I like you to familiarize yourself with the origins of Africa. Since this is your terrain now, you should know the background of what happened here. To know the history enables you to get into the minds of Africans here and to experience what actually motivates us. If you like I will arrange it today. It will only cost you at most two days or so. Did you know there are caves with very old San (Bushmen) paintings there? This is something you really should not miss now that you have the opportunity," he said.

They approached the field where a light fixed wing aircraft was waiting for them. Two other people, foreigners, jumped in with them and moments later the small plane took off. The pilot, middle aged Zimbabwean smiled and told them what to do so that they had a good chance to take pictures:

"I will approach from the river then turn left to fly over the falls. You can then take pictures from the right side when I bank. Then I will turn full circle now on the right side so you have the falls under you from the left side. I will do this two times and then change to the right. Then I ill fly into Zambia so on the return you will have the view on the water expanse just before it drops in the river."

Off they went to fly right towards the thundering falls. Jeanie saw the bridge she had stood on and where she almost had attacked Muga. He noticed and smiled at her understandingly.

Sharply up then the pilot climbed over the falls and to avoid the vapors of water coming up from the splashing wall of water, he made the first roll to the left. Looking down from their right as the plane glided the right wing down to give them a full view, they saw the water thundering right beneath them. An overpowering sight it was, not for those with weak knees. Jeanie felt completely overwhelmed by this natural phenomenon. This was excruciatingly beautiful and she could feel the surge in her body. The fear and the power she felt. For a moment she thought: 'what if the small plane comes down to crash into the falls?' Though she quickly try to brush this thought away but Muga had seen it and gallantly took her hand to lightly squeeze it amicably. Then, before she knew it the scenic flight was over when the pilot directed his aircraft back to the runway again.

"Magnificent," Jeanie exclaimed once they had touched the ground and had alighted. The pilot readying the plane for another ride as they talked and Jeanie, in the office on the field she noticed a poster stating some 8 flights were organized daily, "this is quite an exasperating experience Muga, remarkable!"

"Come I will take you back. Have you decided?", Muga asked.

"Yes," Jeanie said, without actually thinking about it. The idea had attracted her, yet the turmoil in her head practically prevented it until Muga had spoken in a way she could not possibly refuse. .

"I knew that," Muga smiled and when back at the hotel he handed her a train ticket, I knew you had the good sense of exploring. My people will fetch you from the overnight train. Take a rest on board. I have reserved a sleeper for you."

After their final meeting later that day knowing she would some diversion still at Bulawayo Jeanie's mind came to rest now as it was like she had come to terms with the troubles ahead and was prepared to face the consequences of her actions. She had known about them, but had never anticipated they would be so far reaching. Now convinced she decided k she would talk to those who had assigned her to do what she had done. For it was now only she felt she had been set up by them and this angered her tremendously. Once back on her post, she would get in touch and blast the hell out of them. Well, only one person really it was, but she would tell that person how she felt about him. This much she was certain of.

After all was said and done Muga took her to this an antique station:

"Such lovely place Muga this is, just like and old English station," she remarked happily while he put her on the train reassuringly saying:

"I know you are troubled, but when you apply your mind to it like I know you can, I am sure it will work out well for you dear Jeanie."

"Thank you so much my dear Muga, we will meet again," she said to him tenderly and she smiled at him then kissed him on the cheek. As the old train began to move out of the beautiful station Muga and her parted but she was followed by a wink and a smile. On the train and not yet quite dark she saw some of the landscape they slowly passed through. Jeanie enjoyed the trip very much and as she had time to think she reviewed her decisions which had led her into this odd predicament. Dusk came and fell over the fine and true African land which was so close to the Kalahari Desert of Botswana. Moving slowly she pondered and rethought things along the route while having a beer in her dark coupe. To turn in when it was pitch black outside, she went over to the sleeper, got undressed and fell asleep minutes later. But she woke up several times as she was tossing and turning. The worrisome things ahead passed through her mind time and again until she finally fell into a sound sleep. The next morning at Bulawayo station two rather nonchalant men met her. They had whispered her name and waited for her to confirm it was her they had been looking for. They whisked her off to a hotel when Jeanie revealed it was her indeed they had been waiting for. The local chapter of her counterpart service had come to meet her and once in the car they told her about the program which Muga's orders had been set up for her:

"Have a few hours rest Ma'am," he said, names here remain undisclosed, "we will come and pick you up later. Refresh and say at 10 am we have a vehicle ready for you, will that suit you?", he asked.,

"Excellent," Jeanie answered.

"Then in two hours from now we are ready for you," one o the men concluded and left with the other, the silent one. Jeanie took the opportunity to take a bath. She dried off and now nude looked at herself in the mirror. She put on a robe then fell on the bed and almost immediately slept.

The bonking on the door plus the room telephone ringing at the same time woke her up. Apparently the men had been knocking for some minutes already, the men said after they had marched in with a smile of surprise on their faces.

"We were beginning to worry that you had either left, or were assassinated," the leader said in earnest but soon after sported a smile on her his face, "good you are alive I would not want your death on my conscience," he roared with laughter.

"Give me five minutes and I am with you," Jeanie said quickly, equally smiling.

So, the men left and Jeanie, slightly embarrassed now, jumped up and hastily dressed. She picked up her purse and then, after locking the door behind her, ran outside. She was about to join the men in the lobby when she realized she had not drained the bathtub and went back to do so. Reappearing in front of the men she heard:.

"Hello Ma'am, we have an interesting journey ahead of us. Did you bring your camera?"

Jeanie checked her purse where she normally kept a small digital which had high resolution so she could take good quality pictures.

"Oh yes," she smiled, glad she had not made another foolish mistake the men could embarrass her with.

"Are you all right?", the man asked.

"Oh yes, let's go," she said, making it almost sound like a command let a smile accompany her words. Without a further word she hopped in the van and off they went. Driving south soon Bulawayo was behind them to enter into what was once a bulwark of the British and a large area stretching deep into northern Botswana.

"Are you comfortable Ma'am? We will be passing mountainous areas and with a lot of strange boulders, many people are infatuated by them?", one of the men said.

"Yes I am fine, I am used to many things, I can assure you," Jeanie smiled.

"The train got you though," the man smiled with her as they came into a plain with some extravagant but beautiful rock formations.

"Oh it is beautiful indeed," Jeanie exclaimed when the van stopped to allow her to get a view closer up and especially for taking some pictures of the sheer beauty and strange boulders around.

"This is bushmen area, well was," the man said, "we shall be heading towards a cave which has the shape of a vagina you know," the man chuckled, right next to it you will see the ancient Bushmen paintings on the wall."

"That would be interesting," Jeanie answered. She confirmed that a second time when they had reached the caves to be stunned indeed by the sight of it. Next to the cave with the Bushmen paintings and illuminated by softly striking light these she saw indeed very apparent labia, clitoris and anus. They were large, very large. She looked at the sculptured like features for a moment then asked:

"This is shaped naturally by water, I think?"

"Indeed it is," the leader of the team accompanying her smiled, "quite a few women come here to prey for fertility."

"Oh well I can imagine that," Jeanie laughed as she took some pictures.

"The pictures you take in the cave here," the man said as he walked towards it with Jeanie and the others, "will be much better if you don't use flash. By this time of day there should be enough light to actually see good contrast in the drawings," he explained.

"That is a good idea," she answered and walked into the cave. There on the right side she did immediately saw them and was drawn to them. Rather large and extending over some three meters she on the wall of the cave gradually she saw several hunting expeditions visualized in red. Very interesting this is, Jeanie thought, and saw giraffes, buffalos and other animals depicted, men among them with spears.

"Quite a natural tableau right?", the man asked, :"we do not have bushmen here anymore, but they are still masters of their environment in Botswana and Namibia I am told.

"Really?", she asked.

"They lived here centuries ago. I can show you some lineage done by the Bulawayo museum later on if you like," he explained while Jeanie watched the drawings intently.

"Yea that would be nice," she said.

"Shall we go to the Rhodes memorial then too?", he asked, "I am sure that will impress you too. We certainly do not quite like the man who was responsible for the subjugation of our people that and more so for the negation of our people who built Great Zimbabwe."

"Let me take a few pictures still, some close up," Jeanie said.

"Of course," the man said and waited patiently for her to take it all in. When on their way again they first passed a manmade lake made to ensure irrigation in the fields nearby and to regulate water flow in this very dry area. Then they went into the mountains again, this time going up. After a while they reached a point of no return and the leader said:

"We just have to walk up a little to get to the monument. For that trouble you will be blessed with a good view," he teased.

"I should be able to do that. I looked ahead and decided to put on sneakers rather than high heels," Jeanie smirked back at him.

"Of course," he said and the men laughed with him. Up they went and reached the top in about five minutes. The scenery looked splendid.

"Come," the man said, "you cannot see it from here, but a bit further there is placard in stone, honoring the memory of Rhodes."

"Hmmmmm," Jeanie reacted, r I am not so sure many people are in the capacity of honoring that memory. It is far away from everything and I do not think you people are not excitedly trampling to go and pay respect to this man?"

"You are very right," the man smiled, "to us he was not good. We lived in peace, well amongst ourselves and we fought other tribes but we did not take the land like the white Englishmen did. I cannot say we are too happy he did not acknowledge Great Zimbabwe either but said that these buildings could only have been constructed by people out side Africa. He did not think in our past we could have created such unique structure. If you have a chance you must go and see it!"

"Well, well, you are a man of your own culture," she laughed, "and I admire that. In time I will take you up on that suggestion," she assured him, but focused on both the memorial stone and the surroundings of this low mountainous terrain. Jeanie had a look at the memorial embedded in the rock for a moment but was not impressed, rather repulsed she felt about it. While on the way back at her request they stopped a few times to take some more pictures. Finally at round four in the afternoon they rolled back into Bulawayo. It was far too late for lunch but Janie now realized she was starving. In fact she realized she could not quite remember when she had eaten last. This was good, for she realized too she had very much been taken in by what she experienced on this short trip and so had forgotten to eat. She was about to say something about that when the man asked:

"We must eat, but it is not a good time. Let me take you to a place where we can have some barbecue. Men I am starved, how about you Jeanie?"

"Indeed, yes please, I was about to ask you!"

He ordered to driver to drive to a street where they could sit outside. Minutes later they were served plates full of freshly barbecued meat and salad. And, that they were all hungry was obvious for they all of them devoured the food..

"We have arranged a flight out for you, tomorrow morning. Later you will connect in Harare for your flight to London all right?", the leader announced when he saw Jeanie was quite satisfied.

"It is fine, I think I am being spoiled," Jeanie smiled, but the leaders showed that for him it was routine and he did not react to her flattery but said as a matter of fact:

"You will be picked up and eight and the flight is at ten. Please feel free to spend some private time tonight, but then again, if you want someone with you dear Jeanie, we can take you out and go for a drink and dance."

"No, I am fine, thank you very much, I feel too much obliged already. Don't worry I will be okay on my own."

"As you please," the man said, "but let me tell you in the evenings this Tudor kind of looking hotel, I agree it is a bad copy of the English style, has dances. So, if you want to mingle, feel free, but be careful?"

"It is nice of you to think of me, I shall look after myself though. Thank you very much for showing me around and please feel free to go?"

"All right, we just want to make sure you are not lonely if this for you strange land. I will post two men around the garden and the bar for your security. That much I feel I should do. Please do not argue with me," he laughed when he saw Jeanie's face.

Okay, thanks. Be well," she said and after they had delivered her to her hotel, she turned, waved and walked in to go to her room. There she was alone again and well prepared to return. This short tripe had done her good. She felt rejuvenated and decided to take another bath to rinse of the dust she felt she was covered in. to dress herself up. She had the urge to look beautiful and in command and dressed herself accordingly. On top of things now, but with spite in her heart, she looked ahead to deal with the things to come, the things she could not share with Marius. The next day while flying to Harare and on to London, little did she know about what was in store for her!

Chapter 3

Indian Rebel leader shot dead in Manila suburb

A Naga rebel leader was shot dead today in broad daylight, Isak Chishi Swu the chairman of the National Socialist council of Nagaland while trying to catch a taxi in frantically busy Cubao received multiple shots in head and body. Fired from a passing vehicle, he died on the spot. The police who were on location within minutes have not been able to apprehend the killers yet. Swu, who was part of the collective leadership has been running a revolutionary government for decades as its president, was brutally murdered far away from the Nagaland he was exiled from. From his base abroad he directed his very successful Naga Army as they put up a fight against the Indian Armed forces for many years.

The Naga saga began really with India taking over the British Empire to form the union of India. Since the tribal Nagas opposed to be part of the of this emerging nation, they at first peacefully objected. But then when in 1954 India sent its troops into the region, the Nagas resisted and have done so ever since. What strikes many about this murder though is that the Nagas were negotiating with the Indian Government to come to a solution for this long time conflict. Already a cease fire in operation for some ten years both parties for reasons unknown (the talks are held in secrecy and without policies made public by the Indian Government) the progress in the peace talks that followed, were left to be desired. Consequently all eyes are on India now or the adverse Naga Forces which are supported by the Indian Armed Forces as many a Naga accuses India of foul play, of hiring an assassin to murder this revered leader.

India categorically states that it has had no hand in this assassination but says it will leave no stone unturned to find the culprit(S) to bring them to justice. The people of Nagaland are in mourning and after a coroner has examined Swu's body thoroughly, it will be flown to Nagaland where the Naga nation will be enabled to pay its respects for this great leader. The big question now is, should India through stooges be found to be behind this what will happen then? The Nagas are reportedly furious and there is no telling what would happen now. Naga people.

The Indian Government meanwhile urges the whole of the North east to stay calm but puts its troops on high alert and ordered them to be vigilant. Already the people of Nagaland termed it an outcry what happened and pointed to the secret service of India who was believed to be behind this assassination with the aim to undermine the peace talks once and for all. Reuters news June 26 2006 .

Oh my goodness, Marius howled while reading this newscast. This cannot be true. I can't believe the Indians stooped this low. Having everything under control and able enough to keep prospectors and onlookers at bay, they have been able to stall for time a decade already and aimed at weakening the spirit of the Nagas to fight again. If this is true, he promised to himself then I will join forces with others and will I hunt the assassin down to find out who ordered to kill Swu. This throws a different light on the situation, he thought. To connect and start the search I will have to get in touch with quite a few people, he realized. This is shocking, he said aloud and grabbed the phone to begin to connecting; first to make sure that this really had happened, second to see whom he could work with best. Marius was sure quite a few people would be planning to get on the trail of the assassin, but he knew too that as many would frustrate the search too. To unravel what was behind the assassination, by catching the killer this was really what Marius wanted to do. After the few calls and after sharing information and having make some appointments, he sat down, hands in face. He had lost himself in deep thought.

"Who is this Isak Chishi Swu?", Mairus asked his counterpart at the bureau. He had just returned from Douala and checked into the office that morning.

"No idea, some Indian with a Bangladeshi passport, I am told. What is it to you? Just one of these Manila murders you know. I believe they have a few hundred a year, drugs related, gangs, extortion but also macho but drunk policemen killing each other frequently," Bram told him.

"Do you think this has anything to do with the new Peoples Army?", Marius asked Bram who was the South East Asian specialist.

"That is hard to say Marius. Nothing much is known yet you know. Just an Indian was shot, but I must say the man has an odd name. What do you make of it," he asked.

"Well, it reminds me of someone, but I can't be sure. I will look into but if I am not mistaken, this could be a grave situation."

"Oh how so," Bram asked.

"Later, I want to be sure first," Marius answered reluctantly for he suddenly felt quite sure, but did not want to make a fool of himself in case he should be proved wrong, "you know," he continued, "I am going on a long holiday soon and it is an area rarely visited. I am drawn to it. Do you know anything about Nagaland Bram?"

"Of course Marius," Bram smiled now, "Nagaland State is part of India bordering Burma and China, the north east, you know that chicken neck?"

"Oh yes of course, but don't you call that Myanmar?"

"The old guards don't like to call it Myanmar for it is ruled by the military junta against the will of the people. Everybody there calls it Burma still man," Bram smiled.

"So, Nagaland is only a state then?", Marius asked.

"Well there is some turmoil there, domestic in nature. Lots of tribes fight both the Indian military and each other. Containing the situation there Marius I am afraid the Indian Forces are not doing a good job. You want to go there? Why man? You most likely do not even get in!"

"Oh how so," Marius asked Bram feigning he had no idea.

"They locked it off from the outside world. Nobody gets in without some kind of permit, without which you do not get. But why do you want to go there man?", Bram asked again a surprised look on his face.

"I have met this woman called Lisa here some time ago Bram. She told me stories and the culture now fascinates me. Do you know more? Can I rely on you to give me access to what you know, what I can expect? It is purely for an adventurous holiday and you will oblige me to return this favor."

"Hmmm, interesting Marius, but it is neither your area nor is it mine exactly. Not much is known about it except for some museum people who are quite interested in these cultures. There seems to be a lot going on there, but it is all of domestic nature. Don't go and poke your nose into that. When you get implicated you could be involved in some diplomatic difficulties. So, be careful and don't get into anything without me knowing about it, Marius.This is my territory in this bureau!"

"This is my private interest and please Bram do not act defensively or is it there is something you are not telling me?", Marius asked but with irony.

"No, no, no," Bram laughed catching Marius undertone, "do as you please but be prepared. It is a wasp's nest there. The Indians keep it under the table, they see it as their domestic problem and the Dutch Government officially has nothing to do with it."

"What do you mean 'officially' has not?", Marius asked.

"Well there are talks held here in the Netherlands between the Indians and the Nagas!"

"What?", Marius exclaimed.

"Yeah, there is tacit understanding between our government and the Indian one. No press conferences Marius. No newspaper articles," Bram told him.

"Why is that?", Marius asked.

"The Nagas have resisted the Indians for many years and came as far as peace talks. Now on the basis of a cease fire these talks are held outside India and the Netherlands just facilitates and is a venue for the talks, nothing more and nothing less, Marius."

"So, only a venue and no third party participation?", Marius asked

"Right," Bram answered.

"Tell me Bram, if nobody knows about this and India has been pressed to negotiate but cannot win that war. Why did it actually start it negotiations anyway?. When India for so long has tried to subdue that insignificant tribe. This exercise seems to be futile?"

"Well, all I know really is that for reasons of its own, India wants to keep it's affairs under the table. It could be as you said, they act out of fear to be humiliated. There could be of other reasons too, for regarding this conflict nothing much is known about the policies of the Indian Government."

"So, Bram, when I go there, will I encounter a lot of nosy military? Will they prevent me from experiencing the culture, restrict me in my traveling?", Marius asked.

"You need a permit to begin with. I understand it is easier now to get one. Just get a group of four together and the Nagaland State Government can issue those permits. I also heard married couples can get that too. But please Marius you better verify first man?"

"That I will do of course, I will go well prepared. It should be an adventure in itself. Anything I should pay special attention to?"

"Just see to it that you get your permit. I don't think getting arrested is much fun. The people I am sure are friendly, but it is a volatile area. Better take some precautions Marius. Who knows what might happen to you,."

"What kind of precautions Bram?", Marius asked.

"I suggest you find a woman. Compared to a man alone in a group a couple does not raise that much attention. Catching my drift Marius?"

"I have been thinking about that too, but where can I find a woman who is daring enough to get into this kind of adventure Bram?"

"Oh come on Marius. You have your ways. Tell you what, hire yourself one on Bangkok and tag her along for a few weeks. You will have fun and you can travel safely too."

"Are you serious Bram?", exasperated now Marius asked.

"Of course," Bram smiled, "it is a suggestion. Spend a few days in Bangkok and find one who speaks some English then go as a couple. She will be your ticket of going around unnoticed. Of course you will reward the woman?", Bram laughed.

"It is an idea man, but I do not feel like using a woman for this kind of exposure. For the Thai woman it will be work of course and for me that could be a very interesting holiday. Still I cannot ask that of any woman, prostitute or otherwise," Marius said getting irritated with Bram.

"There are thousands there Marius and you will do the woman a favor. You will pay the one you choose and she will be delighted. It is not too dangerous then and in the process you have a nice and gentle companion. Anyway it is just a suggestion Marius."

"Thank you Bram, I will consider," Marius concluded, cutting him short on this matter..

"It is your call, Marius, just be careful. This is unknown territory for you. You cannot predict too much. You are right man; this is going to be quite an adventure for you."

"I am already looking forward to it," Marius answered Bram, signaling implicitly their talk on his proposed trip had ended.

"I wish you well on that journey. Let me know before you go if I can be of help still?", Bram asked in friendly tone and winked, "I still think you are crazy man!"

"Well, perhaps I am crazy a little, but I would like to see this woman again too. She made quite an impression on me you know. And, why not do something adventurous once in a while? Are you not a daring man Bram you decided to work for this agency man?"

"Well, well, well, you want to have the last word hey, Marius," Bram chuckled. Marius let him be and walked off. On his way to his office Marius already thought it was time to begin the planning, In Manila things were going into a strange frenzy.

"As if I do not have work enough men," one of the lower echelon policemen said, "Madre mia, now we have to find out about the background of this man. We have to check immigration and we know how cooperative there people are there."

"Let's get an order so they cannot refuse. I am tired of this kind of corruption. As police we can't even get them going unless there is something in it for them."

"Jesus, Maria and Joseph, it is sick, really, let's go man," Eddie said as he grabbed a jeep from his post and rode towards the meandering Pasig River in Manila. On the bank facing Intramuros and in between Manila Cathedral and the Main post office the immigration office was situated. Eddie drove through dense traffic via busy Quiapo, which is known for its church and plaza Miranda in fro not it but more so because of its with its hundreds of jeepneys dropping off passengers right there in the middle of the road. Once they had passed that bottle neck, they passed over one of the many Pasig river bridges and turned right to pass left Liwasang Bonifacio and right the post office. The Press Club office was next when the men in the jeep saw the walls of old Manila on their left before they stopped in front of the immigration office. After they entered they whisked off the many runners who were about to make a handsome amount acting as go betweens and went straight into the office of a high ranking officer. Though some guards tried to stop them, they just flashed their badges and told them off saying:

"This is police business not yours," before they stepped in. Once inside they caught a surprised the officer on duty who was literally teaming up with a secretary. Well secretary? Still in a kind of indisposed position, while stumbling over his words he flared up saying:

"Don't you people know how to knock This is unheard of?", he shouted.

"Do you think you are paid good public money to receive hookers in your office man," Eddie, the older policeman said, "we do not come to ask you for a service, but to commit you to so something for us, the police. So, get ready. Is that understood?"

Shocked by what he heard and realizing this was not a simple thing he could address quickly to get back to fondling the woman, he summoned her to get out. He did so in the way that it appeared the woman had seduced him, like she was responsible for putting him in that position. But, as long as the officer did what they had come for the two policemen could not care less.

"Get into your files on computer and check this name pronto. We want to know all that is known about this man. Failing to do so, will cost you your job this time. Now get on with it," Eddie said. As the woman sneaked out and the other policeman told her to get some coffee, the officer said:

"Yes pronto!"

'This time we were lucky', the young policeman thought, 'now that we caught him in the act the man could not resist.

"That is quite an attractive woman," he said within in earshot of his secretary who was hurriedly leaving the office.

"Just find out rapido," Eddie said and both of them left to wait outside.

"Well, it is good, this way he will do as ordered and we do not loose time in using other means. Besides, now we can take it easy. Give him half an hour?"

"Yeah, fine," the young man answered and they both went outside to have some coffee at the newly opened American Starbucks café opposite but part of the old wall of the city. .

"Odd to see that here in the wall itself," the Eddie said, "how could they have tolerated this to be built here. Ridiculous!", he exclaimed noticing another chain had taken root in the Philippines

"Modern times it is man, we can't always look back," the younger man answered.

"This is heritage," Eddie answered in defiance. Don't you realize the bloody Spaniards lived here in these walls and subjugated us? Do we really have to pay lip service to the Americans then by building them a Starbucks in this wall here?"

"Well, swell, calm down man. You may be right, but the coffee is a treat on me, okay?"

"Gosssshhhh, man this is expensive. Coffee is 40 peso here. We can't afford that on this salary," Eddie said.

"May I offer you a coffee on the house, a croissant with it?", the woman behind the cash register announced. Surprised, but pleasantly, the two men instantly recognized policemen had to be regular guests here and no ordinary ones."

"Yes please," they both said at the same time.

"I have not seen you here before," the young lady continued.

"That is right," the young man answered sizing her up, "but thank you."

"Pleasure of Starbucks,' she said not venturing further but keeping an eye on them. The men sat down and after having shared their surprise about this expensive set up, they discussed the case.

"You have seen the body right, riddled with bullets," the young man asked.

"Yes, Eddie answered.

"What is so special about him then?"

"Well, he had a suit on. Who wears a three piece suit in Manila?"

"You tell me,' the young policeman prodded the older one.

"he could be an official going to some diplomatic meeting?", the man answered.

"Yeah, yeah, something like that," the young men said.

"If it is a diplomat and we will hear about it, but for now we have to find out what he was doing in the Philippines."

"I heard he has family near Santa Lucia, so he lives here in Manila!"

"Yeah, may be an Arab arranging things for the South, Abu Sayyaf, The MILF?", Eddie suggested thinking out loud.

"And then officially living in Manila, that would be too simple to trace,' the young man said trying to make a sharp remark.

"You can be officially Christian, but unofficially you can be and do something else, of course," Eddie mocked the younger one.

"That's right indeed, so the question is why would he do that?", he asked.

"If he is a Christian of course buddy, we do not know is he was a front for the South, or a go between or a financier," the older man said, " he may be acting as a Christian but could also be a Moro who gets weapons. But let me cut you short. We are here to get some info so we will see some light in this tunnel. We may have hunches already but we really know nothing yet."

"The detectives are working on in right?", the young man spoke in awe of themselves.

"Yes we are the errand boys investigating and scraping up some info to fit in to the puzzle. Solving a murder is like solving a jig saw puzzle man, I know that much," Eddie said.

"Okay let's go back then, I am curious now to know what that fool has dug up."

They nodded to the lady who showed a fancy smile. They walked back to the immigration building and went up again to barge into the office of their officer.

"Well, well, well, quite a person, men," the immigration officer began when they had settled down in chairs in front of him, "the man is Indian, well officially. Judging from his picture here," and he showed it, "he does not look Indian to me, but officially he is. I have just talked over the phone with someone of the Indian Embassy here and they assured me there were people looking like us in India. Can you believe it?"

"I do not know what to believe, but go on, "the Eddie said with authority in his voice.

"I have asked what kind of people look like South Asian peoples in India and he answered this: the north east of India bordering Burma and Bangladesh has many tribes who look kike South Asian people and surely not like Indians. He assured me this man could be one of them!!"

"Did he come up with a name of these people, or do we have to go to the Embassy ourselves?"

"The officer there told me their tribal name was Naga. He said these people have been at war with India for a long time. They are rebels," he stressed, "and he told us to be very careful for this could be a big thing."

"We don't have to be anymore, the man is dead," the young man dryly said.

"Really?", the officer exclaimed.

"Really," the young man said.

"But there are more here, families and their children go to school. There are wives and husbands. Did you know that?"

"Good work," the older policeman said and by the tone of his voice it became obvious he had forgiven him, "now get us the names of the people with similar background man."

"Okay, I will print out a list for you to go on," the officer said.

"Okay we will wait," Eddie answered.

Back at the station the two policemen triumphantly explained what they had achieved only to find out that all these particulars were already known and the people concerned were being interviewed in their homes by detectives. The families of the deceased were shattered but had revealed a few things the detectives may not have had full knowledge off. It was then decided to investigate some more, this time in the documents and relations of the Nagas that were recorded there.

Meanwhile at the main police office in Manila proper the men were gathering and their meeting was disturbed. This, they realized, that this was not an open and shut case at all. The highest echelons had to be informed and some already suggested that this kind of thing could have political repercussions. As soon as the word was out an Indian citizen had been murdered, the Indian Embassy had enquired with more than just the normal interest. This murdered man apparently was somebody important, they learned. But then the wondered, what was Nagaland? For them this was the question now, more so when they thought of why anyone should want to kill someone from an insignificant country nobody here had ever heard of? Was this not a purely domestic affair for India? Was it some Indian had done it. The deeper they were diving into the matter the murkier it seemed to get. Here was a gentleman, an older man, apparently the chairman of a rebellious people, a nation, but part of India. It was a people which had been fighting to be free of that same India.. Considering how he lived in Manila, the police was still checking that out, and the Christian attitude an behavior he had had, it was hard to believe he was a violent man, no evidence but to pinpoint him as a religious man. The director of the investigative unit had assigned three of his crew to do research on Nagaland and on the man's position in that country. The result of that research astonished the heads of police. In short this was reported to them:

The Nagas were a people consisting of no less than some 40 tribes. They were, but partially, colonized by the British and about one third of their land was in Myanmar, formerly known as Burma. These tribes shared a common ancestry. Millennia ago, it was not known when, from two places in what is now Manipur's India and Sangaing district in northwest Burma, they had swarmed out to settle into what the British had called the Naga Hills. As far as the men could see from the pictures those were no hills but really mountains. The people founded villages on the hilltops and were quite self sufficient, and this also meant in governing some themselves. Thought they fought amongst each other there were no records of tribal showdowns. This is how the British came across them when they marched into Naga territory at around the 1830, but it took them some 60 years to actually come to an unsigned agreement with a few Naga tribes. More than two third of what the Nagas now remained un-administered and the British called the people there Free Nagas. Later, when Britain was preparing for decolonization, the Nagas told the British time and again to leave them alone. They said they just wanted to live the way before the British had arrived and had insisted to control and to rule over them. Though there was a lot of recommendation from British administrators to make provisions for the Nagas to rule themselves, the British did not do that and the Indian Union took over. This in spite of what Mahatma Gandhi had assured a Naga delegation visiting him as quoted:. "You have every right to be free." Unfortunately for both Gandhi and the Nagas he was murdered and things had taken quite another turn. The Indian chapter had begun.

After some verbal skirmishes and talks with both the Assam rulers and the central government in Delhi, Jawarhlal Nehru decided to crush the Nagas and moved his troops to occupy the Naga territory. The war began in 1954 and the Nagas hastily put up a guerilla army to fight back. In spite of their expectations the Indians could not win the war against the Nagas down and resorted to dirty tactics like divide and rule and corruption. During these 50 years of incessant war lots of things happened, but in spite of mounting pressure and ruthless torture and killing, the Nagas defended themselves against the Indian military invasion. They felt they were intruded and wanted the Indians out of their Homeland. Though they could withstand the overwhelming majority of some 200.000 Indian soldiers, but were not capable of driving them out. To this day the Nagas are still in a state war. The latest is that there is a cease fire and peace talks going on.

"The second cease fire I read here," said one of the directors.

"Yeah, second one followed by peace talks too. Yes it began in 1964 but did not lead anywhere then too and already these talks have lasted over a decade," commented a researcher of the University of the Philippines, who had been called in to help the police.

"This old man was shot because of that?", asked another high ranker.

"We do not know that, but we do know he was the president of a Naga Government in exile. You know they ran their own government under the nose of the Indians!", the researcher remarked

"How is it possible for them to hold out so long? Guerilla warfare like our New Peoples Army can be put out Americans tell us, but not here that is possible. We have so many islands where they can hide. There is should be easy, don't you think men?"

"Could be, but we don't know the situation," the researcher answered, "in any case because of that military stalemate eventually the Indian Government could not do much else but to suggest a ceasefire. Since that cease fire is almost a decade old and no progress is made, I wonder if this has something to do with it. Don't you think he could have been taken out by their adversary, in all likelihood India?", he suggested.

"Let's not jump to conclusions. We will call on the Indian Ambassador here of course and we will question the man. But, as far as I know, it could also be a rival group which felt compelled to kill him for. When researching I came across factions which have created their own armies," the researcher informed.

"Men, we really need to look into this. This is getting more complicated by the minute!", a director from nearby San Juan said.

"Yeah, however if I am not mistaken bystanders said they thought they had seen a blond lady in the car. This blond late had opened fire on the old man, killing him instantly."

"We can't be certain about that. It could have been a wig too. Has the get away car been found?"," the Quezon City director asked. t

"Yeah the forensic investigators are taking it apart," said one of them, "but if it is a white woman, then I suspect she was an assassin and we have to find the people who gave her that contract."

"First things first, there are too many angles now. It is puzzling. This is going to be a political thing. If the Indians actually killed a man on our streets, I am sure our Foreign Affairs want to know about it. Listen men, until we have more concrete evidence for the moment let's keep things under the table?" the highest in command concluded and formally ordered..

"Yeah," they agreed.

"I had a call from the Foreign Office," said the police commander from Quezon City which had Cubao in its jurisdiction, "from the report in the papers they wanted to know if they should know what happened. I just said I do not know yet, but will let you know when we know more!"

"Good work, I will take over from there and give them a call about it, just not today: the man grimaced.

"Well men, if there is nothing further now, let's get to work and see to it that all stones are turned and what we find under them will surface. I am beginning to believe we have quite a strange but significant case here!"

Because he wanted his money Bailung had just called Sean. He was reassured it was on the way. Not by bank transfer but in cash so it could not be traced. Bailung had done some precarious work but was running low and so he put the screws on Sean.

Sean and Bailung knew each other well, very well and though Sean after their shared experience had fled into unscrupulously making money Bailung had gone down hill. As soon as he had put down the phone, Sean realized that Bailung could be a deadly weapon all by himself. They had been both friends and soldiers for a long time and though Bailung had never really had any ambition but to live his life to the fullest, he was skilful and could be trusted. Bailung of course trusted Sean like no other too, but needed the money badly. Not because he spent a lot on women, but much more so because he recently had been gambling rather stupidly. In the Philippines where he was very much at home, he could not control himself and had lost heavily. He knew he had to stop, but he had become an addict instead and without help he knew this was quite impossible. He knew too he needed someone badly to finally work through the misfortunes he shared with Sean so he could start a more regular life. There was a time he thought this could have been the woman he had guided, Jacky, the assassin. Jacky like him too, he knew that. And a hell of a woman she was. Mentally very capable, sensually seductive, but foremost she was cunning. So cunning even, Bailung smiled, that she was quite sure not get involved with him. Yeah, he thought if he would change his life then he could have a chance with here. He noticed how she had sized him up, remembered how she had teased him and how she tried to make him fall for her, but in the way she would firmly remain in command. No, Bai thought this could not the woman for me.

Over the phone Sean had told him the person with the money would come to see him tomorrow and would arrive by the Thai flight landing at three pm. Well, this should be good then, he thought for this money should launch me into another life. I will go back to the roots. But, this one night and this night only I will go to Angeles City where the women serviced the air force personnel when Clark airbase was there but serve the tourists, the cheap ones, he decided. I will avoid the casino or the back rooms and will just watch the women in the go-go bars and the odd tourists and expatriates there and will return the next day. Adding practicality to his decision he went out to take a bus to Angeles thinking of submerging himself into the night life there. Though similar in nature this nightlife in comparison to Makati or Pasay City in Manila, was more straightforward and less overdone. He rode a jeepney to the Philippine Rabbit bus company near Quiapo and boarded a bus heading to the north. Going through the busy streets of Manila to reach Edsa where it finally would reach the four lane highway toll way up to Dau. It took more than an hour for the bus to hit Balintawak where the highway began and the toll station slowed them down. Once on the highway finally the bus could drive fast and in less than an hour he was dropped off at Dau near the entrance of Clark Airbase. Because the Americans had left when Pinatubo, the volcano, erupted it was not called that anymore. Then all Americans were ordered to vacate the damaged base, both Subic Naval Base and Clark Air base with satellite city Angeles. This city like Olongapo adjacent to Subic Bay served as Rest and Recreation Centers of the American troops. Bai got off at Fields Avenue, the narrow road with perhaps a hundred bars. Though it was early still from a distance already he could see the pre nightlife, just about seven, was already in full swing. The neon lights were on and the bouncers outside quite active. Before he checked into a cheap hotel Bai decided to look only first and walked up to an ordinary quiet bar with a terrace to sit outside. He went for a Red Horse, a special beer stronger served in a bigger bottle and an older heavily made up girl, as all working women were called here, brought it to him and he asked her with the memory of the base on his mind before it converted into a commercial centre with an airport:

"Did you work here when the Americans were here?"

"Oh yes," the woman smiled. She was clearly no youngster but in her late thirties perhaps forty already, "I used to work at Bubbles," she disclosed shyly to him.

"Now you are a waitress?", he asked.

"Yes, just waitress unless I find the man of my dreams," she giggled.

"Oh, la, la," Bailung laughed.

"Yes, there are many old men here and I have two children to look after," she continued. Bailung felt a sad story coming but then she had a happy and radiant face, so he wondered where this would lead to and asked:

"Do you think you can find such man here? Watching the scene I feel these men are on a night out and just go for cheap thrills?

"Yeah, that is true, but there are some nice ones too, these are the ones you can trust," she said with determination.

"Well I hope you will find one dear," Bai said to her as she opened the Red Horse.

"Right away Sir," she answered dutifully but then asked him, "would you like a younger girl to sit with you?".

"Don't you worry about that," Bailung laughed, "I can decide that by myself, but I do thank you for offering me!"

"Okay Sir," she smiled and left to entertain others. Bailung looked around him and noticed some old-timers hanging around in this joint. They were talking to some young girls and acted like they owned them. Out on the street lots of people were passing; vendors of all kinds of wares but primarily food, girls in skimpy outfits and boots on a break to or before going to work get something to eat on the street, jeepneys, trikes (tricycles), beggars primarily children and also quite a few people had come out for the night already, invariably European, American, or Australian men they were. Many were in their sixties, some even seventy or more. There ones in their forties or the youngsters at around thirty were a minority. Though the bars with terraces had only a few customers the scene outside looked quite busy, Bailung thought, Sitting there and watching the crowd, his mood changed. He wondered what the hell he was doing here. Was he chasing fata-morgana's? Woman after woman he had had but no love to hold on to give or to take he could find. To find purpose with someone dear to him was impossible as his soul eluded him because of the unrelenting turmoil lodged in it.

Suddenly the feeling of having gone mad struck him. This environment of poverty of the women and families, of plastic seduction, of cheap sex and with men who could easily afford a woman ate their service every day was the living injustice of what people do to each other. Here on the surface it looked like the people involved did this voluntarily, but Bai knew very well that the circumstances had led the women here to a life it was impossible to escape from. The men, formerly the American soldiers now the expatriates or tourists profiting from this organized out of balance situation which, once you were in it, seemed to be as normal as could be. Bai indulged himself being here because of his need to feel he needed punishment. Being a worthless person after the stint he shared with Sean In Rwanda, he could not come to terms with himself anymore. Coming to Angeles for him was a way of showing to himself how low he could go, how low people could go.

This, he felt, was a way to purify himself of his sins. Sins that haunted him, for ever since Sean and him had committed the worst human crime one could think of, he had not been able to be at peace with himself. Not just the world, he knew, but he himself had gone mad. Bailung was convinced he had no purpose in life anymore. To consume, to have fun was what he had inherited from the warfare he had been part of and had participated in. To be here was like and escape from the horrors he had endured, horrors which haunted him beyond control. He knew Sean was suffering from that too. They were friends, but Sean had taken another path to deal with this trauma. Quite successful in shady areas every now and then Sean had something for him Out of Sean's friendship Bailung knew he was given just tidbits not based of merit. Why the hell did he facilitate that assassination and so why did he agree to pave the way for Jacky? What could have been the need to kill this innocent man? These memories and questions shot through him while watching the transparent game in front of him, women parading men reacting, and drinking his Red Horse. Because Bailung was not unattractive and the women suspected he had money on him, they tried to catch his attention continuously. Absent minded about the world around him, he grew increasingly disgusted with himself. Within him several voices were talking, each and every one trying to get the upper hand.

"No," he angrily said to himself aloud and so startling the women sitting at a table beside him. Completely immersed he did not pay attention to them, more so they had their eyes on him. Now fully focused and oblivious of the women staring at him, he forced himself to decide on his future. Speaking to himself his inner voice said:

This has got to stop. You want a future Bai? Then stop drifting, stop feeling sorry for yourself, stop fucking around. You are a nobody now, you have no purpose in life, you have no perspective, you lost your convictions, and you do nothing but to escape from your painful reality.

"Shame on you!", he said out loud again and realizing the women heard this, he laughed. The women looked to see if they recognized him to be a madman. He saw their startles faces, glanced at them briefly then showed his captivating smile. He knew now he could withstand them. He had decided and he felt some strength returning to him. Now things appeared to be a lot easier as he realized too they would also be much more difficult. Just the idea to have to stick to what he decided would take tremendous stamina. For years now he grown into and led the life of an escape artist and now he had to leave that. He knew well enough that old habits don't just die but, with determination, could fade away. And there was one thing to his credit he remembered vividly now. Though he had acted on the spur of the moment, Bai realized that this small act alone would bring him the redemption he had been seeking for so long. This seed sown in fertile earth would change things, he thought.

"When this seed bears fruit," he said aloud, "the road to my redemption is wide and open. If I can stick to my decision, this will set me free!"

The ladies next to him gasped but when they saw him covered in smiles they realized they saw a confident man and reacted like they were used to. They shifted their attention and with renewed vigor began to seduce him. Bai felt good now. He too felt some new energy was flowing within him and though he reacted gently and warm he firmly showed the ladies that their efforts would be in vain.

"You better point and shoot your love arrows on the men who are willing to be hit by your beauty. I am pretty sure your charms will be appreciated much more," Bai said. The women played along but without giving up on him yet indeed began to focus on the other men, who they obviously deemed to be much easier game for them. Relaxed now, he observed their moves and watched the street too. Sipping his beer now, he saw a stunning lady passing. Right in front of him she looked and Bai felt a sting of recognition. He immediately threw the thought of remembering this lady he once knew far from him because the lady he thought he recognized could never have been part of the scene here in Angeles City. The lady saw the transformation on his face and instantly realized he had recognized her as much as she felt a jolt too. Her heart jumped as she smiled and winked at him. Bai's heart stopped when her direct look hit him and he for a second frantically tried to act like he was not interested. Jesus, he thought. I have been tested already and was found to light. How can this be possible? Then the lady leaned over and smiling still she said softly:

"I think I know you!"

"Oh," Bailung said forcing his thoughts to change dramatically. He looked at her knowing that no matter how he would have wanted this, he would not jeopardize the happiness of this exquisite woman he had known so well. The decision he had made stuck in his mind and was strong. Remembering her well he felt drawn towards her, but he realized he should not indulge. He had left her because of the tremendous difficulties he had gone through. Oh, he had loved her, but knew then that her love, because of his predicament, would cause her tremendous pain. That is what he wanted to save her from, to save her from him. And, now here she was in front of him and again he was completely taken by her. He did not know what to say but heard himself slowly uttering:

"Hhhmmm, I am not sure I had the pleasure of meeting you!"

"Can I be mistaken?", she asked aloud engulfing him with a golden smile but knowing she knew that he knew they were meant for each other.

"I think you must be," Bailung answered nervously and knowing that she knew. .

"Cannot," she laughed, "I have changed. I am a lady now Bailung. May be you do not know me as a lady? Look again," she commanded, "look me straight into my eyes!"

"You know my name and I do not recognize you?", he lied and blushing as she knew.

"Yes, we knew each other some 5 years ago and spent some time together," she knew and to be sure now too Bailung went back in time and he could match her face with a name.

"You don't look like Celia!!", he exclaimed

"Right," she smiled, "but look again and you will see it is me!", she smiled.

He looked and banking on the instant recognition now, he realized what she meant. He had known her as a young woman, very much like one working here in Angeles City and the reason why he did not recognize her fully was that she was indeed a lady now. She had nothing of a giggling girl anymore, but was a woman in full command of herself. It now dawned on him that Celia was the woman he once loved but was too afraid then to share his life with. This is strange, he thought as their eyes met and the old feelings resurged, just now I made a sweeping decision which changes things dramatically in my life and here comes Celia. This cannot be a coincidence.

"What are you doing in Angeles?", he suddenly asked thinking she might be working as an hospitality girl.

"No, no, no," she laughed again, "visiting some friends with some restaurants. I am in the restaurant business now. Angeles is expanding again Bailung so we are opening some," she explained. Bai looked at the lady in her tight business suit, not too high heeled and with a smile he could resist. Yes, he knew her well, he thought.

"Gosh," he said, "you Celia, I would have never thought you could pull this off."

"That money you gave me Bai when we sadly departed I pout to good use. First I did some courses in business management and what was left of it I bought myself into a restaurant. Now things are moving along nicely."

"I am glad to hear I did something of value," Bai smiled.

"You caused me to cry and to be happy. You taught me to fend for myself but you Bai? You look like you have not changed man, still rough nut? What are you doing here? Are you after some cheap women? I am sure you can afford," she said mockingly.

Bai smiled knowing very well she tried to draw him out, her heart still with him.

"Believe it or not I have changed too, come sit with me," he said softly.

"You are sure you want me by your side," she laughed covering her uncertainty he noticed when he saw her face twitching.

"Don't be silly, it is good to see you again, so we should talk. Are you married?", he asked without thinking for this revealed much his inner feelings. Surprised about this question Celia looked at him:

"I know you well and I know you know when I come sit next to you I will be helpless. Have changed Bailung?"

"Come sit with me," Bai smiled and felt helpless now too.

No, I am not married, but with a good man would like to. Unfortunately you are not a good man. Well good for a night or two!", she mocked him again.

"You think lowly of me. And, rightly so," he smiled again but now with some confidence, "come sit and have a drink, I promise I will not seduce you, okay, you can find out for yourself if I have changed?", Bailung pleaded now. Strange he thought, normally I would not stoop to that. On the contrary I like it much better for women to go after me so I am in control. But for the fact that he had liked her much more than any other woman at the time Celia was no exception then. Mentally he had felt drawn to her but oh now he remembered her body too. He knew it had been good for her he had told her off when she declared she wanted to be with him. And, he recalled the horrible scene. She had cried her heart out throwing at him he loved her, but denied himself the bliss of this union. Bai had been furious, but he knew she was right. He feared to ruin her life, but how could he tell her that? He decided to leave her something so she could get a start in life but he had never seen her again. And here she was standing in front of him, teasing him and he thought, could this mean a second chance? "What are you thinking," she asked in a tone like she felt he had changed their tension was subsiding. Bailung with a lump in his throat said:

"Sit down, we will talk!"

She looked at him, her eyes ravishing but attentive. Without a further word, neither one to tease nor to be serious in, she gained trust and slipped beside the table sat in the chair next to him. She looked again and saw he did not try to hide the lump in his throat.

"I have been stupid," he said to her.

"I know," she answered softly this time not to put him down but to show empathy.

"I have done many stupid things," he went on, "even if we could come together again Celia, I do not quite deserve you. You were once so close to me it was frightening," he said and he felt a tear welling and tried to remember the last time he cried but could not.

"What is wrong darling", Celia asked, the people around the bar looking up for the word darling was common but for Celia's special sound. They saw this woman clearly cared about that man.

"Nothing really Celia, I am just pulling myself together and made a decision," he said wondering why he told her. He just made it and it meant nothing yet. Did he feel he wanted to make an impression on her, he wondered.

"You were always pulling yourself together," she laughed then ordered a drink from the older waitress. The normally confident looking Bailung due to Celia's nearness turned shy now. A stunning looking woman by her appearance alone she commanded attention from everyone. Like Celia Bailung, overwhelmed by her presence had only eyes for her:

"Goodness," Bai said, "I stood still and you went ahead. You are a radiantly successful woman and I was where you left me," he smiled in modesty.

"Ah come on macho man, you are just hoarding your strength to make a big jump again. May be you don't know it yourself, but I always felt that from you. God how I loved you man," she said without any restraint. It is so good to see you Bai."

"Friends for life I remember saying," Bailung said.

"Yeah," she agreed.

"But I am in no state to be your friend," he said.

"What do you mean? Let me help you then man," she said decisively.

"I don't know if you can. It is not money, though I have been stupid with that. I have gone down a road I should have gone."

"You said you have changed now," Celia tried.

"Well I decided that only today, it has no form or direction yet," Bailung answered.

"Then let me help you?", she asked in a way which left little room for denying her.

"Where do you live?", Bailung suddenly asked.

"Your drink lady," the older woman said posting a soft drink on the table.

"Thank you," Celia said and smiled at her then focused on Bailung again:

"Manila, Makati," she said, "a far cry from my province you know. Now at least I am capable to do good for my family and I do," she said.

"Apartment?", he asked.

"Yeah, but it is large enough to have my office there too. Do you want to come and stay with me," she asked off hand like this was the normal thing to offer a friend.

"I am not a long lost friend you'd like to help out dear Celia," he said reading her thoughts, "oh, I would love that but then I have to tell you what I did not tell you when we were together. I am not sure you don't like what you are going to hear!", Bai said.

"You are an untrustworthy man, a man without honor?", Celia asked in turn, "rubbish, never mind about that. I know I am safe with you. Come let me drive you back to Manila to spend a few days together in my place. I am dying to know how you fared, about your escapades. You have always been an adventurous man," she laughed.

"You were just about to go back then? I just came by bus you know, Celia!"

"Never mind, if you want to stay then come and visit me later. Do not go around here unprotected," she giggled, "buy some Trust condoms?"

"I did not come for that, but to see how these foreigners move around, people I once fought for and are now only taking advantage of a country in difficulties. The solders of the American Army gone, now in contrast to Olongapo, Angeles City flourishes as a tourist centre. There is nothing to see but a volcano and of course scores of women.. I felt like studying the behavior of the men."

"Hmmmm, okay, if you want to stay here studying for a few days, then do so, but remember I want to see you. You owe me some time with you."

"Well I think you may be bored very soon and kick me out Celia," he smirked.

"Here is my card and address, yes I finished university thank you for your help in that. I owe you big time too man," she whispered.

"You do not owe me anything Celia, whatever makes you think that?", he asked.

"You gave me strength man," she giggled, "and I know what love is. That is why I am still alone, nobody, no man stirred me like you did. I could only let you go because you needed to be free. Oh come on, how are you now?", she asked.

"I Can't say I am fine, I am still searching but downhill. If I tell you what I do you do not want to see me ever again, I am sure of that Celia."

"Where did that self assured but honest man go? I can't believe you have become dishonorable, have you indeed?", Celia fumbled.

"Yes I think so," Bailung sighed.

"Let's go to my place or is it you came to have a last look at the seedy life?", Celia asked. "I am sure of that indeed, Celia, though when I decided to come here, I was not aware of it really. Now I am. Yes let's say goodbye to this kind of life forever!"

"Right," she said and got up, "let's see a few bars together then go to my place, she said and called the waitress to pay, "a friend of mine owns a joint here and is friends with both the governor of Pampanga and the mayor of Angeles. You do know there are no more shows here, just bikini go-go?"

"No, I did not know that," he said and followed her.

"You will see," she giggled and by putting her arm in his she showed she was with him.

"Okay," Bailung said, now shy again

"Good," Celia answered and walked along with him till they turned left into a side street leading to a square full of bars and open air restaurants.

"The Chicago Hotel is still there so if you like to spend the night there, you are right in the middle of things," she giggled again. "What? Being with you, do you actually think I want still another woman?", Bai asked.

"Oh," Celia exclaimed as if she was surprised. Do you mean it past time lover of mine?"

"Of course, what do you think?" Bailung laughed now, "no one here can even stand in your shadow. Such a long time Celia, I did not think you liked to be close to me."

"Yeah, but do you feel any different? Now be honest," she smiled but seriously.

"It did not enter my mind, because I am in not way worthy of you Celia!", he whispered.

"Rubbish, you were my man and I loved you with body, soul and mind. I know you did love me too. You only could not give yourself the way I do. You pulled yourself free and caused pain for you and me. But, that is in the past now. Oh Bailung, whatever happens man, let's be friends at least?"

Bailung did not quite understand how it was possible she cared for him that much still. Here she was a woman of standing who had grown in her beauty and was now in command, while he was just a bum he thought. Of course they had had a deep rooted relationship, but as soon as she had come so near to him to want a future with him, family and children, he had fled in fear. God, he had thought then, I love this woman dearly, but with my mind not together and a wandering spirit I cannot promise her that, not with my Rwandan background. And, when he told he could not follow her, she had cried, , she had been sad and angry, became violent and she had shouted. 'You deny yourself a future with me', she had cried out. 'You deny yourself to yourself; we are destined for each other. You know it, I know it. Why do you fool yourself? We are one in spirit. We belong together; you are free still in being one. When do you leave like this, throwing away half of your?' she had cried out angrily. And, she had been right, but still he could not go back to her. Not because of pride or passion, not because of fear of being rejected, but what he had gone through during that bloody war, he could not share. He would never be able to share with her. So, here she stood on this bordello bar square among hookers, vendors and johns, and she looked at him wanting him to acknowledge they were friends:

"I have deep caves of strange memories hidden in me. I am so glad to see you again and of course we can be friends Celia. I cannot say no to that, but I have lived an erratic life and you deserve better than being with a battered man."

"You are a silly man, you know that?", Celia giggled, but she was happy he had agreed.

"Well, I know that very well Celia," Bailung smirked.

They approached the club of Celia's friend and the bouncer who knew her opened the door for both of them. There must have been some 15 girls dancing on stage all in bikinis. Fire station it was called and it was quite dark, only the stage was lit up and black light lighted up white shirts in ghostlike manner.

"Hello Celia," the floor manager began, "you brought a handsome fried. Come I will seat you comfortably. Some beers?"

"That's fine," Bailung said for both of them. In the dark and with loud music they could hardly talk but Celia took him by the hand and asked teasingly:

"Which one is to your liking Sir?"

She said that in the tone of a floor manager would when a man was suspected to be either to shy or had no idea of how to approach

"Only you tonight," Bailung said teasingly and looked at one dancing before him.

"Only tonight?", she teased back.

"We need time to talk Celia. I am profoundly happy that you even want to talk to me. Do you know that? After what I have done to you I did not think you would."

"I know what you go through. I have listened to you sometimes at night when you had your nightmares you know. I can't pretend to know nothing even though you do not easily talk about it," she said trying to talk through the blasting stereo installation.

"I want to talk to you, perhaps now I can. This is going very fast. I never expected to meet you again and here we are. Oh, oh darling this is too good to be true perhaps. I am not sure I deserve this," Bailung said

"Then you must tell me everything Bai. Let's go back to Manila. You will stay in my place!", she said. Her friend the owner appeared for a chat. Bai let them be and looked around to calm down. He felt overwhelmed now and still could not believe Celia was actually sitting right next to him. He watched but did not actually notice silly foreigners trying to make an impression on a bunch of girls.

"This is Bailung, my friend and once my dear lover," Celia introduced him to the young woman in charge.

"Hello to you," Bailung said:

"Once he was?", she asked quirking a brow, "you never told me that Celia!"

"I do not advertise," Celia giggled.

Bai saw them talking to each other and his attention drifted to the foreigners, obviously expatriates who were living here, not just visitors. They were having a disagreement over some women and engaged using big words of derogatory nature. The women with them, not knowing what to do, looked on in despair. He caught some of it through the flaring music when it was not so loud:

"Look Jerry, you fart, I paid for this girl the other day. I want her now, so no way fucker you can get her. Get lost!"

"Big mouth fat George is talking," Jerry reacted with contempt, "just because you had her does not mean you owe her low life Australian outback sicko who fled here to get what you can't get at home. You do not order me around, got it!"

George was ready to jump on the smiling Jerry who had the woman they were fighting over by his side, but he was held back by both the bar personnel and the floor manager when he cried out like a wounded animal:

"Who the fuck do you think you are mocking me retard? That woman is mine!"

Jerry still smiling came up with a compromise, but one it looked like he was sure to feel good with and proposed:

"I believe the woman concerned has as much say in this as you or I. Shall me make her preference decisive George?", Jerry asked.

"She has nothing to do with it you fool; she is paid for the services. It depends on who buys her service. Man you are stupid!"

"So, you don't agree," Bailung heard him saying and thought 'God these people are like children, they fight over a person they can buy'. This is really a low way of relating realizing he had indulged in it too, only to get rid of the numbness in his brain and only this helped temporarily. Now that he saw it with a fresh mind, the mind of a changed man, he loathed the way these people were talking about the women they were fighting over. He looked on:

"I am not bound by foolish pride George," Jerry said, "so I tell you this. If the woman here decides to be with you, she will go with you, but if she wants to be with me, no more word is said about it. I do not ask you to agree anymore. This is the way it is going to be," Jerry said looking determined.

"Fuck you," George replied, but Jerry took no notice and turned to the girl who being the center of attention now looked frightened and fragile in her bikini.

"You may choose whom you want to be with," Jerry said gently to her, "either way you will be paid!"

The girl looked at both of them, fear in her eyes, less fear as she looked at Jerry. Clearly more frightened of George than Jerry she said:

"I like you Jerry. George very rough," and dropped her head for she expected a fight to erupt. But nothing happened. George looked at her like he could tear her apart, but knowing the whole bar would jump on him and knowing the girl had fairly chosen, he counted his loss, turned and ordered a beer and that was that!

Celia and her friend were still talking. Bailung had expected her to intervene, but she did show trust in her personnel to let them handle the potential danger. She had looked every now and then to check on things.

"Okay, let's go Bai," Celia suddenly said.

"You finished your conversation?", Bai smiled.

"Of course," she smiled, " I do not feel like these fights. Some men are straight from the gutter. Just because there are women available, they behave like they own them all. It is horrible to see this," she said, her friend nodding. Bai would have wanted to talk to her, how she got into this business, what she did expect next to making money and so on, but Celia wanted to go. She was elated they found each other again. Bai had to admit he had the same feeling, but did not know how to deal with it. Celia was spontaneous but Bai was withdrawn, overwhelmed. He knew he did not deserve a woman like Celia. Not now, first he had to make sure he could pull himself together. He felt this lovely meeting had come to soon. He had not experienced redemption yet, if this was ever possible for him, he thought and was ashamed. This time I will be man enough to tell her all, he promised himself, then she can decide, and he rose with her to say goodbye to her friend.

Outside she took his hand and glanced at him. Feeling good about that Bai said:

"I have to tell you who I am and what I did."

"You never looked down on yourself, why now Bai," she replied defiantly, "why should you look down on yourself?", she asked.

"Okay, let's go to your apartment," he answered and I will tell you all about it. It is time to come clean and face myself. You will be surprised and will see me in a different light. I wonder if you still like me or love me then!", he said hesitantly.

"My car is parked on the Macarthur highway," she simply said and took his hand to walk that way. They did not speak again until they reached. Bai go in after she unlocked the doors. Still without a word said she drove off. Only on the Superhighway past the bus station at Dau Bai said:

"I remember you so well Celia," he sighed and looked at her.

"I am not stupid Bai, I knew you then and I knew the troubles in your head. I knew too you could not stay with me to build up something together. But I know you love me like I love you. This is obvious to me, so obvious that it feels like you are in my body. I do not need sex to feel it."

"In my head and body I am with you all the way Celia, but there are doors in me I cannot open. Only now when I have the courage, or I think I have, I can show you. I am sure you will be flabbergasted what you will discover behind these doors, my love! Because I love you darling, I could not stay with you. You cannot understand that, but it is true!"

"Well soon we are home," she said and you can talk about it all. I assure you I will not reject you, even though you might deserve it," she said:

The Ambassador of India was called in by the police and when he arrived, guards swarming around for his protection around him, the first thing he asked was:

"What has India got to do with this murder?"

"Good day to you," said Efren. "we called you in to inform you about what we know and how it possibly relates to your country, but we want to ask you a few things too."

"Oh you do?", the man said showing some irritation.

"Yes, this murdered man we found out was a Naga. We understand Nagaland is part of your country. The man lived here with his family. There are also some more Nagas here. We want to find out why this man was killed in broad daylight. We like you to help us."

"I know nothing; of course I am aware some Nagas have taken refuge here, but other than that, nothing I know. Are these Nagas a nuisance to you?", he asked.

"Not at all, they behave well. They are registered as religious people, Christians. Let me ask you this, I am sure you are aware that the Nagas do not want to be part of India and that your army has occupied their territory right?"

"Yes of course I know that," he said reacting like he was going to be cornered.

"Can you tell us about that relationship?", Efren asked but not revealing what the Manila police knew already.

"India took over from Britain," the man began, "so it took over all that was the British Empire then in South Asia. The Nagas did not want to be part and had to be shown that they were Indian. The first Prime Minister Nehru ordered the Indian military to take over and so the troops were sent there," he said in a tone like he was lecturing.

"Okay," Efren nodded, "but as I understand it, the Nagas fought back and still don't want to be part of India. India did not conquer them yet right?", Efren asked.

"What has this got to do with the murder?", the Ambassador asked in turn.

"Nothing and everything, we are trying to find out Sir," Efren answered, "but tell me have the Nagas agreed to be part of India?"

"Not that I know of," the Ambassador said reluctantly.

"I understand there are peace talks now between the Nagas and India?", Efren asked.

"Yes indeed," the Ambassador nodded.

"And, this murdered man was one of the highest among the Nagas. In fact he was part of the negotiating team, isn't that right too?"

"Is he?", the Ambassador played dumb, "has his identity been confirmed?"

"Yes we have been able to do that. This man is the chairman of the organization which leads the fight against India. He is also the president of the Naga Government in exile. His identity has been confirmed."

"Oh gosh, this is very unfortunate then," the Ambassador exclaimed.

"It is indeed, for at first we thought this was just a murder like many, murders for money, jealousy or passion. But this one is not. Do you have an idea who could profit from this assassination?", Efren asked looking straight at the Ambassador now, but talking in a gentle manner still.

"If you are referring to our Government I can assure you India will not stoop to this kind of level. Have you checked on the rival organizations? I am sure they may profit from the disarray that will come after it is known the highest man of the Naga Army has been assassinated."

"Has the news spread in India and Nagaland already?" Efren asked.

"I will look into that," the Ambassador promised but evasively.

"Tell me more about the rival organizations," Efren asked. Of course they had come across some of it already, but he was not sure what this Ambassador was relating to.

"Well, there is the old NNC, the Naga national Council, which was the first organization representing the Nagas and had its own army and government too. In 1975 the Indian Government closed a deal with them called the Shillong Accord and we thought all was settled then; the Naga Army was being disarmed and the people would be part of India."

"You mean they had been fighting all this time for nothing?", Efren asked.

"No, no, no, of course they would have some kind of autonomy. Mind you they already had a state of their own. This one was inaugurated in 1963. Gosh what more did they want?", he wondered aloud.

"Obviously some among them did not want that kind of compromise and carried on but since the NNC you mentioned had sold out, they went ahead under a different name. I read somewhere that this murdered man was part of that NNC too?", Efren asked.

"Yeah right," the Ambassador replied visually showing he was under pressure now.

"Tell me Sir, if it is not the Indian Government who profits from the murder on this man, can you distinguish to whose advantage it is? I am asking you about motive. Killing someone in a strange country presumes planning, so the motive must have been quite strong, don't you agree?"

"I am sure, but I think if you want to look into it further and I do not see why you should, then look into the motives of the rival factions!"

"Hhhmmm," Efren reacted.

"Was that all, Mr. Efren?', he asked.

"Not yet," Efren said firmly, but smiled, "this is an Indian citizen who is killed on our soil, don't you feel a responsibility to solve this murder?"

"I don't pretend to know about these things Mr. Efren, I am not a detective, but I like to reassure you we are taking things seriously."

"Oh how Sir Ambassador?", Efren asked.

"I have requested a team of detectives to come to Manila to help you out. This should be beneficial to us and to you, but I am sure more so to us than to the Philippines."

"To us?", Efren asked trying to grasp what he meant and asked:

"Well when the murder is solved I am sure it has nothing to do with your nation, but everything with India. The Philippines has been used as a venue and you only get into it now because you are a policeman, a detective, who wants to solve this murder."

"Yeah, it is a puzzle and it could be a political murder too!!", Efren remarked.

"Could it? Let's not come to any conclusions but get the facts first, shall we?", the Ambassador remarked now gaining ground as he felt he had taken the initiative back again and smiled a superior smile.

"Police detectives go by the facts. They produce likely theories, and then discard them one by one until they get to the most viable one. Do not underestimate the power of police work Ambassador," he replied curtly looking at the man straight.

"Right, can I go now, it may surprise you but I still have other things to do!", he quipped.

"I would like to give you an assignment," Efren said discarding his remark, "I would like you to get in touch with your government in Delhi to supply us with all the information we need to solve this case."

"I already promised you a team of detectives," the Ambassador said.

"That is good, but not good enough. I like you get us direct communications between your police and us via Foreign Affairs. This is more than a request, we require this!"

"Are you giving me a fait accompli?", he asked and smiled.

"I told you we require this and you are here in the Philippines. I would not like to venture into diplomatic repercussions should you decide not to honor this request," Efren smiled.

"Your wish is our command," the Ambassador smiled back, "we are guests here. We may be diplomatically immune, but we feel warmly welcomed and are very much motivated to help you out. It can only lead to helping ourselves in the process," the Ambassador smiled again, "I will do anything to assist you!"

"You were apprehensive at first, this is quite a change," Efren dryly said.

"I needed to find out how serious you take this case. After all as you said it could have India targeted in a way this murder is used against India. Let's be fair?"

"We will be, it is our intention to solve this murder by finding the right culprit, not a scapegoat, though already I think we may be directed to a few first!"

"You could very well be right in that," the Ambassador said and got up, signaled his guards. This time without Efren's intervention or his fellow police men, but he did say:

"We will keep in touch. And, oh yes, do not hesitate to pick up the phone if you have no time to come and visit us, all right?"

The Ambassador turned, smiled, looked and said:

"Right, we will work together!"

In Delhi there was some tension the Home Ministry and Foreign Affairs were besieged by questions and it looked like soon the Prime Minister was required to make a public appearance on the matter. Within Foreign Affairs there was disbelief over the murder. In the Home Ministry too but since this ministry was responsible for the internal security together with the Ministry of Foreign Affairs; the first thing the civil servants thought about was to keep this news as lukewarm as possible. Certainly not, like some newspapers already suggested, through their stringers in Manila that the Indian Government was involved in this. Because phone calls on the matter could not be avoided instructions by their ministers were issued to the spokespersons to categorically deny any involvement. They were to tell the newspapermen and TV reporters that a full investigation was under way. The Philippine Ambassador in Delhi had been instructed to come to talk to the Foreign minister. When he had arrived he was immediately led to the Foreign Minister.

"Good to see you Alfredo, welcome," the Foreign Minister began, "it has been a long time indeed. Please sit down!"

"Greetings to you Minister Patill," said Alfredo in return. What seems to be the hurry? I am sure you did not summon me for some chit chat!"

"Oh Alfred, you know of course," Patill smiled.

"Oh, I have a hunch," Alfredo smiled back," we are not altogether too foolish you know."

"I asked you to come right away for we have a situation here, one that may go out of hand. Not in the Philippines of course, but here it will and we need your country's cooperation. Can we count on that?", he asked in serious manner now.

"Normally you can, but a man has been murdered on our soil. We have to find out what this means Mr. Patill; I cannot say anything before we know more. Besides I am under instructions of my Government. I am sure you understand!", Alfredo explained.

"Of course," Patill answered, but you see it has nothing to do with the Philippines. The Press may come to you and talk, or ask, or accuse your people. This could turn ugly, you know," he said:

"I don't see why it should. I am sure Philippinos have not done it. It was no murder for money, or anything else. But it could be political too," he explained.

"Well it looks like it and the press here wants to know who was involved. I understand a team of detectives has been put on the case, Alfredo?"

"As far as I am informed yes indeed and I understand your people have decided to send in a team of your own, Mr. Patill?"

"Assshhh," Patill sighed, "news travels fast, the order was only given a few hours ago and communicated to our Ambassador in Manila," Patill laughed.

"Like I said Patill, we don't have our heads in the sand. Now be open and tell me what this is all about? My government likes to know and I am sure when it is appeased, I will be directed to cooperate fully!", Alfredo said hinting at the consequences.

"Your men have discovered a lot already and at first suspected our side, without knowing what level or circle, to be responsible for it. It is obvious of course to think along those lines. It is a person important for the peace talks and a leader of a people India is at war with. So, to take him out could lead to instability. But Alfredo, like you and I can readily conclude, is that this would be far to obvious. No government will be that stupid to go through killing an adversary in a foreign country for it would only to be accused of destabilizing right away. No, Alfredo we are not that stupid here, but the ones who actually planned it, I am sure wanted it to look like the Indian Government is behind it."

"If we can think that Patill, don't you think a Mastermind, a real plotter, would not have foreseen this? No Mr. Patill, already I am rather convinced it is more complex than this. I can sense it. This is a murder to elude us all, but the right people will be blamed."

"Oh Alfredo, and according to you who are the right people?", Patill asked sharply. Alfredo laughed noticing how Patill showed he felt like he was bitten by a snake:

"Implicitly I said it may not be your Government Patill. Yet tell me, are all in your government and across parties in line with those responsible for the peace negotiations?"

"Oh gosh, you know about those too then," Patill said in surprise.

"I live here Patill. Nagaland may not be known in the Philippines or anywhere else in Asia, but I do read the papers and I did take an interest when the leaders, of which one is killed now, came to Delhi last time. From then I read up on the background of that long conflict. In fact I took special interest, because we also have a long standing conflict going on. With the New Peoples Army we have not even been able to come to profitable peace negotiations. I took interest in this conflict because we may learn from it," Alfredo smiled gallantly now. Patill did not trust him of course and reacted:

"In what way are you learning?", he asked.

To name one thing about the negotiations, the skilful give and take of course. Look Mr. Patill, it is obvious the Indian Government is forced to talk. It cannot win the war and it cannot talk the Nagas out of their right to self determination. Both do not give in an inch. So, there are a lot of pointers. Returning to this assassination, you know well enough that this could have strong bearings on the talks. Many things have to be scrutinized before we can find the plotters," Alfredo smiled, "The assassination could have political implications. It also depends on who is vulnerable and who will take the fall," Alfredo smiled, "it is a well thought out game, I suspect. Don't you agree?"

"You may be right, but then again you may not be. Who knows," Patill equally smiled.

"We had something like this too, well not too similar, but something like it. For all to see a presidential candidate was shot dead on the tarmac of the international airport in broad daylight. Still the police could not pinpoint the perpetrator and though all fingers were pointed at Marcos, then the president, never enough proof was uncovered to actually arrest him as the plotter of the murder of Benigno Aquino."

"So you have are interested to find out how we work to solve the case Alfredo?"

"Yes, but also how certain elements of the investigation are bound to disappear. Evidence that has been discovered, can disappear you know!" he said.

"Are you suggesting something of that sort can or is going on here?", Patill asked trying to control himself as to what he felt was an impertinence.

"Not at all, but I am sure you will agree that this case has all sorts of elements in it which when fully known would harm certain people in power?", Alfredo asked his face blank.

"It is a reality perhaps, but Alfredo I can assure you now, but don't have to, that we here at the foreign ministry will leave no stone unturned."

"That is a sound style of working and the attitude I like and is just, but you are not alone in this, there may be predators," Alfredo praised Patill.

"Okay then, Alfredo, thank you for dropping by at such short notice. We will keep you informed," Patill said in a tone like he dismissed him. Alfredo did not mind for he knew they had a watchdog and Alfredo wanted to play openly. He got up and said:

"Thank you for you hospitality and openness, it was a pleasure as always Patill," he smiled gently and left.

Once Alfredo had left, Patill called the staff of the Foreign Ministry together then phoned the Home Ministry people to come over for a top level meeting. The top secretaries arrived less than half an hour later. The offices of the ministries were laid out close to together, all in the same Government area and faced the big monument, the gate of Delhi. Parliament house was nearby too. But here they were, now all secretaries present Patill explained why he had called for this meeting:

"We may be facing a grave situation," he said and he looked at the secretary who watched over the Internal Bureau (IB) then at the another who had the Research and Analysis Wing (RAW) to deal with, "if this is not solved, if we do not find the killer but more so the plotters, we may have to bear the brunt of this murder. Since the Government is responsible for the talks with the Nagas all eyes will be on us. Now let me be very clear," he paused and looked around so the meaning of his words would have impact and sink in, "I want you all to beat the grass to get the snakes out. I want to make sure no government agency, no individual, nor are cooperating agencies involved in this. And since the situation is grave I want that be sorted out as of yesterday. Now is that understood?", he stressed, "I want to be absolutely sure the Indian Government is not implicated. When we are actually certain of that, we can go after the real culprits and plotters. Do not think of what I say as just an advice. I am deadly serious and we must get to work to be sure."

The group of men and a few ladies had not realized how serious Patill was. They had not seen him like this before, not this deadly serious.

"Are there any questions?", Patill asked searching the room for faces who were either too docile or too evasive or perhaps too eager to come up with something..

"I have one," said a rather young man working in the Home Ministry close to the IB and Raw offices, "what will we do when it appears to be indeed an inside job? You did not rule out that possibility I think?", he asked.

"Well what would you advice the Government when indeed this is so?", Patill asked.

"My task will be to find who, not to tell the Government what to do but to report the culprit, right?", he asked, feeling somewhat cornered.

"You are right, you can leave the decision making to us, but my actual point is, what will you do when you find out the Government, when it is responsible, will put that knowledge you provided under cover again?"

"Oh Gosh," the young man said, "this means I should not like to be the bringer of bad news. My life surely will be uncertain then if the Government will not get the killer."

"You are right, so rule out there is anyone in our ranks responsible for this mess, okay?"

"Okay," he said while looking at the others who looked a bit sheepish. The young man was at loss too but had made up his mind and did not ask further. He knew now what to do, but did Patill know what he just had done?

Chapter 4

The great escape

It had been a busy night at the high class Bordello, called The Bordello, cum escort service Amsterdam girls and Jacky had just returned from Bangkok. She felt good. Oblivious of what had transpired in Manila and Delhi, she had been with Sean for a good rest until he had directed her to return and to go back to work as usual. Reluctantly she had done so, for though very independent, she was quite close to Sean. She knew he felt for her, but he would not ask her to join him for good. There was something about him that made him refrain from having a deep relationship, something she had read in Bailung's eyes as well. She had thought then to face him and draw him out but fearing the consequences had thought the better of it. Jacky, her real name Jacqueline, loved her independent life, but had grown more towards Sean than she did like to admit to herself. She knew Sean knew that as well. She knew from his eyes and from their lovemaking. Having worked again for a few days she was back to her usual self. It was three in the morning when she had a call from Amsterdam girls:

"Would you like to go to Brazil Jacky for a week or so?"

"Hmmmmm, Brazil, what for?, she asked, "I just returned from a trip to Bangkok Madam Desire," she laughed as that name alone was one of her many nicknames.

"And, if things go well another week in New York?", Desire went on like she had not heard Jacky's question.

"What do I have to do?", Jacky asked.

"Be a day and night escort for a politician from there. He was with you once. I think you liked him. He is a good client. He pays well," Desire said in her usual way of praising a client for his financial capabilities and her cut as a go between.

"I will consider it," Jacky smiled for she as usual with Desire did not want her to control whom she would be with. Not that she did not like

Desire, but she had too much of a clout on her girls and Jacky wanted to be free of that.

"When will you tell? The man wants to know and arrange it," persistent Desire said.

"Look it is three in the night; it is bad enough you bother me with this request. This man should not come up with it at this time. Is he a spoiled brat or what? Let him think for a while. I will tell you later, when you tell me who it is?"

"Hmmmmmmm," Desire thought aloud, "well it is up to you, but I tell you it is a good chance this Latino who works for the United Nations."

"Does the UN have money now?", Jacky giggled and hung up.

I think I know who it is and he is fun too and not too demanding. Besides through him I may get to know something, Jacky thought. Her thoughts were cut short by a stocky fellow who had just come in to the Bordello. An ugly man he was, but apparently with loads of money. After he was made comfortable by the hostesses and had scanned around the place, he went straight for Jacky and without further ado said that he wanted her. Though money was not the option here, it was not for Jacky either. She did not mind to please an ugly man, after all those men did not have much chance to be pleased but there was something about him that made him irritating. Belle de Jour (Beauty of the Day), he had said to her and Jacky instantly related to the idea of the French movie. But today she did not want to entertain anyone she did not know or instantly felt good with. And like in Belle de Jour she did crave the unknown man to take possession of her and it the case of Catherine Deneuve who played Belle Jacky's Sean was the man Deneuve had, while she was part of that bordello in Paris, but voluntarily like Jacky. So, she thought, what the heck. Being in this business I might as well enjoy it, so if I think who that man is, then yes I like to go to Brazil and the USA. Of course as along as he does not want anything more than some really well paid intimate fun. She smiled at the ugly man but not in too much of an inviting way. She wanted to go and leave him, but without offending him. This was not possible. He laid his hand on her arm and looked at her pleadingly, but met a look of disapproval in Jacky's eyes. He changed and now held her arm in iron grip. So much so in pain she gasped. This man was one rude but strong bastard the thought shot through her and unlike in Belle de Jour totally put her off. This is why I hate this otherwise quite interesting a job, she thought and with her left foot, a pointed high heel on it, she kicked the man in his balls. The man screamed and realized he had gone too far. The doormen and a guard came running towards Jacky. The men and removed him immediately. A Bordello cannot use disturbance. The adagio of course was that this would put people off. More than real advertising bordellos exist on mouth to mouth recommendation, Jacky laughed, knowing this time she could get herself out of a potentially difficult and dangerous situation. She decided to call Desire for now she had made up her mind to take that journey:

“Who is that man I know,” she asked her.

“Why do you want to know now? Don’t you like surprises,” Desire giggled.

“I love surprises, but not those that put me in danger, Desire, so ahead with it woman, or I won’t do it,” Jacky said.

“Okay then, it is that Surinam leader who has been accused of the coup there in 1982. He has this name just like,” she said.”

“Oh him, fuck him,” Jacky laughed, “I don’t do drug money.”

“A pity, he is going to New York too,” she still tried to persuade.

“I will tell you this Desire, you gave me an idea. I would love to go to Rio and perhaps spend a few days in Amazonia. I will call Sean and tell him to go with me to Rio. I like to check on our Bordello in New York too.”

“Okay, okay then, so you won’t do it?

“Of course not,” Jacky smiled, “you know I am not fool Desire. I won’t have anything to do with Surinam, not anymore, darling!”

“Go to sleep, I can’t hear you anymore Jacky. You are not good for our business,” she laughed.

“Well, Desire I am more of a manager than a high geared pleasure provider. I do it for my pleasure too, not just theirs or only for the money. I don’t like to be forced or dependent, you know that, so do not aggravate me,” Jacky said and hung up on her and scanned the reception room with the oval bar of the Bordello. She saw the few well dressed but sexy women hanging around and some customers, but she had no inspiration. Too early to call Sean, she thought. I am going home and call him from there. Five hours later so when he runs the office, I will find him there. Or, I will call his GSM, his cell phone:

“Get me a taxi Kees,” she said to the bar man. Kees grabbed the phone as she got ready to leave the luxury bordello.

“Taxi will be here in a few minutes Jacky,” the barman said and she went for the door. The bouncer winked already to show her the coast was clear. The taxi had arrived.

“That was quick man,” Jacky winked, “do you have them parked in front just in case?”

"Hahahahaha miss Jacky, always a joke ready. Yes a deal with them, how did you know?", he asked laughing.

"I know you and this joint, what else is new?", she replied head up haughtily, "pffffttt."

She heard him still laughing when she slipped down the stone stairs of this famous Amsterdam Bordello and got in. Then zoomed away from the classy Herengracht to get to her place not much more then a few canals away, over the Rozengracht to reach her own place in the Jordaan.

Sean was angry. He had just been woken up early by a phone call from someone tapping the wires in Manila. The man had warned him that a full investigation was under way and that the Ambassador of India had been called in by police headquarters. Well, that was to be foreseen, he thought. I should inform Jacky and Bai about this though. I do not think the police will find them; all traces had been wiped out. But from the other side it would be possible still, the side of the people who forced the contract and information on him, people like Jeanie. Of course Sean knew that he could be sacrificed by any of them when the ground under their feet would become too hot. Then they had to deflect attention. After all, when the assassin and her immediate boss were to be given up, the trail to them would be cut and so it would end with Sean. If worst came to worst they would not hesitate to kill him either, Sean knew. Though he had made precautions, like copies of letters and put them in a safe, letters that police could decipher as leads, he was sure that if things would turn sour this was not nearly good enough. Oh, they were handsomely paid. Too well perhaps, he thought One millions dollars was quite a sum and he had shared it with Jacky and Bai. They did not know what he was offered before he took the contract but he had allocated to them two hundred and fifty thousand each, cash of course. Bai already had received the money and had stashed it somewhere. How Sean had received the cash? Simple, it was handed personally through an intermediate; no doubt it had come through more than one intermediate. The responsibility for it was on them until it was delivered. But what is money when you can loose your life? He did not like to jeopardize Jacky's life either. Thinking of her, he had come to the conclusion to settle down with her. He knew it was much more than liking her, he knew he loved here, but could not fully connect with this burden he carried. But it was time she stopped this rubbish like working in Bordellos, he thought; time for her to be a madam now, if she likes being in that life, no longer as an escort. He thought about her and the last few days they had relaxed Bangkok when he, disturbed by the potential consequences of that phone call, heard the phone ringing again:

"Sean here," he announced.

"Hello darling, Jacky here. Let me tell you something," she began.

"Okay shoot," he reacted, "I have something to tell you myself," he answered.

"You want to tell first Sean?", she asked.

"It is up to you, yours cannot be worse than mine," he laughed ironically.

"Is it that bad my man?", she asked.

"Not that bad Jacky, you can go first honey," he decided.

"Well Sean, I was offered an escort job for two weeks with a Surinam leader, you know who, to Brazil and the USA, Rio, Amazonia and New York," se explained.

"Oh nice for you," he laughed, but fumed inside. It is time to stop her now, he mumbled to himself, but half aloud:

"What are you saying now Sean, you don't want me to do it?"

"No, no, no, do what you must do, so for two weeks, when are you going?", he asked.

"I am not going," she said.

"Oh, why did you turn it down Jacky?"

"I don't actually like the man who might be responsible for some murders, but that aside it gave me an idea and I wonder if you like it," she asked.

"Let's hear it," he said.

"I was thinking of you and me going to these places. I want to see more of you. You are busy but what is two weeks, you could use a stand in. There are enough capable people."

"That is a nice idea and there is lots I like to talk to you about, so okay let's do it. Give me a few days to wrap things up here, so the operation will be run smoothly in my absence and I will come to Amsterdam."

"What you mean it darling?", she asked thinking he was teasing her.

"Yes I do. I can use the time of and I think it would be a wise thing to think some more about our future. If we want to stay together of course," he smiled.

"Good idea and we can do that while relaxing and planning a few things, but tell me what is going on? You have me worried about you man!"

"Hhhmmm, you are not going to like it and it is another reason, why we should be together and get prepared."

"Go on tell me what is it?", she asked with voice full of unrestrained curiosity.

"The news is out and already Delhi knows that a full investigation is under way in Manila, something we hoped would not happen," Sean explained.

"They will not find a trace of us," Jacky intervened.

"That may be true Jacky but think; the ones who assigned us might get cornered and may give us up. Then we will be caught. They will just leak info about us and we will get arrested. What then?", Sean asked.

"Oh God, yeah that is a possibility,' she reacted.

"Also this case is much more political than I thought, so the plotter, not Jeanie I think, who is an intermediate, could leak just so that attention on the case is growing. I want to prevent that by taking some counter measures," Sean suggested.

"Tell me what?", Jacky quickly asked.

"No, no, not over the phone, I will now disconnect and be sure I contact you in a few days in Amsterdam, arrange tickets for the destinations you mentioned," he explained and hung up immediately.

Jacky was stunned by these developments. Elated because he wanted to talk about the future, but cautious if not frightened because of the fall out of what they had planned and she had done, the assassination. Sean, though he had been precautious felt a stir and converted that into planned action. He went on checking everything and tried to detect possible loopholes and actions that good be taken to fill them up so there would be no damage. In the end he knew he had to depend on what the ones who commissioned him for the assignment could do when they would be cornered or what not. All tangible things he had on them he collected, copied and put both in a safe in his office and in a safe in his bank. He intended to leave a copy in Amsterdam and New York too. Feeling slightly more secure now, he called for the madam of the Bordello Bangkok, the front office for his other operations. Oh these operations were all legitimate and had much more to do with international trade than with anything else. The Bordello he had opened for fun and in such competitive place as Bangkok he knew was not much more than a niche he filled to make some good money. Since he had implemented some stylish ideas and also some non Thai beauties, the classy atmosphere had attracted a sizable number of high rollers and the name Amsterdam, though not exactly in the name Bordello present, was already renowned. In fact some well run and known massage parlor managers were sent over to him to sniff the atmosphere and the methodology on how the clients were treated. This to Sean was a great compliment.

"Yes Sean," said the madam to him, a real Thai beauty of impeccable taste and elegance, when she entered his office, "is it not too early to have a meeting?"

"Yes it is,' Sean smiled, but it is urgent unfortunately. I have to go for a couple of weeks and I know you are quite capable of running the show. So, I would like to ask you to take over from me, you know the drill," he explained.

"Yes, I do and I am honored you trust me," she thanked him.

"There is one important thing and it could undermine your authority. I won't have it, for when I say you are in charge you are, all right?"

"Of course I will be, but what is it that worries you?", she asked.

"Half of our staff is Thai, so the other half is European. Thai men come here for the Europeans; you know they kick on that. The Europeans know they will be really spoiled by the Thai escorts, right?"

"Oh yes," she agreed, "it is really it is!"

"Well then the European will try to outwit you and undermine your authority. If they dare to doubt your authority you fire them. Let them go somewhere else. No way do I want them to rule over you. I will tell them myself. As soon as I have spoken to them, I will get ready. I will attend to an emergency and I will take some holiday. When I have returned, you will have a deserved holiday on me, agreed?"

"You offer me a holiday?", she asked.

"Yes I do, I want you to take a rest too. You have to show your authority and when you succeed as I think and trust you can, you have deserved it?", he smiled.

"Then I certainly will," she said in her melodic voice and made him a smile he thought only Thai women can do.

Later that day after he made phone calls to instruct other people to control his trade interests and when he had managed his affairs he got in touch with his friend Bai and told him about the situation, warned him too to be prepared for eventualities.

"Come on man, I am Indian and I don't know who did that contract," he reassured Sean.

"No man, you are not Indian, but a Philippino of Indian descent. Nobody knew that. This is not about what you know, but what they can do to you. Wipe out all traces if there are any. That is your responsibility he had said over the phone. Come to Bangkok after I have returned, but take your time now. We have to straighten things out."

"I can come to Amsterdam too, if you like," Bai said.

"No need, I am sure you like to lay low there in the Philippines hey?"

"I met an old lover, and the fire is back," he said, "I am thoroughly enjoying myself, I was not ready then, but it looks like I am now. What we endured Sean was the reason. We are friends but we must talk about what we did man. I want to change my life."

"That is funny," Sean said, "I am about to do that too, "it has been enough to do shady work. We have to be able to live with ourselves and you and I could not do that for a long time. I am glad you break loose Bai, you are encouraging me."

"That is so good to know you are honest with me Sean. You are encouraging me too. It feels like my life has meaning again."

"Well Bai, for a long time it had not. Let's face it you and I were successful in running away from ourselves. We did all sorts of things to mask who we really are. Now I feel strong enough to face all we did, the consequences too. I love Jacky you know."

"You did not have to tell me that. To me that is obvious from both of you. You should stop playing the spider and she should stop being an escort, right? Is that why your going to Brazil is about?"

"Yes, but not only. Also to try and make sure we are not going to get caught should we be given up on by the planners of this bullshit, man. We are not going to take the fall for them. This is planned in high places."

"We will talk later on then," Bai said knowing too the phone is easy but could be tapped. Not yet perhaps may be but calls are registered and appear on bills for potentially future reference to investigators.

After talking to the European escorts and getting their full cooperation and to Bai Sean handed over the affairs to his chosen Thai madam, he booked a direct flight to Amsterdam for later that evening then went home to prepare his things there.

Marius was waiting for Jeanie in his office in The Hague. He did not need to fetch her from Schiphol International Airport for Jeanie knew her way around the Netherlands well. She had called him and he could expect her any moment now. He was answering his official emails and his personal when he discovered one sent by Lisa. In that email she told him she had reached her rehab centre and from there would prepare an exposure trip for both of them. She told him she had already gotten in touch with some of the leaders so their ways would be paved both for the underground and the official journey. She also had sent him an electronic kiss and a picture of her smiling eyes, eyes only. It made him smile too and he still smiled when he heard a knock on the door.

"Are you ready to go?" she asked him in smiles and with a big tease on her face.

"Go where?", he asked not right away getting what she meant.

"To Nagaland of course, stupid man!", she laughed.

"Good heavens silly woman that is why you are here. We can leave in a couple of days. I booked flights to Delhi. We will be with some people there first then we get a flight to Guwahati from there, okay?"

"Okay, I am already exited. I have been reading up too on the way over and I am very much looking forward to it now."

"The reason why I do not want to book through flights is because I want to talk to people in Delhi first. It will deflect them from the notion we will be stopping by Nagaland. The friends in Guwahati will arrange the Rap. I do not want anyone to get ideas to follow us around you know!"

"Good, good. I am sure we will be safe. I can count on you like you can count on me. Are you going to meet Lisa?", Jeanie asked.

"I was just reading her email to me," he smiled, "so yes; she is planning things out for us like getting in touch with the leaders and the Naga Army."

"So we will be able to get in?", Jeanie asked.

"Nothing is sure yet," Marius laughed, "but it looks good."

"So we will go?", Jeanie asked, masked pain in her heart for the two reasons of being involved both with the assassination and Marius. Both she had to come to terms with.

"We will," Marius smiled.

"Let's get ready then," Jeanie replied.

"I will finish my work here and then you will stay in my place. We can talk there and make arrangements. If necessary I will do a last minute runaround. Does that sound allright?", Marius asked.

"Excellent, but do I need a tropical outfit, you know with helmet and khaki shorts and shirt," Jeanie laughed.

"It is summer there too and higher up it in mountains I am sure it is cooler so just bring summer things and a few sweaters and long trousers?"

"Delhi will be hot?" Jeanie asked again.

"Oh yes, of course Delhi before the monsoon could be very hot and damp," Marius said and sent her outside for a stroll around the centre of The Hague, the Peace Palace.

"Come back in an hour and I will be free for the next three weeks Jeanie," he said, "leave your stuff here?"

"Right I will have a coffee then, see you later," she smiled and walked out. Marius went back to work, made a few phone calls and sent a few emails before a last minute meeting with his team and went over to the board room where the others were waiting:

"Welcome Marius," the director said, "for a moment we thought you were not able to make it here in time man. Your head is already focused on your holiday to a strange land? I had a look it up too, remarkable," he joked.

"A man has to do what a man has to do," Marius smirked.

"Oh you did," a young operative in training, a woman, asked, "I also did and I was surprised we know so little about what is happening there. Frankly speaking I was astonished about learning this war has lasted more than 5 decades already, unbelievable. No wonder Marius wants find out, unofficially of course, what goes on there."

"Yeah," the director agreed, "the Indians mastered in keeping it behind closed doors."

"It is unbelievable the peace talks are held here," the young woman said, "no doubt you read about the Cease Fire?"

"Did you check with the Foreign Ministry?", the director cut in, "when held here in the Netherlands the Foreign Office secures visas for the Nagas so actually they can attend the talks. I am sure you were aware of that?"

"Of course," the Marius reacted, "but India is a friendly nation so when we are asked to be a venue, we will oblige. From the international level it is a domestic problem and officially we have no opinion about it. We don't investigate and don't to intervene."

"That is all officially said of course," Bram agreed "I am sure you don't mind telling us what we do unofficially?", he asked

"Well, Marius is going there, that is unofficial," he teased, "and because we do not keep him from going, it surely shows it is unofficial indeed."

"Oh come on, seriously," Marius laughed, if I am on a mission I am required to report. Now I may or may not, depends on my discretion, so I am only going unofficially when I am assigned to do so."

"Hence this meeting," the director said, "the team here will monitor what you are doing and from now on it is a full scale unofficial mission, but an important one," he said.

"Oh! How did that come about? I don't want a personal thing to become unofficially official. This I supposed to be my own initiative," Marius cried out loud, stumbling over his own words.

"We did not know if you were going to be serious about this or that you were following a whim of your heart," the director explained, "this is now a mission because knowing you, you will discover a few things. And we can't really afford to leave you you're your experiences. It is more important than we thought. Jeanie's trip will be unofficially official for her too. She does not know that yet, but we informed her superiors."

"You organized that?", Marius asked.

"What do you think?", he smiled asking in return.

"This is quite a change of heart. What else do you want to tell me?", Marius asked being quite surprised.

"Now you are suspicious and you need not be. Let's just say we have taken a renewed interest in what India and Burma, oh sorry Myanmar, are doing?"

"Really now," Marius mocked him.

"Well, to be honest Marius, I was quite impressed by your story of the woman Lisa you came across and fell in love with," said Bram and he smiled too.

"Fell in love with?", Marius exclaimed getting irritated, "I told you no such thing. Surely I should know that myself?"

"It was obvious, your infatuation for this woman made you want to ho this Godforsaken place," the director smiled.

"Well, first it is not Godforsaken but strangely God-fearing instead; second I am taken very much by these people who, being in their right can hold up against a large army and not for just a few days, but 50 years. That is more than enough reason to get me interested in going on an adventurous holiday, but under cover," Marius elaborated and now had the others stunned. Overtaken by the turn of events, but for the young lady who had done research on the background of the Nagas, seemed to grasp Marius' motivation and said:

"When you actually see what the Nagas, this virtually unknown people, are up against and how controlled they are, how the endured severe provocations, it is not too hard to be on their side. They are the under dog, a dog which has been held captive and in isolated, yet with enough teeth to keep a big army occupied. Read that history and you feel for them and admire then too. By the way their culture is unique and interesting too. They would attract lots of attention when they come to introduce their culture in Europe."

"Sure," the director said, "and because this may be the case we have another reason to be prepared for what we are going to face in the future," the director said.

"What do you mean?", Marius asked.

"This Naga International Support Center in Amsterdam is planning a Naga exposure in Europe, seven countries and under the slogan: Naga Call for Peace, a Cultural Exposure. A cultural troupe will tour key cities, press conferences, seminars, symposia, documentaries, exhibition, you name it the lot. You did not know this Marius?"

"I head about them, but did not give it much notice for it is a rather small organization. How will they finance this then?"

"You will be surprised. They are applying for subsidies, the European Union and others for the troupe to come and stay here, but affiliated organizations will take over to get them booked in theaters all over. Those organizations will pay for the rest. The EU has to have some strong and valid arguments to turn this application down, for that NISC is well versed in politics and can expose the Nagas will be denied subsidy on the motivation of fear of India. So you see it will be a testing matter. We may be called in to see what this NISC is about and how to prevent them from pushing through, even though the Netherlands cannot stop them from organizing such events."

"Our government fears possible repercussion from the Indian Government?", the young woman asked, "I know this can affect the trade between the Netherlands and India of course," she said.

"Exactly, but I am sure that is not their only motivation. I suspect they have a lot to hide regarding what they have done there. Human rights were negated by black laws for instance. There have been accused of genocide too."

"That bad it is? Oh my goodness," the young woman exclaimed.

"More will be revealed later, but I wanted you and Jeanie to know that it is no longer a holiday, but a paid holidat," the director smiled, "so if there are no more questions I would say we can end this meeting!"

"I do not quite like the way you operate," Marius said, "I think you should have discussed this with me. You do not call a meeting and drop this on me like a bomb. Now, please do not make that your policy for I am on the verge of refusing to okay?"

"I can assure you this is an exception Marius. This will not happen again. The official okay I got only a few hours ago also. So, do not get angry. Time was limited."

"So noted," Marius answered, "do know this is not the way things are to be handled."

"Yes, we know," the director said, "now let me wish you a fruitful and safe journey?"

"Thank you," Marius said reluctantly but with less enthusiasm accepted the well wishing from his colleagues

Jeanie enjoyed her stroll. The last time she was in The Hague it had been raining heavily and she did not like the dreary days. It was nice and sunny now as she walked from the dead center of town, opposite the houses of parliament to walk the street leading to the Mauritskade and passed the canal towards the Javastraat. There she turned left to see the contours of the Peace Palace rising above other buildings. From the Javastraat then she crossed the street and turned right. Less than two hundred meters she walked to stand before the gates of this now world famous building, a building with allure and not only because it stood for something: it was the embodiment of peace world wide. Of course London had much more grandeur, Jeanie thought, but this Peace Palace here had something too. The international community was here, vested in this building. On the other hand it was still it was just a building, an edifice, a symbol. Not too heavily guarded she wondered, if she could just walk in and asked the guards:

"Oh no lady, don't even think of it. You are required to have a visitor's badge, which you will get here when you can show an invitation, a valid one," on of them said when she approached them with that question

"Well I cannot, but tell me. Are there guided tours then?", Jeanie asked.

"Yes there are, but not right now and please book in advance?", the man answered, "I will give you a leaflet which has the info on it," he added.

"That is all I wanted really, I don't have time right now anyway. Thank you very much for your information," Jeanie said.

"At your service my lady," the man smiled; clearly glad he got rid of what he thought could have become a persistent customer.

"Jeanie walked back passed the flower display in front of the gate and took a few pictures of the building. Satisfied now, she saw a small coffee shop on the other side of the road at the Laan van Coppes van Cattenburch. She did not think twice and crossed the road in front of the tram stop. Then again at the Laan with the long name and sat down outside to enjoy some rays of the sun. It was a good day and possibly better things were to come. She was ready for an adventure too. Well, not that her work was without exploring and venturing but this was something new and she felt it was something which had nothing to do with an assignment. Her coffee was served by a young lady who after school earned some money as a waitress, something many young students did.

"Thank you," Jeanie said..

"Would you like a newspaper?", she asked.

"I am a afraid I am not so fluent in Dutch," Jeanie said smiling.

"May be I can find an English one for you," she answered and left to go back inside to get her one. Jeanie drank her coffee and when her cup was just half full the young lady returned to bring her the Guardian:

"It is yesterday's but perhaps still good enough for today?", she said and laughed.

"Should be fine," Jeanie smiled back at her and leaned back to scan the front page. Nothing there she did not know already so she browsed page two and three. When she got to foreign news she was drawn to a small report which had the word Naga in it. Close reading told her a man had been murdered in Manila, a man who was identified as a Naga leader. A full investigation had been ordered and the report on the facts ended with the question why the man was murdered there in Manila and who could be benefiting from this assassination. Of course the potentially obvious culprits were mentioned; the Indian intelligence, the factions among the Nagas themselves. The conclusion in the short report was that the case was an enigma yet. Jeanie knew that this put their entire trip in jeopardy, for not only was it so that it was already difficult to enter the Naga areas, now with some suspicion on the Indian Government the borders could be much more firmly closed to who could be judged as intruders, visitors and tourists alike. When she had fully grasped the content and finished her coffee, she went inside to ask the girl if she could have the page of the paper:

"You could take the whole newspaper. You were lucky we did not chuck it out yet," the girl giggled.

"Well thank you, you are kind," Jeanie said, paid her coffee and left. This was something she should show Marius immediately, she thought and hastily paced back to his office near the centre. So excited she became she had passers by looking at her. In the lobby of the office building she had the receptionist call Marius. The meeting had not taken long but Jeanie had stayed away longer than an hour and he had been waiting for her. He came down right away and walked with her to his place. She showed him the short report and he read it while walking and looked at her inquisitively. Ten minutes later in his apartment while brewing them coffee Marius said:

"We have to be careful now. Before we go tomorrow I will check my sources and find out about repercussions. Use my phone here to check on yours, all right?"

“Yes, of course, you think too this should not stand in our way?”

“It should not,” Marius laughed.

“Then we are on,” she concluded and took the phone to call London.

The next day just before they were due to take the train from The Hague Holland Spoor to Schiphol Airport directly, they sat and compared what they had found out from their counterparts in the different countries. The best source had been the one in Manila and the one in Delhi. London did not know much, neither did the AIVD.

“The Indians are sending an expert team to help investigating,” Marius said and you tell me that your Indian sources came to know all indications are pointed at Indian intelligence? I think they sent that team to try and cover up. What do you think Jeanie?”

“I think that would be too obvious. If the Indians are responsible for the murder what can they cover up in Manila? They can pay to deflect attention or their team can frustrate the investigation? I think it can’t be the Indians but because they will be under suspicion they want to find out who or what is behind it!”

“Hhhhhhmmmm, could be yes, what do you make of it then, when only two parties could benefit from the local disarray. I am sure we will come into some turmoil when we are there. It could become tense with the Nagas suspect the Indians, or when they deflect and accuse the factions then it could spark a civil war there, among the Nagas. I must get in touch with Lisa She should know more about the situation on the spot.”

“Why not call her now? I am anxious!!”, Jeanie suggested.

“Form the airport then. I want to be sure we are checked in,’ Marius answered..

“Okay,” Jeanie answered and soon after they left by the Brusselaar, the dark red train which connected Brussels to Amsterdam. A fast train it was and because it did not stop in Leiden they were at the airport in less than half an hour. After they had gone up to the departure hall, they checked in and passed immigration then leisurely walked over to their gate. With more than an hour to go Marius picked up his phone and dialed Lisa’s mobile number:

“Hello Shilu,” Marius quickly said, “we are on our way but read the terrible news.”

“Oh hello Marius,” came Shilu’s voice, “good to hear from you and that the trip is on. Yes our leader has been murdered in Manila and there is a lot of disturbance about it. Everybody suspects the Indians are behind it and when they heard a team is sent to the Philippines, they just know they go there to cover up. Perhaps even to get a fall guy to confess to that murder."

"What do you think? Have you got an idea who could be behind it?"

"Well, if it they were the Indians, it was rather a stupid thing to do. The Philippines is not involved so only with money they can be kept silent. On the other hand it has already been reported, so people all over will wonder."

"I am sure all kinds of security organizations are monitoring on what transpires or are sending in their people to find out what this means!", Marius said.

"People here are angry. I am sure it is reason enough for the military to call for some state of emergency. This again may have serious consequences. It may even come to them stating nobody can enter for they cannot guarantee the safety of visitors," Shilu said, "oh Marius I hope it will not come to that!"

"Well, we are going anyway and we will see what happens. This may not be something small and when the Indians try to subdue it, we can at least see to it that the word is out. Perhaps I can mobilize some journalists to pay attention to this. I think this may have some severe consequences, don't you agree?"

"It could be, but I hope not. I hope they soon find out who did it and that it is not anyone from us, for any of us will be lynched. If it is planned out by the Indians and the world forgets us, the war will be on again and it will be bloody," Shilu said almost crying now.

"I hope to be with you soon Shilu. This trip must be made," Marius said with conviction.

"Yes I hope so," she concluded, "until soon then."

Marius turned to Jeanie and briefly explained what Shilu had said.

"This is going to be serious then," she remarked.

"Yes it will be," Marius grinned, "does it deter you Jeanie?"

"Not in the least, but I will admit I would not have gone alone Marius," she grinned too.

"I can imagine," he smiled, "now we can go for a drink over there. We still have more than half an hour to go before boarding. I can do with a beer, you?"

"I will have a glass of wine then," Jeanie smiled.

They walked over to the gate bar and sat down after ordering.

"Geez man, this is going to be an adventure,' she said.

"Swell in Delhi I am sure we can connect with the human rights groups there and perhaps some coverts too. We will see, I am not yet afraid of anything!"

"Do you think this may me part of a grand plan hatched somewhere?", Jeanie asked, remembering her part of it and blushed.

"It could indeed be more complex than what it looked like. It looks too obvious the Indians have plotted this out. If done wrongly it will affect their position in the international community. Surely this conflict will become much more prominent then. What they have been able to keep in isolation will burst out into the open and they have no idea how or the means to contain it then."

"That would not be to their advantage right," Jeanie agreed and while sipping. In though they were lost for a while assessing the implications. When the boarding call came they were back on track together and boarded.

"I am tired," Jeanie said when the plane was up and dinner was served and hour later.

"Yeah, we should try and rest. The flight is just over seven hours and we will land in the middle of the night. A good nap will do us good," Marius said as they were both enjoying an after dinner wine.

"Right," Jeanie agreed. Jeanie covered her eyes with a blindfold provided by the airline to facilitate undisturbed sleep. Marius wanted that too, but there were too many things playing through his head. Who profits from the death of this Naga leader? Questions like recurred and sang through his head. Had this been accidental and the work of a lunatic? Could it be someone with a grudge against the leading movement, against the religious leader himself? The rival factions had been very vocal too lately. Or was it the Nagaland State Government who, fearing there would be no future for it when a settlement was reached and peace a fact? The former Nagaland Chief Minister Jamir, a vassal of the Indian Government, could be behind this. Had he had been by propping up rival factions? Marius knew that all was possible, no party could be ruled out yet. He was wondering though if he had forgotten any party. What could have taken this leader out emulating a planned reaction which would in turn be beneficial, a party Marius did not know about? Marius's mind kept on going and he nursed himself with a few glasses of his favorite red wine before, already half way, he knocked.off and fell asleep too.

Chapter 5

The Journey begins

In Atlanta, United States of America, the influential Baptists were gathering. Peter Uhllriche was one of them, the well known John Baterson as well. Already in the 1830's the Baptist missionaries had come to Nagaland at the time the British were making their presence known to the Nagas. Both Baterson and Uhllriche knew this very well. Baterson had been to Nagaland once and was quite impressed with the religious level and the spread of baptism amongst the Nagas, his forebears had initiated. In articles, where he had reported about his journey, he spoke quite highly of the people who lived, according to him, in dire circumstances still. He did not mention the war at all and did not explain the departure of the Baptists from Nagaland and the consequences this had for them. In the United States in Texas, Fort Worth he ran a seminary. There he had a dozen Nagas among the students who were being groomed to become ministers. Baterson was a good friend of Uhllriche, who was more of a scholar, a thinker, a man of the world who aside from his Christianity did more than studying the implications of the religion, implications like the effects of missionary work. At the conference in Atlanta where many religious Baptist leaders had gathered, they were talking about the participation of the Nagas. Only two parties had come; namely the remnants of what once was the powerful Naga National Council, the organization which up to the 1975 Shillong Accord represented all Nagas and the Kaphlang group, the group which had separated from the National Socialist Council, NSCN, of Nagaland in 1988. The large NSCN, more powerful and more influential party had not come. This was quite a setback Uhllriche then thought, for the reconciliation quest they had embarked on thus had fallen though.

"I am pretty devastated by the events man," said Uhllriche to Baterson during a break.

"Yeah, I expected too we could convince all parties to reconcile, so when together there would be strong to the Indians to talk diplomatically. Now it is the Indians who win with their game of divide and rule. Why they did not come, I don't know?"

"They told me that they did not want to discuss this with people who sold out their homeland out and certainly not with those who are sponsored and kept alive by India itself, weapons and money. To them that is treason and they feel they are obliged to talk to traitors then," Uhllriche told Baterson, "but this is in the past now Baterson," he added, "now one of the leaders has been murdered. I think we could contribute by coming up with a plan of action."

"I am sure there is truth in that. I think it would have been nice though if they could have talked it out in the open," Baterson replied, "now that a leader has been murdered there could be severe consequences too."

"That may very well be so, yet with that coming out nobody here would know who spoke the truth. No Baptist here knows the background well enough and neither does the press. All remarks, attacks, defenses, accusations will be taken seriously here and besides us and a few others you tell me Baterson who knows how to place what will be said?"

"You may very well be right there," Baterson replied, "yet I think they missed a good opportunity to show themselves and explain their stand. After all who understands the Nagas are capable to stand on their own? Certainly our men, who, in line with what the Indian required of them, fled the country and left their Naga brothers behind to fend for themselves."

"Yeah, to me that is a black page in our missionary history, it makes missionary work rather a one sided affair. On the other hand it is understandable too, but for one very strong reason," Uhllriche said.

"Do you mean that the Indian section of our missionary work could be at peril if our missionaries would have gone against the eviction drive of India?"

"Precisely, you know as well as I that the Indians would have given the other Baptist communities in India a hard time. They did not want to take the chance that all our missionary were going to bear the brunt," Uhllrich replied.

"Yeah, so it was decided to sacrifice the Nagas," Baterson said.

"I don't know if it was done on purpose, but the Indians, on the basis of accusing our missionaries working there, said it our Baptists incited the Nagas to stand up against India and to fight them. To the Indians our Baptists instigated the resistance. They thought it could not have come from the scattered tribes of the Nagas themselves."

"This, I think, was not true!", Baterson readily remarked.

"Well, at most partially, we did support the drive to be free of India, but you can hardly conclude that we instilled what was already there. You know as well as I do that in 1929 when the Simon Commission came to meet a Naga delegation which extended their wish to regain their freedom when the British left. So, the Indians used that notion against us, the problem is that we did leave and did not stand by them."

"Should they have risked their neck then for something that could not be won?", Baterson asked in earnest.

"If they would have assessed it that way and had made it known what that decision was based on, okay. Then to save other Baptist communities in India, you can accept that they left for a very good reason," Uhllrich said.

"Yeah, that is what I thought too!", Baterson smiled.

"Okay, don't smile like you are victorious already," Uhllrich smiled too, for now you tell me, when they had returned to the USA, could they not have raised the alarm? They knew what went on there. They knew the Indians had invaded and were killing people like flies. The Naga Army was just formed to engage and contain these soldiers who had just one command, to subdue the Nagas with might. Our missionaries saw the people they Christianized being driven into a corner, they were murdered. Now tell me also Baterson, when we advertise ourselves as a tough nation, one that stands up for peoples rights, then don't you think that the tough should be going when the going gets tough?"

"That is a good one, Uhllrich, but I do think you did not assess the implications, well not fully anyway," Baterson brought in.

"How so?", Uhllriche asked, but did not stop, "because of political implications in the USA or Baptist fears of intimidation of other communities? I said already that these considerations could be valid enough to leave, but something is missing here," he said.

"Really? Well, what would that be? Did I miss something?", Baterson dared Uhllriche.

"Are you testing me?", Uhllriche smiled," or are you playing ignorant?", he retorted.

"Let us just say I am being ignorant," Baterson reacted feeling Uhllriche bite, "so tell me what is on your mind?"

"Oh come on Baterson, this is elementary to me and irritating. Given that we think they left their brothers and sisters on a valid ground, then you tell me when they had returned why did they not raise hell? Why did they keep quiet? Why did they leave the Nagas hanging? They could have created quite a disturbance in the USA to disclose there was a war going o, a simple people were paying the price for wanting to be free of domination. Why did they not do that?"

"Yeah, you are right. I was thinking about that too off late. Having been in Nagaland and meeting these people who act more Christian than those who brought the Good News to them, I was wondering too why we let them down. Do you think there is more to it than what we are thinking now?", Baterson asked. Uhllrich smiled as he listened to Baterson talking then reacted:

"Well, well, your mind is active Baterson," Uhllrich said ironically, "but I think indeed something happened that prevented our leaders to throw the Naga case into the open. I think they were very vulnerable to political implications, implications of our own government. I think they have been asked, perhaps even ordered, to shut up."

"Jesus man, what does it mean what you are saying?", Baterson asked.

"Well I have no proof, but I tell you this stinks and I intend to find out what makes it stink. I am determined to do that," Uhllrich said.

"You are talking like the CIA is involved man!"

"Would you be surprised?" Uhllrich asked.

"No, not really, but I cannot imagine our government paying lip service to the Indian Government. Does it do so now?", Baterson asked.

"I cannot say it does so now, but there is something within our Government which prevents the Naga case to be known. Even among us the issue has died out. Very few of us know about it and its importance. But now something has happened. I can feel it has to do with this stalemate in the peace talks. Something is bound to happen, Baterson."

"Jesus Uhllrich, what are you saying man. What kind of things are you talking about? To break a stalemate is something major, it must be right?"

"Right," Uhllrich agreed, "what else can I say?"

"Are you going to investigate?", Baterson pushed him.

"If I would do that, do you think I would tell you?", Uhllrich asked him.

"Come we are friends you can tell me," Baterson tried to persuade Uhllrich.

"When you are so raving about the level of Christianity Baterson and on a kind of paternalistic horse advocating that, even though we are friends, I would not be able to trust you enough. You might very well be connected to some of the hardliners here. I think you know who I am talking about?", Uhllriche smiled.

"You are not serious now, are you?", Baterson reacted.

"Very serious," Baterson said, "I am deadly serious. That is why I can be your friend. I can talk serious matters with you."

"Thank you Uhllrich, but you don't trust me enough. I am sorry man!"

"Well, it is not a personal thing, not only. There might be other people's lives at stake and why should I run a risk with those. You need not prove yourself to me, for that would be an unfriendiy act. I just have to take the precautions required."

"Good heavens, this means you cannot even trust your fellow Baptists," Baterson said.

"Don't be naïve Baterson," Uhllrich shot out, "you very well know how religion is used in politics. As long as the voters are satisfied the politicians are happy; at election time they will kneel, they will bow. Among us you can point them out, all the way up to the highest in the land," Uhllrich explained.

"Yes, you are serious, or are you paranoia perhaps a little too?", Baterson tried him out.

"I will leave that for you to decide on," Uhllrich retorted.

"My, oh my, you are slippery my friend. Let's stay in touch, I like to know more on what is transpiring," Baterson suggested.

Uhllrich having sent Baterson on his way back to Texas then recalled his meeting with the Kaphlang group. He briefly met Kaphlang in Atlanta but much more vividly he remembered a more recent encounter, one in a forest hide out:

"Hello, hello," one of the aides who had come down to fetch them said, "they are already waiting for you and happy to talk. Please follow me!"

Uhllrich followed and when they arrived at the camp after a long walk Uhllrich could not refrain from posting a joke. He smiled to the men gathered there and said:

"Lovely, I take it you chose this pristine forest for its resemblance to the seventh heaven. I am sure we are all feeling close to God now," and looked around to make eye contact, "I am Reverend Uhllrich," he continued. The men looked at him like they had not expected such introduction.

"Please sit with us and have a drink," a relatively young man said known as Kaphlang's interpreter. Khaplang himself was the oldest among them. He began to speak to the young man once all were seated and tea was served:

"Thank you Mr. Khaplang," Uhllrich said, "it was good of you to receive me at such short notice. I am sure you are a busy man."

The young man translated and he saw Kaphlang nodding.

"What are you here for Reverend?" the young man asked on behalf of Khaplang.

"If Mr. Khaplang does not mind, we would like to know from him how the split in the Naga forces came about and also what the objectives of the Khaplang Group are. We are ill informed about that and thought this to be a good opportunity," Uhllrich began.

"Yes," the young man said, "it should be. We are in Eastern Nagaland mostly, so it is quite inaccessible there and communication is erratic. But, Mr. Khaplang does not like to talk about the split itself but about the objectives of The K-group yes."

"Oh," Uhllriche reacted in surprise, "we heard only one version of that and thought it would be good to hear from you too. You were there, so you can elaborate and possibly refute something too?", Uhllrich said keeping some pressure going. Kaphlang looked at Uhllrich hearing the translation and looked like he wanted to look straight through Uhllrich, then hesitated and talked to the young man again who then said:

"Kaphlang thinks it is not relevant now. It is more important to talk of the future for all Nagas. He just tells you that the Tangkhuls cannot be trusted. Too much has happened and we would be sitting here for days if you hear it all."

"Okay," Uhllriche conceded, "I do not know why he cannot give a brief explanation or why his version has not been written so it will be known what happened according to him, but let's move on to the future then. Does he have objectives, a goal and when it is reached a Nagaland can be governed by its own people democratically?"

Again Kaphlang gave him a look, a fierce one now before he talked through the young man, this time much longer:

"I was as much part of the NNC as the leaders now. I did not abandon the cause of the Nagas, no less than sovereignty, I say. Nothing short of that, but I do not see this integration issue to be important. Let me tell you this, the others have always neglected the Eastern Nagas and it is the Tangkhuls who did that. Tangkhuls are from Manipur. Let them belong to Manipur. In the future we can do without them. They think they represent all Nagas, well the Nagas will decide that when the time comes," he nodded.

"How will you do that? I mean when they have reached and agreement and say Nagaland becomes a nation of its own, don't you think all Nagas will like that?"

"Well, what makes you think they can talk for all Nagas? There are those we represent I told you and there are those the NNC represents. The Nagaland State people want to belong to India; they want the money and some power. So, what then when they have an agreement? We will just carry on where they left off."

"I do not get that," Uhllrich said, "when the nation becomes independent then is that not good for you too? May be not for the people running the State Government, but I am sure that in the end they will agree too and will play another role in the administration of the new sovereign nation Nagaland?"

Now Kaphlang looked at Uhllrich, narrowing his eyes before he spoke:

"You may have been responsible for Christianizing the Nagas, but you can't fool me," Khaplang shot back, "I shall tell you this. We share the same ancient history, but some tribes have tried to be bigger than themselves; the Angami's led the NNC but did have the Eastern Burmese section on the same level, the Tangkhuls are like dictators. They infect everyone and if you do not do as they want you too, they will make you. No, Tangkhuls are not Nagas. I have said this before. It is nothing new."

"In a free Homeland they will have to make sure to be elected in a Government office just like anyone else who aspires that, right?", Uhllrich remarked.

"Well," Khaplang reacted, 'if the constitution were up to me this would not be so," he said, "in the East we do not think like that!"

"Oh?", Uhllrich said, "you don't want a democracy in Nagaland then?"

"We will have elections, but we cannot have it like they do in the south and west," Kaphlang explained.

"I do not get that, for in a Naga nation you can have your own party. What is wrong with that?", Uhllrich asked now.

"Up to the administrative level that is fine, but they cannot challenge an Ang you know. This is our heritage and I am an Ang, even an Ang who leads others. I will be the leader of the land," Khaplang said and looked determined.

"Is this the heart of the matter, a culture clash? I am sorry Mr. Khaplang but I cannot believe this, the majority of the Naga tribes have the village state democracy as their heritage. How can you think they will agree with your point of view?"

Quite relaxed Khaplang looked at both Uhllrich; his men with him did so as well. For a moment there was an eerie silence, but then he spoke again:

"You do not know the history very well; you missionaries have been only with those who became Christian, the Indian Nagas. Your missionaries did not come as far as the tribes in Eastern Nagaland. I am an Ang, a leader, this is my heritage and I will lead the Nagas, like I led the Federal Government of the NNC and now the K group. I will use all and everyone to achieve independence and this includes the Indian Army and the Assam Rifles. Sure the Nagas will be independent and I doubt if the others will be successful in their peace talks. They are talking for a decade now. Do you think their talks will bear fruit or will they go on forever? I don't think so either way," he said, "the fools think the Government of India will concede. When they realize it is not possible it will be clear all Nagas will turn to us and we will save them," Kaphlang said, again with determination.

"So you have given up on the talks then, yet the others are much better equipped to go back to war than the K group, is this not true?", Uhllrich asked.

"Do you know our strength? Do you know what equipment we have, who would work with us What do you actually know?", Khaplang asked.

"Are you collaborating with former Chief minister S.C. Jamir?", Uhllrich suddenly asked in an effort to derail him.

"I just told you we take support from anyone, so from him too. We do some work for him to keep the funds flowing. But if you are asking do we support him? Then the answer would be no. No, we do not support treacherous Nagas either. We fight for all Nagas who will work with us to create our own nation. Yes, he supplied money and weapons to secure his position, but we pull his plug, he will flush down the toilet," Khaplang smiled.

"So, you have S.C. Jamir is in your pocket, while he thinks you are in his pocket?", Uhllrich now asked him.

"You can see it like that," Khaplang laughed.

"Back to the movement now please. What is your relation to the old NNC? Have you combined forces with them?", Uhllrich asked.

"Read the above well. We are not in favor of this Shillong Accord; disarmament of the Nagas is no way to become independent. Never mind the Accord, they say, it was never ratified by the NNC. What counts was that it was implemented. I realized too late and was too power hungry then and when I was briefly the president of the Federal Government of Nagaland, the Federal meant that Eastern Nagaland was in the Federation.

That is why I joined the new organization with the Tangkhul and settled for vice presidency, only to discover they called the shots and plotted a Naga future I did not agree with. The other one is a puppet and is more religious praising the Lord than anything else. That is the main reason why I broke away."

"I am told this was very bloody?", Uhllrich said.

"Yeah right, but there was no other way, we had to tackle them this way. They had summoned me for a meeting I did not want to go to, for I knew they were going to fry me and my people. They came to Eastern Nagaland and we attacked them. We should have killed them all, but we failed doing that. Even their leaders could escape. A pity for else we were not having these problems," Khaplang was telling and Uhllrich could see him growing in his role sensing Uhllrich was listening intently.

"So, in your assessment it was the others who were not able to listen to your reasoning, right?", Uhllriche asked.

"From the perspective of the Eastern Nagas it was them who determined what the movement should be like," Khaplang answered through the young man.

"I understand there are Konyaks in the Naga Army of the other side too," Uhllrich said.

"There are renegades everywhere Reverend and we will deal with them in due time!"

"I am sure you will," Uhllrich laughed, "however recently a Mr. Bawi, Ao I believe, crossed over to you from them. This I heard is also a leader of stature though not as absolute a ruler as an Ang. Isn't that right?"

"Yes, that's right, but what of it?", Khaplang asked.

"I heard he had some personal problems and did some money tricks, was he power hungry too?", Uhllrich remarked.

"Of course they will say that, but can you check what is right?", Khaplang quipped.

"Well, is that not a correct thing to ask? That is of course the problem, nobody can check anything and so you can say whatever you like," Uhllrich smiled.

"So can the others or do you believe what they say was the actual background of the split in our forces?", Khaplang said.

"You are pleading here loud and clear for an impartial investigation in the matter?", Uhllrich now asked.

"Ha, ha, ha, good one, yes of course," Khaplang laughed, "but how will you do it? How can it be organized reliably? It is an empty statement now, only words!"

"Let's go back to the future then," Uhllrich continued, "suppose there is an agreement and more than just a simple majority will abide by this. There will be a first Government and some temporary laws will be introduced. A tribunal will be organized to deal with the past once and for all. There will be many traitors, killers, collaborators running around free and a new society has to deal with them. This of course will have bearings of what you have been accused of too, will you submit to this kind of tribunal provided it is guaranteed it is impartial and has full powers of investigation too?"

"Of course not, we will not accept or condone a Tangkhul Government; no tribe will rule the Nagas alone. Freed of fighting the Indians we will then fight this blood stained Tangkhul led Naga Government. We will fight them!", he said grinning.

"Even with a majority of the people being happy that there is peace with the dignity of living in a free nation that will determine its own future?", Uhllrich pushed on.

Khaplang looked at him straight again, swallowed a few times, looked around and said:

"You do not seem to understand. Tangkhuls cannot be trusted. We sent them a quit notice, meaning that they have to leave Nagaland. They are not welcome here."

"Yes I have seen the bitter almost racial action you initiated, but you also had a meeting with Jamir, who is governor of Goa now. I think he wants to return to Nagaland as a puppet of the Indian Government he wants to deploy you again. You know the man is quite rich, right?", Uhllrich now in a mood chanced to bite into his face.

"Where did you get all this nonsense?", Khaplang laughed, "even when it is true it is good enough a plot. S.C. Jamir we can use, he has money and hates the Tangkhul too. So let him make a come back, we are prepared. And, when Tangkhuls behave like terrorists, they deserve to be evicted. That is not racial That is justice!", he grinned.

"We are to believe you of course Khaplang?", Uhllrich asked him mockingly. Not deterred in the least Khaplang answered:

"But of course," he laughed out loud.

"One last thing then," Uhllrich said.

"Go ahead," Khaplang smiled victoriously.

"Is your problem solved if the organization of your opponent, say the Tangkhul leadership is removed; either by persuasion or by force?"

"That would be helpful yes, but what do you mean by 'by force'?", he asked now quickly sitting up attentively.

"Now you surprise me," Uhllrich smiled, "you surprise me indeed now Mr. Kaphlang," Uhllrich repeated slowly and all felt the tension rising till Khaplang asked:

"Are you thinking what I think you are thinking Reverend?", he asked.

"But of course," Uhllrich smiled to encourage him to say it.

"You think I will stoop so low as to kill them?", he asked.

"I cannot say how low you stoop or are capable of doing. What I do know is that innocent Tangkhul Nagas have already been killed by your forces. It has been reported and that you cannot deny I think?", Uhllrich said, his men listened and looked at Kaphlang:

"Mistakes are made Reverend; we have already given the order to stop these mistakes made by our forces. We have issued a statement saying that innocent Tangkhul have nothing to fear from us. They can leave without being harmed," he stressed.

"Then let me ask you this," Uhllrich intervened "how do you determine innocence. Do you leave that to your soldiers?"

"No of course not," Khaplang retorted irritated now, "all those who persist and want to stay in Nagaland, will run the risk. When they go they are safe."

"That's ethnocide, ethnic cleansing," Uhllrich concluded aloud and silence fell. Not one talked and tension rose quickly. This is not good Uhllrich thought, this may turn to violence. Feverishly he thought of a way out now and came up with this, not very strong or convincing it was, but possibly enough to let him go unharmed, he thought:

"It is a point of view of course and one stemming from within the Naga circles. I like to thank you for you very open answers on my questions. I am sure this was not easy for you. What you said took courage. I can see you are a confident man and I thank you again," Uhllrich said hoping that he would feel flattered. Kaphlang's eyes mellowed. He proved to be not insensitive to flattering.

"It's all right," he said curtly, "it is good to speak my mind every now and then. I can imagine what goes on in Nagaland is little understood, if you do not know the Nagas well enough. It is not your fault, you are strangers in our land and you should have helped us, but you were scared and left. Now you want to know, that is good. I thank you too!"

The cold atmosphere was gone and with the interview over all men relaxed. Uhllrich was about to leave when Khaplang laid and arm around him showing he took Uhllrich for a clever one and said:

"Come have a drink with us?"

"Just one beer," Uhllrich answered to show he was as fearless as Kaphlang and his men.

They drank more than one and sang till Kaphlang inquired if Uhllrich needed a woman. Thought Uhllrich declined the offer he made him think he would have liked as he said 'forbidden fruit'.

"I thought so," Kaphlang laughed, "reverends I hear can act holy in public but know their way around in the dark. I will save you from sinning Uhllrich and will say goodbye to you now!", and he gesticulated his man to take Uhllrich back. Out of sight now Uhllrich felt free to assess the situation and said to himself: 'oh man, for a moment I was frightened. I felt how dangerous this man can be. True I was prejudiced against him, but I felt he was confessing what he did while he denied at the same time, a very odd feeling.

'I could feel his power and it was not the power I like and trust!'

With the investigation gaining momentum in Manila the police was briefed and helped by the Indian team. Jeanie and Marius were brought up to date in Delhi and Sean had landed in Amsterdam. In London the Quakers had a meeting. There was a member from the Netherlands present too, but it was the English chapter which had ties with both the Indian Government and the leaders of the Naga Forces. Bamamurthy of Indian heritage had met both leaders a couple of times and was briefed throughout about the backgrounds and the prospects of the Indo-Naga conflict from the Naga perspective of the NSCN. It was their, more or less, regular meeting and they were discussing what route to take to while operating in the shadows. It was their background task to facilitate the peace talks. Most in the group had visited Nagaland. They knew the culture well and this had reinforced their interest in the people. Because the news on the murder was not yet widespread, it was found insignificant by most editors in Britain or at most judged as trivial news, Bamamurthy was going to break what had happened. Since they were all volunteers and had jobs to attend to, in their spare time they would when possible focus on their topic of interest, so they could not have possibly known the news on the demise of the Naga leader already. So Bamamurthy opened the meeting by saying:

"I have something to tell you. It happened a few days ago and it concerns the Nagas very much. In Manila, in broad daylight the Naga leader you all know and have met was murdered. Nobody knows yet who did that and what the motivation behind it."

"What?", the Dutchman reacted leaving the others with a puzzled face too. The Englishman with his base in Sri Lanka asked:

"Good heavens man, has this been confirmed?"

"Oh yes, though you have not seen this in any paper in full, it is true. I am sure they have treated this kind of news as domestic. After all as I understand it, this is just one of the approximately twenty murders which are counted in that big metropolis every day. I can assure you though that it is confirmed. I have spoken to his wife earlier today."

"Who would want to assassinate an old man," the Dutchman remarked, "already I think this is a politically motivated murder?"

"That could very well be," said the man from Sri Lanka, "Bamamurthy, did you check if robbery with this fatality as a result has been excluded already?"

"Nothing was stolen and our friend was gunned down from a moving car. The Indians sent a team to Manila to help out with the investigations. This looks like a carefully planned execution. Most likely hired killers did the job and disappeared. Now the Manila police try to get to the plotters, which is why the Indians sent a team," he explained.

"Because they themselves are under suspicion?", the Dutchman asked.

"Of course it will be established who benefits from this murder and then from there on the trail to the plotters will be followed. Hopefully there will be no dead ends."

"This must be quite a blow to the leadership of the Nagas then," the Sri Lankan Englishman said.

"I hear the Nagas in Nagaland are already reacting. Of course they suspect the Indians are behind it. They think they wanted to sabotage the peace talks. It could also be one of the rival factions of course. But then only the NNC here in London might have the international connections to hire an assassin and deploy that person minutely in Manila," Bamamurthy explained further.

"This reeks you know, it stinks even. What do these plotters hope to achieve then Bamamurthy? A resurrection, so the Indians have a legitimate reason to crack down on them? Do you think this could be behind it?", the Dutchman asked.

"It is hard to say at this stage," Bamamurthy answered thoughtfully, "I am shattered by this news too. I take it personally for we knew this man, a soft spoken religious man, not a man who would intentionally harm anyone. How many times did we talk to him and his colleagues?", he asked rhetorically. The others understood that and kept silent till the English Sri Lankan smiled a twinkle in his eyes and cooled English type humor he said:

"You know my friends, I think our advice may have had greater impact than we envisaged. The Indians recognized the Nagas to be strong at the negotiation table, so they had to find other ways to gain the upper hand over them again, and so ultimately we are responsible for this."

"This is quite a sardonic and egocentric remark," said the Dutchman who laughed out loud nevertheless. He looked at the others, then launched an idea of his own, "since you think the impact of the Quakers is that far reaching," he said, knowing very well the Englishman meant the opposite but he harped on it, "when I look around and spot your faces I think it could very well be that we have a master plotter among us. One of us who could be compelled to, still from the shadows, influence the situation to break the dead lock. Just an idea," he laughed.

The five men looked at him in despair, a despair that could hardly be acted and this was exactly what the Dutchman wanted to see. He was now relatively reassured no one among them was connected to any plotting.

"Okay, okay," the Dutchman laughed then, "just wanted to make sure that no one among us took things upon himself. Since we are in the dark and it is too simple to think the Indians are behind this, I thought of testing you a little, all right?"

Gaining confidence again now that the sting was out of the remark Bamamurthy on the basis that they were friends in this voluntary work said:

"It could be you too Dutchman. You could have used this remark to deflect attention, right? And, now that you think the Indians are not behind this, who may I ask, do you think is capable of plotting this. Who or what organization has an interest?"

"Oh, oh, sharp Bamamurthy, very sharp, you are good. Now shall we send our condolences to his wife and family to the Naga Organization and to the Naga People?"

"That is a good idea," said the Englishmen, "but it should not reach the papers remember?"

"Of course," said the Dutchman and laughed again, "prominence would mean we could become a target for the investigators and I do not like them on my back. Certainly not now that Bamamurthy has singled me out," he laughed.

"I am shattered," Bamamurthy reacted, "here we are talking about the Nagas and the one person we know very well has been brutally murdered. Of course it is good to talk about motivation, but we know nothing and we are speculating. Jokes on suspecting I do not appreciate either," he said.

"I am shattered too," the Dutchman reacted, "that is why I act like this for I am certain this breaks open what is deliberately locked. We can pay lip service to the Nagas of course by talking to them, but they think we stand by them. Yet, tell me what we can actually do? What have we done to help them?"

"You know of course that we do not intervene outright, but contribute to at least the idea we take the Nagas seriously," said the Englishman.

"This makes us suspects you know. I think we should be prepared to be scrutinized. I am sure the police will question us. It is just a matter of time," the Dutchman said, "and I encourage this openness, one way or another the Indo-Naga conflict will come out into the open because of it."

"Was this the motivation of the plotters, do you think," Bamamurthy asked.

"I am beginning to believe that that was the motive behind it, hence my thinking that the Indians are acting very cleverly for once. They are taking the wrap first hand, but will deflect it to organizations like us. There are more like us who are operating from the background," the Englishman said.

"What about Adinno's NNC? She as the president of the old and defunct NNC has condemned the other organizations in very strong words, traitors she called them if I am not mistaken? I would not be surprised if there is a coalition of some sort through which she planned and ordered the assassination?", the Dutchman suggested.

"My oh my," said the lovely looking secretary who was a full fledged member too and of English origin as she spoke on the matter for the first time, "I remember the leader very well so I ask you can we leave these speculations for another meeting and talk first on how we shall pay our respects to the Nagas. I hear the suggestion of sending condolences and I heartily agree with that suggestion," she said.

"You are right," Bamamurthy agreed, "let's do that indeed and call for another meeting within a week. Perhaps we know more then and can act more to the point, all right?"

"Yes, that is right Linda, we got carried away," the Dutchman agreed too and the Englishman joined ranks. So, they got to work on the text and the ways to reach the Naga People and the family of the slain leader. They put in their agendas when they could meet again; one week later same time, same place then fully equipped with information.

Patill was negatively exited. He had just returned from the Home Office, the Home Ministry, where he had long talk with those responsible for the intelligence units of India, Raw and IB. It was common knowledge that both organizations had ethics of their own and were not just working in their specific fields of interest only, but often checked on each other too. This was a euphemistical way of expressing that in fact they were rivals of each other. This became apparent to Patill right away when he was talking about what exactly he could coordinate with the Home Ministry. He did not get an answer right away, first it had to be established which of the two were eligible to be involved, was involved already or had to be deployed according to what the Home Ministry deemed necessary. So, here he was, with a team of police present in Manila to help with the investigations, but to get to the bottom of this he was pressed politically to deploy secret agencies too. Since this was something concerning the Foreign Ministry, not the Home Ministry, he got angry when he was sent on a run around. Still empty handed he stormed into the office of his counterpart, the Home Minister himself:

"What are you doing man," he began, "is there something you are holding back. I am running the Foreign Office and I am dealing with a rapidly spreading international situation. You should tell me everything you know. Now is any of the two involved in it or not? Darn it, the whole Government, heck India could be blamed for this. Do you want me to make it a cabinet matter?"

"Yeah, I am aware of it, no, no please don't," the Home Minister answered thoughtfully, "I have a possible resurrection of the Nagas on my hands because of this already and I have been frantically searching in our own organizations what the involvement is. There are no leads, I cannot come to the conclusion that the deed was done by one of us," he explained, "but I had to be sure before I come to tell you as you have to defend it to the outside word, while I face the questioning here at home."

"Well this is at least something, but I will tell you man I will have your skin if you are lying to me. The Philippines is full of questions now. They ask how it is possible an Indian citizen has a Bangladeshi passport and is a leader of an armed movement against India. Our ambassador is under fire and cannot say anything. Now I will officially declare there he can say we have no involvement whatsoever, all right?"

"All right," he agreed, "but there is more, you know the he more is known about the murdered man, the more we will be questioned. Later on and within a few days the Government by word of the prime Minister has to come up with a statement on the matter. I am pretty sure now, that neither the IB not the Raw planned this."

"Do you actually mean only that no order was given officially?", Patill asked.

"Of course," the Home Minister said.

"Well then you should still look into the possibility of some unit acting on its own. There are a lot of disgruntled people in this country. So, let's not be naïve and check all your sources, ask your people, question them about their whereabouts. Check their records against what they did. These are secret agents and could have their own agendas. Your RAW men are at my embassies. Of course I know that," Patill said.

"Well," the Home minister replied, "we cannot keep anything from you, can we?"

"Joker," Patill laughed, "but seriously now this is something we have to clear. I do not want these mopping up procedures afterwards. If we are not careful this will go out of hand," Patill emphasized but good natured now.

"I wonder how we can pacify the Nagas though," Patill," the Home Minister said; "this is my major concern at the moment. Any ideas?"

"Hhhhhhmmmm, let me think. How about going there, well may be not you, but an even more credible person, who explains the situation. Go on television there, speak to the people, show you are very concerned, offer your condolences and show you are with them in their grief and anger. Let them know you understand their anger."

"Good idea Patill, but still I am not too sure they will believe a man of my stature. Don't you agree?", he asked.

"That should depend on what you do and yes better it is you who does it. The government should go out, via you, to show the pain is shared. Tell them you will leave no stone unturned to find the culprits? Instead of threatening the people with your military give them something they can believe in man, something tangible. You win their hearts with honey, not with your bombastic show of power," Patill said and smiled.

"Are you saying I am a bombastic, a man who shows power?", the Home Minister asked now with anger in his voice.

"Don't take it personally; you represent security you have to use the stick at times. But in this case when you use that you may create an angry mob and the consequences can go out of hand. It could attract international attention too and of the kind we do not want, the kind we cannot handle. We will be questioned internationally. Don't forget the Nagas are a tenacious people. It may even happen that they come back together and our work of divide and rule goes down the drain. I am sure you do not like that scenario," Patill rubbed in as he explained.

"Thank you for your suggestions," the Home Minister rounded up, "I will confer with my director generals, but already I am convinced the way you showed me in dealing with this predicament is of value. I have taken it seriously. Let me work on it now!"

"Okay, I am sure you realize I have lots of things to attend to too. Perhaps I fly out to Manila myself to show we take this case very seriously and it would of course reinforce what you can do in Nagaland," Patill said.

"Oh yes, that would be a great help it would prop up our credibility. Okay then, I will go to Nagaland and do all needed to win the people over, provided you do your bit in this process we set out just now!", he concluded.

"You have my word, I will make arrangements to go to Manila to give the operation some weight and credence," Patill concluded with him, "but again man, I want to see your announcement on your departure to Nagaland for paying respect to the bereaved people, okay?", Patill asked to exclude a misunderstanding.

"Agreed, you will have it by tomorrow," he said.

Patill nodded and left the Home Ministry. Back at his own office he arranged a flight as well and phoned his people there to announce his surprise arrival. He also ordered his staff to get in touch with newspapers, well the media in general, Indian, the Philippines and the foreign correspondents, so his visit to the Philippines would get wide coverage.

The Scorpion was getting anxious. What he had been planning and plotting was coming together. He had feared Manila was not the best of places where he had set out to start the ball rolling. He thought the ball could have been stopped somewhere unnoticed and the whole idea would perish, worse for then the assassination had been futile and the Naga leader would have died in vain. He had already had the idea to lead the police to the assassin and helper, even to expose and Jeanie and even Sean, the man who had taken on the assignment. But, things were moving, he noticed. With the ball in the court of the Indian Government now, a test for them how to get out of this mud pool, some time or other the trail would go further and all contacts of the slain leader would be checked. Anyone suspicious would be questioned, including the Scorpion himself of course. But I will enjoy how things will unfold and when the exposure is lacking I will feed some info to put the investigators back on the right track, the track that would lead to maximum attention on the Indo-Naga conflict and minimal attention for the planner, the one with a heart for the Nagas. The plotter was the one who was not afraid to propel things even though ethical principle were held high by him, the Scorpion as he called himself. Now let's see how far we are now, he said to himself, when for the first time he saw the story in the international press. He smiled not because of the story, but because the man with stature of a Minister of Foreign Affairs found it necessary to go Manila to address a well attended press conference in Delhi then in Manila. The press, though it really had no idea of the importance yet, did realize something important was in the cards. The scorpion was excited now to see things were moving. The assassin out of sight for quite a while, the suspicion would be on the Indian Government. He cheered, but also was rather taken aback by bouts of guilt. Of course he did it for what he thought a good cause, freeing the Nagas from the iron grip of the Indians, or at least making the Naga cause know so that they could expect help. Either way, he thought it would put them on the map when the case was out in the open and India would be held accountable for what it had done and most likely Britain too for what it had not done. For many years now he had been sitting on the sideline seeing this conflict was dragging on and both the Nagas and the Indian populace were paying the price. Irresponsible and arrogant Indian leaders they were, he thought and he dwelled back on the words of Jawarhlal Nehru who quite harshly converted his words, born out of anger, into action and reality. He was the one who had unleashed the war on the Nagas, the successive leaders in his wake had not been capable to stop it or resolve the conflict. They deserved to face accountability, he knew that. But he was not satisfied with himself. In his enthusiasm while plotting things out and laying the contacts he had not taken enough time to assess the impact an assassination he decided on had on himself. It was one thing to plot things and move the pieces like playing chess, another to see the consequences. A man had been murdered and a man had been murdered by his command. That reality he felt stronger than ever, much stronger than when he was plotting, moving the pieces and calculating the likelihood of the different outcomes of the deed. But then it had been a just something of a plan on paper. He had been so enthused and involved that only when it was really in motion and he had given the order it was that he had realized there was no way back. But then he had realized indeed that by his command a murder was on his conscience and his conscience played up. In fact it was heavily playing up for guilt was consuming him as he was diametrically opposed to the success of his mission. The feelings of elation and guilt consumed him, yet his planning went like clockwork He felt tremendous the Nagas were getting closer to what they deserved, but at the expense of a slain leader. Who was he the Scorpion to decide over life and death? What arrogance did reside in him, the arrogance of world leaders who, with the stroke of a pen, set things in motion with consequences they could not even have thought of? He thought of the past wars unleashed on people through which millions had died. The Second World War one being hatched in the mind of a man who thought the German Arians were super beings. The conquest that followed had far reaching consequences indeed. Now, but for others reasons and many wars later, the war on Iraq was declared and executed on the premise of weapons of mass destruction being present and the supposed ties of dictator Saddam Hussein with the Al Qaeda network of Osama bin Laden, which terrorized the United States of America as it flew commercial jetliners into the skyscrapers of New York and the Pentagon, killing almost three thousand people. For them it was reason enough to begin war in Iraq that was, a war in which already thousands of lives were lost. An eye for an eye, the Scorpion thought and an eye with far reaching consequences indeed it was. He quivered because no matter how exciting it was what he had set in motion, the consequences he could not control. And, if a civil war would break out and the Indian Army would be commanded in to contain, control or seize the moment to subdue the Nagas once and for all, it would be on his conscience. How could I have done this, he asked, I am a Christian myself and I killed, not directly of course but through someone. I gave the order, I am responsible, he knew. But then soon his desire to watch how the events, he planned fell into place, took over. And, that he did not have things in hand to control after the assassination would soon become apparent. By releasing info when the sequence of events would get stuck he had some control of course, but what was about to happen, he could not have thought up.

After a day or two in Amsterdam and having fun together Jacky and Sean sat down before their trip to Rio de Janeiro:

“I have to tell you Jacky. Now that we are getting serious with each other I want you to know, what I know already,” Sean began.

“I want to know all about it and it,” she smiled remembering these last few days had been bliss. She knew that Sean was indeed the man she ever wanted. They had gone out and she had felt that he had captivated her so much that she had lost her wild hairs she always kept whenever she felt a man came to close. Because of her feminine attitude, her beauty and her casual ways, she was spoiled by men. Yet she seemed to be available and open till men found out when in close proximity of her, they were with a very strong woman, one who would be capable of all and anything but on her terms. Now she asked:

“Well, what do you want to tell what know then Sean?”

“You are a bloody warm hearted, attractive, in command of yourself woman,” Sean laughed, well educated, strong willed a sense for feminine exposure too. Should I tell more?”, he laughed.

“Of course,” she laughed.

“Well, men are like flies around you and after your honey, very genuine, very Dutch?”

"You forget one thing Sean, quite an important thing I might add?", she mocked him.

"What there is more?", he smiled, "okay wait, let me think. Hmm, I know, no matter how bad you are, and you can be very bad, you are my woman. That's it!"

"Right," she exclaimed and flew into his arms and after a minute of caressing him unabashed, she took off his shirt as he opened her blouse. They looked at each other like they were seeing each other for the first time. They hectically, feverishly rather, undressed themselves while looking and giggling. Jacky finishes first and helped to take of his shoes then tore of socks. Now nude he said:

"Over the phone I promised you something and now is the time, but I can't with you so menacingly seductive in front of me."

Jacky said nothing but wrapped her arms around him and they made love passionately and compassionately. Long after wrapped up in each other Sean heaved and whispered:

"Jacky, now is the time to talk to you and it will change our lives because I have decided to change mine."

"You are serious indeed," she said noticing that he had waited to talk until after their lovemaking. She sensed it could have been their last time if that she was going to hear would break them up.

"Yes, I am," Sean answered, looked and began, "I am not the easy going man you think I am. I have lived an outward and inward life. You know the outward one. That life is a front for what I am ashamed of and because I am I did not much care for the life of others. I could deploy you only because of that and Bailung who was my mate and experienced all this with me during the few years we were together knows this too and suffers the same fate."

"My goodness, what is wrong then Sean," she asked and her poise was gone now. Nude they laid close to each other but both sense the change in atmosphere, their bodies showed that and without realizing they separated them:

"During the war in Rwanda and Burundi the bloody Indian Bailung and I went crazy. We lost our minds and we not only saw horror, but we took part in it. I must have gone mad. Both Bailung and I were part of the intervention force. During that time we were stationed there, we felt so unreal and we must have been influenced by it. It still haunts me everyday. I am so ashamed of it that the only way I am able to look myself in the eyes is to be of service. The Bordello because it has style, the political influence to destabilize and justify things, to put them back in order, but also to prevent people from being killed. When I received that contract to assassinate this Naga leader, the one who issued the contract could not know I knew the Indo Naga war and agreed to the assassination. I did this because I knew due to the stubborn unwillingness of the Indians it could change something in this stalemated war. I will come to that later but first now what actually happened in Rwanda. I am sure you know about the mass murders which took place there?", Sean asked.

"Of course," Jacky answered with a serious face.

"Well then, Bailung and many others saw many people being hacked to death, many discarded dead bodies. It was genocide and it happened right before our eyes. We could not intervene. You cannot imagine it, you cannot imagine the devastation and to this day I cannot comprehend it, even less about what we did, not just Bai and I. I don't know if it was team spirit, but we lost it completely. We, the soldiers did the very people who were there to prevent atrocities indulged in them. Jacky, we raped women in the camps over, we beat men up. We behaved like animals, like life had no value except our won life. We felt nobody could touch us and nobody did. I can't tell you why Bai or I joined in. Oh, we did not instigate it. It just happened of course and some believed in that stupid but classic saying. But, Bai and I know very well we were sucked in and I fully admit to you we did this. We came close to killing people too, we were so powerful, we could do anything and we did, but at least we could stop at killing people. I thank God and I kneel before him that we were spared doing that. The unit we were part of was not finished with it but went into frenzy. Bailung found me to make a stand. You cannot believe what we were up against this group of men in frenzy, looting, raping and killing. When that happened Bai and I could draw the line and we fought it out. We were cowards Jacky, abusers. We were the lowest kind people, I know, but I also know now how difficult it is to withstand the force of a group when all systems go. We fought our own men and this was serious, for we had to fight for our lives to break that terrible spell. When they realized what we had been doing they were afraid we would expose them. They were right of course and because what we did was too terrible to describe in words, we could not turn them in. We were too ashamed ourselves. Here we were this Philippino/Indian and I standing up against our men afraid to be held accountable. To make them stop raping and killing we conceded the promise we would tell. It is the most stupid thing we promised of course, but it saved our lives and possibly that of perhaps a few Africans. Now both Bai and I concealed all we know. And I tell you that this is to big a burden. I keep my mouth shut about it and not just for feeling ashamed but also because of some of the group who come to check on me in the

Bordello sometimes. Jacky I liked you from the beginning; you were like a soul mate to me. Yet I thought I could never tell you my dark side and I did not deserve you because of my past. This is why I did not care why you were the high class prostitute. It is the reason why I knew I would not have to commit to you. It is crazy of course, but you and I have known from the beginning we would be together yes?"

"Yes," Jacky whispered without hesitation.

"And, when you say yes again it will seal our bond. You know that too and you will leave that profession and we will both leave the Bordello and lead another life, so Jacky say yes now and we will do it," Sean said and looked at her.

"Yes," Jacky said, "but now I must tell you something too. Are you as ready for that?", she asked trembling with anxiety now too.

"It would only be fair," Sean answered, "you are not turning away from me now?"

"A man, a woman who lands in something he or she cannot control cannot be fully blamed. To me something of the same, something similar, happened. I don't know how to tell you. I never told anyone, perhaps that is why I am so extravert," Jacky said while to avoid his look, putting her head in her hands,.

"Compared to me it can't be worse," Sean said to encourage her.

"May be, who knows, but how will you judge me when I blindly follow your command? How can anyone actually kill someone else? I did as you asked me to do. You deployed me. I was your assassin, your weapon. What self respecting person will do that? The answer lies in my past, my past of abuse and the masquerade to hide what is my dark side. Oh I am not a dark person, you know that. But what happened to me formed me and it lies hidden and made me the reckless person I am now, like I want to punish myself for what happened. I know very well I am not responsible and a victim. I could not defend myself, I was too young to even know how to, but I do blame myself for not being able to stop it."

"Were you abused then?", Sean asked.

"My stepfather treated me like a slave; I think that says it all. I cannot tell you the details. They are too abhorrent and I do not want to cry," she said but tears came to her eyes already, "oh I was terrified of him but he sent me to school and I had a good education. I still did everything he said. My mother found out he was treating me like this and being enslaved by him herself, it was very difficult to go against him. But she did and admire myself for the strength I showed once she knew. Stepfather was furious but because of me, my mother did not yield. I was released, well I released myself and when I was seventeen I left the house. I could not stay there anymore. Don't ask me what I think of my mother, she is still with him. Being away from my stepfather made me very happy, but –and I do not expect you to believe me- also sad. He had me for some years and you cannot empathize what it means to be in that relationship, you learn to want it. You learn to desire it, even though you know it is wrong. I became a prostitute to support myself, finished my education and now had what I wanted but did not realize; sex that I had learned to crave but now in command I determined who with and no one else. The Pavlov effect?", she asked and laughed, "I learned this through my studies at the university, clinical psychology. Push the right buttons and I would be wet already. Being like this, is how we met, remember? Here I am a relatively attractive woman, attractive enough to a category of men who want to pay me for my services and a woman who decides for herself what to do and whom to be with, until I met you. Now you know about me, like I know about you. for the first time with you I can be naked, mentally of course darling."

"You don't reject me?", Sean asked.

"Reject you? Why should I? I love you silly man!", she laughed.

"But have you been listening to what I told you? I have been an extremely bad man and I am fully responsible for what I did."

"Of course you are and you told me, you are my man. I am surprised you don't reject me!", she cried out.

"Why should I do that, you are closer to me than ever before," he simply said.

"Oh gosh," Jacky reacted I could not have dreamed this but it is true and we are not even in paradise. We are going to Rio, to Copacabana!"

"Yeah," Sean laughed, "that reminds me, we have to get going. We have less than three ours to fly off Jacky, but we have much to talk about still for I want to leave this life behind and now that I know we can be fully together, will build a life with you."

"Yeah," she reacted, "and we will change. We will put things together and reject what we did. I feel we have to make amends," she said.

"Precisely, it could lead to that, And we will be accountable for what we did!", Sean said.

"What do you mean now Sean," Jacky asked.

"Let's go on holiday first, all right. If we are true to ourselves we will face many difficulties and we have to plan to reemerge clean," Sean said.

"I have an idea what you mean," Jacky said, "but please let's enjoy each other first. On holiday we can talk about all and everything, but in each others arms, all right?"

"All right," Sean smiled.

A few hours later they were up in the air and like a couple of newlyweds they held hands practically for the duration of the flight. Their dark sides now known to each other, they could focus on their more attractive inner feelings. Later on the beach at Copacabana after a day of sunshine and making love late at night on the veranda of their hotel as they overlooked the bay Sean said:

"I am quite certain now I will stop all this shady business. I will sell the Bordello and the chain around it, the Bangkok Chapter too. And, I want to look into what made me accept that assassination contract. I want to know who is behind it and what the reason for it was. This leader was a leader of the Nagas, a people fighting for their freedom. I want to see what is behind this murder, one we both committed.

"No, I pulled the trigger,' Jacky said, "I could have refused."

"You did it under my command and because you did not refuse, I am responsible as well, so is Bailung who made it possible. That reminds me I should really get in touch with him. He too is going to change his life. He found the woman again, he once left. He is in love and finally, like us, ready to change his life forever. Oh Jacky, I am so happy that we finally are able to experience some redemption. This is such a big burden, my woman."

"It still is Sean," Jacky reacted, "I agree we should do all to redeem ourselves. How do we find the one who issued the assassination contract?,' Jacky asked.

"Normally the money trail will lead us to him or her," Sean suggested.

"I am sure the person is clever enough to frustrate that trial man," Jacky said.

"We will have to begin somewhere," he said.

"Yeah right," she agreed.

"How did you get the contract Sean? Who made contact?", Jacky asked.

"Though she never disclosed her real name I know it was Jeanie," Sean said, "Jeanie is a cover operative working for the British Intelligence. I know her through some other channels," he explained.

"Can we get in touch with her?", she asked.

"I am not too sure she knows I recognized her, so she might get a fit when she realizes I could be on her trail!"

"Should you think of her?" Jacky asked.

"No, of course not, but I don't think she is the plotter, however she could lead us to the one with the contract," he explained.

"When you get hold of her, then grill her, I suggest to you," Jacky said.

"In person I can do that yes, but I have to find out where she will be first," he answered.

"While here you could do that indeed," Jacky pushed him.

"In New York I have some friends Jacky, who could help out without exactly knowing the details yet, friends who can be trusted," Sean disclosed.

"Then we will go to New York of course," Jacky said, but first our holiday, right?", she asked and without waiting for an answer threw herself in Sean's arms, laughing out loud.

In Manila things had become a little hectic meanwhile when the news reached that the Minister of Foreign Affairs, Patill, was going to come the reverberations were felt:

"Hmmmm," Efren said, "we cannot have strangers looking into our operations. They will see we are ill equipped and overburdened. At that level and certainly when the man has a bunch of journalists in his wake, our country will be criticized for being negligent. What can we do to prevent this gentleman shifting some of the blame to us?," he asked the team of investigators he had handpicked.

"Well," said Eddie the one on the spot earlier, "we can of course shield off some of our work. It is an official visit, what harm can it really do? We already have an Indian team here and they have eyes. I noticed they do not keep them in their pockets, yet can't do much in our environment. Heck, they do not speak our language. They are useless.. To feign we are better may work against us. Rather than focusing how we come across I suggest we do our work well?"

"You are right Eddie, but we will get clobbered from above if the Indians complain. You know how it goes," Efren said.

"Of course, but we have nothing to fear. They sent a team right? That team is responsible now. We will provide them with what we know. So, let's talk about where we are now, shall we? The man only comes tomorrow and I am eager to know as much as possible before that."

"Okay Eddie," Efren agreed.

“Now let’s see,” Eddie continued, “what the Indians come up with?”

“They only told what they know about the Indo-Naga conflict and placed that against the murder. Like us they don’t have no clue really. Let’s face it,” said one of the investigators by the name of Felix, a clever kind of man according to Eddie.

“Right, we are in the dark, but we must assess what we have found and assemble the pieces of the puzzle now that it has blown out of proportion and has become an international issue,” Efren commented.

“Let’s get to work,” Eddie agreed, “and put up a chart so we can visualize what we actually do know!”

Not waiting for an answer he picked up a stand with big paper from another room and when he had returned he began:

“The man was shot from a moving vehicle in Cubao. Bystanders saw practically nothing. That is one. We found out the man is a leader, has a Bangladeshi passport, but Nagaland is part of India and Burma, so the Indian Government is on our doorstep. We interviewed some bystanders and family members, who told us they have no idea who could be behind this but pointed at some possible parties. And, some bystander said there was a blond woman in the assault car.”

“Yeah, Felix agreed, but that is suspicion. We do not even have a lead on the assassin. Blond leads to either a white person or one with a wig. True, the family and friends rightfully pointed at the Indians and their own kind for we know now that there are rival factions at work too. Did you find out Eddie who benefit from this murder yet? Aside from the two possibilities you mentioned, I have been thinking. Could it be the people themselves, some clever mind perhaps, who thought this up?”, Felix suggested.

“What purpose?”, a shocked Efren asked immediately.

“Well, think of the exposure the murder will get, who can contain it now that the Indian Foreign minister feels he should pay attention personally. Have you read what the murder evoked in Nagaland itself?”, Felix continued.

“Is that the reason for this Foreign Minister to come here?”, Eddie asked.

“I think so,” Felix said, “especially because the Home Minister will go to Nagaland. That Indian Government comes under pressure you know. No wonder they want this solved regarding the confusion with suspicion on the Indian Government?”

“The Nagas of course,” Eddie said.

"Well, then we do have to look into this and I suggest we interrogate some father family members. Did you not say Eddie there are other Nagas living here?", Felix asked.

"There are a few indeed," Eddie answered.

"I suggest we interrogate them, but not the family. I am sure the family would not sacrifice anyone, but others might or might know something," Felix suggested.

"Good idea, we can do that today of course," Efren agreed.

"There is something else I have been thinking of," Felix continued, "when we have no leads, we should try and find them, right?"

"Of course," Efren and Eddie laughed, "so you have an idea?"

"It is a long shot and involves work, but who knows what may turn up," Felix said.

"Shoot," Eddie eagerly said.

"Let's do two things or three perhaps," he began, "first let's check all Indian names on flights coming in to Manila up to three days prior to the murder. Check by the way for any irregularities anyway," Felix said.

"That is one," Efren said, "continue!"

"Well, what seems interesting too is to check hotels and especially the ordinary ones, tourists ones with the same recipe. Come to think of it. I don't think this is done by one person, unless that person is Philippino. You know why?", Felix teased them.

"I have an idea," Eddie smiled, "may I?"

"Of course," Felix chuckled.

"Cubao is a busy place. The target lives in a suburb. You have to know the city well and how to move in this traffic. The assassin then had the task to kill, a helper was the guide and paved the way for the assassin?", Eddie suggested

"Excellent," Felix praised him, "so there may be three involved here now: an assassin, an Indian and a Philippino. It could also be that we have an Indian living here in Manila who knows the city like no one else. Perhaps we should check that too. Let's get to immigration and check the records for that. An Indian who lives here long enough?"

"Okay," Efren, "good thinking Felix. What is your third?"

"I think telephone companies with their advanced computer technology register all calls. We can demand to release all calls with the words Naga from them, the name of the slain victim, or words identifying relations to the murder. Then we can perhaps find out, who actually made those calls?"

"You are darn clever man," Eddie laughed, "now we suddenly have a lot of tedious work to do again. Let's split up and divide into sub teams, each taking on a task. Let's report by this evening, all right, Efren?"

"Okay, this is sound thinking Felix, yes we can get full steam ahead now, off we go," Efren concluded.

"Wait, wait, wait," Felix laughed, "what will we do about the Indian team? We are due to meet them later today?"

"They have gone off on their own now right? Let them be for a while. I doubt if they can come up with something. I am sure there are some secret agents among them. They will have their own agenda," Efren said.

"They have to come up with something to share," Eddie said, "or they will look stupid and there will be suspicion befalling on them."

"On the other hand they might come up with something to steer us in the wrong direction?", Efren suggested, "let's be careful anyhow men."

Chapter 6
Nagaland revisited

In Delhi things were moving rapidly for Jeanie and Marius as they were planning to go to Dimapur via Guwahati. They had just returned from the Delhi chapter of the Naga Peoples Movement for Human Rights, NPMHR, and were back in their hotel room to review what they had accomplished so far. They had connected with people and made appointments for when they would be in Nagaland. Of course Marius was eager to get in touch with Lisa and he had phoned her as soon as he could. But it was not only Lisa who informed them of the rising unrest in Nagaland, the unrest that drove Patill to Manila and which made the Home Minister announce that he would come to Kohima.

"Do you think things go out of hand," Jeanie asked one of the Nagas. I hear from you the Indian Army is preparing already?"

"It all depends how they will act," the NPMHR member said, "if they do not exert power but only intervene appropriately then I am sure nothing major will happen. On the other hand we fear the worst. The people think it is from the secret service or the military themselves who are behind this and they are furious. It is good the Home Minister goes to Kohima but then, it depends really on what he is going to say there."

"Yeah that may very well be right indeed," Marius said, "Is there anything we can do?"

"Not yet, but soon I think you can," the NPMHR man said, "I am sure you will be close to where things transpire in Nagaland and you can make it public. You will be an asset to us if you can do that."

"If we can we will," Jeanie said, but winked at Marius knowing that as covert operatives it was practically impossible to show their face in public.

"I want to call Bram," Marius said to Jeanie.

"May be that is a good idea. He may have found out something of course!"

Marius picked up the phone and dialed the 0031 access code for the Netherlands:

"Bram here," Marius heard,

"Marius here Bram, listen we are in Delhi and soon on our way to Nagaland where an uprising is in the making. This is getting more serious by the day, so tell me, do you know anything?" Marius asked.

"I know something, but it is not much. I know in Manila they are checking flights, hotels and phones for Indians who live in the Philippines. What is more important is that it is buzzing in our world of covert operatives, but no one is allowed to go out and investigate, only the secret services of India."

"The Raw?", Marius asked.

"And the IB too," Bram said.

"How do you know that? Normally they will not tell this kind of info?"

."We have our ways, but this is a really simple our men. For something else we had to get visa and they talked to the RAW man at the Embassy," Bram explained.

"Even then, the man disclosed?", Marius asked.

"It was more like he wanted to make sure the Raw had nothing to do with it," Bram said.

"Will this not actually lead to more suspicion Bram?"

"I thought so too but in this case no, I don't think so. Our man innocently asked, for he had said he read that the Nagas were rising because of a murder of one of their leaders. The man then asked, how did he know that? Well our man replied to him, that it was in the papers, the English ones and he added that he would think it would be in the papers of the Netherlands soon too. The Peace Talks are held here, so there will be some interest!"

"He evaded the Indian involvement, or was he told that the Indian Government was suspected to be behind this?", Marius asked.

"Not exactly, it went more like this Marius. Our man asked if he, while on official business in Delhi and Bombay primarily should be taking extra precautions. He clearly stated he would not go anywhere near Nagaland but expected both secret services and the Indian Army on high alert. Of course, like a pro he stated then that all was under control. But then our man remarked that the Manila people, the police investigators there, thought India was behind it and that appeared in the local media, hence the uprising. But then the Indian Embassy man vehemently went against that and said his government and his secret service would not do that."

"Of course they would say that Bram, even when it was the killer himself you spoke to there and then man."

"Right, but here it comes, as a joke our man said that if it was a really secret service then even the Embassy man would not know about it. But I do, he had answered, so when our man then said, in that case two plus two is four, the Embassy did not deny, but signed the visa and let our man out."

"So, to you it is so that the Embassy man is part of the Raw or the IB?", Marius asked.

"Yes, I have heard it before and this seems to be a confirmation," Bram answered.

"Do you really think he will tell you the RAW or IB are involved if he knows either one of them are Bram, come on man?", Marius laughed.

"I would be too naïve Marius, if I would go just for that, but there was something, like he knew all was going against them and he did not know how to defend. I don't think he could have faked it, it was too sudden. But, I will tell you this, I will get to the bottom of this, I will tap the wires here and there. Get back to me in a day or two? I will have my Philippino friends on it too. They are closing in to the police and one of them owes me a favor, okay?", he suggested.

"Well, if you can draw them out. But think, if they are they will try to cover up like never before, this is going to be serious. If it comes out it is them, the Indian Government bites the dust man!", Marius chuckled.

"Right, a day or two, if I can get you on the phone from Guwahati!", Marius concluded.

Briefly Marius explained to Jeanie what he had heard, she knew half but not what Bram had said of course:

"This might be a breakthrough if they can isolate the Raw and IB being involved or not and make it known, then they might be able to defuse the potential uprising too, "Jeanie assessed, "let's talk to the Nagas tomorrow about how likely these ideas are. They, I am told, know the Raw very well,"

"Good ideas, yeah, we will do that then," Marius agreed.

The next day when they had a breakfast meeting before they were taken to Delhi airport for the domestic flight to Guwahati Jeanie popped that question. Now it was one of the Naga Student Federation, Delhi chapter, who eagerly answered before anyone else could:

"These Raw and IB agents are a treacherous lot, the Raw is in all Embassies and they keep tabs on everyone whom they feel is worth their attention. The people of the Naga International Support Center in Amsterdam for instance are on their list of attention and I heard from their secretary that the Embassy man has regular meetings with him, unofficially."

"So in the Netherlands they screen people who are involved with the Sikh, the Kashmir and the Naga quests for self determination?", Marius asked what he knew already.

"Yes indeed," the student leader simply said.

"What do they do here?", Jeanie asked looking at the others too.

"They are the architects of their great divide and rule game," the young man said, "they have money and they scheme. They deploy and they bind, you name it they do it."

"That is their job I suppose," Marius said.

"To make life difficult for the Nagas, yes that is their job. Both work in the dark. They are not accountable but to the home office and to the Foreign offices only. Of course those ministries are part of the cabinet, the government, so ultimately it is the Government of India who scheme through these two agencies."

"Yes, we understand that," Jeanie said looking at Marius who nodded and continued:

"Thank you very much, that was quite enlightening."

"We better take you to the airport now for your flight, our people will be at the airport of Guwahati to fetch you, to make you comfortable and get you the Remote Area permits. From then on you are free to roam around Nagaland, Arunachal Pradesh and Manipur," the NPMHR representative said.

"Good, let's go, and thank you all again," Jeanie said.

In the Home Ministry the IB and Raw head offices were buzzing with activity. Both were very sure there had not been any order received with the idea of taking out one of the Naga leaders, but now both were facing questioning of the highest order. Since nobody in either ministry had a clue who had murdered the Naga leader and suspecting either there were irregularities in either secret agencies, or worse that they had been acting on their own, things could go out of hand. Of course it could also be that neither had been involved, but that was not the first and foremost thing that was thought about, yet it could not ruled out altogether either. So when the Home Minister called for a meeting first with IB and later with RAW, all in the Ministry remotely connected to either agency, had the jitters. The Home Minister opened the meeting by stating that due to the brutal murder in a foreign land of an important Naga leader the country was in the process of facing a crisis. The heads of the different departments of the organization called Research and Analysis Wing, in short RAW, were all present when the Home Minister addressed them in the meeting saying:

"Welcome ladies and gentlemen," yes ladies were represented in this covert operatives set up, "you know what happened and I ask you directly and bluntly now first in this meeting and later in one to one questioning what you know about this. You know we have sent a police team to Manila because we want to find out for ourselves what really happened and who is responsible for this mess. Now tell me is anyone of you involved?"

Having said that the Home minister looked around and studied the faces. No one did come forward to state their Raw unit was involved indeed. So he went on and asked:

"Does this mean that the Raw is free of hatching plots and is oblivious of plots hatched by others, plots the Minister should know about for he accountable?"

The head of the Embassy section rose slowly. Quite shyly the, in this case a man, when standing, overlooked the room then addressed the Home minister:

"I hope you do not mind me being frank Sir and I cannot talk for others, but allow me to say this to you, if there would be anyone among us who is responsible for this, I cannot imagine that person to stand up and admit this. So, I suggest you select your most trustworthy people and unleash a full scale investigation on all of us. Of course you should not make it public to us who these people are, for that would alert the culprits, provided these people are among us of course. May I suggest checking all computers, all communication between members of our covert staff and the people outside they get information from, the people we pay off on the outside, the running programs and plans that are in operation but in which sidelines a plan like this could have been hatched? Perhaps we should check our ties with the other Naga factions too and may be find that instead of the responsible Raw operatives the tables were turned and some lower operatives have taken bribes and hatched a plan of their to create this mess Sir?"

"Go on," the Home minister prompted the man.

"That is really all I can think of now. It is elementary, anyone could have told you this perhaps for the tables could be turned situation," the man humbly said.

"Okay, okay, anyone else who wants to contribute? No, has to contribute because it is your duty as heads of departments?"

"No, no," the lady who handled research and would file everything said. She led a rather large unit which took on lots of tasks on request. It was actually really the heart of the Raw, "I fully agree with our Embassy man. Yes we should check all contacts for the word Naga or the name of the slain leader. We will screen, preferably in combination with Manila. We should have the results of that operation very soon," she concluded.

"Very soon, very soon, woman we have a crisis on our hands, an uprising, and soon everybody looks at us here. They will say we are responsible for murdering this Naga leader and I must be sure what I am going to say when I am in Nagaland. You will give me a preliminary result of the likelihood of your operation by tomorrow at the latest. Now as for the control unit, all of you know now that I appointed the Embassy man as the leader to check all units. His deputy will take over. Man, you will pick the team and you will bring me the list. Now, is that understood?"

Satisfied with the outcome they nodded and the Home Minister added:

"Now all go to work and fast for this is no child play!"

And they did. In front of him too a similar meeting took place with the IB staff an hour later and now that the Home Minister had some expertise on how to set it up this self scrutinizing procedure, he first let them come up with it then rapidly took over what he thought to be effective. All at work now for his purpose, he got in touch with the Nagaland State Government to tell he would be there a day later than planned.

The Scorpion, alert on remote sensing, detected three networks now. Through his sources he knew the Manila network was making progress, slowly, but he was certain sooner or later there would be a lead in solving the murder on the Naga leader. That was network one and it was connected now to network two, the Indian network itself. Besides his own the Scorpion discovered another network. So, he had come to the conclusion there were four already. Next to his own net work which had put everything in motion, there was the Dutch network of Marius. He knew he had nothing to fear from the Indians he had for he could easily lead them astray or when needed put them on a track to where he wanted them to go. The Manila network connected to the Indian police, though it was now politically connected because of the high level visit by Patill, did not worry him either. That was all in the plan and so far it worked wonderfully well. The threat of an uprising also would lead to what the Scorpion was ultimately after. The unsecured factor now, he thought, was what he called the Dutch network. Through his sources he learned that some covert agents had come to India to try and find things out in Nagaland itself.

What could he actually expect from this network he hardly knew about? What were these Dutch people after? Due to Naga exposures in the USA and his on visits to the land the Scorpion was well connected in Nagaland. He had come to know and like quite a few young and promising Nagas, many of which were either members of the NPMHR or the NSF. So, when he carefully inquired about those Dutch people this is what he learned from those sources; Marius and Jeanie had planned this trip before the Naga leader was assassinated and this apparently had no connection to it. From the people in Delhi he also learned now that Jeanie was an operative from Great Britain, or the United Kingdom as it was now called. Marius, the Dutchman had met a Naga woman and got interested in the stories she told. She inspired him to come to Nagaland, both because of the Indo-Naga conflict and of her. Marius and Lisa had come to like each other he heard and Marius had talked about this frankly and openly. They expressed their dismay about the murder, but did not seem to know much more. The Scorpion was not quite at ease with this simple piece of info and he had two reasons to feel that way; first of all the pair were covert operatives without a mission but their own interest. Secondly, things were happening in itself, this immediately would raise their interest professionally. The Scorpion calculated that this personal interest could rapidly become a professional interest. This is a large and important but yet dormant network, he thought, one he had no way of connecting with, yet with the potential of, when involved, becoming influential. Not just for contributing in solving this murder, so to get to the Scorpion, but to raise interest in the Indo-Naga case world wide. He was thinking about what to do. Should he try and feed info so they would do as he envisaged? Should he shield himself so as to avoid getting caught? Then hopefully things he put in the cards would indeed work out. This was the question he raised and had to answer. Leaving this network out of the general picture could be a grave mistake, he thought. Besides, this network was one which had tentacles in the USA as well and when the European operatives would inform their counterparts in the USA, they would eventually find him. The Scorpion, if at all he wanted to be found, wanted to set time and place himself so to achieve maximum effect. He knew this was too early to consider yet. With his my sources in place I can stay near to these two and like that I might just be able to assess what their exposure in Nagaland is about. Where they would go and perhaps more importantly, where that would lead them to. So, he forced himself to think about his own network now. After the deed he had lost touch with the assassins and their intermediate. So, it was strange to see Jeanie, the intermediate connected to the Marius network as he called it. He had given out the contract to a well known and trustworthy person; one with connections in different countries and on different levels, but Jeanie was only the person who was to set up Sean. So, directly he had no connection of any sort with Sean or Jeanie and certainly not with Bailung or Jacky. In order to keep himself fully informed and to be sure that it would be the Scorpion himself who would set time and place for the revelation of operations and if needed motivation, his organizing friend in the background had the names to that effect. This friend was a mutual friend of both Sean and the Scorpion. Of course neither of them knew each other personally. So, the only connection really was the one through the mutual friend. This link could prove to be an important one, because if this friend would be arrested and forced to talk, then the Scorpion would be detected and his identity revealed. Since he did not know Jacky, Sean or Jeanie but wanted to know those who had done the Scorpion required, he ran a check on them. Apart from what Sean did in the Bordello business and his connection of personal nature with Jacky he was especially interested in their background and consequently their motivation. He stumbled on what Sean and Bailung had gone through in Africa and thought in the end these people could be a liability. They had done things which made his heart turn and he his trusted friend had indeed chosen the perfect assassins. He concluded that because of that background they were truly reliable. Since it was practically impossible to catch them, the Scorpion decided, if this was opportune to do, to lead the teams of investigators to the assassination team. Not now of course, he reminded himself, but when needed he decided that remorse for giving them up would not stop him. Considering what they did not think twice. Okay then, he reviewed, what are the weak points? How can I make them stronger? Well, first of all tension should rise in Nagaland, the international press should be compelled to dive into this and travel with the Home Minister, who was expected to try and pacify the people only without giving them any perspective. So he wanted to make sure the word of a Naga people being taken for a ride by the Indian Government would be out. More and more nations would have a look into what was happening then. Interested parties, especially human rights and cultural organizations, would decry the situation and blame the Indian Government for letting things go so much out of hand. History of the conflict would be studies and the oppression of the Naga people would become a topic. This would also lead for governments elsewhere to put the Indo-Naga conflict on their agendas and moreover those governments would begin to look at India with different eyes. Some, like perhaps France, Germany or the whole EU and the USA would question India on the matter. Should there, for any reason, be a flaw in the proceedings, the Scorpion was determined to release clues to keep the interest going. While for the moment it would serve his purpose, in the end though he did not want to blame the Indian Government for what it did not do,. Only later, when it became apparent the suspicion on the Indian government had fully served its purpose, would he think of leading the investigators and so the eye of the international community to the real killers. Yes then would he give the assassination team up, he thought and grinned.

Little did he know then, while planning and plotting, that realistic dynamics would eventually determine the outcome! Like, he could not have counted on the changes taking place in Sean and Bailung, changes that would send ripples through his plans and so soon he was forced to take drastic measures, measures which would reel his sense of justice. The ethical principles in him he had struggled so hard with would come under severe pressure. For now, the Scorpion was content with the proceedings as he quietly tapped the wires, yet withholding any information which would, at a later stage, lead the process in his desired direction.

In Guwahati when Marius had gone for a walk with some of the Nagas who had received them and arranged their Remote Area permits, Jeanie was thinking of Sean. She needed time to think about things alone. From her schooling days, she had known Sean, so for a long time. Once, they even had had something together, yet always remained friends. Jeanie had been very angry with him when she learned about what he had been doing in Africa. Astounded she saw the person in him was full of remorse and now lacked self respect. Instead of turning her back on him, she tried to help him out. In vain this was, for he himself who had declared to her that he was beyond repair. His life was over and he would not know how to relate in any way trustworthy way again. When he had been suicidal, they had talked for days. Eventually he had found some sort of basis when he, as a front for other activities like intervening in conflicts, started the Bordello. Sean after all was a very well trained commando. He had introduced her to Bailung too, but she did not quite what to make of this man with his prying eyes who had gone through that ordeal with Sean and possibly, according to her, was the instigator. Sean denied that and took it up for him by telling Bai had been the better man. Meanwhile Jeanie was very conscious about her double role. Jeanie knew a lot more about the Indo-Naga conflict and when Sean had sought her advice on this matter, she had given it. She had heard from Sean since 'the deed was done', and had discussed her opinion regarding this assassination. She recalled when they met in London that time Sean had said to her:

"I get this assignment through you, a mediator, and you do not know who gave out the original contract, but Jeanie when you see the history of these people and you see the historical involvement of the British, our people, and now the Indians keeping them in deadlock while trying to outwit them, I think this could be a golden opportunity to break through. What do you think?"

"Let me think on it," she had answered and later she had entrusted him that he must go ahead, but without telling him she in turn was compelled to do so. In Africa shortly afterwards Marius had launched the idea about going into Nagaland with her, as a couple. And she knew things were already moving and could not be stopped. Now in spite of the fact Marius was lost for her, Jeanie did not want to either. Now she was interested in the effects of the assassination and consented to go to Nagaland with him. She was eager to find out too who the person or group of persons was, the initiators of the assassination, for it looked like they had similar ideas as she had about the effects. Now though she focused on Naga life and what the assassination brought about, how it shaped the perspective of the people realizing the Indians could benefit from this. The looming uprising, the man in the street talking of nothing else, was the talk of the day in Guwahati. Just to feel the pulse of the people it was no wonder both Marius and her were looking forward to get into Nagaland as soon as possible. Before Marius returned she wanted to get in touch with Sean to learn if there was more news on the investigation in Manila. But she was surprised when he answered his cell phone:

"Hi Jeanie, there is something I must tell you. Jacky and I have sent ourselves through hell. Finally and only because we could encourage each other we decided to deal with our past. I know what I have done, I will never forget it. What we are doing now is an ethical conflict too. I am sure it will change for the Nagas; this murder made this possible but to completely redeem myself and Jacky we may have to do something you might not like," he announced sort of solemnly.

"What do you mean now Sean? I just wanted to know how things are developing in Manila and you come up with a thing of your own now?"

"Right you are,' Sean said but not just with discernable sincerity in his voice but with seriousness she only knew from him when he was uptight, "now listen Jeanie. This may be our chance to redeem ourselves. We will both look at what transpires, we are responsible for executing the assassination contract. You know that. My point is that we cannot take that back, but what we can do is to intervene in the process. We will bank on a flow favorable to the Nagas. When it is not I will come clean and tell what really happened in Manila. I want the whole world to know about the importance of this assassination. I want to deal with all my guilt, not just with what I was infected with in Africa."

"Sure I understand, but you could have been more dependable you know. And, depending on what you are going to do, I may have to turn against you. I do hope you realize that? I will come after you and if necessary take you out," she said menacingly.

"Look Jeanie, you are good friend and a fine woman, but after many years I am back on the right track or, so you will, trying to. Don't you go threatening me It won't help you to change my mind," Sean said before hanging up.

"Got you," Jeanie said then thought of the repercussions if Sean indeed would reveal what he had been responsible for and executed.

Meanwhile Bailung and Celia had the time of their lives. Through her, his self loathing had come to an end, his redemption had begun. Resisting it at first, for he could not quite believe he was capable, in the seclusion of her Makati apartment, they had begun. Oh, he knew he loved her like no other, but he could not show that to her, not yet:

"I am so unworthy of you Celia," he had said time and again but not in a way she should take pity on him. No, when she finally had wrestled the African devastation out of him, he went through and felt responsible for, she finally understood what he felt:

"I have been such a low human being, there is no forgiveness. It does not matter if I love you. I am not worthy of your love," he had stressed again. But Celia had not given up:

"Yes, you have been a very bad man, due to your lack of backbone you went through with it. Now you will grow that backbone back. You can be sorry for your weaknesses, contemplate them, but you will grow out of them. You are a strong man, but a stupid man at times, your weakness was that you not only felt sorry for too long but that you let yourself be led by others when you knew it was wrong, very wrong."

"It is horrible. I know that well but you know what? Once you are in it, it feels normal, very normal and now I realize why I came to Angeles City, the city of Angels."

"Oh come on Bai, what has Angeles got to do with rape and indiscriminant murder?"

"I am not talking of the what but about things becoming normal when they are not and in Angeles this is similar though not as deadly," Bai tried to explain.

"Tell me more," Celia demanded as she did not understand it at all.

"Okay," Bai smiled thinking how he could get through,":the first time I came here as a young man the American Air Force was here, do you remember?"

"Yes I do," Celia said, "go on please."

"Well then you know of course that the 'normal' life was the life of a town solely catering for men on the base and they called it Rest and Recreation?"

"Right," Celia agreed.

"That first time, years ago, I felt sucked in just like many of these Air Force and Navy people from Olongapo next to the naval base Subic Bay. Every day became some sort of frenzy, mob like if you will. Here were normally shy young men opening their big mouths who could do anything there what they could not dream of at home. They were like children in a candy store and they could have all the candy they wanted. Now Celia picture those young men fancying many and different ones every night and because they had money, they could get them in real and the sexual frenzy was normal. It was 'abnormal' when you did grab a pussy and would fuck like a maniac. You would be called a queer, a nerd, a faggot if you did not. Now, I was not part of that but I did see how these young men, barely twenty years old behaved with our women. Consider too that this candy was handed to them cheaply and in abundance and I mean handed for it was all organized on high level between the Philippine Government and the leadership of the American forces. Of course it was poor or rejected women who flocked to Angeles and Olongapo to try and make a better life for them. You are a woman so tell me then how a woman feels when she has become dependent on this? Those men would hardly ever venture further into the Philippines than Angeles or Olongapo. This was their home away from home and to them this was the Philippines, one big brothel. That was their reality and all their colleagues were doing the same. But, we know that outside Angeles and Olongapo it is a different world, the real one. Angeles then was the world of beer and women and the only existing. Philippinos you could not find, only those working for the Rest and Recreation Industry, so for you, the soldier When you know the world outside, you know that this cannot be the real world but a realistic but separate world of make believe. Being part of it you will submerge in it," Bailung said.

"Not every man is strong enough to resist that," Celia said with compassion.

"I can only tell you that I have fought hard and did not come up, not on my own. I regret many things I have done Celia. I went to Angeles again to find out about that feeling of this world upside down which felt so very normal when you are part of it."

"And you have learned, now we can be closer than ever before?", she whispered.

"After all I have done you still believe in me?", Bai asked.

"Because of it, I know you are sincere and though your slate is not clean, your experience has made you a better man. Now you are my man. I have faith in you. Because you told me your dark side, now I think we can try again. I saw it in your eyes, you are a changed man, No, not beaten, but to make this move after all these years shows your resilience. It shows that, deep inside, you are a good man. Your life now really has begun."

"My things of the past when I was a younger man are haunting me, how can I get rid of that feeling of being insignificant? Why do I feel this urge to prove myself? It can't be because I was discarded as a child and grew up in foster homes," Bai said," I always had a need to show I was not bad. But now it is over. Now things are falling into place. I need you by my side to share and to remind me that I can be of value too," he said.

"Oh silly man, I have loved you from the start. I know and felt it many times you were deeply troubled but could not show me. I also felt that you wanted to protect me from you, from your dark side. And you do remember how I tried, but the more I did the further you withdrew. I felt hopeless and tried to satisfy you with sex. That was at least something you could relate to, if only for a moment."

"Yeah I remember, the more I grew closer to you the more frightened I became. My future felt bleak. Loosing you was too terrible, yet I knew it was inevitable. So, I kept it to myself and thought it was honorable to separate from you, so you were safe from me."

"That feeling was horrible," Celia said.

"Yes, for me too, but it was then the only thing I could do, to protect you from my terrible anger which I knew could get out of control."

"We are back together now Bai and I feel it stronger than ever before. Now I believe in you and you will prove it too by telling me about that last act of yours and how to make amends, how to repent too," Celia said warmly.

"Yes I will," Bai said and he began to unfold the story of the assassination in full. He talked for as much as half an hour on how he had been called to talk about it with Sean and how to conduct things when they accepted the assignment. For weeks he had been laying in waiting after they decided to go ahead with it. Sean had convinced him it was for a very good cause and he had shown him the extent of the Naga struggle, so doing something bad, in relation to the good it was relatively small, he was glad that he could at least do a lot of good for a good number of people. So, he trusted his friend and went ahead and. Around Manila he had gone to find out the ways of this Naga leader, like where he went and at what times. He had been reviewing lots of possibilities, to strike at his home or in public. At it was too dangerous for there were children around he did not want to take that chance. It was too dangerous too because they may not be able to get away unseen. When he knew by overhearing that he would attend a meeting on that day, he had prepared Jacky for that fateful. Jacky had been in Manila for a couple of days to get acquainted with both the people and how they act in the streets as well as with the traffic. Bai had stolen a vehicle and he had dropped two get away cars. They had checked into the Manila Hotel for two nights to show they were high society. After Jacky had gained some experience on the Manila streets, that day she had changed into assault gear and they had driven to Cubao. It had been not been very difficult for them to single out their target, but because of Bai's calculations on the spot they had been right on time. Slightly away from the corner where Bai saw the man emerging from the Light Rail Transit station to catch a taxi they had waited for only a minute or so.. That is when he told Jacky to make her move and she had done exactly how they had rehearsed. She shot him while he drove and they rapidly had disappeared to get to dump the stolen car two blocks away and changed it for the one they had parked there. Then only they heard the traffic deafening traffic and they realized the shorts could hardly have been heard. Bai had thrown the gun in a ditch after Jacky had wiped it with a cloth. The gun Bai had arranged from a friend of his', one that could not be traced. Again two blocks and they left the care to go up to the light rail transit bound for Monumento. They switched to the one going to Rizal and Quiapo over Taft Avenue and alighted at United Nations Avenue to leisurely walk, like a couple in love, towards Manila Bay and the Manila Hotel.

"That is how it went," Bai said to Celia, "now how can I repair anything without jeopardizing the lives of Jacky and Sean?"

"You can talk to them that is one, perhaps for I think they feel something similar. As you said to me it seems they have found each other too and there was a change going on?"

"Yeah that's right," Bai agreed.

"Now, the Indians are under suspicion and what has been planned out is happening, the Nagas are rising too. With a lot of attention, international too now, drawn to this murder, something is bound to happen. If there is anyone who could have done it the Indian Government will try to pin this on someone within its own circles. If their internal investigation comes up dry, they will try to pin it elsewhere," Celia was thinking aloud.

"If I give myself up and the others, it would mean the plotter will go free. Should we not try to find out who ordered this first?", Bai wondered while he looked at Celia.

"Good thinking man, yeah get in touch with Sean as soon as possible and suggest that to him, he is the man who could possibly trace the plotter though the communication he received. He could also try to follow the money trail. It was delivered in cash right?"

"Right," Bai answered.

"So, it had to come from somewhere. Do you have any friends in the international police circuits, access to databases? Can you get some people on it, you have money now and so you can put it to use too, you do not need all that money. We have enough together," Celia suggested.

"Lots of money and we can use that of course," Bai said.

"Get a laptop and I have an internet connection here, so get to work. I have to too and we will see each other in the evenings. My place is yours and will be your office, but you do the work and we will review every evening. If need be and Sean agrees we will release some info at time, just to keep the investigative teams on the right track."

"Tomorrow the Indian Foreign minister will arrive and this will bring some commotion," Bai said, "perhaps a good scan of the papers will give us some info."

"Don't forget to get in touch with the foreign press too; there are a lot of correspondents and stringers around. The Philippino stringers will gladly listen for a small fee, you know," Celia suggested.

"Very good, we are already a team," Bai smiled.

"Of course my man," Celia smiled as a sign of warmth, an implicit invitation to be intimate.

"My soul overflows when I look at you and you call yourself my woman Celia. I mean it. Though I am not convinced yet, I do feel much more confident that we are together and a team too. Is it a dream come true darling," Bai whispered and Celia moved closer to touch his face. Moments later they were undressed and as if coming together for the very first time, they merged to come together as one. The fierceness of their joined bodies did not express desperation, but the opposite. It was lust to share beauty and forgiveness, the acceptance they extended to each other, the giving and taking in mind the yin yang principle literary they became. After they were both exhausted and their passion had subsided they laid relaxed, touching en enjoying their souls enveloped in their bodies. They realized they were into each others veins now, never to be separated again.

In Guwahati Marius and Jeanie had been around town for it was their once in a life time chance to see the Bramaputhra river, the mighty river which flows down into Bangladesh to empty in the Indian Ocean. They had had meetings and had talked about their route, whom to meet and what places to go. The news about angry Nagas wanting to fight the Indian Government spread like wildfire and it was now urgent that the Home Minister should come to explain all so he could take the sting out of the shattered Naga feelings. Demonstrations in Mokokchong, Kohima, and Dimapur were going on already and Haflong in Assam, Uhkrhul and Senapati in Manipur and even the Tirap district in Arunachal Pradesh were following suit. What struck most people was that for the first time since 1975, (Shillong Accord) and 1988 the second split over leadership, the Nagas stood up as one. Never mind background and conviction their leader had been assassinated and all Nagas were enraged.

"This of course is a good thing," a representative of NPMHR said during one of their meetings, "even though there is more than strong suspicion on the other two Naga organizations, funded by the Indian Government, their rage now all come together as one in. To the Nagas this is the ultimate insult and since there was no other adversary but the Indians or our own people, all eyes are on Delhi now," he said.

Though the Home Minister announced he would come to Kohima to be with the bereaved Nagas, the postponement of his trip did not fall well at all. The Naga people saw this as a way for the Indians to elude and evade and the mobs in the cities cooled their anger by attacking Government offices. They took to the streets, shouted slogans, raised banners and finally attacked set fire to government offices. Things were rapidly going out of hand and there was no one left to pacify the people. Not that anyone had tried yet, not even officially a condolence was sent. Primarily in the press only the State Government had vented its feelings. The people only reacted with contempt, they were disgruntled with the studied way of reacting by the politicians on this type occasions. Years of grinding teeth had come to an end and it was like lava now flowing freely from a volcano made to erupt by the Indians.

"This assassination was a cowardly act and meant to influence the peace talks," the NPMHR man said, "this is terrible. This is a treacherous act which makes it almost impossible for any Naga now to trust any Government. The sincerity has been buried along with our leader," he remarked bitterly, "this could be the beginning of a dark age."

"Unless you break out of this gloom and make the Indian government responsible internationally?" Marius suggested.

“We have no means to let the international community know what happens here,” the man said, “we depend on people like you to make it known how we are treated here.”

“It could be,” Jeanie cut in, “that this uprising and the assassination will catch the international news. We can contribute to keep it there,” she said.

“You can?”, he asked not believing a single word of what she said.

“Well, I cannot guarantee but we can do our best to play our part,” Jeanie said slightly less convinced now.

“We can pull some strings,” Marius smiled, “but something major has to happen before the international news agencies will think of covering it in a grand way?”

“Like hundreds of people dying by the hands of the Indian Army when our people they recklessly resist them as they are told and pressed to go home but instead persist in demonstrating against the Government?”

“That is one option, perhaps we can think up another and in line with that orchestrate for maximum effect. I hate to think that people have to die always first to catch any kind of attention,” Marius suggested.

“That may be good thing to say, but in practice you have to come up with some good ideas. We don’t know how to catch attention. True when the international eyes are on the Indian Army I am sure they are ordered not to turn against our people. The Government could be afraid of the bloodbath they created for it will then be held against them?”

“Yes, so we have to give them some pressure from the outside. Let me make a few calls,” Marius said and then to Jeanie, “yes you can do that too. Instruct your home people to get in touch with the media for a disaster can strike here any time, all right?”

“Right,” Jeanie agreed but she knew too that this was a hard thing to accomplish. The British secret service after all does not control the media.

“To work then,” Marius announced and withdrew to a phone which had international access and began. Jeanie too did so and called Sean in Rio plus some key people in Britain. Marius called Bram and some counterparts in the USA, the UK and some key European countries.

“This is the networking I like to see. A concerted effort to get media researchers interested so they will produce news items and background info, credible and reliable of course,” Jeanie said, “and when they do not find the indo credible enough nor can double check, they should feel inspired to gather credible info themselves.”

"Most just copy from each other here," Neichu, a representative of the Naga Mothers Association remarked.

"They do that everywhere. News is something you can buy, do that and it is cheaper then gathering it yourself," Marius laughed, "on the other hand there are some credible agencies too of course and it is those we should get into gear so they will investigate. Because they are credible, they are quoted."

"Like, Reuters, UP and AP?", Neichu asked.

"Yeah," Marius acknowledged.

"Those agencies again use stringers here and are persistent in nonsense too you know,"

"How so," Jeanie asked now.

"An example," Neichu said, "Reuters consistently quotes the number of 25.000 causalities over the years of the conflict. This is a number once quoted by the Assam Tribune. Nobody knows what it is based on, but when the Nagas say and we have documented background so it is reliable, that Nagas alone have lost lives amounting to 200,000 to 300.000 people, then I would think researchers the basis of this gap alone, would be inspired to investigate. Reuters, in spite of the info we have sent them does not even acknowledge the reception of such information and keeps on quoting what it deems fit. So, Jeanie, does it look like we can actually take the international agencies seriously."

"Not even the BBC," asked Marius.

"Especially not the BBC," Neichu reacted sharply.

"I learned the BBC is a well documented and impartial?" Marius asked teasingly.

"How can you actually say that, when it is the BBC especially, knowing the history of the Nagas, which has knowledge of the legacy of the British? They act like they don't know anything really and only publish something when it has to do with some actuality. Hardly ever do they go in depth and besides also quote dutifully the 25.000 casualties. No, I believe they are restricted by the Indian government too, to say as little as possible about Nagaland and our people. The British are accountable. They caused of this conflict here, but there is nothing the BBC does, to show that. They keep quiet and so adhere to what India wants them to do, which is nothing at all as far as the Nagas are concerned."

"I think Neichu is right there Marius," Jeanie admitted, "until recently I knew nothing about Nagaland and this for a woman of the world should be unthinkable, when you know it was once under the British. That only a people in Great Britain know about it means that India and Britain have been successful in sweeping their dirt under the rug."

"Yeah, apparently it is still there now, but we are going to change this. I phoned a few people and they are setting things up. Slowly there is news seeping through in Europe too, of an imminent uprising. Due to the brutal assassination of one of your leaders," Marius informed them.

"I have been able to push some buttons that still function," Jeanie said, "let's see what happened in the near future. Who knows, with some pressure from Europe on the Indian Government to come clean, things might take a different turn.

"That would be nice for a change," Neichu smiled, "it is arranged you can go to Nagaland tomorrow. I will travel with you to make sure you will not get unwanted questions from the Indian army or Assam Rifles. I ask you to play dumb when any uniform comes up to talk, all right?"

"Agreed," Marius smiled, "playing dumb is not that easy though."

"Right you are," Jeanie agreed.

"So, you will come with us all the way?", Marius asked.

"It is not that far. We will travel by train to Dimapur and Shilu will meet you at the station," Neichu smiled.

"Oh that is nice to know, but how do you know?", he asked.

"She knew I was here and she knew you were, so two plus two is four," Neichu giggled.

"It is good to know she can count," Marius laughed, "and that I can count on her," now they all burst into laughing. We will be on the night train?"

"I think you better get prepared," Neichu said. The Raps are with you and we will reach Dimapur station early morning. You will have some time left to run around town and see the sun sink in the Bramaputhra. Would you like a guide to take you around town?", she asked concluding the conversation.

"We have seen something and I am eager to get to Nagaland but like to get some more of the word out right now. So we will relax while doing that all right?"

"Please suit yourself, I have things to prepare too," I will pick you up in the evening then," she said and left.

The BBC World Service and other international media got wind from what was about to take place in Nagaland. They felt the buzz going around and got that from nervous civil servants, anxious politicians and busy ministries. More so even they received from unreliable sources and what those communicated had to be verified. Unfortunately all those in the ministries were nervous and tightlipped. To Anirbaum from the BBC this was a strong indication something was brewing and he suggested to his editor to dispatch a few reports to Nagaland:

"We have neglected the region long enough now," he said, "with the assassination of this Naga leader it looks like a can of worms is opening now. The Nagas will resurrect and we should be there to cover the situation on the spot. I propose I will go there myself," Anir suggested to his boss.

"Let me check with London Office," Greg (nickname) answered.

"This is precisely the problem I should think Greg," Anir reacted like he was stung by a bee, "are we not capable of judging what is important here? Always London has to check on things. Do you remember this Naga international Support Center accusing us of the use of leading language? That time the London Office had to yield, for rebels the word we used to describe the Nagas was technically incorrect," Anir said.

"Calm down Anir, I am just following the rules. I don't make them and you know it. Yes sometimes it is better to get some fireworks from the outside. I agree with you there, but we are bound by the terminology and the editing plan."

"Then tell them Nagaland will be burning soon and we need people there. It is ridiculous that we are still listening to the London people, as if they know what plays here and how to interpret it," Anir said.

"Okay, okay, you go then, I am sure they will agree. It is usually more a matter of informing them rather for then to decide on things. Anyway, concerning what is really happening now and brewing up, how do you assess it Anir?"

"To me it looks like the assassination has made things move again. The peace talks like a ritual without any progress, now it is possible the eyes of the word will look into this crucial matter too. They will see the incompetence of this government to deal with a relatively simple conflict. If they were really willing, this conflict could have been solved long ago. I have talked to many Nagas who say they have nothing against India, but they don't like to be treated badly. They want to be heard and taken seriously, but their land has been invaded for how long now?"

"They say it is the longest running insurgency of modern times Anir!", Greg said.

"Rightly so, but it is also an unknown war. This war is fought and can be fought this way because it is fought in isolation."

"Does that mean we are responsible too? I faintly sense you are working towards this perspective Anir," Greg smiled.

"With a London Office on our tail, how did you guess Greg," Anir laughed.

"Perhaps this time they cannot keep it under the table and okay let me say this whether the London Office approves or disapprove, just go. I will just save my neck by saying you left unauthorized should I be held accountable for you," Greg roared with laugher now. Anir looked at him for a moment thinking Greg had been serious:

"You are such a coward," Anir shot out now red faced although this was difficult to see on his black Tamil skin.

"I am joking man, calm down," Greg still laughed.

"Well, well, well, of course, what makes you think I am not?", he laughed now too,

"you are so serious about this? Normally we have a lot of leeway and we only are checked afterwards. With the Nagas and Kashmiri's they like to know beforehand."

"We need to do what is required, as good journalists of course. We should be impartial but we should report on state terrorism and black laws too. We should show that these two matters have nothing to do with democracy right?"

"Oh yes, that is right, issue oriented and without any vested interest to serve, the ideal situation for a journalist. Ah, but is this so, but can it be so? How can it be guaranteed it will be so and it will remain that way."

"Officially there is the freedom of speech and the freedom to access information, to acquire information, right?", Anir said.

"Yeah, but it is one thing to have the freedom on paper another to have it in practice,' Greg said dryly.

"This Naga International Support Center is monitoring the situation closely, Greg. They do press releases and they are involved with the UNPO and the Parliamentarians for National Self Determination in Britain. We cannot neglect what is happening here, when they are on top of it man. They are spreading the word and it is what we should do, the credible word of course. What news agency are we if we can't take our work seriously?"

"Yeah, check this NISC and PNSD out then and see how they connect to what the assassination evoked. No, you go to Nagaland, I will check them out. I wonder who really did this. Nobody claimed the murder right?"

"No, no one did, this is why the government is scared now. Everything points in the direction of the Indian Government or any of its stooges. Do you think the Internal Bureau or the Research and Analysis Wing are involved here? Could they have been acting on their own?"

"Very possible but I would not think we would see a frantic government then. If they did it I am sure they would have some scapegoats ready to put the blame on. No, I think this took them by surprise too."

"Hmmmmm, interesting thought, so you think it is an outside source. Okay while you are away, I will look into some other things too. The Home minister will get to Nagaland first thing tomorrow to see if things can be defused. So, you better get cracking I will handle things here and hold the fort okay?", Greg concluded.

"Okay then, you will have my first report by email after the speech of the Home Minister plus the general feeling of the Naga public," Anir said.

"You put me up with a lot of work while you are happily off to the field like a good reporter should," Greg laughed.

"You have lots of important things to do and I will stay as long as is necessary," Anir retorted, "oh yes this time I will try and get into a camp and talk to one of the leaders," Anir announced.

"Please check too how things are among the opposing groups. It was reported there is going to be a general uprising, the rival faction will join too, though it was not directly their leader who was slain. Check out what that means Anir, see if the old feuds are a thing of the past and the dive and rule police of the Government of India since 1963 with the formation of Nagaland State finally failed?", Greg put to him.

"Good idea, I think we are getting into the right direction again. Working as a team but as real journalist has always been my ambition."

Chapter 7

In Nagaland

You can call me Shilu now Lisa said. I use Lisa only when I am abroad, too much talk on explaining and unless there is some real interest, I don't bother to explain," Shilu giggled.

Neichu had escorted Jeanie and Marius to the train station and on the train itself talked about the Naga Mothers organization with fervor, but also about her travels in foreign countries like Israel where she had spent some time and had acquired a good grasp of the Palestine/Israeli conflict. The train itself was an imported one, an oldie, and it looked like it was bought from the Dutch railways. Though essentially not a bad one, it was the maintenance which disturbed Jeanie and Marius because some electric wires hanging loose from a compartment in a corridor looked dangerous. Nobody cared though and nobody cared either for the way the tea man too, who came around selling his fine cha (tea) in paper cups, discarded the cups after use. When Jeanie and Marius asked Neichu about this it was reason enough for her to stress the differences between the Nagas and the Indians in a very practical way:

"Oh Jeanie," she had begun, "as you probably have noticed in Guwahati but Delhi too, I can assure you that this can be much worse in many other places around India. You see lots of beggars in the streets clad in rags and I do not mean the sadhu's who do this on purpose so they deny themselves all in material life to go to the nucleus of living. No, I mean the many poor people, the people without rights, the people who live in slums, I mean the people nobody cares for. You see them peeing in the street, working in garbage and throwing rubbish anywhere. They don't care and they have only manners to each other when on the same level. The people you see are dalits, or outcasts. They are nobody's and can used for anything. So, you see them sleeping in the streets. Now do you think self respecting Nagas want to be part of this?", she asked rhetorically for she continued immediately, "can you imagine what it would mean if we agree to be part of India?" Neichu asked.

"I am sure if I would be part of the outcast people, I would not like it. I wonder though if you have never known anything else, if would you really know that there is actually something else?", he asked.

"They all want to be reborn into a higher case, since they believe in reincarnation and know that they cannot move out of their castes, they cannot do much else but to accept." "Yes indeed they don't know anything else, but I say they have every right to be treated humanely and mind you, I am speaking of some perhaps 300 million people?"

"That is quite a few people. How do the Nagas relate to dalits?" Jeanie asked in turn.

"Nagas are tribals in the eyes of the Indians. We are not part of the Hindu religion like dalits are, well know they are part of, so when not even Hindu and tribal for that matter we are even lower than nobodies. To the Indians it is normal to subdue us. Can you imagine someone whose mind is engrained with the idea of being very much higher than a Naga, a savage, to treat us equally? Translate that to the Indo-Naga conflict and on that idea alone it is very difficult for the Indians to come close to what the Nagas know as their Homeland. "

"So, you fear this is the real background of the conflict Neichu?," Jeanie had asked.

"Of course there are more factors involved, the integrity of the borders, for India fears China due to the annexation of Tibet and it fears too that when they give in to such, in their eyes, insignificant tribe the rest of the country falls apart, just like the USSR did."

"You have a point there," Jeanie agreed.

"But we cannot let power hungry Indians take our rights from us. The Nagas do not want their women to be raped at will, just like the high cast Indians do because they own the outcasts and make them work for next to nothing. They take women and use them but find them unclean too. They have double standards and they use one standard over the other when it suits them."

"They rape women?", she went on asking.

"It is practically normal Jeanie. The Indian Military does that to our women too, what more can we expect when we are part of India for good?", Neichu spoke in defiance.

"Do the Naga women and mothers have documented stories. Is this something I can document on perhaps," Jeanie asked.

"Of course you can, I will lead you to some who have been through these ordeals, young women they prefer and they took many. I will get you to some women who are older now and some young ones," Neichu promised.

They talked till late in the evening, but Neichu reminded them they would have to be up early again so it would best to take a nap. The bunk beds were folded out and now, they traveled first class and were not besieged by families with children, luggage, chickens and what not, to lay stretched out so they could turn in. About half an hour before the slow train, later they found out the bus ride was shorter, the gentleman like conductor came by to wake them up.

"Close to Dimapur now, just one stop to go," he had whispered to each of the three. It was dark still when the train pulled into the station and stopped at the platform. The eerie atmosphere reminded Marius out the bomb attack that had taken place there, a year or so ago and he said to Neichu:

"Goodness, I feel the ghosts of the victims of the blast are around me."

"If it would have happened at this time at least there would have been fewer victims," she dryly answered in a wry smile. It is still not known who were responsible for it and what they wanted to achieve."

"That was terrorism then," Jeanie said, "innocent victims and not even done to attract attention for a noble cause!"

"Right," Neichy agreed as Marius offloaded their luggage and out of nowhere Lisa had appeared. She ran up to Marius who was so surprised he could only sheepishly laugh. When he had gathered his senses he said:

"So beautifully overwhelming you are Lisa, I am glad to see you."

Lisa greeted Jeanie warmly and Neichu whom she already knew said:

"Hello Shilu, you must have gotten up early, just like us."

This is when Lisa had said: 'You can call me Shilu now Lisa said. I use Lisa only when I am abroad, too much talk on explaining and unless there is some real interest, I don't bother to explain," Shilu giggled.

"Come I will take you to a hotel. Let's just hope we do not get checked this early morning, but you will never know, right Neichu?"

"That's right Shilu, keep your passports and Raps near you," she said.

"It is not very far, walking distance in fact, but perhaps because of the luggage we need some transport?", Shilu suggested, "perhaps for you Neichu? Are you going to stay around in Dimapur," she asked.

"No, no, no, I will get me some transport to Kohima. I want to go home as soon as possible. Lots of things I have to do. I just need to go to the bus station."

"Do you need any help?", Marius asked, "we can dump our things in the hotel first and then help you to get your transport?"

"Excellent," Neichu reacted thankfully and off they went. Marius as expected the more heavy things, but Shilu too took some excess baggage from Jeanie and Neichu.

"It is really not that far," she said while they had been walking for about five minutes, "it is just around that corner there."

She had not yet stopped talking when it happened. About five uniformed men appeared suddenly and surrounded them. There was no way to go, well they could not have run away with the luggage on them, so they stopped and looked. The two Naga women had been through this kind of drill may a time and heaved their heads to wait for the leader of the uniformed men to speak. Marius was not frightened but he thought it to be odd for it was not clear to him what kind of uniformed men these men actually were. The uniforms were green and looked just like those of the police in Delhi and Guwahati. The five men did not say a thing and only when a sixth man appeared things got actually started:

"It's just five o'clock in the morning, so tell me what you are doing here," the sixth man asked in not too unfriendly tone of voice. Marius felt his blood rising, the impertinence alone he thought. They were carrying suitcases and it as obvious they had come from the near by train station, so was he doing actually, checking or chit chat. Because there were six of them, he thought is better to not talk but let the ladies, the Naga ladies handle it. And they did. Quite composed Neichu answered:

"I think you addressed yourself to me so I will answer you," she said slowly, "I came on a long journey. These two foreigners came with me from Guwahati and this is the friend of the man there. We are going to the hotel on the next street. Does that answer your question Sir? Was that sufficient?"

The officer smiled but not too relaxed: "Do these two foreigners have RAPS," he suddenly asked scanning the faces of all four of them, with the other five soldiers standing by but alert. Marius felt uneasy, not so much because he did not want to show the RAP, it was a requirement after all and these men were just doing their job. It was the way the officer jumped from one thing to the other that worried him, so he decided to answer the question himself directly followed by another:

"Yes we have, now tell us Sir in what capacity are you that you ask us this at this time of the morning? If you follow us, you will know where we stay and you can check all you need to, but right now it is rather inconvenient."

He looked at Marius then sized up the three women as if he was weighing what to do. Should he accommodate convenience or just do as he pleased and check them there and then. To help him deciding fast Marius added:

"I read in the paper that the Home Minister will make his appearance today. Are you here checking to make sure security is safeguarded?"

"Precisely Sir, we are jawans (soldiers) of the Indian Armed Forces and required to check everyone, especially those who travel. But for your convenience we will accompany you to your hotel," he said and told his men in Hindi to take some of the luggage so walking there was easier for all. Jeanie sighed. Neichu and Shilu smiled. Now eleven people were on their way to the hotel which they reached less than five minutes later. The luggage was placed before the reception and after that the jawans took their distance. To Jeanie's surprise the five jawans withdrew as she noticed the hotel people were ready for action, but did not like the soldiers inside. Shilu explained they had just come to check their papers and would be on their way again and called on the receptionist for the reservations. Meanwhile the officer for the second time asked for the RAPS and both Jeanie and Marius showed passport and the RAP papers.

"All is in order," the officer smiled, "yes there is a lot of checking today and in the days to come. I am sure you know why. Are you a journalist Sir?", he suddenly asked.

"A journalist?", Marius asked surprised.

"You have interest in our Home Minister and you are informed. Journalists are like that," he smiled.

"The culture we come for," Marius quickly answered and produced a smile along with his explanation, "we did not realize the Nagas had the attention of your Home Minister but the papers are full of it?"

"Yes, that's right," the officer said as he checked the papers of Jeanie. He had no interest in Neichu or Shilu at all. The hotel people sighed when the group of soldiers finally left after bidding the travelers goodbye and wishing them a pleasant journey in spite of the rising tension. Jeanie decided not to get into the hint of the man though the word 'tension" itself almost had both Marius and Jeanie asking what he meant. When they had gone they were assigned a room. After all, Jeanie and Marius were to be a couple now. They brought their luggage to the room and returned to help Neichu to the bus station.

"Not so far also," Shilu said as she picked up the small suitcase and Marius the bigger one which the wheels. Shilu had frowned when she saw Jeanie and Marius going off to their room. Though she knew it was for appearances sake, obviously she did not like it. In good mood nevertheless and with the sun now up over Dimapur they all left to take Neichu where she wanted to go and bid her goodbye. It was pretty busy at the stations with early morning buses ready to go all places. Neichu bought a ticket on a straight through bus to Imphal, the capital of Manipur. Long distance buses were often the target of many an armed organization, for there was only one road to Imphal and the capital could only be reached by plane or bus. The animosity between the Meiteis of the valley and the Nagas of the mountains sometimes burst out the seams and in reaction the road between Kohima and Imphal would be sealed off by the Nagas. This had the result that all trucks would be held up and the shops and stores in the city would run out of goods. This was one means of pressuring, Shilu explained. The buses too were held up, not just by the different forces, but also by the Assam Rifles and police. Checking people on the buses could take quite some time and when there was a blockade it could take lots of time before reaching the destination. To Kohima however was not far and it was the capital of Nagaland state. The road from the plains, Dimapur though in Nagaland is not in what was called by the British the Nagas Hills, led towards the foothills of the Himalayas and so soon after leaving the commercial hub called Dimapur the road would enter the mountains, strangely according to Marius called Hills here still.

"We hope to see you in Kohima again Neichu," Jeanie said as she embraced her, "I am sure you can take us to the Naga Mothers and perhaps introduce us to some villages too?"

"Without a shadow of a doubt," Neichu smiled and as she boarded the bus shortly afterwards, Shilu waved and Marius showed a similar gesture.

"See you in Kohima," she said as the bus moved and was soon out of sight.

"Now our time has come," Shilu daringly said, "oh I mean I have arranged a few meetings with people here. That is one. But now that the actuality plays an important role I suppose we should be at Kohima ground to see what the Home minister has to say to us. You two are not too tired?", she asked with a smile and a wink.

"I could do with a nap," Jeanie said as she truly felt the strain of the last few days.

"I am not 100% either," Marius smiled, "but I am so glad to see you. Jeanie how about this; Shilu and I will talk elsewhere, so you can take that nap?"

"Excellent," Jeanie answered but with a bit of a sour face. It was clear to her now that Marius had eyes for Shilu, not for her. It was useless to intervene or compete. She should have shown her affection for him much earlier. Now it was too late, Marius clearly was taken in by the cheerful Shilu. And, since they were both considerate about her welfare, still she could not leave them just like that. Now it was real and she felt compelled to do something. But before she took up the idea of a nap Jeanie sneered:

"So, the lovebirds want to be alone and will separate the couple?"

Blushes appeared on both faces but Marius joyfully snapped back:

"Such an understanding notion Jeanie, see you later sweets!"

Jeanie turned without a further word and left them alone but with turmoil inside. Not too much but enough to regret she had not made her move long ago. What is the matter with me; she thought as she tossed and turned in bed and could not sleep thinking of those two having a good time. When she finally dozed off, she had no idea what Marius and Shilu were doing.

"Okay Marius, let's go for a walk and see what is going to happen today all right? Let's have some breakfast first?", she asked decisively.

"Okay, okay, you lead me Shilu," Marius agreed and followed her as she walked off into the crowd. Stopping at a cafeteria where people had gathered enjoying the morning talking, gesticulating, drinking and eating,,:

"Here we can have coffee!" she announced and she pulled him in laughing. Seated among the people she ordered coffee and a bite to eat. Marius noticed a fair number of mongoloid looking people, but there were quite a few Indians there too. Shilu caught on with his observation and without him asking answered the question on his mind:

"Most of the Indians here are traders. They are the commercial people around here. I think there are as many of them as there are Nagas. Dimapur is the commercial hub of Nagaland," she explained..

"There is quite a difference between Nagas and Indians. I see only few Indians and Nagas talking amongst to each other. Do they actually mix, have relations or even marry?"

"Most Nagas do not exactly fancy Indians. Many have migrated here. They have come relatively recently. Their culture is so much different from ours and it is difficult to relate their religion. They do feel they are of a different order too," Shilu explained.

"In the past they were not around?", Marius asked.

"Not in these numbers. In Mokokchong, where I grew up, I never saw them, but now there are many there too. We fear it might go like Tripura.

There the native people are outnumbered now. This is why the State Government tries to curb this influx Indians. We understand that there are many people in India, but it should not lead to many of them coming here to live and act like they own the place," Shilu said.

"Once here they take over?", Marius asked.

"Well, in the towns they control commerce. In the villages there is no way they can take over. They settle in the towns, or try to get some land in a village to farm the way they are used to. Many of them have no experience in high land farming though."

While sipping their coffee which was served with some friend eggs bread, Shilu kept on talking about the situation. Marius felt was like she avoided talking about themselves, but then she shifted and talked about the trip.

"We will go and visit the organizations which will map out the trip for us. You should be able to visit the rehab camp Marius. The former general of the Naga Army now part of the negotiating team lives in Dimapur too. Would you like to talk to him?"

"Should be a fine idea indeed," Marius said, "I understand the other leaders are living abroad and in exile?", Marius asked.

"Quite so," Shilu smiled, "that is a story all by itself, but for later," she answered.

In Manila things were happening fast. What was discovered could be called a breakthrough. While checking what Felix suggested, Eddie had been able to narrow down a few things. The people of Indian descent were quite numerous but not those who were of naturalized Philippino nationality. Checking the hotels in Manila had been a tedious job too, but with the help of some ladies with qualifications for this type of work, he had come up with something. Then the records of the phone companies showed some interesting things too. He had found names which matched some parameters of the search. Eddie rather excitedly informed Efren and a meeting was called. There in the head office Eddie and Efren told what they had found out and suggested then what had to be done. Eager to know what was to be revealed, the Indian team was present too. Quite proud of their status the investigators did not avail much on the help from the Manila police, yet independently they had not been able to make much headway. Excited they were, now that they might get a lead too just before the arrival of Patill, the Foreign minister. Though they could not show that, for fear of the Manila police keeping something important from them and their Government, they had more or less demanded to be present.

"Well, it looks like the hunches Felix with Eddie working on them have paid off. So, I like them to explain what they found," Efren began as anticipation on what was to come was expressed in silence, but Efren deliberately paused till Eddie took over from him.

"Our hotel search gave us a couple of names," Eddie disclosed, "at first we were searching in the blind but when we assumed they could act like high profilers we looked into the less shady hotels and checked names against those who had come in on flights around those dates. First we checked flights in the region, the Bangkok flights from three days before the event. We found a Dutch woman traveling alone who checked into the Manila Hotel with a Philippino of Indian descent. She checked out and left the Philippines straight after that. Let me spare you the details, which by the way came to a tremendous amount of work, but give you the results. This lady phoned quite a few times to Bangkok and other places and had quite a bit of money on her. She met the man of Indian descent in the Manila Hotel. We checked hundreds of couples before we came to the conclusion that this couple had the characteristics of the profile befitting the assassins. When we actually could get hold of phone calls and checked the numbers by calling them, we knew we were on the right track. Then we checked out their movement of the recent past and found the Indian Philippino had been around South East Asia, but primarily Bangkok. We get hold of his contacts and we checked his past. Unfortunately we could not find much on the woman, but that she was part of a high class bordello ring and was flown around. We are sure though that the Indian/Philippino was not one of her customers. She worked for The Bordello in Amsterdam, which has a subsidiary in Bangkok too. This Indian man was in Bangkok too and we know through his phone calls from Manila he was in the Bordello. Now about his past: quite colorful and not only positive. The man was a commando, highly trained and sent out several times by the United Nations on peace keeping missions. He returned to Manila from his UN time in Africa he became fully disillusioned and he did not move professionally ever since. Though born here I am not surprised however if he has more than one nationality. About the woman, she stayed with him until just after the assassination. They checked out together, the woman Jacky went straight to the airport and flew off to Bangkok, the man disappeared. We checked where he lived, thanks to births and deaths registration office for his address. We checked his ordinary house but we found nobody there, yet all his things are there and left like he could return any moment and we expect him to do that for we think they think they have nothing to fear. When he does we will get him for questioning," Eddie said and took a breather, leaving the people in front of him speechless. Nothing was said and so he continued:

"We are thinking, but it is conjecture yet that these only two people committed this assassination. The woman was flown in, the man was here in the Philippines preparing for it. The man does not actually work, but has enough to sustain himself. We checked his bank records. We are checking his life and behavior from the moment he returned on our soil from Africa. To prepare for the assassination he had ample time to arrange, so the enigma is the woman. Actually we think she was the assassin. Considering his marine past this Indian man, by the name of Bailung, is very capable of doing so, but the woman was not here for his pleasure. The hotel people told us that Jacky is a very attractive lady but more like a companion, a person to work with, not a lover. We think they formed a team and were launched by someone in Bangkok, an Englishman named Sean with Bailung preparing and Jacky pulling the trigger. Because they were well prepared and quite elusive, we think these people will not be easy to catch. They are professionals and may carry different passports from different countries. They could even change their appearance and vanish. Though we did find the getaway vehicle not too far away from the scene of the crime but it was a stolen car and other than those of the original owner it had no fingerprints," again Eddie paused and Efren took over.

"We will do everything to catch them, but one thing is pretty sure; the woman has left the country, but it is likely that the man is still here. There were personal effects in his house, a rented home, and unless of course he smells we are on him, we are sure he will come back for. Now for the sake of further investigation we have to ask you to keep all you heard today confidential," he said and looked around. He saw a few fingers going up for questions but Efren shook his head saying:

"Wait a moment please, let me finish first and this is important for our Indian colleagues too," he stressed, "although we may be on to our assassin and accomplice, we do not think that these two people murdered the Naga leader for no reason. They had no motivation, well none that we could think of," Efren smiled, "we think in fact that they were hired assassins and that the motivation to kill this Naga leader here was hatched somewhere else. Since we may have the name of the assassin, the woman Jacky of Dutch heritage, we took the liberty of following her trail. Through our airlines research we found that she left for Bangkok shortly after the assassination. More importantly is that she stayed there a couple of days, but not in a hotel. We learned that from our Thai counterparts who were accommodating enough to check her against the hotel records of Bangkok. Of course you will say, the woman could have stayed outside Bangkok and perhaps she did, yet we think she has been with the people who are running the Bordello, the subsidiary of the one in Amsterdam. The person who manages that Bordello is the one called Sean. We think that this Sean is connected to the plotter, for the woman Jacky flew to Bangkok but she could have taken a flight to Amsterdam straight too. Right?", he asked rhetorically for he continued, "From Bangkok Jacky left for Amsterdam alone and Sean followed her a couple of days later. Checking airlines again we found out they are together again and now in Rio de Janeiro. Well ladies and gentlemen this is how far we have been able to reach, but the question now is this: even if we are capable of getting them, do we have the real culprits, the real perpetrators on our hands, or a decoy? Let me be frank with you all. We have come to the practically inevitable conclusion that this murder was orchestrated, perhaps by this Sean, but we really think it must have been someone or a group who or which hired Sean and through him the assassination team. When we know the motivation of the plotter or plotters then we know how to find them. It is imperative we get to this Sean and I call on our Indian team here to move diplomatically to get the Brazilian government and thus the police there interested in questioning Sean. Perhaps a small team of you should go there?", Efren suggested.

"Does this mean Sir," asked the commander of the Indian team," that it could indeed be this Sean where it ends or do you rate this Sean too as an intermediate?"

"I wish I could get you off the heat you are facing," Efren smiled compassionately, "but I am afraid not. Considering what we found in the house of Bailung we can't imagine that this man knew who he was actually going to kill or to help to kill. Considering too the check we did on this person Sean, we could only find a direct connection to Bailung. Both of them served in the UNO forced in Rwanda, Africa and are friends. So, we do not actually think these two had the motivation to kill a complete stranger. We think Sean took the contract and so he is the key to those who are behind this murder."

"So, this means that the Indians are still under suspicion then," the Indian team leader concluded.

"Not really, for these were not Indians but hired assassins and so not just the Indian Government could have deployed the assassins. I must tell you though that other than Bailung being of Indian origin we found no evidence of him being connected to any Indian agency. The man has been out of your country for a very long time and has little or no connection to you. He was born in the Philippines. To us it looks like a contract to assassinate the Naga came from beyond the man called Sean. This is why I asked you to wrestle on who handed him the contract the out of the man!", Efren stressed.

"Yes Sir, that is sound advice!", the leader of the Indian team answered.

"But one last thing," Efren interrupted, Eddie in the background now smiling proudly, "we think too but we cannot put our hand in the fire for that, for it is really yours to find out, that the plotters have been operating with a very, very strong conviction. I wonder if the Indian Government could have given an order to any of its agencies to do this. I am not saying it is impossible, but we think it is improbable."

"Oh," the Indian leader of the team reacted, his face lighting up with that good news, "what makes you think so," he asked.

"Well, all points in the direction of the Indian Government and its agencies. Now I suggest you inform your Minister and urge the man to take action to check his own departments and agencies for contacts with this man Sean and if I were you and there are codenames involved, imaginable don't you think when dealing with professionals, then get that out of the man when you are in Rio de Janeiro. As for me I think there is a third party sitting in the background which pulls the strings," Efren concluded before the informal talk began. They were complimented by both their own kind as well as the Indian team. Once more Efren stressed not to leak anything for that could jeopardize all operations. Soon after they had concluded the session and has answered all questions, the Foreign Minister was fetched from the airport and brought to Police Head quarters. There, before meeting the press, in the presence of the highest commander of the Metro Manila Police and the Indian team, Efren and Eddie told their story again but then only with what they thought were the results and warned him for the margins of errors.

"This is good news," said Patill, "yes get a small team together and have them dispatched to Brazil, he agreed immediately granting their request for swift action, "this is quite something indeed and yes all the names you have mentioned, I will have thoroughly run through our operations."

"There is more," Eddie patiently told a nervous Patill, "be very careful what you release to the press. You must realize that it may work to you advantage in the long run when you do not mention you are on the trail of the killers."

"Really? We are facing a crisis man, a resurrection," a baffled Patill answered.

"So, you are saying the political directness should go before finding out who and what is behind it," Efren asked as he stepped in.

"How dare you ask to suggest this," Patill's eyes shot fire now, "do you know what is at stake here. Please don't be shortsighted with me," he stressed.

"Please be so kind as to explain," Efren said feeling anger rising at the impertinence, or at least it is what he felt, and now trying to control himself feverishly, "but let me tell you that to us it is rather obvious your agencies cannot be behind this, unless they want to bring down your government," he explained grinding his teeth.

"Well, I am sure you are not aware of the Naga people who will rise and many people could be killed when the forces are pressed to maintain law and order. This we want to avoid at all cost, so we must release the information we are hot on the trail of the assassins. We will stress that these assassins are not Indian, so the heat is off the government. From there on you and our team here will become very important again. We will send our team to the Rio in Brazil and you do your thing here. I will instruct our people that the Manila police will be paid for the efforts, but I will tell you we will not have people killed because we withheld information to them. We do not want a blood bath," Patill concluded.

"I am sure we could not foresee the political implications," the police commander commented, "of course when tension is high, it is better to use what we know now to defuse, but do realize we may alert those who are behind this. If it is a plot to undermine the Indian Government, I am sure they will seize the moment they created."

"True," Patill admitted, "but I am afraid I have no choice, You can only see things from the direct repercussions of the assassination. I have to take into account what this assassination evoked in India itself. So, please do not feel I am overriding or criticizing your approach and dynamics of handling this difficult situation created by this, I see now, well planned case. In fact I like to encourage you. You are doing a wonderful job."

"Thank you," Eddie said, followed by Efren. We will do that we are as puzzled about this as you are," Eddie continued, "now that we are possibly closing in, it becomes excruciatingly important to uncover those who have been plotting this."

"Yes from a professional point of view you feel challenged," Patill smiled now, "rest assured, I can easily relate to that. The Home Minister will be in Kohima today, the capital of Nagaland and he needs this information so things can be pacified. I hope you do not mind I will phone him now with the latest. I know you will grind your teeth, yet I am sure that our countries and agencies together will find a way to catch the culprits. Your work is greatly appreciated. I want you to know that."

"You can use this phone," the Commander said and took Patill away so he could talk to Nagaland directly and without being disturbed. The Indian team meanwhile after hearing Patill's order listened to Efren and Eddie for the latest details like possible addresses and how to approach

Sean and Jacky and assigned one of them to arrange the trip to Rio de Janeiro. This was not an easy think to do, for soon they were facing the dilemma of going over the Pacific and so via the USA, or through Europe with straight flights to Latin America. But, when they found the swiftest route to be via Tokyo and Los Angeles and from there straight to Rio, they soon decided that and booked for the same day.

The Home Minister had just landed in Dimapur where he was received by local dignitaries showing proper decorum but also by a demonstration of hundreds of Nagas booing him. As the police kept the angry demonstrators at bay, they were shouting murderer, one of his aides handed him a cell phone and said:

"Important Sir, Manila for you. Patill wants to talk."

"Listen carefully," Patill began, "and do not interrupt or argue. Jot down the particulars so you will not forget," he said as the Home Minister gesticulated to his aid to get him paper and pen.

"Okay," the Home Minister answered dutifully realizing Patill had come to his rescue and jotted down fast when Patill began to talk rapidly what he heard from Efren and Eddie,

"Be sure to mention the good work of the Manila Police. They did the work to find the trail of the assailants," Patill said when he had concluded.

"Of course," the Home Minister, "this should do it. Good heavens thank you Patill, I feared the worst man!"

"Well, I am glad it may not be one of us, but we can still not rule that out. We are going to do a full investigation of our own ranks too. This you must tell as well, both in your speech as well as you must tell it to reporters. And, the team assigned to do that, will be as impartial as possible, agreed?", Patill asked.

"Agreed," the Home Minister confirmed and when he had said that Patill hung up.

The street of the hotel where Jeanie and Marius had checked in was full of demonstrators now. In fact many people from all over town and the villages around were converging. They knew the Home Minister had arrived and they were convinced they should stop him. Jeanie woke up from the sounds in the streets. Before she slept she had opened a window for some fresh air and though there was noise, it had not bothered her, until now.

A Naga leader had a megaphone with him and shouted slogans like: Indians out of Nagaland, Indians out of Nagaland. In no time the crowd around him followed the sound of the slogan which was loud and like it was a song and easy to relate to.

Jeanie had woken up from these recurrent bustling sounds produced by the voice of the leader shouting India out of Nagaland. Oh, gosh, it is happening, she realized and not realizing she was half naked rushed to the window. The bustle in the street had grown and now the sign to move to the road here the motorcade of the home minister would pass. She did not know that yet, but it was the intention of the leaders of the crowd to block his passage and demand accountability from the Home Minister. She looked down and saw the leader with the megaphone commanding the crowd to follow him. As it began to move Jeanie, all excited now, moved away from the window, quickly washed up and dressed then ran off after she locked the door behind her. As soon as she entered the lobby she felt the suspense for it was full of people persuading each other to follow, but it was easy not because the police outside prevented that.

"Is there another way out," a heated man shouted I want to be with the crowd. It is time for the Indian bastards to leave and never come back."

"No, no," the personnel of the hotel busily shook their heads.

"Oh come on all. All hotels have more than one entrance," he shouted again and a stampede was now at hand.

"I know where to go," a young man shouted loudly and began to move in that direction, all went after him. In no time at all the lobby was practically empty and there stood Jeanie. She thought for a moment then opened the door saying to a frightened policeman:

"I was going to see my husband at the restaurant over there. Let me pass please?"

The street was clearing out and now from around a corner the guests of the hotel came running by. The policemen went after them, leaving Jeanie standing there. Strangely she could just walk away and decided to after the disappearing demonstrators. The crowd passed the restaurant where Shilu and Marius had taken breakfast and coffee and since there was police protection there too, they only could move when the crowd had passed.

"Hey," Jeanie shouted for attention when she saw them standing in the doorway of the restaurant, face towards the crowd. They looked up, smiled and Jeanie ran over to them.

"I think they are planning to stop the Home Minister, you know," she said.

"Yeah, I think so," Shilu answered.

"This could be the beginning of a resurrection," Marius said as they followed the crowd from a safe distance. That crowd consisted of Nagas; the bystanders along the route were Indians with worried faces. They were shopkeepers, laborers, or officials.

"Don't the other people join in to support the Nagas now," Marius asked.

"I am sure some would like to, but when they do they may be criticized and even loose their job, who knows,' said Shilu, "others of course don't want the Nagas to do anything against their interest. And, I can assure you there are Nagas too who don't like to see the Indians leave forever."

The crowd was moving fast and to keep track they paced too. When they reached the main road, the Minister's car was to pass on its way to Kohima, while they had stopped to wait it was now Jeanie, not Marius, who came forward with a question,.

"Shilu? There are Nagas who like be with the Indians who oppress their own people? Why, I do not get that!"

"Opportunists, politicians, commercial people who are indebted to some, they have all kinds of motivations. Some believe we cannot win our freedom. It is better to take what the Indians are prepared to give. At least there will be peace then and we can start building our society, not free we are but we will have some kind of cultural freedom and dignity they believe," she answered.

"Opportunists for position and money," now Marius asked.

"Like in India," she smiled, "the Indians brought corruption and like a child on a breast of a woman, they are in need of being nurtured like that."

"So politicians are involved in scams then?", Jeanie asked.

"They are at the heart of it," Shilu answered but was distracted when a roar went through the crowd and they understood the motorcade was nearing.

"If they are wise, they would send a decoy motorcade and let the Home Minster go a different route unseen," Marius laughed, "this to me seems like asking for trouble. They know already the Nagas want to stop him?"

"Hhhmmm, I am sot so sure about that Marius. Remember in the restaurant we were told there were hundreds of Nagas at the airport. There are thousands here. The Nagas at the airport would have signaled the switch you talk about "

"Good heavens, how would he get through then? A furious crowd may lynch the man and then the Army would clamp down on them. This is going to be a showdown!"

"If the man is wise he would climb up his car and ask for the megaphone. If he has nothing to say he should apologize, if he has something to say which to some extent may clear the Indian Government from the assassination, he should speak. I think only that can calm the crowd now," she said earnestly.

The crowd was cheering now and the slogans were going in staccato, quite threatening as they were all targeted against the Government of India and the prime target, the responsible minister was now in their midst. Make no mistake this crowd was talking business, no threats but a stern warning to leave Nagas alone.

Then it happened. Some bold young men stormed the cars to find out which held the Home minister. The police closed in but the crowd and surrounded the cars and shielded the police. There must have been twenty rows of people around the cars. They did not budge, not even when the police started using sticks. The visibly frightened Home Minister was pulled from his car and put in front for all to see him. On command of the leader with the megaphone the first rows retreated to make room for him to stand alone. The policemen now a few dozen perhaps hundreds already were fighting their way into the crowd, but did not dare to drew a gun. One Naga leader spoke through the megaphone before handing it over to the Home Minister and said loud and clear:

"Dear Home Minister we believe you are here to delude us. Our supreme leader is slain. We do not believe in an eye for an eye, but we also do not believe you can act devilishly to design a plan to kill our leader and get away with it. The Government you represent is a murderous regime. You will address this crowd now. If you can inspire the people here, we will let you go and you can resume your journey to Kohima. No harm will come to you, but do know now that you can only vanquish the Nagas and have your way here if you kill us all. Well Home Minister, will you speak?"

As he took the megaphone fear disappeared from the eyes of the Home Minister. These people are fair, enraged but fair, he thought, as he sensed he would not be killed by a mad crowd. Now that he heard he could talk, he knew he would be safe personally. Armed with what he had just learned from Patill, he knew he had nothing to fear. He thankfully smiled and said:

"Shall I stand a bit higher so all can see and hear me and I can instruct the police not to interfere?"

"Please do," the leader with the megaphone said.

Jeanie was utterly impressed by the dynamics of the event. Marius eyes popped out of his face watching the restraint of the Nagas around him and with the leaders in charge in particular. The Home Minister was handed a stool. He climbed on it and he took the megaphone then began his improvised speech:

"Dear Nagas, it is a pleasure to be here. It is just sad we have to meet under these circumstances. I truly must say I am with you in your mourning of your great leader. But, I have also news for you. I am sure your thoughts went out to the Government of India which you suspect to have had a hand in the assassination of your leader."

"Booooooooooo, murderers," the crowd roared with one voice. The Home Minister waited patiently for the roar to die down, he smiled, and then continued:

"I can tell you some of the results of the investigations in Manila. They will be fully reported and can be checked for credibility," he said. Because it was not what the people had expected, the Home Minister had their attention. The demonstrators were all ears:

"The Manila police tracked down the assassins. They have their names and it is reliable information," he said as he waited for the crowd to react and for him to assess how to continue. The people kept their breath to hear more and Shilu gasped along with Marius and Jeanie. Before they could actually discuss it the Home minister continued:

"They are a man and a woman dispatched by someone in Bangkok and they are of British, Dutch and Indian origin. The Indian man had the Philippine nationality and was born there. It does not look like he has anything to do with India itself," he explained.

This was a wrong move apparently because the crowd did not believe him yet and booed him again but now steadfast, he rose to the occasion and carried on. He called on the agitated people now, "let me please tell you this. At this point we do not rule out anything yet for it looks like those three were together and formed a team of assassins. They most likely had a contract to assassinate your leader. More importantly now is to find out where the contract came from. Let me stress that we do not rule out that it has come from our own Indian agencies," he said.

This sank in and made the restless crowd move. To even admit that the order to kill could have come from sources within the Indian Government felt like victory already, so though apprehensive the crowd hesitated. The leader of the Nagas for all to hear asked him loud and clear:

"You are going to catch the assassins? You are going to look into your own circles?"

"We will do better than that. As I speak to you now, a team is formed to check on all our agencies to find out if the contract has come from within our administration. I can assure you however, no one in the

Government came up with the strategy to undermine the peace talks by killing your leader. But, in India there are disgruntled people who might have acted on their own. Surely the suspicion goes out to us. I understand that very well, but the Government of India did not do it, some people or some Indian Organization could have done it and we will leave no stone unturned to find those who did, certainly when somebody plotted this in obscurity, but right under our noses," he promised.

"All will be out in the open then," the Naga leader asked.

"Yes, I guarantee that to you personally. We have just learned that the assassin left Manila and via Bangkok teamed up with the Englishman in Bangkok. From there they went to Brazil together. We have ordered the Indian police team to go to Brazil. They are on their way now. It is from that end that we will find out who ordered this, either from India or from another party who wanted to frustrate the peace talks," he explained.

This was big news for the crowd and most people did not know what to believe. No representative of the Indian Government had been very open in the past, but instead had schemed and plotted against those who defended the Naga principle, the Naga stand. The fierce anxiety about the loss of their leader directed to what was thought by practically all Nagas as orchestrated by the Indians now came into a different light. The Home Minister showed a different perspective. Now the point was, could they trust him? The leader vented these thoughts by asking him:

"This is not a small thing you can wash off by telling us tales. Should your words have no value and just meant to pave the way for your personal escape from this predicament you will be met with the rage of the Nagas. What are you going to do now?"

Since the man was confident now and he radiated it too he calmly answered:

"I have told you the truth about what we know and what we are doing and going to do. Let it be written so you can hold me accountable to what I have said and mean. Report and put in the media, all media. This is not worth to risk more lives than the one already lost. There will be no scheming to destabilize the relations between us," he said and did sound like he was genuinely serious.

"Then let's call on some journalists before you go. Tell them on air again what has been discovered and what the Indian Government plans to do, or I fear that once in Kohima the crowd will turn against you there. Do you agree to this fair proposal," he asked.

"Yes that is fair and I will do that right away," he agreed, "but let's not continue this forced gathering now for I am sure the Military and the

Police here are nervous. They are here to secure my safety too and we do not want anybody arrested or even killed by some very dutiful officers who are trigger happy."

That the man thought of the safety of Nagas did wonders for the people in the crowd who were already astonished by the words of the Home Minister. They had not expected this turn of events and the anxiety which could explode in aggression had subsided. Marius, Jeanie and Shilu felt the sigh of relief going through the crowd:

"He is good," Shilu commented, "I wonder if he made that up because he was closed in and had nowhere to go, or if what he said is the truth. He did sound rather convincingly, don't you think?"

"In that position facing a furious crowd, I am not too sure if you can make up a story like that," Jeanie responded, "but I do not know how the Indian leaders handle crowds. What do you think Marius?", she asked.

"He held up well under this kind of tension. I have never seen such well controlled yet furious crowd which was led very well by that leader there. To keep composure like he did and to not get angry or create confusion shows statesmanship in a time of crisis. I think he meant what he said," Marius answered and had hardly finished when he was pushed away by a contingent of soldiers forcibly moving into the crowd. Marius resisted instinctively and realizing it was Army soldiers acting on command, immediately anger rose. Since the words of the Home Minister had made the crowd no longer hostile to him, had pacified the people at least physically, this intrusion was felt as an anti climax and all eyes were on the Home Minister to do something. When the man saw the soldiers moving in creating havoc, his voice rang out through the megaphone again

"Stop this immediately, this is an order of your highest commander," he shouted, "retreat instantly or I will have you and your superiors in custody. Retreat now," he said, noticing Marius and Jeanie he now looked straight at them.

The soldiers hesitated. They were ordinary jawans and most likely had never laid eyes on the Home Minister but knew disobeying and order from their officers could lead to severe punishment. The Home Minister seeing this said loud and clear:

"Call your officers and send them to me!"

Only when hearing this they did retreat and moments later the crowd opened to let the responsible superiors through. Quite subservient and with fear in their eyes they passed, but the Home Minister smiled when they came up to him and the crowd realized it was ordered as a matter of fact and not meant to disturb what could now be called a rather cordial meeting.

"Comparable to what could be called the Naga village state democracy in action," Shilu smiled quite relieved too that the moves of the military had not led to violence, "this Home Minister is remarkable," she continued, "of course he brought pacifying information but to be cornered like this and able to speak openly, undeterred by the threatening situation, shows he is in command and yet compassionate a man," she remarked. The crowd saw the Home Minister talking to the officers:

"When you see the situation is under control, you better don't move in," he explained, "it could create something you cannot control. The risk of innocent people dying here as well as your men is great. Assess the situation firs, don't go on blind orders which are not relevant to what you see in front of you," he advised and then dismissed them again. The Nagas in the crowd never actually saw a superior, in this case of the highest sort, publicly corrected and slowly some people began to clap for the Home Minister who in turn raised his hand to speak though the megaphone again:

"Dear Nagas gathered here. I have been as frank as possible and I have come to you share the good and the bad news. It was my intention to tell all in Kohima, the famous ground there, but in your eagerness to know what is going on, you did ask me to tell you all here now. Now that you know, I will continue my journey to Kohima. We all know that force will not lead us where we want to go and you Nagas are the proof of that pudding," he smiled now as he referred to the fact that no matter what kind of force the Indians had applied on the Nagas over the last fifty years, the Nagas could not be subdued. The Naga leader then grabbed the megaphone and spoke:

"The Home Minister has spoken. We will take him up on his words. Now let him go with his entourage. He has an important job to do in Kohima too. Spread the word."

Chapter 8

Top meeting with the leaders

After the Home Minister thanked the crowd calmly the people dispersed. The Home Minister got into his car and soon the motorcade moved like nothing had happened. Of course there had been some stringers and journalists in the crowd and those had run off to get to phones and on line computers to signal something major was happening. They told Kohima and beyond the Home Minister brought big news and the uprising was defused.

"Let's go and have a drink in a house of one of the leaders," Shilu to their surprise suggested.

"Just like that?", Jeanie said and smiled, "that informal?"

"No, no, he is expecting us. He wants to see you two," she smiled.

"How does he know us then?", Marius asked.

"Of course, I told him, for I want you to see him too. He is one of the highest in command in the organization, was the highest in command of the Naga army once, a general and is part of the negotiating team with the Indian government."

"Oh, yes you mentioned him already. So, an important man he is. I am sure he is well aware of what happened here," Jeanie said.

"He may have been here, but I did not see him," Shilu said.

"Well there must have been a few thousand people, so it is easy to go unnoticed," Jeanie said, "yes let's go. That could be interesting."

"All right, I am sure he will surprise us with coffee. Gosh I have not slept much, Shilu laughed, "so I would love some more. I am happy though the potentially bloody confrontation has been averted. And, although the man looked genuinely honest, I am not at all convinced the Indians have nothing to do with it."

"Neither am I," Jeanie said with Marius nodding.

The three of them walked to the house of the Naga leader but when they arrived there they were being introduced to the almost complete government of Nagalim and some members of the steering committee.

This is quite a surprise," Marius smiled to the men after they had exchanged introductions and greetings.

"It is for us too," said Latem, the former general, "we love to have some people from the outside interested in our plight. We have been kept in isolation for too long. We must break out and seek support from the international community."

"We are only ordinary people Mr. Latem," Marius said, "I came across the Indo-Naga conflict through Shilu here and I am, like Jeanie my wife, overwhelmed by the events taking place. The history of he conflict alone and then the actualities right under our noses, we had no idea the murder of your leader could have this impact."

"You need not tell you are married to your friend Jeanie," a man called Gaising smiled, "Shilu told us everything about you and so we know you are only so called married so you could get the RAP. And, we checked you too dear Mr. Marius and you need not be too modest. We know you can do something. Likewise your British friend Jeanie," Gaising smiled, now openly.

"Oh you know about that. Good, then you know that we, behind the scenes, might be able to rally up some interest in Europe."

"Of course," Gaising said with Latem and the others grinning now.

"Well we will do our best of course," Marius said, "but do not overestimate our capabilities. Come to think of it I could phone my people later to find out what we contribute for brewing things up in Europe if you like. I can report to them what happened here today. We are eye witnesses after all," Marius smiled.

"Please do that," Gelos, a man who was part of the steering committee, a kind of think tank for the unrecognized government of Nagalim stated, "and tell them we are not yet fully convinced India had nothing to do with it."

"Yes," the finance minister contributed, "because the Indian Government devotes a lot of time, effort and funding to split us, it may be possible that our rivals have been used to assassinate our leader."

"Yes, all is possible still," Jeanie said, "but I offer you my condolences with your loss!"

"Thank you very much indeed," they all said and nodded.

"When Shilu told us you were coming we were quite eager to meet you," Latem said.

"What honor you do bestow on us?', Jeanie asked.

"We do not get too many foreigners and we should be quite convinced that this long standing conflict, it is international attention which could contribute to solve it in an honorable way. Ultimately we think we need the support we deserve," Latem explained.

"I think we should like to know about your future plans," Marius said, "the S for socialistic could be easily misunderstood and so when you come to a settlement, an agreement then I think it should be clear as to what kind of society you envisage?"

"Right, but Gelos can easily tell you this, he is the architect of the democratic society we have in mind and desire. I think I speak for the majority of Nagas," Latem said.

"Yes," Gelos took over, "perhaps you know that most of the Naga tribes live a kind of democratic life, more so in their villages than in the tribes. Fighting occurred between villages primarily. Contrary to what many think, it was not the tribes fighting each other," he explained but then interrupting himself: "oh I am sorry, we are not good hosts. Would you like a drink? Shilu is a coffee addict and told me you were one too Marius?"

"That is right," Marius laughed, "yes coffee is excellent."

Latem winked one of the younger men, their security guards, who rapidly disappeared.

Gelos continued, "in the villages life was complete in the old days, in the sense that the people were self sufficient. Only little trade took care of what could not be made by the Nagas themselves. All in a village had say in the daily affairs and in planning of some future events. A village was led by a village council and a headman led under the guidance of this council. Then the village was represented in a tribe council which in turn sent representatives to a Naga Cultural Council in which all tribes and subsequently all villages are represented."

"I read there are also tribes with different systems? Did that not lead to some animosity?", Marius asked.

"Well, the tribes you talk about were partly in Indian Nagaland, but more so in Eastern or what we call now Burmese or Myanmar's Nagaland. Yes these tribes like the Konyaks and the Poumai have a system of practically absolute rulers, called Angs. There are also tribes with hereditary leadership, the Sumi are such example. If you want to form a nation however you have to have a system of law with regard to culture which covers the rights and duties of all people concerned."

"Yes, I have read extensively about the village state democracy as you were explaining, yet I see some dissension along tribal lines with the remnants of the NNC combining with the Kaphlang group. Those two are against you. In a democracy of a nation would this normally translate to parties which are elected by the people?", Marius said with the others listening carefully..

"That is the idea indeed, but no arms by any party then and we need some kind of reconciliation procedure when the time comes," Gelos explained.

"You mean those parties which have collaborated and have committed crimes against their own people?", Jeanie asked then as it was her field they were talking about.

"Well, we have had some terrible incidents in out past and they are still dividing the Nagas. I am sure you know which ones I mean. These incidents caused fratricide amongst us and of course when they collaborated, those people deserve to be tried in a court. We may have to install courts for that purpose alone. Our society must be purified of elements that have been going against the will of our people and have killed or shed blood to protect their selfish interests. But, we have to be very careful about that, democracy and freedom of speech and expression are first and foremost. Yet, we must protect our nation too from those who want to sell out," Gelos said with conviction.

"Oh indeed," Jeanie agreed, "you have some interesting example fn this in South Africa. They had a very difficult operation there too, their checkered past had to be cleared too."

"We have studied that Jeanie," Gelos answered, "and we take their experiences very seriously indeed."

"Let's return to the actualities," Latem suggested, "what we saw today at the blockade was a remarkable performance of the Home Minister and I think this time he may have been a righteous man. He was composed and did not fear."

"That is also because he may have rehearsed what he knew and could expose to the crowd," Gaising said, "so I am not too certain yet."

"Well that may be but the man would be a hell of an actor," Jeanie laughed, "have you seen him operating in public in other situations?"

"Well, I must admit under this kind of siege and devoid of anyone to protect him, he stood his ground," Gaising smiled, "yet I cannot convince myself the Indians have nothing to do with this," he said.

"That is indeed difficult to believe, but our man did the right thing. If he had not shown the Home Minister the benefit of the doubt, the crowd could have gone outrageously wild and perhaps would have lynched him. The opportunity was there."

"Yeah," Latem agreed.

"But if he would have behaved like he was guilty or had spoken arrogantly, which he did not, then I think nobody could have saved him."

The coffee was served by the young guards as they talked and Marius sipped and asked:

"Either way, rightly because the man and so the whole Government is involved in this, or wrongly for the plotters have to be found elsewhere. Lynching a man of that stature would have had an adverse effect. You would be judged as bloodthirsty people. Certainly when you are proved wrong then the real killers or plotters can be tracked down."

"Yes, I am glad it did not come to that, but I felt the tension man," Latem smiled now.

"I think we may have lots to talk about," Jeanie said, "is it possible we can freely move around and meet your people and army too?"

"By all means," Gaising said with a surprised look on his face, "I thought Shilu here told you we will arrange your trip here?"

"Yes of course she did," Jeanie acknowledged, "our time is limited can we talk about it and set up a program?"

"We hammered out a program for you already," Gelos smiled, "I hope it will cover your interests as well as ours. It is culture, every day reality and the reality of being alert through our forces. If you like you will stay a couple of days in one of our camps?"

"That would be excellent," Jeanie grimaced with Marius nodding and smiling.

"Here is a list of suggestions and the days it will involve," Gelos said and handed the piece of paper. Jeanie and Marius studied it and Shilu, knowing it covered all they felt like, gleamed because she had talked well to Gelos about it and had convinced him of the necessity of their exposure.

"We will be seeing a lot of each other the coming days and I know you must be quite tired of both the traveling and the multitude of impressions," Gaising said thoughtfully, "so I suggest your will retreat and take a well deserved rest now. You may not be too surprised that we too have a few things to take care off."

"Very well indeed," Marius answered, "and what I see on the list looks promising. I wonder though if the authorities are alerted. The Home Minister once looked me straight in the eyes. He may have thought some international press may have covered the event?"

"We should not be too afraid of what the Indians may do. They can be erratic. The lower officers are eager to show off to their superiors. They could question you. We will shield you from them as much as possible," Latem explained his strategy.

"Does this RAP cover all areas? We are free to move?", Jeanie asked.

"They will interfere with your travels when they think it isdangerous for you, more so for them," Gelos answered, "they are jittery now that the whole population defies their authority, so with foreigners around they may be on their best behavior," Gelos smiled.

"Well, we have to take our chance," Marius smiled.

"Shilu can stay with us, or is it you would like her to be with you," Latem asked cheekily.

"Well, we are tired," Marius laughed, "sure I would like her to be with me now," and he winked at Shilu, "but we better keep up appearances. I am sure we will have ample opportunity to discover more of each other?"

"You are right, Marius, we don't want unnecessary intervention. Have a good rest, one of our boys will take you back," Latem concluded.

Shilu waved and threw Marius a hand kiss. Jeanie smiled and both turned to the door, their young guard leading the way. Out on the street the buzz of the event was heard loud and clear. In passing people were discussing openly what had happened. There was police or was it army moving around to. In contrast to what, like their guard pointed out, people normally would do like ducking away and keeping their mouth shut; now they did not. They talked and looked at the soldiers or police like they were intruders. On a TV in an electronics shop they saw the Home Minister had arrived in Kohima and was giving a speech there and a lot of people were watching the screens from the street. The news on what happened in Dimapur had reached Kohima before he had actually arrived and so a much bigger planned demonstration on the grounds where once the Prime Minister of India Nehru saw 10.000 Nagas walking out on him, looked friendlier. Obviously the demonstration organizers there had opted to listen to his explanation.

"I wonder how this news is received elsewhere," Jeanie said, "I suggest you call your people from the room, like I will mine?"

"Yes of course, I was wondering the same thing," Marius said, "perhaps we can find an internet café. I would like to check the international news on this too!"

The guard heard what Marius wanted and without a word led them to a café near the hotel. There only he opened his mouth:

"You can do it here. I am also rather curious to know how it is received," he smiled.

"Okay let's give it half hour," Jeanie agreed, "but then I insist we call the European counterparts and take a nap all right Marius?"

"Sure thing Jeanie," Marius laughed and entered the café.

Forty five minutes and some emails later they emerged from the café and walked over to the hotel. There Marius picked up the phone and reached Bram right away:

"Hi man, things are happening here. Has the news reached you?"

"What kind?" Bram asked.

"No uprising, at least not yet," Marius said, "because of the Home Minister making a narrow escape."

"No, I know what Manila released and of course the Indians could still be behind this, though it does not look like it now. I have been looking into the affairs of Sean and Jacky. You know the Indian team has been sent off to try and catch those two?"

"Yes, that Home minister mentioned that, but it is hard to believe. He also said he would purge his own agencies, squeeze out all info and has put a team on it," Marius said.

"Yes I have that from Patill. He said that in Manila."

"So the Home Minister got all that from Patill?"

"Yeah, the Manila police did great job. But we cannot stop there. They booked flights to new York you know!"

Who?", Marius asked..

"Sean and Jacky of course man," Bram laughed.

"Oh Gosh I don't hope the Americans are behind this," Marius exclaimed, "we will have a hard time getting them and it will become too political too."

"It is a political deed man. This was a contract with a purpose. Someone wanted an uprising," Bram said as Jeanie was listening and thinking. Jeanie was thinking about her own involvement now. She could not really call her sources with Marius around. This was far too dangerous. She had to think of some time alone. Not bad, she thought, Marius is with Shilu sometimes so I can get in touch and check things out.

"Yeah I think you are right Bram. And the lead to get them is via Sean and Jacky. Is there anyone we know in the region? We should get at them before the Indians will?"

"I will do my best," Bram said, "call me tomorrow all right? Oh wait, do you have a number I can call?"

"I will get a Sim card for my mobile phone, so will do and call you from that one!"

"Good, till then," Bram said and hung up.

It was Jeanie's turn now, but she, to avoid she could be checked who or where she called she suggested getting Sim cards right away:

"Important Marius, for then we can be informed any time," she explained.

"Please go and get me one too, Jeanie. I am too tired and want a rest. Let's get some dinner after my nap?"

"Okay," Jeanie answered realizing that being on each other's lip could lead to some complications she did not want. They should be able to operate separately but for the outside world they should still be a couple. Only when in a village or so or in the camps the people could know the marriage was just for the RAP. They were to be married for those who would check their papers, nobody else really. Marius looked tired and without a further word took off his shoes and, still clothes on, as soon as he stretched out fell asleep. Jeanie took her chance, went down to find a telecoms shop to buy the Sim cards and to call Sean:

"Man, they are on your trail. Did you know, Sean?"

"No, not yet, what happened," he asked.

"The Manila police traced you all the way to Brazil. You better change your name and use another passport. An Indian team is on the way to get to you. I am sure they want to know who assigned you for this assassination. Do you actually know?", she asked.

"I might be able to track the person who gave me the contract, but it is through you too, so why don't you find out?" Sean answered.

"I am in Nagaland Sean and I am limited in what I can do without anyone getting suspicious," she answered.

"Okay, I am free here for the time being. Yes I will change house and name!"

"I am observing the real idea behind this assassination Sean. The plotter wants the Nagas to go against the Indian Government. They want a resurrection. I think there is even more the plotter has in mind now that things are moving fast. Did you know about this?"

"I know I should never have taken the assignment. I know it had to do with getting the Nagas better positioned. I have done a few stupid things in my life and it looks like this one of them. On my behalf Jacky too feels she has done something terribly wrong. We are together now Jeanie and it has to stop. Finally, like Bai, I have found myself again. We are going to stop this life and redeem ourselves. Perhaps we should give ourselves up so we can go after the real plotters. What do you think?", he asked.

"If you are sure you can lead the detectives to the plotters, may be you should consider this indeed. But beware, when the plotters find out you two are on the trail to expose them, your lives will be in danger too."

"Yes I am aware of that. We will disappear now for a couple of days until we are sure to know what we will do. You can use this number, but only you Jeanie. You will be the only one who can contact us."

"Okay Sean, thank you for your confidence in me, but beware I might have to give you up too. Considering the circumstances or pressure I get or will get, I might have to. I will inform you beforehand though, agreed?"

"Well you are a covert operative and we are friends. The two cannot always go together, I understand that. But I thank you for letting me know when it comes to that. Already I am telling you that our lives need redemption. We are yearning for it, so it may be that we are going to do that by ourselves anyway."

"Do what?", Jeanie asked, not quite understanding what Sean meant.

"Give ourselves up of course," he laughed nervously like he decided already to do this.

"Oh, I see, yes. Well that will be your choice then. Right now from my side I have no urge to come after you. You are my friend and you have done some dirty things. I am in it as much as you so I am in this one too, but for a purpose right we did that? Wait before giving yourself up, who knows we might be able to get to the plotter after all."

"If you mean you are going after Bai I have to disappoint you. Bai is my friend; he did this because I asked him to do so. When you are thinking of taking him down to get to the plotter, I will bare all. I will expose all I know."

"I did not intend to, but I think the Manila police may get to him. You may not be able to stop the search Sean. You can hide in Brazil, but when you show up in the USA like you planned, I think you will be caught man!"

"How did you know that?" Sean asked. Jeanie laughed and replied:

"We have our sources Sean. You of all people should know that not all things can be done in the dark. There is always some light which could expose what is done. I will soon give you a number to use here Nagaland, dial 0091 for India first?"

"Okay darling," Sean answered, "I will reconsider going to the USA, but do know also we want to know who the plotter is!", Sean said.

"Don't we all now," Jeanie laughed before she hung up.

Chapter 9
Manila revisited

Eddie was pondering. He had his men watching Bai's rented house. For days now there had not been any movement whatsoever. Of course they had interrogated the owner, but to no avail. Bai was last seen before the assassination and after that there was no trace of him. The investigation now hinged upon Bai's return. Eddie was sure Bai would return, for the personal effects which by the way did not offer much of a clue but did offer some insight in the background of Bai himself. So, Eddie delved into Bai's past and discovered a once successful man, a marine, who after his time in Africa had become quite a less ordinary but solitary man. There was o trace of a woman, so they had nothing to go on from that side either. The only thing they could really do, Eddie thought, was to wait till the man showed up. The Indian team had arrived in Rio de Janeiro and tried to find Sean. They could cooperate with the Brazilian authorities and learned Sean and Jacky had stayed in a hotel in Copacabana, but had left the very day the news broke in Manila about their flights to Brazil. So, Eddie thought, they must have been tipped off. Would it still be the Indians who had done that, he wondered. No one in his force had any interest in doing that. Or, could it be that when the news reached Nagaland, as he had seen the local papers on the imminent uprising which was expediently defused by the Home Minister, the information had come into the hands of other people who in turn had tipped off Jacky and Sean. Well it could be, he thought. So, for now, Eddie could only wait and meanwhile concentrate on the other murders in this city where there was hardly a lack of them. Yet, Eddie had a secret, one he had not revealed yet and it was a secret he shared with the coroner of the morgue.

Bai and Celia in her apartment were oblivious of what was going on in the offices of the Manila Police or what was happening in Nagaland. They were engrossed in each other and had no need whatsoever to focus on actualities. They had found each other and though Bai was well aware his old life had come to an end to begin anew he had to face the consequences or the music as he used to say. He knew now he could not yet bring himself to the point of staying away from Celia. Because Celia no longer could get away with being ill, for the first time during their time of bliss Celia had gone to work that day. When she announced she would be away that was the first time since they had found each other again. Bai could think again and he used the time to see if he could plan a road ahead. But then his mobile phone rang:

"Hi Bai, it's Sean. There is something you must know man!", he said.

"Good to hear your voice. Did you make it to Brazil for your holiday?", he asked.

"This is less of a holiday now Bai, we are on the run now," Sean said.

"Oh, from what?", he asked.

"Listen carefully Bai, for it concerns you too. First of all the Manila Police seems to know we are behind the assassination. Remarkable, but true, they have traced us to Brazil and the Indians sent a team to get us to talk. I am sure they want to know who gave the order, who handed the contract."

"The plotter?", Bai asked.

"Right," Sean answered, "they are after you too. I am pretty sure they know who you are and will be on the look out. You said you are in Celia's apartment right?"

"Right," Bai acknowledged

"Then know that they most likely watch your house. So, now it becomes important as to what we want to do. We talked about this before. I am very happy with Jacky. We finally found each other. I understand you have similar feelings for Celia?"

"I know my life is destined to be with her," Bai said and was surprised about his own words, the conviction he felt from them.

"We will do away with our life the way we lived it, I mean Jacky and I and knowing you, you are contemplating the same right?"

"I have a purpose in life again yes," Bai answered.

"Well then listen. I think I am going to give myself up, us up. It looks like you cannot escape either, unless you are helped in getting out of the Philippines. In any case you will have to forget all about your things in the house now," Sean said.

"I figured that out and we have discussed that too Celia and I," Bai said.

"So, my question is when you get caught don't worry about blowing the whistle on us. You don't know or have no connection to the assigner. I might have. Though not directly but some good detectives may be able to use the leads I have."

"So we have decided then?", Bai asked.

"Yes, I have, we are going to give ourselves up and if you do, you can reveal all you are required to do. Don't feel bad about doing that. It is time for Jacky and I and hopefully for you too, to redeem ourselves."

"I hope it is not too late for your soul and mine," Bai said, a tear in his eyes, really doubting that he could ever be redeemed

"It is never too late Bai. Let's be glad that this assassination and the women whom we love, either directly like yours and indirectly like mine did show us that we can still live and pay for our sins of the past. Let's do it man and face the consequences?"

"I am glad you called. Was it Celia who gave you this number?'

"Yes, she knew I am your friend and wanted to know about you from me and our time in Africa, so I called you back here."

"Okay, I will do it even though we will be separated from Celia, perhaps even forever."

"Don't you think of that? When you cooperate with them I am sure when we both talk and lead the detectives to the plotter, we will get some credit for that."

"I hope so," Bai said, "leaving Celia again will be the hardest thing for me to do now!", Bai said and practically cried just thinking about that idea.

"Oh, I know how you feel; it is really the same for me. We are in bliss man, but the strange thing is, because we are so certain we must be clean to deserve each other."

"That is a heartwarming thought, the idea we are not alone in this at least strengthens me a little," Bai agreed.

"Okay, give my regards to the lovely Celia, your woman. Go to your house in a few days. I am sure you will be arrested and taken inside out. Tell everything you know, meanwhile I will do some investigation of my own," Sean concluded.

When that evening Celia came home, she sensed a change in Bai. At work she had read the papers and learned that accomplices of the assassin were still here and others had fled to Brazil. Celia knew enough then and planned to talk to Bai about it, details included. Yet, when she saw him she instantly felt he was going to give himself up, the question which remained was then only, when would it be. So, she decided to live it up with him before it was too late and when she came home sensing the atmosphere she instantly felt so attracted to him that she jumped into his arms.

"I have cooked you some Indian curry," Bai smiled as he gently kissed and touched her, then they took off her clothes, "we can eat soon!", he said.

"You rascal," she laughed now in her fine lingerie and with Bai's eyes on her practically devouring her. Celia felt the same and reciprocated by taking off Bai's clothes too. Like he had stopped at her lingerie, so did she when he was just in his underpants.

"Now we can eat darling, my dear Celia," he smiled. And they did. They fed each other morsel by morsel and laughed and drank a bottle of San Miguel.

"We are in heaven, my sweet Bai," Celia murmured and smooched his chest tenderly. Bai in turn touched her and soon effortlessly raised their sense of intimacy to unknown heights.

"I love you Celia," Bai whispered and took off her bra then burying his face in her breasts. Celia's heart jumped and the moments after were filled with passion for each other. Their lust now unleashed, it gently took possession of them and they came together enveloping each other. Then fiercely and eagerly while giving themselves away, took possession of each other. It must have been some two hours later when, wrapped up in each other and Bai stroking Celia, just said as if it was an ordinary thing to talk about:

"You can tell now what is bothering you Bai, or what you have decided my love!"

"Oh, you knew all the time, ooh," he whispered, "who is the rascal now?"

"I know there is something," she said, "and you should share it with me!"

"Of course darling, I just wanted to postpone so we have this lovely time together. Soon that may be a thing of the past!"

"Oh," Celia feigned as if she had no hunch, "tell me?"

"I have spoken to Sean. Both Sean and I have decided, because we want to change our lives for good, thanks to you too darling, to give ourselves up."

"Really? So, it is definite now!", Celia exclaimed

"Yes, but it is very hard, now especially with you in my arms. I may have to give up you too my sweet," Bai whispered, sincerely meaning that.

"Why should you need to give me up," Celia asked,

"Going to jail will separate me from you. It is as easy as that," Bai answered.

"Yeah, that is true, but you will come out again," Celia concluded.

"After how many years, I will be an old man then and you will have married a much better man," Bai replied.

"Oh, come on Bai, we are soul mates, I am with you all the way. Let me suggest this then. We will stay here, together, for three more days to explore all we feel for each other. Every centimeter of your body and every thought in your mind I want to know. Is that clear," she laughed,

"Yes and phrased better," Bai laughed.

"Well then, we will live three days and nights in bliss and then only you will go to your house to get your things. If you are not caught then, you will drop your things here for me to look after them and turn yourself in. We will go together. But, and that is likely from what I heard as they are on the look out, you will be caught while you are in your house and then it begins."

"Yes, Sean told me to reveal all. He is now busy to find out more about whom he took the contract from,' Bai explained.

"Good, we are getting closer to really loving each other," Celia said.

"What do you mean now Celia?"

"Well dear Bai, only when you have tried to purify yourself and accept you need to repent, you can love. We are coming close now because we desire each other so much I could devour you too, but we really come together if we can look each other in the eyes and be innocent and full of love, my darling. Then our love will flourish!"

"Yes you are right Celia. Yes, okay three days to plant the seeds so we will meet again when I have repented," Bai agreed.

The Indian Army had come under severe strain. In Kohima high alert was given, but because of what happened in Dimapur it was thought things could be contained. Now to be sure all precautions were taken and with thousand of men in the small city around Kohima ground it looked like an invasion rather than a visit.

"Was this absolutely necessary," the Home minister said sardonically to the head of police who accompanied Swio, the Chief Minister of Nagaland State:

"We can't risk you being molested," Swio grimaced, "for then these soldiers here would clamp down on my people. Of course it will be bad for you, but much worse for us. So, it is better to contain them," he said while thinking he would have loved to let it go out of hand, so that this terrible tension would come to an end too. Swio had become the Chief Minister by way of a coalition government and was the successor or the powerful S.C. Jamir, a man famous for her allegiance to the Indian government and part of the then group of Nagas who were the architects of the 16 point agreement which led to the foundation of the State, the first of what is now called the Seven Sisters. They were looking at the crowd assembling when the army general joined them:

"We have it all under control Sir. You can speak freely."

"Well, what would I do without you," the Home Minister retorted with the same kind of venom he had served the police officer with," you obviously forgot about proper protection when I was in Dimapur. Or, is that not within your jurisdiction?"

"Oh, it is Sir, but we were unprepared there. We did not know such crowd would go that far," he said in his defense.

"Their leader is assassinated, the feelings run high, they suspect the Indian Government is responsible and you think they do not do anything? Don't you know the Nagas man, perhaps it is a good idea to have you replaced."

The general said nothing but had shame on his face, not the kind of shame that goes with a sense of feeling guilty, but the shame one feels when being exposed in public, but he had to say something:

"You did a wonderful job Sir, speaking to the crowd and pacifying them!"

"That is right," the Home Minister agreed, "but let me ask you these two things. Why do you have so many men here, when you know with the news I brought and will elaborate on here, you know the Nagas will not do a thing? And then, the Indian Armed Forces are ultimately under my command, if I find out somebody under your command has been plotting this I can assure you many heads will roll. Now tell me is the army on some level involved in plotting the assassination of the Naga leader?"

"Oh, no Sir, I know of no such plot," he said and with fear in his eyes.

"Well withdraw your forces; make them unseen, they are very conspicuous now. This might infuriate the Nagas again and they will see it as if I have personally ordered this. They will think I have been lying. Now that is a risk. Redirect them instantly, at least 80% per cent of them and pronto."

"Right away Sir, directly," he said, sighed then ran off to shout orders to his officers.

"What do you think Swio? Doesn't the presence of so many soldiers aggravate the Nagas here? I think it angers them and they may not believe what I say.

Well most of that I am sure they know, but hear that again now with thousands of soldiers containing them?"

"Right you are," Swio smiled, "it is s good thing you did that," but you did come down hard on the general," Swio laughed now.

"Sometimes these people have to use their brain, don't you agree?", he asked.

Swio thought a moment on being his Naga self and shoot back at the Home Minister or to be diplomatic. Oh what the heck, he thought, he acts like he is in command of the situation but in fact was rescued by his Foreign Minister, or better said, by the Manila Police so Swio smiled at him and said:

"Sometimes all of us could do better when we use our brain. Before we realize we become too haughty and think it is all about us?"

The Home Minister laughed and thought what impertinence! Who does this Swio thinks he is? Instead he smiled back realizing Swio put a finger on a weakness many politicians suffer from.

"Are you referring to me being briefed and could actually could say something to avert an assault, a stampede?", he asked wondering what Swio knew.

"I must say, that it was very convenient for you the Manila police came up with some indications directing suspicion away from what the Naga people thought. The Nagas do have some bad experiences with some Indian Governments unfortunately."

"Well trust is being built again and I am sure that, unless some people in our agencies have been plotting things for themselves for whatever reason I like to know. For, we did not decide to commit such blatant murder. So, dear Swio, I am indeed looking for others who have done this, are behind this."

"I can say I believe you of course," Swio smiled, "but we are talking frankly and I think you deserve to know how things are. So, let me tell you this, I am not entirely certain that Indians are not involved. I am not saying or even thinking this means it is orchestrated by the Indian Government, in casu yourself, but is it possible that some people in your vast country took it upon them?"

"Possible of course Swio and we will find them, our record and our relationship should not be up for grabs now. We have worked hard to come to where we are now in the talks and I am glad you have openly stated you are for integration of all Nagas."

"No, I did not say that," Swio smiled, "I said I am for reunification of all Nagas. We like to have our Homeland reunited, the land, which as you know, was arbitrarily divided between two country and four states."

"Okay, granted, the Home Minister said. Shall we leave it up to the negotiating teams? I have to get ready to deliver the speech, one I hope will lessen the chance for an uprising. I don't like to see our Armed Forces being deployed against your people. It may be a bloodbath, let's do all to avoid such unfortunate event," he stressed looking serious now.

"One thing perhaps before you go on stage Home Minister," Swio said but in tone the man could hardly say no to.

"Yes please Swio?"

"Just a thought but tell me did you calculate too that in the event the Nagas would rise and you had no alternative but to deploy the Army against angry people, that a bloodbath would catch international attention? Is that not something the Indian Government would want to avert too?"

"Hmm, Swio, of course when this happens I am sure we would be internationally held accountable. Why did we have to come down on demonstrators, bloodbath in with perhaps hundreds of people dead? The blame would be on us, yes we will be answerable. You are right we do not want that. Neither do I think would you like to sacrifice hundreds perhaps thousands of your people for that purpose?"

"Of course not, but come to think of it, there could be some very angry people among Indians and Nagas alike. I would not be too surprised if the plotter is laughing about what the assassination brought about. There may be something left in the planning still."

"Yes, I have been thinking on that too on my way over here. Let's talk about this later? Right now I am due to speak."

Swio nodded slowly but then confirmed with a full: "Yes Home Minister, the crowd is waiting and the people are restless."

The Home Minister nodded in turn looked at Swio straight, sized him up and decided he had done the right thing to talk about this with him. He turned and climbed on to the stage. The Kohima ground was full of Nagas. Kohima, already in the hills the mountains began not altogether far from Dimapur, was the home of the Angami Nagas and it was here where the battle against the Japanese was fought. The Japanese from Burma side wanted to create a passage so they could pour into India, Kohima being the gateways if they could knock out the British. The Nagas fought alongside the British and because they were the Masters of their terrain, they were able to drive out the Japanese. Lots of Japanese lost their lives in this fierce battle. The military graveyards are visited every year by many relatives on both sides. Of course Nagas lost their lives too. Swio walked over to his people and his ministers to listen to the speech of the Home Minister. Though the ground was packed, the tension felt in Dimapur had practically subsided. The news of the Dimapur confrontation had reached Kohima by radio an when it was confirmed by the publication of a special edition of the Nagaland Post, the people knew that at least it was not certain the Indians were behind it. In the newspaper a journalist reported they had phoned the people in Manila to double check what had been said by the Home Minister and concluded he had not just done to save his neck. The telephone inquiries were also broadcasted so most were certain indeed the Home minister had not lied. Of course there were always some people who could not believe and were convinced the Indians did it but had hired assassins to do the job. Since this was a plausible explanation and the people did not quite know what to believe, it was now imperative for the Home Minister to come across as a man not just of stature, but as one of honesty. However, most Nagas were willing to at least give the man the benefit of the doubt, something which they would not have done, if the Dimapur confrontation had not occurred. So, when he began he did hit a positive nerve instantly when he said:

"Dear ladies and gentlemen, I am honored to be here with you and I have something important to say. But first of all I offer you my deepest condolences. The lost of your revered leader to an assassin is very difficult to bear. The Indian people as a whole are with your in your grief,", he said pausing for a moment to see the effect of his words. When he saw the people were not getting enthusiastic yet, he continued:

"I very well understand your first thoughts were on the Indian Government which I represent. If I as a member of the government was behind that you have every reason to suspect me," he said and slowly was applauded, "I am responsible for that too," he continued, "but that it not all. From the police in Manila we learned that the assassins of your leader are on the run. It is likely they were hired, deployed and the reason for this we do not know. Already in Dimapur I have said, that the Indian Government has nothing to do with it, but we cannot rule out that there are plotters among us and we cannot rule out that others have an interest too," he explained and paused to let his words sink in. The crowd, apprehensive still but showing willingness to listen waited for him to reveal more and he did. He came up with some more details on the prospective assassins and asked the exited journalists swarming the field too, to check on his words. NDTV was there, Star TV too, most of the major national newspapers like the Times of India, the Hindu, the New Statesman, the Deccan Herald, the Telegraph were present. They were kept in check by the local ones which were, normally speaking, better informed, but not on this issue. For the local dailies checking of what the Home Minister had been telling would be difficult, not so of course in assessing the impact of the assassination on the Nagas as a whole. The Nagaland Post was there, the Assam Tribune, the Morung Express and newspapers of the other states of the North East too like the Kangla, the Sentinel and the Sangai Express. Many in the crowd, because of the presence of the media, did realize that the outcry of the Nagas against the assassination was now big news in India, but would it reach elsewhere too? Stringers of the BBC were seen and a journalist of the news agency IANS which had its news on Yahoo too was seen taking notes. The Home Minister meanwhile kept on talking on the lines he had set out namely sharing the information on the assassination and promising that all would be done to find the actual killers or the plotters so their motivation would be revealed. The question on every one's lips after all was: 'Why was our leader murdered?'

Right after his speech the pacified crowd felt reassured things would be done and even the Indian Government would be thoroughly checked to see if there were renegades operating on their own motivation. The press besieged the Home Minister and his aides had to keep the journalists at bay. Since the Home Minister realized the importance of the press in this he let his aides make half an hour appointments with some of the journalists and so spent the remainder of the day being interviewed on the burning topic.

Meanwhile in Dimapur when evening fell Shilu had come to wake Marius up and Jeanie who had finished her separate talks had returned too.

"Come I will take you to dinner," she announced, but first dirty man, you should take a shower. This afternoon you slept with your clothes on and you are smelly!"

"Good idea," the still groggy Marius smiled, "yes I feel like I could use a bath!", he said and jumped up to disappear into the bathroom. Jeanie and Shilu then talked about their mutual female interests, but both carefully avoided the subject of Marius. Shilu because she instinctively felt Jeanie had, beside the professional connection, some interest in him and Jeanie because she knew that both Marius and her were here because Marius was attracted to Shilu. Well not only of course, Jeanie knew Marius too good for that, but surely she had been a strong factor for him to decide to come here. When Marius, refreshed now, emerged from the bathroom in a towel to take his clothes, they both smiled as he went back in to get dressed. When Marius was ready to go, they found a restaurant and when they had something simple to eat Shilu told them about the program they had put together. Out on the street they found things had calmed down and had gone back to normal. Shilu announced that they were going to leave tomorrow:

"The leaders have made arrangements for you to visit a Naga Army camp. You will be free to talk to anyone there and see some of the trainings too," she said, "you can stay there a day or two if you like. Then I will take you to a few villages where you can experience Naga life and perhaps talk to some people about culture and what they endured. I will have to go to work soon, so after that I will take you to the rehabilitation center. You can see what we do and find out how youngsters are led to be hooked on drugs. From there it will be arranged for you to go back to Dimapur." Shilu explained, "if you need or want to do some other things, please let me know and I will try to connect with those who can accommodate."

"That looks good," Marius said, "we don't have too much time so this will cover most of what we had in mind, right Jeanie?", he asked.

"Yes Shilu," Jeanie smiled.

"The leaders have provided us with a vehicle and driver, so we are free to go around as we see fit, but first you will be taken to the camp. Is it your intention to get into the Burmese side of Nagaland?", Shilu asked.

"To tell you the truth," Jeanie laughed, "I have not thought about that. Is it possible?"

"It is possible indeed, but we need time. We have to walk many miles, not all villages are connected by roads and especially the ones in Burma are not," she explained, "but I can ask some people of the organizations to accompany you there. You need guides and porters with you."

"Oh I would love to do that," Marius said, "may be we can plan that on another visit?", he winked at Shilu implicitly letting her know he was serious about her. Shilu understood and smiled too when she concluded:

"Well then let's make sure your exposure to Nagaland will be fruitful. You will have many impressions anyway from this short trip. The villages we are going to visit are on the way to Mokokchong, my home, in the north towards Arunachal Pradesh," she said.

"It is all new to me," Jeanie smiled, "so I am open to anything Shilu."

"Well that is a positive attitude in these dark times," Shilu smiled back at her while Marius sensed Jeanie had some hidden feelings she tried to control but could entirely prevent them from coming out. Jeanie felt Marius could realize and suggested to go back alone to arrange some female things, usually a good excuse for anything.

"I shall be back in an hour or so too," Marius said. "we have to get up early right Shilu?"

"I was thinking of picking you up at around eight and I will have the vehicle ready for you then, bring all your things Jeanie?", she asked.

"Of course," Jeanie answered, "and do me the honor to let me pay for this meal?", she asked in turn. She did not wait for the answer but walked up to waiters and asked for the bill, paid, waved and left.

"Finally alone," Shilu smiled, the official face now leaving her.

"It is so good to see you Shilu," Marius replied, "I did not think I could be so attached to you already. For some reason I feel rather close!"

"You better don't joke about these things, I do take you seriously man," Shilu smiled, "and to tell you a secret, I have been thinking about you."

"I am with you," Marius stated warmly.

"Tell me Marius," Shilu asked inquisitively cocking her head, "you feel for Jeanie?"

"What do you mean Shilu? Jeanie I have known for a long time. She is a good colleague, a loyal friend and an attractive woman," Marius smiled.

"She is more than a friend to you Marius," Shilu said.

"What are you saying?", he asked.

Well, may be not to you, but I can certainly feel she does not like me to be with you. I hope this is not going to turn into an awkward situation?", Shilu asked.

"What are you assuming now? I have never had anything with her, I carefully avoided that. In my line of work this is dangerous. Oh, I like her, she has a sharp mind too," Marius explained.

"She may be all that, but she wants you," Shilu smiled.

"I seem to be stupid then," Marius laughed.

"Yes you are," she smiled back at him.

"Oh, you mean it?", he asked now totally surprised.

"Yes, of course, it is obvious," Shilu said, "all signs are there!"

"I carefully avoid anything when I am professional," Marius said, "so if there are signs I chose not to see them."

"Are you sure she went with you just for the purpose of adventure, to help you out with the RAP. I cannot get rid of the idea she has something else, something we do not know about. I like her too, don't get me wrong and I think she is professional too, but I feel she has something up her sleeve, perhaps a connection you do not know about!"

"This has nothing to do with some kind of envy, some jealousy?", he asked baffled by the insinuations of Shilu.

"To be honest Marius, no I don't think so. I think she wants you, but she also realizes because you came to see me she has no chance and consequently will not share anymore what she knows or wants to find out," Shilu explained.

"Gosh Shilu, you are worse than a secret agent," Marius laughed, making light of things.

"No Marius, I can feel there is something. Let's see if we can check her out. I am not worried I think she means well, also for you. She is just feeling sorry she has not moved on you I think. Now it is too late, you are all mine," Shilu joked to defuse the serious talk.

"If you are right, I will have to keep an eye on her indeed," Marius replied and pondered, "but I know her much longer than you. I feel so open with you and I trust you too, now I wonder if I can."

"Oh, what have I done," Shilu reacted, "perhaps I should not have said it and let you discover for yourself."

"No. it is all right. I do like her a lot and perhaps in the way I like you too, but I would never do anything when we are connected professionally. So, may be you are right and she feels bad, but I am with you Shilu. It is you I want to know!", Marius stressed.

"And I like that too; it is just unfortunate she is with us most of the time!"

"Let's focus on the time we can actually spend together Shilu?"

"Yeah, let's do that, I am sorry but I thought I should talk to you about it!"

"As long as we can rule out we do things out of jealousy then of course it is all good we talk openly about what we feel!", Marius smiled.

"That is what I thought too," she smiled and both could very well feel romance could blossom now. Like young students they looked and smiled and were infatuated and ready to discover each other in any way now. They had longed for these moments, moments of togetherness.

Chapter 10

The Scorpion moves

On his way to New York for another conference plus subsequent seminars and personal meetings the scorpion felt quite excited. He was reading the latest news, reliable news, not the headlines only but the details. That was fast he thought that Manila Police must have had a stroke of luck. To get to Sean so fast was remarkable. Both feelings of elation and setback were on his mind. What was happening in Nagaland elated him but that the police were so quick to move and ultimately would get to him, depressed the scorpion. The developments were as he had predicted and planned. A setback was this cunning Home Minister, he thought would have been molested and this would have triggered the Army, Police, Assam Rifles to jump into action. Saved he was, in the nick of time.

He had hoped that the action of the uprising, not the possibly many lives lost during that confrontation that India finally would not be able to avoid to be questioned. For that was his goal, to expose India as nation which leaders' committed state terrorism. He had so carefully planned the assassination so he could direct the downfall of India, internationally in favor of the Nagas. Though on the right track, but just to curb the influence of the Indian Government, he felt he had to move again. He reviewed what he could do: he could give up the three people, the three he had hired. They would not know how to find him and eventually with them in custody and having no explanation for anything but just that they accepted the contract, they would cease to follow up on the scorpion. But, he was not worried about that, he was more worried about the effects for if the Indians would escape suspicion, again they would go free and in spite of the atrocities they committed, especially in the past, things would return to normal. He felt furious about that. So, yes, he would give up Sean, the actual assassins he did not know. Though Sean had never met him as the person who assigned him to the contract he knew Sean well. Sean knew him in another capacity, a capacity he did not quite admire. Sean did not know him as the scorpion of course. It was odd, because he had been with Sean in Africa just after his failure took place. The Scorpion then part of the UN rescue operations had taken out quite a few UN soldiers who had gone mad. So, the Scorpion knew this was something which had shattered and unbalanced him. When he felt inspired to plot what had been on his mind as an idea only it was Sean who had been playing a major role in it. Knowing what he had done in Rwanda made the scorpion feel unreserved about sacrificing him for the good cause, one he wanted to materialize at all cost. The Scorpion loathed repressive the Hindu system. He did so not only because of the persistent caste system, no, not just that though after all the majority of the outcasts were really shunned Indigenous Peoples, it was on his conviction that his heart was indeed those peoples and with the Nagas in particular.

Moving on the subway he was now with his thoughts on Nagaland. He remembered the time he spent there and the feeling of guilt he had because of the Baptists in 1956. Then the American Baptists had left their brothers and sisters when the missionaries were expelled because the Indian accused the Baptist of instigating the Nagas to rebel against India. This led to the Indian Government asked them to leave the country and thus the Nagas. Though they did not want to go, they eventually did leave for as they reasoned: If we would have stayed on we would have jeopardized all other Baptist Missions in India. That is all nice and well, the Scorpion thought, but back in the USA they could have highlighted the plight of the Nagas. They could have helped them in other ways, like taking them out of obscurity. That is what you Baptists could have done, but you did not. You left them and let them fend for themselves against an overwhelming army. You are also responsible for the Indians killing so many Nagas, he concluded, as he recurrently had done many times. Over the years but from a distance he had intensely followed what happened and saw how the Nagas evolved in spite of all that was against them. He admired them for being able to stand up to this pressure, even when the adversary, the Indian Governments implemented their divide and rule policy. Beginning with the formation of Nagaland State, which was created without the consent of the Naga People, then with the Shillong Accord and the terrible split which was caused among the people up to the bloody separation of the Kaphlang group from the then leading armed organization called the NSCN. The NSCN is still standing firm on the Naga principle, the principle that would set the Nagas free, the principle of self determination, of sovereignty. And now, already almost a decade now the Indians and Nagas are talking peace on the basis of a cease fire. Yes, India plays with the mouse, he thought. The big cat plays until the mouse is too wounded or tired to move. The cat has moved the talks into a stalemate and keeps it there. So, what I have in mind is to break this stalemate. One way of doing that is to create havoc which enables the Nagas to be known and the Indians are nailed to the cross of the international community for committing state terrorism. It was after all their general stating that India could only win this war if the Indian Armed Forces were to annihilate all Nagas. This is why I intervened and interfered, he thought. But then, things might go wrong. If the Home Minister can wriggle himself out of the very difficult situation I put him in, he may be able to sway the attention to others. This is why I have to think and steer the suspicion right back into his direction and with him the Indian Government as a whole. What can I do? When I can give up the assassins they would be caught but the Indians would be off the hook still. Sean did not know much about his motivation or the Nagas so he had no motivation to murder the Naga leader and, the scorpion thought, this motivation other than from a Naga himself, was important to blast the Indo-Naga conflict out into the open. Suddenly he thought of something and he said out loud, of course that is it, I will move, I will sew some confusion and I will make sure the tables are turned on them again. The Indians should feel what they have done and repent, he said to himself. Satisfied with his thoughts, he stepped off the underground at 42second street and before attending the conference outside he looked for a phone booth. When he found one he used a phone card to make a connection to Sean.

Marius and Jeanie were picked up by a jeep that morning, one of the Naga Army and have a good natured smiling driver and a soldier on board.

"Off we go," Shilu smiled after she introduced the two young men.

"Wonderful," Jeanie reacted and had Marius smiling too.

"We will go to the camp then?", the driver asked.

"Yes, as arranged previously," Shilu confirmed. They had just left and were some fifteen minutes on the main road when they were stopped by a contingent of Indian soldiers.

"Good heavens," Shilu hissed, "there we go again."

"Papers," the Indian soldier said. The Naga soldiers were dressed in civilian clothing of course and acted like they were just some simple peasants. Dutifully all produced their papers, Marius and Jeanie also the RAPS.

"Where are you heading?", the man asked, his subordinates standing around the jeep, toting their guns.

"Direction Mokokchong," Shilu said, "my friends and I are going to stay in my parent's village. We will stop at a few villages on the way!"

The soldier looked stern, checked all the papers one by one not saying a word, handed them back to them saying:

"Okay on your way then!", and he made gestures as if he was in a hurry suddenly. The driver reacted immediately, pushed the throttle and off they were again.

"Hebron camp is not very far," he shouted, "we will soon be there!"

"Good, good," Jeanie smiled who was still impressed with the conduct of the soldiers on the road. It did not take them long to reach the gate and it did make Marius wonder aloud how it was possible to have camps as large as this one so openly manned by the Naga Army and practically in sight of the Indian Armed Forces.

"It is cease fire," the young soldier said to them, "now we are free to move and the Indian soldiers cannot touch us. Well they do occasionally but we do raise hell and we have a cease fire monitoring group too. Plus when it gets really serious then it is talked about directly at the peace talks too!", he explained when they reached the gate and moved into the camp. The driver led them to headquarters where they were received by officers who were informed of their arrival.

"We were asked to make you a two-day program," one of them said, "but I am also told you like coffee in the mornings Marius and Jeanie, so," let's enjoy that first?"

"A marvelous suggestion," Jeanie said.

"Yes, we did not even have time for breakfast yet. We got up too late and rushed to meet the time we had agreed on," Marius smiled.

"Oh really?", the officer smiled, "in that case allow me to offer you something. You are our guests and it is our honor to look after you," he smiled cheekily.

"This is a pleasant surprise indeed," Jeanie, who enjoyed being pampered, said.

Shilu winked at Marius, she knew of course how the Naga Army would treat their guests, but her smile was meant for Marius. After their coffee and some light breakfast the exposure as Marius and Jeanie had named their visit could begin. The officers introduced them to the young men and women in training which surprised Jeanie and she asked:

"I am astonished you have quite a few young women here. Like the men do they volunteer to join?"

"Of course," the accompanying officer said, "no one here is forced to be part of the Naga Army. All feel it is their duty to stand up for our nation. You can ask them yourself of course," he explained.

"So you have women officers too then." Jeanie asked further

"We have indeed and I will introduce you to one if you like," the officer smiled.

"Are you training them the same way as you do the men?", Marius wanted to know..

"Essentially we do not make a difference yes, but we all know that women are not like men and men are not like women. So we do take these differences into account and make the most out of what both can do and fine-tune our training to bring out the best in both."

"That sounds pretty ideal," Marius chuckled.

"They are very diligent in their training and they don't make much difference between men and women Marius, you will see," Shilu remarked.

"I would like that," Jeanie contributed.

"Now with relative peace for a number of years already and with no sign of permanent peace, how do you keep your soldiers motivated," Marius asked.

"This is one of our major problems indeed," the officer acknowledged, 'and it is not something I can give you a simple answer on. We will have to show you the current realities and consequently the troubles we face. These troubles are rather different from the ones we face while in guerilla warfare," he explained.

"I can imagine that very well, for now the soldiers are dealing with civilian life and need not take refuge in the forest. Do they deal with the civilians?"

"Indeed much more than when the war is on," he answered thoughtfully, "during the war things are clear. The Indians are the enemy and they are in great numbers, but they defend their positions. We on the other hand single out a target, we attack, take the guns and the Indian soldiers we set free again."

"You do?", Jeanie asked looking surprised.

"Of course," the officer smiled, "what good would it do to keep them in some kind of custody? We do not have detention centers, prisons or personnel to keep those captured. Also, these ordinary soldiers don't know much about strategies, they are just sent by their superiors. If they know anything at all, they will easily tell. More often than not it is nothing we know already. Thirdly when we keep them, we have to feed them and that again is a burden. I am sure we would have hundreds perhaps thousands by now if we wanted to. Keeping them means we have to have guards in a stagnant place which makes us prone to be attacked again. No, it is not worth it at all," he smiled.

"So, what about this relative peace where there are no engagements. What do the soldiers do to keep themselves occupied?", "Jeanie asked this time.

"We keep on training for we have to be ready when, if that happens, the cease fire is broken. We safeguard the people from intrusions and when they ask to come and protect them we will," he explained, "you do realize we have our own government? This government runs Nagaland, the people pay taxes to us and the tax has to be collected. We cannot run an army without funds," he smiled.

"Oh yes, that is well understood," Marius nodded, "however there are these reports or are these allegations that not just you but also the NNC and the Kaphlang group go around collection taxes. Some say that this is sheer extortion and the people in some cases are taxed by all three organizations. This I am sure could be quite confusing?"

"It surely is indeed," he agreed, "but you tell me what we can do? We can only chase the others out," he said looking troubled.

"Is this what they meant by fratricidal killing?", Jeanie asked.

"That is how it is interpreted," he answered, "but please do realize what happened in the past and what it has led to. We cannot honestly acknowledge either the NNC or the K as the custodians of the Naga cause, the issue is not with them. Why? Because the NNC did sell our people out, I am not just referring to the dispute of the validity of the Shillong Accord, but to its implementation, after all the Naga Army was disarmed. This was the most important reason for our organization to emerge. So from our perspective the Naga cause, the issue, the fight against India to achieve self determination, is no longer with them, yet they do operate be it in small numbers and try to justify their existence. The K group was part of us and of the NNC before that. Opportunities offered by the Indians made this group to align itself with those we fight against. So, according to us the issue cannot be with them either. We have to confront them, because as they have betrayed our people they have forfeited the right to represent them. They cannot forcibly win people over and ask them to pay taxes. That we call extortion, for they are in no way accountable fro what they do. So, yes, to answer your question, it all depends from what perspective you talk if you call it tax or extortion. I am sure the Indians with their puppet state, we do not recognize, call what we do extortion. They reason that only the Indian government can collect taxes and all others are extortionists. I am sure you will realize when we do not recognize the Indian government as the rightful government to rule over us, that we do not accept that government to tell us what to do either. So, we levy taxes and as such we do not accept any imposition of the Indian government on our people."

"That looks rather logical reasoning," Jeanie agreed, "yet the people, at least some of them in overlapping areas may face four types of taxation then. First it is the State Government, the NNC and K then your organization?"

"That's right and so we are compelled to chase the other two out."

"Don't these other two in turn try to chase you out again?", Marius remarked.

"Of course, they want to broaden their base. They do that by forcing people and threatening them. We have to fight back, that is sure."

"So, people get killed during these clashes," Jeanie said.

"Some things are unavoidable," the officer reacted, "when some of our people act shamelessly we can only try to contain them."

"It would be good if you could have a dialogue, for they have accused your organization for having committed atrocities too," Marius contributed.

"This is one of the major problems among us Nagas," the officer agreed, "many accusations are hurled, but nothing can be investigated. In a relatively normal society allegations are taken seriously and those who come up with them are required to show proof, then after proper investigation and trial, people are convicted of their crimes or found innocent. But even now that we enjoy a relative peace I am sure you will agree that this is not a normal society?", he smiled.

"In a land occupied but hundreds of thousands of soldiers I don't think you can expect normalcy in the society," Jeanie said and Marius added;

"It is remarkable how the society is run, of course under the prevailing circumstances."

"We do our best," the officer smiled, "this afternoon we have training for women too. Would you like to see that?"

"Yes," said Jeanie first with Marius following suit.

"Then let's relax now. I will show you around the camp if you like?", he suggested and took the lead by walking along some of the buildings which made Marius remark:

"These look like rather permanent buildings to me. When the cease fire breaks will these not be very difficult to defend, the camp can easily be overrun?"

"Of course," the officer agreed," please do realize that we will not be here then. We can attack an army but cannot hold positions. We are running a guerilla army not an occupation army. There is a big difference there. We want the Indian Armed Forces out, but we cannot drive them out. They want us only to be part of India and we resist. They cannot win when we do not agree. You cannot force people with the gun on their temple. Well may be some people will submit, but not the Nagas as a whole," he smiled again.

"So, this camp will be abandoned then." Jeanie concluded.

"That is more than likely," he concluded.

They passed the barracks of the soldiers and saw the young men and women busy doing chores of the day.

"While in the forests they have to do everything themselves, even getting their own food they have to find. Oh, they may have rice with them, but we teach them how to live in the forest and to get what they need to live on."

"Survival training?", Jeanie asked.

"That is a modern way of saying it, yes," the officer said, "we teach them what the forest offers. Most of them know that for they come from the villages and know how to hunt. Here we teach them how to get vegetables, roots and much more," he explained.

"So, you take them on trips where you test their abilities and their skills?", Shilu now showed her face too.

"Of course we do that," the officer chuckled, "and we make them feel they have to go to the best of their ability. We deprive them so they have only what is around them to live on. While they are busy with that, we will attack them."

"Not for real of course," Jeanie cried out.

"No, mockingly indeed, but with realism so they feel what might happen. We act like Indian soldiers and take them prisoner. We use soldiers for that whom they do not know. This way they are truly tested and they will use all their skills to stay out of the hands of the Indian soldiers," he smiled.

"You said you release the Indian soldiers after you disarmed them. The Indians do not do that with your troops?", Shilu asked as they walked along the training course.

"Here we will do some training in the afternoon," the officer said, then answering Shilu, "no the Indians normally interrogate, torture and lock our men up. It is possible they rape our women. It is what they do!", he explained.

"Yes," said Shilu, "many stories about rape and not just about captured women soldiers."

"No, indeed," the officer agreed, "much more so they do that with our civilian women. In times of cease fire not so of course, but the stories during wartime were rampant."

"I heard so many, you can write a book about that alone. I am sure it is done with the purpose of making the Nagas feel they are lesser beings, but instead of making us submit, it infuriates us," now Shilu explained, her eyes furious

"I have read something about that," Jeanie said, "is it true that Indians would come into a village and drive the people into a field or a building like a church and then rape some women in front of their men?"

"It happened," Shilu answered, the officer nodding in agreement, "it happened many a time more than was documented. Yet the human rights organization NPMHR has documented a lot of these assaults. Perhaps we will find some older people in the villages who dare to tell," she said.

"I am sure little is known about these things and if at all they were reported. In India nobody cared and outside India these stories are not known?"

"Yes, I think that is about right," the officer confirmed, "the Nagas, the victims, were not believed. This is why the NPMHR was founded, in 1978 I think?"

"Yes," said Shilu.

"Well your tour is about complete," the officer said, "we will return here to see our men and women at work. You will see how they harden themselves."

"I cannot wait to see that," Jeanie smiled as they walked back to headquarters building. Since till lunch they were more or less free to spend some time on their own, Shilu winked Marius. When he had gone over to her and was out of earshot of the others she whispered to him"

"Let's go for a walk on our own, Just the two of us?"

Marius smiled and teasingly answered: "Darling I thought you would never ask!"

No words were exchanged when they left to walk up to a forest road nearby and now out of sight of anyone and perhaps some three hundred meters away from any building, Shilu suddenly embraced Marius. With her face on his cheek, but not facing him she said:

"It is so good to see you Marius, only now I feel sure you are really here."

"Yeah," Marius whispered back feeling warm, "it is so strange to have Jeanie around me when I want to talk to you, to continue where we left of in Amsterdam."

"It is a strange situation yes," she laughed now as she pulled back to face Marius.

"Doing that and being alone with you now makes me, no, no further talking now," Marius frowned then smiled and moved to kiss her. Shilu felt him coming and since this is what she had taken him away for answered his kiss with passion. Judging from the merging feelings they felt, they had longed for this moment. Now that it was there it overwhelmed them as it validated what had been simmering in both of them, but neither of them thought it could be true. Now that it was, all brakes, all inhibitions they had evaporated. They knew now they were destined for each other. It was only a matter of time to get to know each other. Standing there passionately and firmly wrapped up they felt the firm foundation was laid. They could feel all safety mechanisms, all decorum, leaving them and with all they believed in and worked for, they transmitted they were to be one.

"Oh Shilu, oh Shilu, I did not think embracing you would open me up this way. I am embarrassed and elated darling. You feel like you belong to me and I to you. I realize that now," Marius said, utterly surprised too he dared saying it. Shilu smiled understandingly and replied murmuring:

"I felt it in Amsterdam but was too overwhelmed and shy to tell you. I am so glad you feel the same. We will do something about it yes?"

"Of course, there is no way back now. All of you I want to know"

They looked into each others eyes, no words needed now. They walked hand in hand and not too long after they returned to have lunch with Jeanie and the officers, before going to the training track to see both the men and the women. Once there what they saw astounded them. They realized that this was no child play.

"First the men come on and had the assignment to use a rod on their mate they were assigned to. That rod was used to strengthen their mate, how much could the person endure? How much punishment can one take? That was the point. And, when one finished the time, then it was the turn of the victim, the friend," one of the officers who was in charge of their training explained, "the women will do the same, they will in this matter not be treated differently from the men!"

"But this is rather a painful exercise," Jeanie protested.

"What do you think the Indian soldiers will do to you?", he asked looking at Jeanie like she was rather ignorant, "they have to endure if they want to survive and they have to be able to inflict too. This is just training; in reality it could be infinitely worse. So, we tell them that if they can take this, they are capable of taking a lot more."

"It is horrible to see,' Jeanie insisted.

"War and being captured is not a game, you can be tortured and killed," he said, "we have numerous examples."

"Yeah sure," Jeanie replied feeling the true nature of a convinced officer. Seeing Jeanie was far from convinced he continued:

"Look it does not mean we are deliberately hurting anyone. We do not beat up Indians either, but if you know what police and Indians can and will do to any of us and more so how they humiliate our women, you'd be glad and more understanding knowing we prepare them for the worst."

"Well, I did not doubt that, I just feel it is abhorrent to see them beating up the other. They must be bruised by these blows, Jeanie answered, "I find it difficult to see it rehearsed. It looks so real!"

"It is real of course. They have to feel they have to go through their pain barrier," he explained further, relaxed a little now for it was more the actual infliction she could not see, rather than that she was unwilling to understand the need for it.

Marius and Shilu looked on from a vantage point the officers had put them. Two rows they saw each had some 15 young women facing each other now. On the command of the officer they picked the rattan rod up and began to hit on the buttocks of their partner:

"Swweeppplop, klatch, sweeplop," they heard, but other than the sounds of the life in the trees nothing else was heard, no cries of pain, no sighs, no yelling or screaming, but just the sounds of the strokes delivered on the flesh. Until the officer commanded the change and the girl who was hit now was handed the rod to beat up and make her the victim.

"These girls are hard," Shilu commented, "I am not so sure if I can endure that."

"Can you imagine what they can do to a woman or man, when their hatred knows no boundaries? I will help you. Think of your breasts, your ears, your things. When you think there, I am sure you already feel it?"

"Oh gosh yes," Shilu blushed and Jeanie who had been listening shivered.

"This is why we do it," he said as they watched the blows being delivered. The blows could be heard from afar and neither the women nor the men held back. In fact they were ordered to show no mercy when they did. Only 15 minutes later the first woman cried out in despair, still the sign to stop was not given. Five minutes later a very embarrassed pair of young women ran off in shame. They had broken down. At first Shilu and Jeanie thought they were gone to have their pain treated, but no for the officer explained:

"We have to motivate them. You see that lady officer will go after them. They feel they have failed and feel ashamed in front of the others. They are proud but they failed. Now we have to assure them that we cannot get anywhere if we do not accept ourselves, we are all different."

"Sure, but will they eventually be able to endure," Shilu asked.

"Most will, it is a mental capacity they will learn to use to the fullest. In the end no one really fails this test," he said.

"Well it is over now and I found it extremely difficult to see," Jeanie remarked, "it looks so incredibly cruel."

"Yes it is cruel, for who really wants to beat someone cripple? Yet Indians do it, what else can we do but to prepare to the best of our ability?"

"Of course," Marius said, "it must be done, but it reminds me how your people grow up. The circumstances are so unreal. There must be a lot of people with psychological difficulties, with the pain off loss and the pain of being under strain, of not being free while occupied. Yet it does not look to me that the Nagas show any hostility. The people contain themselves, are reasonable and hope and work for a better future."

"Like I described to you in Amsterdam Marius, there are a lot of youngsters who are not capable of that. The youngsters you saw here have a goal. They are being trained for something they believe in. Others face these psychological uncertainties, humiliations and more and see no future."

"Oh yes," the officer now confirmed as they walked back with the two groups, young men and women, some so much in pain they could hardly walk and when they noticed they were being watched, they smiled to cover their pain, "yes those go astray, get hooked on drugs, they run away from home, are bored and without education hang around without something useful to do. So, drugs and aids are menacing our society. This is why we decided to run a rehab camp in the country, not in town, and Shilu works there. So, she is doing for society in practice like what we are doing for it to secure our freedom for all of us. We are all fighting the same war, but with different means," he explained. Once back in the camp and the young men and women back into their barracks where they were being taught how to treat wounds and bruises, gunshot wounds too, they were offered refreshments again. It was something Jeanie could not resist to remark on:

"In comparison to what we have seen just now, I feel you are truly pampering us!"

"We are happy to have you here and please do realize, soldiers are specialists. You are specialist in a different field right?"

"That is right," Marius said, "but do not ask what field because if I tell you, I might have to kill you," he laughed.

That evening after dinner when they were savoring some rice wine, the officers volunteered to tell about the wine before they putting a question of relevance to them:

"Rice wine is used by our army in a more solid form as food and as a stimulator. We carry it with us when we have to cover great distances. Fermented rice we stock in our gear, so we can move fast and practically unseen. Guerillas have to make sure they are elusive, so fires to cook food or villagers who are put under pressure where we would otherwise eat, cannot betray were we are. But let me ask you," the first officer said, "our leader has been assassinated. Nobody has a clue who could have done it. The Indians for the time being have been able to redirect the attention. They say they are innocent and the assassins do not seem to have a motive, but money, are possibly being caught. What do you Marius and Jeanie make of this?"

"Oh, oh, you are asking me something there," Marius answered, "let me see. If you do not mind my thoughts, I think like this," he began, "clearly the assassins were hired. They were professionals and they planned things out. So, the one who handed the contract plotted for something to happen. Your leader was a man of importance, the chairman and so a lot of protest could be expected. Now, who could benefit from this? Everyone looked at India. India wants to frustrate the talks. It could still be the plotters are to be found in the secret services, or those services could have deployed the adversaries of your organizations!"

"You do mean the NNC or the K?", an officer asked.

"Yes, but I don't think so. As you saw the whole Naga people rallied behind your leader. Then I think it could be someone from covert rebellious group in the IB or RAW. I cannot rule that out. Yet I have a gut feeling that the people in Delhi were as surprised as we were. So, that leaves us to look for the outside possibilities. I think there are very few however. But, if you do look outside, who would you suspect," Marius asked.

"I have no idea," the first officer replied. The others were racking their brain but could not come up with an answer either. The double edged Jeanie knew who were involved but not who the plotter could be and she shook her head. Likewise Shilu did, she had no idea where to look either. When Marius saw no one could answer that he said:

"First the British I suspect," and he looked at Jeanie, "there could be some old colonialists who feel very bad and responsible for what is happening here. But even so I think those people are too old now. No I am told some 90% of the Nagas are Christians. Missionaries were forced to leave around 1956 when the war had just begun, right? Love your neighbor is a strong principle. Your leader, was he not a 'Praise the Lord' man? I would not be surprised if we have to look for the plotter in that direction," Marius said.

All of them were stunned, even Jeanie. And, it looked like on there faces it was written: has this Marius gone stark raving mad?

Chapter 11

Delhi days and the net closes

"Delhi days and the net closes," said one of the journalists in the national press club, "good heavens man I think IB and RAW must be fully occupied." he chuckled. And right he was this reporter from the Telegraph, for both the Internal Bureau and the Research Analysis Wing were in a state of anxiety, perhaps worse and more like in a state of disarray, "I am sure there is a lot of talk going on there," he laughed, "oh how I would love to be there now men!"

"I am only too sure they would not lift a tip of their veil to satisfy your curiosity," a journalist of the Hindu along with one of the Statesman laughed with him.

"Ussshh, is there no way we can get in to one of these offices," he joked, "Tehelka got itself in a great deal of trouble when that internet newsmagazine publishes some tapes of corrupt politicians, remember?"

"Like yesterday," the Hindu man laughed, "those were the days."

They rattled on and were talking of who could be behind that assassination, but they simply thought that it could hardly be anyone else but the one of these secretly operating agencies or as the Telegraph man said:

"There is hardly anyone who would go at this great length to delude. This is quite a set up and it needed lots of planning and connections, so a secret service I think is the only real option. And, no other would touch this, no country having more interest in this than our own democratic India!"

He could not have hit more directly on the nail by saying 'I think IB and RAW must be fully occupied', for here in Delhi indeed all were in uproar. The directors had had their instructions and now were in the process to form teams which were assigned to check all and everyone of the two bureaus. All were pretty scared, because where corruption is the rule in all sectors of society it permeates the offices of the IB and RAW. And, of course quite a few planners had played with the thought of taking out a leader of any of the peoples who were seeking to independence from India: The Sikhs, the Kashmiri and yes the Nagas too. In the IB especially there was a unit, containing of three teams who were assigned to churn out plans and test those for feasibility. In fact the IB, through teams like that, was responsible for creating diversions, either by assigning or applying funds in specific places to be used by key people, or to cooperate with renegade troops to provide them with logistics and weaponry. This was done in close cooperation with the higher echelons of the Armed forces of India. Though the control team was directed to start with this planning unit, of course covert operatives did not rule out that the plotter would not be in the obvious places or in this case, offices. Yet, they had to rule out what was obvious first to get to the less obvious. This would take time of course.

The same was true for the RAW but the RAW would receive prime attention from the team, because it had its tentacles all over the world. Through the embassies it could tacitly operate in countries where special attention was required. Since the assassins were foreigners as in not Indians, the plotter could anyone even an Indian plotting from within the walls of an Embassy itself. This is what the team had come up with after a day of assessing what they found about structurally adversely organized secret services. To outsiders it was rather odd but the central Government no doubt had its reasons to have two secret services competing with each other. Perhaps this was so organized because through this type of competitions the two would have to come up with the best of what they harbored in intelligence and resources. The news that both organizations were to be thoroughly checked traveled fast and all over the world. In no time all the operatives were informed, not officially via their ambassadors, but through their own direct sources. Of course these operatives, most of them working as embassy staff but usually of relatively high rank, had their own means of communications and when a directive from Delhi was sent it would bypass the official channels but was delivered to the operative without anyone else knowing about it.

"Okay then," said Milke, his codename, to a clerk of the embassy staff, "get me in touch with London, Amsterdam, Bangkok and New York. I want to set up a five minute phone conference with my counterparts there. When you have made the connections, then leave me alone in my office!"

"Yes Sir," the clerk said and went to work on Milke's request. A few minutes later he had it fixed and after handing the phone to Milke, he left the room.

"Hi Bangkok, are the others present," he said when he heard the voice of his Bangkok friend who responded:

"They are here, you can talk!"

"The Home Ministry suspects us," he began, "I want to know if you know anyone around in Europe or the USA, there are two Europeans involved. What do you know about the Brazilian connection? Should we get in touch with our man there?"

"I have no idea Milke. I have asked my informers. They don't know anything. I am focusing on Manila now. I am sure they know something there. If it has gone through them, our man there I think will know?," the Bangkok RAW man answered.

"Anyone else?", Mike asked and received silence. He waited for about ten seconds then asked further, "how about you in The Hague, or anything from New York?"

"The Hague has nothing unless you suspect the plotter is the speaker," the The Hague man chuckled.

"We are all capable," Milke dryly said, "you included!"

"We don't know what is up here," New York reacted, "but there is some buzzing in some circles. Some think it could have been planned from here to destabilize the Government of India. I think it is far fetched. India poses no immediate threat, though I hear that in longer term the Americans are reckoning India could. Our nuclear power capability gives them a headache and the labor power once tapped and managed well, could overtake the American economy. But are they behind this to destabilize India now? I don't think so," the man said.

"You have some contacts in the Netherlands," Milke pushed, "man we are going to be scrutinized so come clean if you know something, even when you judge it as insignificant I want to know The Hague!!," he stressed.

"My sources who are close to some of the Nagas have no idea. I cannot quite see them doing anything either. I did fry them a little to the point of irritation," he said, "one even told me the organization would cease to talk when we continue to insinuate."

"Plotters, my man, do not tell you they are plotting. It is you who should deduct from what you know how they are. Your," and I am talking to all of you now," Milke said, "your task is to find out if any if your contacts behave differently. We are looking for indications, irregularities in behavior. I am sure the investigators which are being deployed to pick us clean, will target us. They will see us as the plotters until proven not guilty. Now please keep your eyes open and report to me before the investigators come down on you, okay?"

"Yes Sir," the answer came by all of them one by one.

The man in New York at the UNO was wrapped up in thought after the phone conference. Racking his brain in relation to his contacts about the diaspora of Nagas in the USA he was thinking of the butter soft organizations operating there. Primarily cultural organizations, the Nagas themselves were either students or had embedded themselves in getting and holding on to their jobs just like other Americans. Perhaps though, he thought, this inertia had led to more aggressive thinking and one or some of those had brewed up that plan. The problem was he had no leads and so he did not know where to look. Of course some of the Nagas and others, affiliated organizations like the one affiliated to the slain leader and the person in charge was given the title of honorary Ambassador of Nagaland, kept him informed. Directly or indirectly he knew what was brewing up. He knew also very well what the slain leader had done while journeying around with the honorary Ambassador to garner support from primarily the Baptist world of the USA. He decided to dive into that, perhaps the Nagas here in the USA and the Baptists knew more about this?

Jacky picked up the phone and heard an unfamiliar voice.

"Yes who is it you want to speak to?", she asked

"Is Sean with you?" the man asked, "I am a friend, he knows me. You don't. Be kind and get him on the phone"

"What is your name? Who are you?", Jacky asked

"I will tell him, if you don't mind," the man said in a sweet voice.

"Okay then, he can judge himself if you are a friend," Jacky answered and shouted:

"Sean, someone is calling you. It's from New York, darling!!"

"Sean here," he said wondering who that could be and how he found that number.

"I see you still use your old mobile Sean?", the man said.

"Oh, Jerry it is you," Sean said, "why did you not tell who you are to Jacky, my woman?"

"I don't know her and wanted to surprise you," he explained, "listen man!"

"It has been quite a while. Did not know you were still alive," Sean chuckled, "okay man shoot and it better be important."

"What do you know about this assassination in Manila, that Naga leader?", he asked. Hearing that immediately Sean went on high alert and decided to be evasive:

"I read in the papers that leader was quite an important man and the result was that it almost led to an uprising in his land. Also I learned that some Europeans are suspects, no names I could come across," Sean answered.

"So, you do not know the names of Jacky and you were dropped, your movements in Manila and Bangkok have been traced, that a team of Indians is here which is trying to find you and that the Indian Government is embarrassed, plus the fact that the Manila Police thinks you are hired assassins and not the plotters of this thing?"

"Whattttttt," Sean asked, "all that is known?"

"Yes, I am afraid it is," Jerry said.

"Then we are finished, Jacky and I," Sean concluded both with some sorrow because of the idea of getting caught, going to trial and his languishing in jail but separated from Jacky. Jacky and Sean had discussed all inside out and they had come to the conclusion to that if they really wanted to redeem themselves, to purify themselves, giving themselves up for a clean slate and suffer the consequences. Rather than having the chance to give up, now it looked like they were going to get caught. Jacky and he had been discussing how to get to the assigner, the one of the contract, so if they knew at least they could implicate the plotter and so perhaps reduce their sentence when they would present the brain behind this. Sean had gone through all his leads, but in order to find out who it actually was they had to have access to databases of banks, credit cards and other sourced of information. They did not have that, he knew they were limited. The primary lead he had was the note he had received where he was threatened to be exposed as a war criminal if he would not take this contract. Since he was then not yet convinced he should change his life, this only because Jacky had pulled him over the proverbial stumbling blocks, he had taken the contract. Out of fear for his skin perhaps, but then he had felt it was an adventurous thing to do too. This shot through his head when he heard Jerry saying:

"Yes it looks like you will be. How about some help?"

"Help? You can actually help? You can't undo what has been done by us." Sean said.

“That’s right,” Jerry laughed, “I think this was the purpose of the assassination, to deploy you to change things for the Nagas!”

“By killing one of then?”, Sean asked.

“Precisely,” Jerry laughed again.

“How the hell do you know?”, Sean asked in exasperation.

“I know, when you think about it there is no other explanation Sean. The motive to murder that man was to create havoc, confusion and you know as well as I do in times of confusion people can do strange things,” he said and he was clearly referring to the time Sean had gone astray in Rwanda.

“How can you help? If they are on the trail, they will arrest us soon. I am sure the Brazilian government does not mind to extradite us!”

“Yes, you could be right there. How about if you can make them a deal? Give them the plotter?”, Jerry asked.

“We have been trying to find out who it is. That man knows enough about me to have me committed to that act,” Sean answered, “so either he did know about me personally or he had information, perhaps from you, so I could not say no?”

”Hahahahaha, you are quick. Your mind works well still. Yes, it could have been me, but why should I assign you?”, Jerry asked.

“How do I know,” Sean answered angrily now, “sometimes friends turn against you!”

“That happens indeed but it is not what I am after. Listen,” he said again, “when you get the plotter, you will get the motivation. For the plotter I am sure it is very important that the motivation becomes known. He wants change!”

“Even when he gives himself up?”, Sean asked.

“Yes, because he gives himself up, the important implications of the assassination will not die down,” Jerry explained, “well at least that is what I think.”

“How can you hand him to me then and how do I know it is the plotter?”

“You will know,” Jerry smiled, “you do not have to trust me but think Sean. Why should I delude you? You are going to prison anyway and you are not going to take the fall for a plotter. Do you have proof you were coerced?”

“Yes I have the printed note of the contract and the threat of detailed exposure if I would not do it,” he said.

"Okay, there you are then. You might be able to work your way out of this then," Jerry led him to believe.

"Why is it after all this time you want to help me?", Sean asked.

"That is simple Sean; you have been unfortunate in your life. We are friends, even though we do not see much of each other anymore. I wanted to help you out when I came to know it was you who was implicated and now that I know you were coerced I want that more than ever. Now listen carefully."

"Okay," Sean said

"Well then. By DHL you will receive an envelope today by flight if you give me your address, or post office box number. No, I will make it much simpler to you. Do you have access to email?"

"Yes," Sean answered quickly.

"Then give the email address to me now!", he said making it sound like a command, "I will send you all the information you need."

Sean gave him two email addresses and asked:

"What is your role in this?"

"I will tell you when the time comes," Jerry said, "get the plotter and a new chapter will begin. Stress the idea you were coerced and you both will go almost free, okay?"

"Okay," Sean reacted, feeling overwhelmed as he heard the click of the phone knowing that Jerry had disconnected. Sean looked at the puzzled face of Jacky. Though he knew from the Manila investigation that they were on the trail, they had already come to terms with that and were living in bliss. Let's pick the day, carpe diem, Sean remembered he had said to Jacky as they again embraced and were taken in by their intimacy. Let's enjoy what we have for soon that will be over. I will stand by you my dear Jacky, always; he had assured her and had been able to take her fears away being with him. This bliss was now disturbed. This new development could lead to a few consequences they had no control over, no grip on. Her face a question mark, Sean quickly filled her in with what he had talked about with Jerry:

"So, all in all, if Jerry keeps his word, we will expose the plotter and because I have this paper, we can motivate our acts as having done them under duress," Sean said.

"Oooohhhhhh that is good news Sean. Instead of a life sentence, the worst, now we may get much less, perhaps we will be free again in a year or two?"

Sean just smiled and walked over to his laptop to get access to his email. After it had started up he checked both addresses, found the message in one of them and cried out:

“Oh gosh Jackie, I never thought it would have come from that angle!”

“What do you mean?”, she eagerly asked.

“Well it looks like it might be someone who is affiliated to the Baptists in the USA!”

“Really? I can’t hardly believe it, how can these God fearing people be involved?”, she cried out.

I do not know, but I am sure the motivation will be exposed,” he answered, pondering what this would really mean.

“It cannot be a Baptist organization,” Jacky said then, “although in Amsterdam there were a few who were frequent visitors of the Bordello and they came on recommendation of others. They really know what they want and by coming to the Bordello they made sure they were not seen publicly in their own USA. That makes me realize these people can be quite sneaky too.”

“Oh Jacky, going to a high class prostitute to do forbidden things is quite different from planning a murder and to force somebody to commit it while planning the demise of the Indian Government and perhaps the Indian state too?”

“Of course, but what I am saying is that they are not to be trusted. Like normal people they have their flaws,” she said.

“Yes you have a point there,” he said, “now let’s think. We must assess what is better darling. To turn ourselves is here, which may not be that easy for nobody here knows about what happened in Manila and they cannot prosecute us here for that, or we wait till the Indians find us.”

“I don’t want to wait for the Indians,” she strongly reacted, “who knows what they are going to do. Perhaps kill us even!”

“No, no, we are their vindication. With us and later when we reveal the real culprit, the planner, they are sure to become heroes even?”

“Heroes?”, Jacky asked.

“For keeping their cool, for their swift reactions, for statesmanship yes, I am sure they like to bank on what will transpire,” he smiled, “but I agree I think we have more control if we indeed turn ourselves in.”

The effects of Christianity and missionary work was the title of an article by the Scorpion he had submitted to the conference and that afternoon a lively discussion on the topic took place in New York. The

Scorpion was happy. Not only did the accountability he had worded in that article come to be discussed, he also had informed Sean. So soon things would be moving again. Of course the Indians would think they were being let off and they would beat their chest with pride. But they had a thing coming to them still, he knew and smiled.

"Accountability for what, for bringing the Good News and then a no thank you Ma'am but planting the idea on us to take care of all of those who have become Baptists?", commented one of the participants, a man of high stature, a man like Baterson, but from another state. The Scorpion thought to react but when doing so already another fired back and it became a real lively exchange of thoughts. The Scorpion thought then when the ideas were exhausted to round up and summarize to where he wanted the participants to go, but did not intervene yet:

"I pretend that you did not actually mean that. Do you know what happened in 1956 with the Nagas? How they were abandoned by us," he asked, "I am not talking theory here, but practice. I think if we want to convert people to what we believe in, we at least could show them a good example?"

"What do you mean, who are the Nagas," the man asked immediately.

"In the early 19hundreds our forebears went over to the Naga Peoples and spread Baptism. Today more than 80% of the people are Christian."

"We must have done a good job then," the man said approvingly

"Yes a very good job, but the Nagas were colonized by the British and when the British left, India took over, in spite of the known fact that the Nagas did not want to be part of India. They said this so many times, but the British were did not listen."

"What is wrong for them to be part of India?", he asked as the Scorpion grinned.

"That is not really the point and really up to them, but to tell you briefly it was like this; the Nagas were never conquered and a great part of them was never colonized. They thought simply like this; when the British leave we are free of them, we have nothing in common with India and we can look after ourselves."

"Fair enough," the man said.

"Yes, but after some insistence and negotiating which failed and after their Homeland was divided by two nations; India and Burma, the Indian troops were ordered to occupy the Naga Homeland."

"This happened? Yes that sounds bad!", he reacted.

"It gets worse, for the Nagas put up fierce resistance and created a guerilla army to contained the Indian Armed Forces, of which Prime

Minister Nehru of India thought and said it would be a matter of days only to crush , but he could not conquer them."

"So, they fought back?", the man asked.

"Yes, and that angered the Indians, so much so they set fire to villages, killed, raped and whatever you can think of. And now it comes," he said, "the Indians blamed the American Baptists for the resistance of the Nagas. They figured that our forebears had taught them to stand up against India and true or not that was, they told the Baptists to leave India. Mind you the war was on and many Nagas perished."

"And you are saying those Baptists left and returned to the USA?" he asked.

"Precisely," he answered and let it sink in. All present, some of the women too, shook heads and thought this could not be true.

"Why don't we know anything about this? This seems to be an important part of our history," a middle aged woman volunteered.

"Well, it is hard to say, but I hear it was a matter of politics," the man answered.

"What, politics? You better explain that man!", the woman insisted.

"It is understandable to an extent," he continued, "you see we had a number of missions in India at the time. The Baptists left for they were afraid the other missions would suffer the consequences."

"So they left to save their missions elsewhere but left those who were at peril?", she asked kind of at loss.

"To make a long story short, yes they did and the war rages till today. The Nagas are still resisting the Indian invasion and for the second time they have a cease fire, one that lasts a decade now and the peace talks are held in Europe or South East Asia."

"What are we doing then for them?", the lady asked.

"As far as I know we did nothing! In fact not so long ago one of their leaders was here to try to get some support. It is the same one who was recently murdered in Manila, assassinated. Everyone suspects the Indians are behind this, but I wonder!"

"Wait, wait," the lady interrupted, "why when the man was here did we not do anything? I can think of a few things already."

"Yes, I can imagine, for instance when they had returned they could have shown the case of the Nagas to the American public. They could have moved our political leaders to question the Indian government. They could have taken the Nagas out of their isolation, but we did not!", he concluded.

"Was this a policy to keep this under the rug?", the lady persistently asked.

"I cannot answer that," the man said, "to be honest? I do not know.

"This is strange,' said another lady, especially when I know now that their leader was here and has not been properly entertained by us. What Baptists are we if we leave our brothers and sisters when they are in need?", she said as she looked around the table to meet the eyes of the other participants. They had no answer too, but felt the Baptists of the USA had something to think about now. Seeing that the discussion had come to an end but without a conclusion for action, the Scorpion then spoke:

"Yes it is rather strange now that we know this I think and propose we should take some action. This I think is a stain on our record, but it is not too late to do something about it," he said and did wait a moment to let it this digest.

"But what can we do?", the lady asked.

"Well I think you go can go back to where you came from and spread the news on the Nagas. To raise attention, begin with the assassination and show that this is a result of neglect, a result of what happens when we do not take our tasks in life seriously. When we all do this, we will become like an oil spill on water and we will spread like wildfire. We should get support in money too, arrange solidarity dinners, and inform politicians, radio and TV-stations, newspapers. Let's make some news," the Scorpion suggested.

"Those may be sound ideas, but we don't know anything about the Nagas and their history and how they relate to the USA!"

"If you like we can provide you with materials. Why not form a committee, so you can stay in touch and I will make sure you will be provided with all the materials you need. Let's work together on this and do so officially?", the Scorpion proposed as he too looked around the room now to see who would be in or who was copping out. An hour later the committee was formed and he was talking to the man who was knowledgeable on the Nagas, a man named Chris:

"I have never understood why we as Baptists don't feel the responsibility we teach through our religion," Chris explained, "and I feel very much that we have let the Nagas down tremendously. The problem is that nobody wants to here about them. To me it feels there are some ashamed Baptists in the higher circles who do not want to be remembered for having made mistakes," he said.

"I feel quite similar Chris," the Scorpion said. Speaking on this some of the others of the discussion gathered around them, "what we preach we should do right?"

"Right," Chris said, "we cannot be just opportunists. This is why I was happy with your paper, because as an example I could bring the Nagas in. I did not expect to get such following and thank you all," he said when he noticed the gathering around them.

"We are inspired Chris, we are going to do something and from you," she said, "we want to gather all you know, publications and such. I think we should make a press kit. Shall we organize this?"

"Good idea," Chris said enthusiastically, "let's exchange addresses and plan a meeting. Now that we know a leader of the Nagas has been murdered, one that was here, we should get an angle with the press on that!"

"Right," one of the ladies said, "let's get to it!"

On the road in Nagaland they were again, Marius, Jeanie and Shilu. Since they were busy by themselves trying to review the experiences of the last two days, as they were driving through the valleys they were not talking much but felt the mountain scenery. Jeanie was thinking how she could come to terms with the situation she was in. Sean was to be arrested soon and she should have an opportunity to talk this over with the bureau in London. She remembered that the British Government had shunned the remnants of the Naga national Council where it could have helped this Naga Organization led A.Z. Phizo, the revered leader of the NNC, but for unknown reasons to her, neglected to do so. There was still an office of the NNC in London which after the death of Phizo, was presided over by his daughter Adinno Phizo, now president of the NNC. Though Jeanie knew about the Nagas, Britain, the United Kingdom, had had so many post colonies to deal with, that this problem of the free nation India, did not catch much attention at all. Since Nagaland was really off limits for most, the leaders of the UK did not feel compelled to make it an issue. So, consequently in her work she had had nothing to do with it. Neither had Marius! But for the remote past the Netherlands after all had had nothing to do with India or Burma at all. More so in the present though, for although the peace talks were held tacitly, the secret service AIVD was informed of course. Living in exile and only using Indian passports for going to India itself, the Naga leaders stayed in the Netherlands often. Marius had actually never met them, but for pictures and he would enable him to pick them out of a line-up easily. Out of interest, he thought, it was a feat in itself such a small and divided nation could keep such a big country with hundreds of thousands of soldiers occupied. Not for a week, a month or a year, but for over fifty years now. He admired them and had read up on their history. In that sense Marius actually knew more than Jeanie. Shilu had told him more about the actualities and before he set foot on Naga soil, he had brushed up to study the history too. Now with Jeanie in Nagaland Marius felt in more ways than one torn between interests. Being with Jeanie would have been nice, if he had not met Shilu. That was one, he thought, two was he sensed that Jeanie had something up her sleeve was and he was not used to that from her. Three was the reality of what he had witnessed and four of course the assassination and its consequences. Slowly now a picture began to form as to where Jeanie and him should look for the motivation of the plotter, hence to find the plotter himself. What bothered Marius though was that Jeanie did not share what she thought or perhaps knew and it bothered him. Shilu increasingly felt Jeanie had become a disturbing factor. She needed more time with Marius, she was certain of that, but how? She fancied that, once she would be in the rehab camp with him or in Mokokchong or in a village, they would have more time to talk. Yes to talk, she thought, for she wanted tell Marius a few things, which were only meant for his ears, no, not about some intimacy. That she was convinced they had already, no she needed to tell him more about the factions, the prime reason to go to Mokokchong. She wanted Marius to meet some K group Nagas. But, before all this Shilu felt like introducing Marius and Jeanie to village life.

As they were driving along, flanked by the mountains on both sides dotted with villages perched on the tops, Marius and Jeanie were in awe with the scenery and bored Shilu and the young cadres with their oohhhh's and aaaahhh's.

"Perhaps we should go and just drive into a village now," Shilu suggested, "that way we come unannounced and the people will not have prepared anything. You can experience village life as it is!"

"Good idea," Jeanie said enthusiastically, the young men smirked.

"Which one Shilu?", the driver asked, "we are in not yet in Ao territory. I think this is Sumi area?"

"It does not matter, any village will do. Do you like to decide for yourselves?", she asked them, "you may have preferences, like one that overlooks a valley?"

"I have no particular idea," Marius laughed, "it is all interesting to me. At random will be an experience. Oh but what do I see there in the distance? Is that a village?", he asked. The driver looked up and seeing what Marius meant without a further word left the main road to follow a sign which lead over an unpaved road up to a village.

"Oh, you are going there!", he said as they steeply went up now. They felt the traction of jeep as it was much noisier. They passed fields and terraces and both Marius and Jeanie looked on. Then they passed the gate of the village which had protective statues in front of it. There were also commemorative megaliths which made Marius remark:

"I would like a closer look at them and talk to some villagers about their meaning!"

"Oh, that can be arranged," Shilu smiled, she was happy knowing that Marius took interest in the cultural heritage of her people.

When they stopped before the traditional house of the headman, already a number of children had gathered around the jeep. Curious but apprehensive they stood there and looked when they stepped out of the jeep to meet the leader of the village. Shilu was to ask his permission to visit the village and perhaps to stay overnight as well.

"Greetings to you all," the older man said when he had come out of the house hearing the noise, "what is your mission," he asked smiling.

Shilu introduced them in Nagamese, the language Marius and Jeanie did not understand and explained what they had come for. Then in English, because the slain leader was from his tribe on behalf of them she offered him their condolences.

"Thank you so much, yes this is very unfortunate. I don't hope this will get us in a lot of trouble, though it looks like it," he said.

"Yes, now all is focused on who is behind it," Shilu replied.

"Yes, we have entered a twilight and we must see to it we will go beyond it!"

"Yes, beyond twilight," Marius repeated, "is that not when the Nagas will actually become free again?"

"You are right," the village headman said, "it has been so long now. Who knows this occurrence will lead us beyond it?", he asked and Marius saw curious villagers walking towards the centre of the village.

"Do you think we could stay here for the night," Jeanie asked, "I would like to see the fields and the villagers working in them this afternoon."

"Yes, see the megaliths and listen to some stories by the elders in the evening," Marius suggested.

"And drink rice wine?". Shilu laughed.

"Yes perhaps hear what people have experienced from the Indians too and the village state democracy way of government?", Marius said now looking at the headman again:

"All that you want to do in one day?", he remarked and laughed.

"May be not all, but at least you know what he have come for?" Jeanie said.

"We will see what we can do for you. You are welcome in my house but I cannot have all five of you. I can tell you about the village governing; others can take you to the fields and around the village."

"That is most hospitable of you," Marius told him.

"Come inside, I am sure my wife will prepare a drink for you. No Shilu not yet rice wine, but if you like I can arrange it for tonight. It is going to cost you some money though, he laughed.

"I am delighted to buy and not just for us," Marius said, "I am overcome by your hospitality, allow me to buy rice wine for all adults in the village?"

"You are a very lucky man," the Headman laughed, "most of the men are out. Quite a few are with the Naga Army also, so we have mainly women and older men here. This is not going to cost you much after all," he smirked.

"But we will have a few drinks tonight then," Marius asked.

"Oh yes, I will personally see to it we will have enough to spend the evening together," he laughed, "but now it is coffee time."

They went inside and some twenty people followed them with their eyes. Enjoying their coffee served by the smiling wife of the Headman Marius, excited now, asked:

"I have read so much about the Naga culture before I came, so I would very much like to know if you still have a morung here and a log drum."

"Well, this is an old village and we are in the process of reviving the morung and what it stands for, learning to become a man and a warrior but now in the modern sense of the word. I am afraid I cannot help you with a log drum Mr. Marius, but a nearby village has one if you like to see?"

"That would be nice; one of your people can take us there tomorrow?"

"I will ask around for that too," he said, "you know how to assign a Headman Mr. Marius," he chuckled.

"I am anxious," Marius announced after they had finished their coffee, "to go out and experience your village."

"Then let's go," Shilu hooked in, "can you find us an old man who could take us to the new morung and who can tell about the megaliths?, "she asked the Headman.

"I have just the man for you," he replied, "wait a moment I ask if he can come," and he signaled one of his daughters to fetch him. Just fine minutes later a very old man came to meet them, a man old indeed but with cheeky eyes.

"It is a pleasure," he said in good English, "I served for the British in the war and the battle of Kohima against the Japanese," he smiled, "so I know some English still."

"Good man," Marius answered, "Jeanie do you want to come?"

"I rather see the fields," she said, "thinking of a way to be alone so she could phone around with her mobile, "I like to see how these terraces are made and what is actually grown there too," she explained.

"Okay, we are quite safe here I think?"

"Oh," the Headman said, "the next Army camp is two villages over there," and he pointed to a window towards the north, "so you are very safe indeed."

"Then who could accompany me?", Jeanie asked. The daughter smiled and took Jeanie by the hand. The driver, who had been patiently waiting, followed them outside. The old man winked to signal he was going to lead them out too. Marius and Shilu followed and they walked over to a newly built traditional house, the morung.

"I am so sorry we do not have a real one anymore," he said.

"Is this one built like they were in the old days?", Marius asked

"More or less," he answered, "like we remember them. I have the strong feeling though that in the past a morung was larger. Or could it be this is because I was much smaller then, a boy?", he wondered aloud.

"Is it being used already," Shilu asked.

"No, not yet, but soon, we are preparing to decorate it in the traditional style, including the ornaments and heads," he explained.

"The heads?", Marius asked.

"Yes we still have some heads from the Japanese times," he smiled, "those were the last of what the British called our headhunting days. To us of course it was not like that. I remember we fought with a neighboring village. When someone died in this fight, the victors will take the head. We believed then the head is the seat of the soul, the spirit. This soul matter is not lost but will be part of our village and the slain adversary is honored because of this. The head of the victim is honored and it enriches our village. The morung is the place where the heads were kept and young men grow up here from boys to men. This is the place where they slept and the elders would teach the younger generations," he solemnly said.

"Just the British called that headhunting?", Marius asked further.

"Well, to us it was normal that the life force would not be lost. The British were much less respectful. They killed people to subdue them and did not care for them. They dumped the vanquished, only paid tribute to their own slain people. So, what can I say, but that we found them brutal? They would condemn Nagas who resisted and when they were captured they would convict them to death, they executed them as they called it. So, what is that? How would you call that?"

"Yeah," Shilu said, "how would the Dutch call that?"

"I believe my ancestors did the same when they encountered similar practices in Borneo or the land of the Papuans. I think those who were powerful called the shots over the tribal peoples. They experienced a culture clash. They put what they saw against their own practices and determined the cutting off of a head as barbaric. They made that known and not the meaning behind it. I think that is how the idea of headhunting was born, as if you people were hunting for heads?"

"No, but it is true that we fought against other villages and other villages against us."

"Villages amongst each other, so they were of the same tribe?", Marius asked.

"Indeed, I cannot remember anyone talked about tribes fighting each other, which rivalry is of more recent date. It was not in our traditions."

"So, it happened only among villages and within one tribe?"

"Yes, that is how I recall it," he said, "of course it was an honor to be the owner of a head and it could be that this was what the British understood as headhunting. We highly valued the heads and the men who took them. Women liked warriors, so if they could get one who had taken a head that man was quite a catch," he smirked.

"I understand much better now how the British and the Dutch could come to the idea of headhunting," Marius laughed, "but may I tell you about a type of headhunting which exists nowadays, but has no connection to your cultural past?"

"You have headhunters too?", Shilu asked, taking the words from the mouth of the old man.

"Yes we have and they operate like this," he smiled, a big company needs some specialists, organizers or managers. They usually have specialized people working if the unit called personnel department, or as they say in modern terms, human resource department. Rather than finding a suitable person for the specialized job, these companies hire a specialist to find them someone who has both the experience and the expertise, for the right price of course. They call these specialists headhunters."

"Yes looking for brains and soul matter too," the old man laughed.

They went inside where there was a hall with a fireplace. The walls were decorated with images and ornaments, likewise on the floor and especially in the corners, carved stools and many other things of value, old too. The morung did smell new, so much so that you could sense no one had slept here yet.

"Now it looks more like a museum," Shilu giggled.

"Yes, soon the first batch of youngsters will come to live here and we will have a big feast to inaugurate this new morung," he smiled, "you should try to be here then Marius and Shilu. It would be very much a nice occasion!"

"You want to see the megaliths and hear a story about them?", Shilu asked then after they had looked around well enough.

"Good idea, lead the way," Marius agreed.

"Okay, you follow me now," the old man laughed and he walked off, steady and sturdy pace. That did remind Marius about what Shilu had told him once about the long walks over the mountain trails and down to the valleys.

"You must have some stamina and very good legs," he remarked, "your stride is still strong. Could you still go from village to village, from valley to valley?"

"It is more difficult now, so I do not go far anymore, but I do miss the long walks, these are good for body and mind," he said as they approached one of the stones erected for a purpose.

"There is a story," Shilu said.

"I can tell," the old man smiled.

"I am sure," Shilu agreed," I have told him something when I was in his country!"

"Makes it easier for me," he said cheekily.

"Okay, you go ahead then," Shilu smirked, "you know much better than me!"

"You flatterer, we will see about that," he smiled then began, "it is a long story but for your sake I will tell a very short version. In the very old days and nobody knows for certain our people came from the North, Tibet, now China and they came into these hills and built a life. Thousands of years ago when they lived in what now is called Manipur and in the Sagaing district of Burma, first they spread out from there to move and live in what became known as the Nagas Hills," he said as he touched the large megalith in front of them. Later in a place called Mahkel also the Nagas there decided to leave that place and spread out too. They built their villages, like this one on the hilltops, so the people could overlook the valleys and built their defense against intruders."

"Yes even from your own tribe, right?", Marius asked.

"Yes, that's right, but let me tell you that in Mahkel the people before they dispersed planted a tree and put up a megalith in commemoration to that important event. This event, or rather these two events are so important because it means that all Naga tribes come from the same root, we share the same ancestors and we believe that one day we will all come together again."

"Oh, that sounds like the forming of a nation. Is this what binds the Nagas in their struggle against India to be free?", Marius asked.

"I know we differ and I know we want to be together," he said, "and I am sure because of the pressure we endure this feeling of belonging together is strong, we know it is within us. So, you may be right when you say that this standing up for us may have been motivated because of this simmering feeling of togetherness. When the need to come together is great, we feel we have to come together as one."

"I understand that there are certain parties who do not like to unite?", Marius remarked.

"There are many reasons why these people and organizations do what they do, but I am no expert in that. I can tell you only that all villages express themselves in stone to commemorate important events," he said

"Skillfully and with great artisanship these stone ornaments are made Marius," Shilu added as the old man nodded.

"There is so much more to tell but let's return, we can do some stories in the evening when we are having rice wine?", he asked and winked.

"Lets go and walk into the fields and look for Jeanie?", Shilu suggested.

"Oh yes the terraced fields yes. I should like to take some pictures too," he answered.

"Take some children with you the old man suggested, they will show you the way and most likely know where your friend is too.

"Good thought," Shilu said but then the old man cocked his head, looked at Shilu straight then at Marius. Suddenly he broke out in a smile and said to both of them:

"Do you know you like each other? Perhaps you are even in love? Or, is it you are trying to hide that from me. I am not so sure now!"

Marius looked at Shilu and smiled, Shilu burst out in laughing as she said, hand before her mouth:

"Is it that obvious uncle?"

"If an old man can see that, what do you think?", he smiled.

"For the cause of the RAP I came to Nagaland with my wife," Marius said,

"You can deceive the Indians perhaps, but I can see in a Naga woman who she likes," he laughed out loud now.

"Well don't tell anybody else then," Shilu laughed along with him.

"Come I will fetch you some youngsters," he suddenly said and paced off. Marius and Shilu, briefly holding hands, followed him.

The boys and girls did not hesitate when the old man asked them to accompany Shilu and Marius and soon they were on their way down and entered the paths to the terraces. Playful the children were as they were elated to show them around. It was the time of year that the rice was growing and although not ripe enough for harvesting, it must have been close to it, the stalks were already turning yellow. In the fields they saw the shape of the terraces built like earthen walls and they must have been hand made for heavy equipment was nowhere to be seen. What was seen and when the children told them they saw it too, was the fish that were raised in the water of the growing and ripening rice.

"Yes fish to eat and shells in the water of the terraces," said a young boy and he pointed out what he meant. They could see for miles and could look straight down into the valley up to the next hill. There they saw a village too and left and right but miles away there were more. It was a lovely sight and they were lucky too for the weather was fine. Marius produced a camera and began clicking. The boys and girls with their enthusiastic faces wanted to be shot too and Marius did not quite want to pass on that opportunity.

"What a pity that we can't be alone here Shilu," Marius said as he pictured her too, "I want to take you in my arms and make love here and now," he smiled.

"A lovely idea," she agreed, "I am sure our time will come. Here we have to be composed, for we do not know if there are any snitches who might tell an Indian that we are to be arrested for having lied about the real connection. You are not married to Jeanie, just on paper, but I am sure the old man would have told you the same about her!"

"What do you mean now," he asked not sure but a hunch he had.

"Well, it is obvious to me that she wants you man?", she simply said as they were watching the sun now in setting mode.

"I thought so too at times and once I thought I should do something about it, but Shilu you came at the right time and place and now there is no alternative but to be with you!!"

This was quite a revelation and Shilu blushed. Now it was out in the open and though she felt quite similar, she had not expected that this Marius, who was puzzling still, could say such far reaching thing to her. Oh she had developed much more than ordinary liking for him. Just the idea that he had come to see her here in Nagaland, that he was true to his word, that he was genuinely interested in the Nagas too, was all very much as she had hoped for. But, now that he was here, he had to keep up some appearance and in contrast to what she had liked, because of Jeanie; they could not spend much time together. This moment together here on the sloping terraces she knew she would savor and when she looked at Marius, she knew he would too. He had chosen to say these words to her when they were in her own environment. A woman of sound mind though Shilu answered him:

"You are a romantic man Marius and there are things you do know nothing about. Let's use the time given to us to get to know each other very well?"

"But of course," Marius smiled, "this is the main reason why I came."

An hour later, with the children practically pulling both of them to return to the village, Shilu and Marius walked back to leave the sunset behind them. They had to pull themselves away because the twilight so overwhelmingly part of them was something the children saw every day, Shilu and Marius wanted to just sit, talk and feel the mountains they were now part of. This made Shilu say:

"The tranquility of this unspoiled nature I do miss when I am with the addicts or when I am traveling. I sit and stare and think often but it is of so different when I am with you, now it feels profound, complete."

His heart jumped and he had squeezed her hand as a sign of unity and now while walking up the hill as they both had completely forgotten where Jeanie was, they knew and felt they were in awe of each other.

That evening after a hearty Naga meal, hot and spicy, for the Headman insisted Marius and Jeanie were to taste the King chilly, considered to be the hottest chilly on earth, the rice wine did flow as promised. And, in and around the house of the Headman quite a few villagers had gathered to drink with these strangers. Stories came out, the ones of old times from even-before the Americans had come to baptize the Nagas, but also of the daring times of standing up against the British. An older woman answered Marius thoughtfully when he had asked her:

"Were you there when the Indians invaded?"

She had replied with a lengthy story which was one that had covered the first six years of the brutal days of conquest and resistance. She had lost many friends, relatives:

"And not just because the Indian soldiers killed our own men, no, because they ruthlessly would set fire to villages and smoke people out. The people, like me, had to run in to the forests, our crops were burned and many died of disease and hunger. We kept ourselves alive with what we found in the forest. We built temporary homes made of leaves."

It was a heartbreaking story, one that she and others had experienced, but she told it off hand, as a matter of fact, without the idea of complaining about how all had abandoned the Nagas. The Headman knowing all these stories too but those from later years of the seventies with the Shillong Accord and the eighties of the K-group and Indian divide and rule tactics told some as well. But not for long as he proclaimed:

"This is a joyful gathering, let's not look back in anger and only to count our losses, let's look to the future and thank the Lord for these moments together. By the grace of God this man Marius is here and bought from us this wonderful rice wine. Let's toast to his health and on that of his wife Jeanie," he proposed, knowing fully well that Jeanie was not really his wife but that Shilu was nearer to him. After the toasting in which many participated, it was Jeanie's turn to be in full focus. The young and middle aged men, especially those who were single involved Jeanie in the conversation and tried to make her drink some more of the rice wine.

Jeanie was quite taken by the scenery she had chosen to be in, if only to be away from the others for a while and to take her chance to make some calls. When she had decided on a spot in the fields and showed that she wanted to be alone, her guides had returned to the village knowing that it was just a short distance, so she could go back by herself. Relieved, she had called the London Office first; collect, because I would be quite an expensive affair otherwise.

"Okay, as long as it does not backfire on us and our neglect for the cause, just go ahead," the superior in the London office said after she had briefly told him what the situation was according to what she knew.

"Do you think then the plotter could be one of us," she asked.

"Nothing seems to be impossible," he answered, "more than fifty years of silence have passed, the men involved there then had heart for the Nagas. But they are old now and I don't think anyone of those will have the power to plan and execute it. But, perhaps a son or daughter could have been inspired? Do you know this David Ward?," he asked.

"No, no, I have heard his name once or twice. Is he not the one who began a support organization?"

"Yes Naga Vigil,' he answered but quite defunct now after he was arrested for the second time and in a prison in Dimapur for some time. He was charged with overstaying and perhaps inciting Nagas. He was freed and returned to Britain.

"That sounds like someone who could have a grudge and so could be motivated?" , Jeanie suggested.

"True, but he would not have the resources, unless the assassin was a Naga or one with enough funds to hire one," he explained.

"A Naga?", Jeanie asked, surprised now.

"Yes, I am told the man is married to a Naga who is close to the K, so it might be that the K and so indirectly the Indians are behind it, but now using the K for that."

"Is that not a little too far fetched?"

"No, I don't think so. The RAW especially but IB too do act quite independently sometimes. They even fight each other, just like in politics when even in the Government itself the different powers from left to right and from hawks to doves fight it out behind the scenes. I am told there is a clean up going on, ordered by the Home Minister, but I think the minister of Foreign Affairs, by the way he just returned from Manila, will prevent the opening of their hidden agendas. So, who knows?"

"But this means the British are free of meddling in the Naga and Indian Affairs, there was no assassination plotted from our circles?", Jeanie asked.

"That is what it looks like," he said.

"Any indication where else I should look?"

"We are trying to find out. Perhaps we know more when the Indians have arrested that Sean of ours? He was the one with the contract and is currently in Rio with the assassin."

"They will be caught and later we can question them then?" she asked.

"I would think so," he said, "but there is not much more I know now. Let's keep in touch. Have a nice time in those beautiful hills," he concluded with envy in his voice.

While Jeanie was thinking about what he said, she dialed the number of Sean. This one could not be collect, so she had to make the conversation to the point and snappy.

"Hi Sean," she began, "I understand they are hot on your trail?"

"Yes we will be caught and turned in," he laughed.

"What?", Jeanie reacted.

"Yes there is a possibility for vindication," Sean said, "the one I got the contract from; the plotter wants to come out."

"To be caught and put away?", Jeanie had asked.

"Yes," Sean said, "he does that because he thinks the effects of the assassination are not going the way he wants them to go."

"He told you what he wanted?", she asked.

"No, but he said it will be obvious that we are let off with a very limited sentence!"

"Really? How?," Jeanie asked.

"Well, my dear Jeanie, he used the Rwanda experience on me and so I could not say no. He coerced me of course and he says he will reveal that too!"

"Where does that leave Jacky?"

"I will take full blame and will say in turn I threatened to expose her too, so she could hardly refuse!", Sean explained.

"Okay, this may work, but does the man hope to achieve by having him arrested while he may face the death penalty? Is he in the USA?"

"I am not too sure but I think he is," Sean replied, "but I think that is not of importance. This is not a government contact with motivation that can be scrutinized. No, I think this is thought up by a small organization or person who feels the Indo-Naga conflicts is a wound hurting mankind and it is ignored. I feel that is what is bothering him and he planned to change this."

"Thank you Sean," Jeanie said, "this is costing a fortune, so I will hang up now man. Keep me posted?"

"Sure will," he said before she broke the connection. Jeanie was thinking about what she had heard and knew. She wondered if the plotter would come after her 'giver her up' too so to speak. After all it was Jeanie who had laid contact with Sean so the contract could actually been given to him. Yes, the plotter could and would not hesitate either, for she knew now that all actors in this plot had been used by the plotter and all had something against them, so this would make it easier for him or her to get any one of them to cooperate, this included Jeanie of course. That evening she kept the info from Marius but was figuring out the implications as she, with the others, had some rice wine.

"Man," she had said to the Headman, "this is pretty strong. I am feeling tipsy already, but it is nice and sweet, may I have some more?"

She was served and because Jeanie did feel she wanted to have time to herself she did not mind. She knew by now Marius had chosen for Shilu which to her was another reason to get a little tipsy."

"Don't drink too much," Shilu warned her, "the rice wine has different qualities and when it is sweet you do not realize its potency," she explained.

Jeanie did not take this pleasantly, she felt belittled and shot back:

"Oh Shilu I am a woman with experience, you don't need to look after me!"

They both left it that that but Jeanie especially knew and Shilu felt that she had overshot herself. Now she had to find a way to show she was not normally like this, for Shilu could think she had just done that out of jealousy. So, Jeanie drank more and was looked after by a few young men, one in his thirties who quite openly showed his admiration for her. Now it was Marius who from a distance saw how Jeanie, who liked the looks of this Naga warrior, flirted with him.

Nagas sleep early and get up early too. So, the party did not last very long. The villagers had a lot of work to do in the fields and they were installing the morung as well, the inauguration of which would take place in less that two weeks. So, it must have been around ten or so when the Headman announced they were all ready for bed. Jeanie a little drunk was still being courted by the Naga, though this could have been her fantasy only too. Marius and Shilu were still talking to the older lady to hear first hand what had happened during the initial years of the war.

"You will have other Nagas who were there then to talk to you about this," she smiled when Marius expressed he wanted to hear more from her, "Shilu told me you are going to other villages?"

"Yes, indeed," Marius smiled, "but I learned one must forge the iron when it is hot?"

"Indeed," she laughed seeing how Jeanie was helped to get to a bed and smiled some more, "she is turning into a Naga too! Who knows there may be another time, but I am sure you will find other people on the way who can tell you more," she concluded.

Early morning after a full thanking session they were off again. The two young men had slept somewhere else and had not taken part in the drinking as, for obvious reasons, that was forbidden for Naga soldiers on duty. So, down they went and after they reached the main road again soon afterwards were going up again to the next village, the one with the log drum. As they passed the gate and the first houses soon appeared they saw the houses here were less modern. There were even a few traditional ones and Marius said:

"I will take some pictures here."

Jeanie acted like nothing had happened and nobody had talked about her getting a little more than tipsy. Only Marius had smiled to her when he had referred to the admiration she had received from the Naga man as he asked:

"Well Jeanie? Did you fancy him?"

"Of course I did, quite courteous a wooer he was," she smiled and Marius knew that she had herself under control again. Marius was the first one to jump out of the jeep and he had a group of children around him in no time. Some women came to greet them and when the Nagas soldiers told them what they had come for:

"Oh you like to see our log drum? Oh yes, we will take you to our morung,: she smiled, "it is a young men's dormitory so women are not really welcomed," she explained but now laughing.

"You better send a man along then," Shilu laughed with her.

"Yes, a man," Jeanie smirked.

"Oh, but no ladies allowed inside," the woman smiled too.

"What are you saying?", Jeanie looked angry rolling her eyes.

"Well, it is a young men's house," she said still laughing, "but let's see the Headman and may be you can ask his permission. You are visitors, he may make an exception?"

"We must be humble of course," Marius laughed with them wholeheartedly, "come let's go and see him?"

He did not have to say that twice and they followed her to the Headman. The children already had alarmed him and he stood in front of his traditional house when Marius approached him:

"Good day to you, the children are telling me you want to see the log drum?"

"Oh yes," Marius answered, "but would you mind making an exception for the ladies?"

"When I can be sure you will not desecrate the sanctity of the old morung in which the log drum is housed, then you may," he said, and to make sure you will not I shall come along with you!"

"That is excellent," Jeanie said, "but of course we will not do anything that might make you feel bad!"

"Good," the man smiled, "come I will take you there."

They followed and in a matter of minutes they reached the morung which was in a dilapidated state.

"Is it still being used?", Shilu asked diplomatically.

"Of course not, but like other villages we are planning to revive our practice. This will help our young men and women not to go astray when they go to the cities."

"Oh indeed," Shilu remarked, "every day I meet young men especially who need guidance for lack of perspective in life."

"Precisely this is why we want our next generation to feel they are rooted in their culture, so they are not lured by outsiders to feel insignificant. We should be proud of our culture," he stressed.

"Indeed," Shilu agreed as she followed him inside. He led them to where the enormous log drum was placed and Marius was immediately taken in by not just the size of it but the craftsmanship it represented.

"This is quite the work of an artisan, that is for sure," he exclaimed, "are there still men around who can carve one?"

"I don't think so," the Headman in all sincerity said, "but again we are training some youngsters to pick it up again."

"Can we try it?", Jeanie asked.

"No, that is not done by women," he answered and I cannot play it either because the drum is used as a warning instrument too, not just here in the village but the sound will reach over the valley and will alert others."

"It is beautiful," Marius said, "thank you!"

Chapter 12
Kidnapped

On the way to Mokokchong now Marius thought back on the brief visit of the last village.After thanking the man profusely Shilu knew well that he had made an exceptional gesture. So, when they had returned to the jeep the smiling soldiers said goodbye to the headman too, but Marius and Jeanie had to promise to return when they were around.

"That I will," Jeanie had said, "it may not be very likely but when it happens I will not forget your lovely village. Perhaps I shall witness then that the morung is back in to full operation, the way it should?", she said.

"We are going back to our own ways. We have abandoned them too fast, so yes. You will see that clearly when you return," he winked a goodbye.

When they were back in the jeep and inspired by the hospitality of the people Shilu was thinking of taking them to Peck and Mon as well. That way they both would have an opportunity to have some exposure on more than just a few tribes. It would be a rat race with time, but at least they would have had the opportunity to experience both differences and similarities between the tribes which, after all, shared the same origin. They were about half an our on their way out of the village, the one they had stopped to see the large old log drum, when a group of men in uniform stopped them on the road. The driver felt uneasy, for although the men were in uniform he sensed there was something wrong. He wanted to drive on but the men had weapons and they pointed these to the jeep as it came in driving towards them. There was no alternative for him but to stop. The four passengers immediately sensed danger too, but could not do much against a rifle. As soon as the driver stopped, the men jumped on the jeep and pulled the Naga soldiers and their passengers out

"Out, out," they shouted, "out!!!!!

There was nothing much they could do, but to do as they were told. So, once out of the jeep, they were lined up and one of the masked men stepped forward asking:

"What are you doing here? What is your connection with the movement? What are you looking for?", then bypassing Jeanie completely and so to Marius alone, "what is this Naga woman doing here with you?"

Marius turned stone cold hearing that commanding voice. He immediately shot back into his well trained operative function but imperceptibly so to those who threatened them. Calmly Marius spoke:

"Your English is fine. I understand you well, but you are asking an impertinent question and in commanding tone. Now, would you be kind and tell us what you actually want? And while you are at it, disclose who you are and by what authority you are doing this?"

"Huhh," the man with the gun pointed at Marius went, "we know who you are and you will be our hostage," he quickly said, no longer that sure of himself.

"Tell me who you are Marius," said again like he was hissing and he looked at Jeanie to see if she was with him should they need to attack these five men. Jeanie looked tense and prepared. The other men sensed that this was not a simple thing, not as simple as they had thought. They hesitated and they could practically hear them think; should they assault them and risking someone could be killed? Should they leave them alone, or perhaps persuade them? The man in front of Marius made up his mind but tried a few menacing words still first as he said:

"We will get you for ransom. We don't tell you who we are. We will take everything from you. If you know who we are we have to kill you."

Marius could not resist laughing at him now, leaving the man both angry as well as puzzled for he had no idea why Marius laughed.

"You said something rather amusing," Marius explained, "what you said comes straight from an American movie and not so long ago we joked about that."

"Are you ridiculing me?", the man thundered.

"Of course not," Marius replied, "what you said was hilarious!"

"What?", the man now fired up in anger but forgot to look at Jeanie and his own men while he watched a very relaxed Marius who was now fully prepared. He felt he was in command of the situation.

"It is only funny man," he said as he like a bow from an arrow hit on his target disarmed him and now held in a firm grip pointed the gun at his own men.

"Get the others men," Marius commanded the soldiers, driver and guard. Jeanie was already in their back and disarmed the four others, who meekly complied now seeing their own gun pointing at them. For fear of getting shot by Marius their guns were taken by Jeanie and the soldiers.

"Oh gosh," Shilu sighed in relief, "I thought they were going to kill you!"

When Marius had rounded them up and incapacitated them, he said:

"We can't have them taking us like meek little lambs Shilu. Besides, I want to know who they are, why they did this. I cannot believe they just did this for the money. Have there been any other threats on strangers like this, for money?"

"No, not in Nagaland," she said and walked over to the men.

"Who are you," she asked, "you are acting like robbers? You said you know us, how? Who told you what to do?"

Quite a few questions she asked, but having lost power, they felt ashamed and did not know where to begin. Then Jeanie to them and said this:

"You can do this the easy way and just satisfy our curiosity, or the hard way."

"We can't tell you," the man who had threatened them spoke defiantly.

"So, you choose the hard option, okay," she smiled, "now tell me this, when your bones are broken and your skin burnt, I can guarantee you what you keep from us is not worth keeping then. Now tell me who are you protecting? Who ordered you??

"We do this by ourselves. We are poor robbers," he said but not too convincingly.

Marius laughed the young soldiers especially.

"We have two well trained Naga soldiers here," Marius smiled, "would you like me to give them a free hand, so they can get some information out of you? They are well trained so I think they know what to do to make you talk?"

The four men, quite sturdy but clearly under the command of the first one, shivered, but the man himself tried to show he was not impressed.

"Hmmm, which one shall we sacrifice first, so the man will talk in spite of the fearless leader here?", Marius said, "come men which one would you like to begin with?"

"I think the fearless one should be taught a lesson and throw the towel in the ring when he knows the game is over?"

"Well said," Marius smiled, "get him then!"

"We can beat him up first, just to see what he can take?", the guard added and he grabbed a piece of wood then hit the man hard on his side.

"No," Marius said, "better take the weakest link. That fellow there is too afraid. He will spill the beans, especially when we separate him. There is no need for violence!"

Okay," the guard agreed as he looked at the man who was squirming in pain, "I did not hit on any vital organ Marius, so he should be well again soon."

The man they talked about and who was shuddering with fear they then singled out and took him with them enough to be out of earshot of the others.

"So, tell," Jeanie said as she planted a hand on his face to encourage him. He kept shuddering and could only talk when he had calmed down again, but then he did and whispered to them like he was conspiring:

"We are from the K-group. We were ordered to bring you in and keep you so some disturbance high and low would be created," he said

"That is all? You were afraid to reveal the K is behind this?"

"We will be punished when we return empty handed. How can we tell we failed miserably and some two foreigners against armed men?"

"Yeah, of course that must be humiliating for the K, indeed," Marius said, "did your commander tell you why they wanted us?"

"No any foreigner, but it was known that you could be some important people and your countries would try and get you free. K would have set you free but only after some time," he explained further.

"What will happen to you when you return and your leader says you have told your secret?", Jeanie asked.

"Severely punished, I betrayed, I cannot return," he said.

"Well then we will take you with us," the driver suggested.

"They will find me," he said head down.

"Well we must make these men somewhat susceptible to what reality is," Marius spoke, "let us see what happens. I can't have you sacrificed. I won't have that!"

Both the young driver and Marius went over to the men. They quickly made a deal as to how they would approach and when the driver said menacingly:

"Okay, if nobody wants to talk we have to beat it out of you or worse!"

"If we say anything all of us will be punished," the man said.

"What kind of punishment do you get for failure in this?", he asked.

"I cannot begin to tell you, but what would you get for betrayal in the Naga Army," he replied asking too.

"You are making it not too easy, but you will change your mind if you see one of your men shot and you will be the next in line?", the young man said and acted as if he would draw a weapon.

"Oh no please not that, so brutal. Punish us but let us go please," he pleaded.

"Even then," Marius interrupted, "you will have failed and they wonder why. What can you say in your defense then?"

"That is true, oh God we will loose either way," he sighed.

"There is a way out, you know," the driver spoke again.

"Really," the man and sighed in relief.

"Of course, if nothing but fear and punishment is waiting for you, what would you do if you can leave altogether? Tell me what are you really fighting for? To me it looks like you are trained to be robbers only. Does your leader tell you what you are robbing for? Or better are fighting for?"

"Against the Naga Army of course we fight, our worst enemy!"

"Worst enemy you say? Is your leader of the organization fighting against the Indians?"

"No we are not strong enough for that!", he said

"If it is the Naga army which is your enemy, then you have betrayed who you are!"

"We do not know that, we are ordinary soldiers and we do as ordered," he answered.

"Well, we do fight the Indian Army," the driver said, "we do not know why we should fight any other Nagas, but we have to when we are attacked."

"If you are punished for the reason you failed to rob us and to take us hostage, I suggest you don't go back and join the Naga Army," Marius said, "that way you work for all Nagas and you escape punishment too?"

The man, they were all without masks now of course, looked at the other three to check on how they felt about that before answering. They were either not convinced or not daring enough to decide either way yet. Marius tried to help them:

"If you are fighting for a worthy cause I would not ask this, but it looks like you are not. You are just a criminal now and you can escape your fate. For your own sake why don't you consider to leave, what is it the K-group?"

Again the man now nervously looked at the others, afraid of making the wrong decision, but then finally one of the three used his brains, overcame his fear and spoke:

"Yes, we are K. We were ordered to do this. The leaders had some knowledge about you people passing by. I don't know why they wanted you, but I don't think it was to get ransom money. I heard them saying you could be important people of some kind. They had a plan and because that has fallen thought, they will be quite angry now. I am a Konyak and I followed because I believed them, they are my people. Now I want to leave them. So, yes if you can manage, I want to be part of the Naga Army," he declared.

The man, their leader, looked at him as his eyes popped for he had not heard him speaking like this before, but he approved as he had said what the man himself found difficult to say, if only because he did not know if he could trust the others. So, he said:

"Good, good, this is what I wanted too, do we all want this?", he asked, resuming his role as a leader. The other two nodded:

"What shall we do with him?", he asked pointing at the man in the custody of the other Nagas soldier and with Jeanie and Shilu.

"You frightened him so much," Marius smiled, "that he could not do much else but to tell who you were. So, we knew already before we came to see you who you were, but we wanted you to reveal yourself. That way you cannot just blame your mate!"

"Yeah, we were all in it and we shall have to make the decision together. Yes I understand we should," he said.

"Okay that rounds it up," the driver concluded, "let's arrange to get you to one of our camps," he suggested and called his mate the guard over to bring the other 'prisoner'. Shilu and Jeanie followed. The young men talked amongst themselves about what to do next. They came up with the following idea; the guard would go in their vehicle and direct them to the next Nagas Army camp, while the driver of Marius jeep would stay right behind them. Though they all assessed them to be not too well trained followers, they did not feel like risking anything. Who knows, Marius had said, is one of them acting dumb so when the moment arises, he could turn the tables on us. So, except for the driver of the vehicle, to make sure nothing would go wrong, they bound the men's hands behind their backs.

"It will only be half an hour or so before we reach, so yes it is uncomfortable," the guard said, "but not for long and in the camp you will be warmly welcomed."

"Really warmly do you think?", the who had spoken before the man did say:.

"Of course man, you are a Naga and you now have decided to join the ranks of those who fight for the right to self determination. We Nagas want to be free; we do not want to live under the Indians. That reminds me, did the K get support from the Indian Armed Forces, or the Assam Rifles?"

"We are with them sometimes for arms and joint operations," he said, "some people from Kohima come too and they have meetings. I saw some money too changing hands," he revealed, "but I cannot be sure what it means. I do not know the policies."

"Well what does it look like when you do not fight the ones who have occupied our land and people for so long?", the driver asked.

"Yeah," itwas all they heard from him.

"Shameless people," the driver said and spit on the ground, "but you can redeem yourself. Don't double cross!!"

"You are going to the camp now?" he asked.

"Yes we will get you there. Tell them what happened, give our recommendations and then we will be on our way again. We will leave you there," he explained.

"They will not punish us, hurt us?", he asked.

"They will tell you a lot of things and they will train you, but as long as you know where you stand for, you will be accepted."

"Thank you Sir, we were very much afraid you would take revenge and even could kill us, thank you for giving is a chance," he said.

"In return you should tell all you know, okay?", the young driver said with emphasis.

"Yes, I am sure we will!", he answered.

The guard, together with Marius, then boarded their vehicle and squeezed themselves in before taking off to be in front of their own jeep. The driver of the jeep kept a close eye on the vehicle in front, for although the men had their hands bound, they were on guard and apprehensive. Who knows they could wrestle loose and flee with Marius and the guard, then they would still be welcomed by their leaders as heroes. This played through Marius' mind too. It could happen. They sighed only when they turned into a forest side road leading to one of the minor camps of the

Naga Army. Nothing had happened they thought when they passed the gate of the camp. Welcomed by their fellow soldiers they were a few of them running off to report the news of the capture of the K men. An officer soon appeared when they had stepped out of jeep and vehicle. Then the driver presented their catch to him. Briefly hey told what happened, the officer asking:

"How were you able to turn the tables of the K-men?"

Proudly the guard told how Marius had disarmed then and had wrestled the info on who they were sent by out of them.

"So, you want to be absolved of what you did. You did this because you were ordered to do so and as soldiers you do as ordered?", the officer asked. The frightened man they had isolated and told them their identity agreed with the reading of the officer.

"Be glad than nobody was hurt or killed, for that would have made matters much worse. Okay you are welcome here, we will debrief you and you will tell all you need to know, before you go into training," he explained.

"So you will not punish us?", he asked.

"Not yet, when you fully cooperate may be not at all," the officer smiled pungently so he could not be misunderstood.

"We will," said one of the men who had kept quiet, "I was afraid you would kill us out of revenge. We were told the Naga Army is ruthless, you people know no mercy."

"This is what they told you?" the officer asked

"They tell us you are our enemy first!", he humbly said

"Why not the Indians?", the officer smiled. Shilu thought these men acted like they were brainwashed or something. They did not talk about the motivation of the K. Why it attack the Naga Army incessantly, not the Indians had the Nagas under occupation. She asked:

"Please tell me, did you ask why we are your enemies?"

"Kaphlang is a very important and powerful leader," the first man, their leader said, "he does not explain himself but he knows what to do. In our tribe we have supreme leaders. It is not the same compared to other Nagas," he voluntarily revealed.

"Are you referring to the Ang system," she asked, "Angs are absolute rulers so when you offer critique you may be heard or you may be discarded?"

"Yes, we may suggest but when it is against policies, we will be put in our place."

"Nothing to contribute you could?"

"Better not try this or that, it could get you in trouble," he said.

"Well, here we encourage you to use your mind. Our nation is a democratic one. Our government is democratic, but our army is different of course. Here you do as your superiors tell you but you can appeal. You can get through to them when you have complaints or suggestions. Unless it is nonsense of course you will be taken seriously," the officer laughed.

"Konyaks are used to it. It is our culture, our leader is supreme," said one of them.

"I can imagine it will not be very easy for you at first, "but I think you will like to be much freer than you were before. You may get addicted to our ways, the ways of the majority of the Nagas," the officer smiled now.

"Don't talk about addiction please," Shilu laughed with him with Jeanie and Marius were keenly listening, "in my work I am reminded quite often what addiction does."

"This is a more positive kind of addiction," the officer said, "come you all deserve some coffee at least. We will take care of the captured K people.".

"Treat them well," Marius said, "I will follow up on that!"

"If they are not causing trouble, they will be treated with respect!", the officer stressed.

"What will you do when they want to go home?", Jeanie asked.

"Hmmm, that will be a predicament," the officer thought aloud, "let's see how we can be guided by the rules in the book and by common sense."

"You have rules about that?", the Konyak asked

"Well of course," the officer laughed, "do you think we just act on our own? I think off hand that when you run off then you will be punished for your former deed. You did capture these people here, after all that is a criminal offense. You are soldiers and were deployed as common criminals, so in that case it is likely you are to be punished as a criminal. However if you prove to be good soldiers, most likely you will be absolved, because you proved you wanted to better yourselves!"

"We will prove you right," they said one after the other. All satisfied now they were served coffee and in smiles accepted a cookie with it.

"We must go," Shilu said, "we are way into the afternoon and it is a long way to Mokokchong still."

"Okay, let's go," the driver said when they had finished their coffee and said goodbye.

"You will look after them like you said?", Jeanie asked

"Come now Miss Jeanie, I am an officer of the Naga Army. I cannot go back on my word. What an officer promises he will do, that is what the Army is about, if you doubt, please feel free to check on me," he said and he wrote down his name and the name of the camp. He handed it to her then in goodbye:

"It is good indeed to not take things for granted. There are unfortunately too many people who take advantage, say one thing but do another. I wish you a pleasant journey!"

On the way to the main road again, Shilu sighed

"This was quite an experience!", and now that she knew it was over and done with, "so this is the kind of people that are with the K. I have seen quite a few near the Assam Rifles camp at Mokokchong," she said, "but did not realize that this is the way they operate. Come to think of it, I don't hope we meet some more of them. I am sure they may know their men have failed and will attempt to do this again?"

"Let's inform our men in Mokokchong so they can keep an eye on them?", the guard suggested and grabbed the phone, a mobile of course, and dialed a number. He finished the call a minute later and announced:

"They know and will look for us, this way we may be better protected. I don't think they know yet that we have taken the others in or that they have surrendered."

"Good, good," Shilu said, "I still feel a little shattered."

The rest of the journey was uneventful but for the scenic road they were on. Marius and Jeanie many a time had the feeling they liked to take a closer look, but unrelenting Shilu said that they had to keep up with their program or it would have to be shortened. When they arrived in Mokokchong, it was already close to sunset, and so Shilu, , directed the driver to her parent's house.:

"We can do some sightseeing in this rural but rather important small town later," she said. Since Shilu's parents took them in as theirs, not just village people extended their normal Naga hospitality, they were received as though they were family..

"We can house you all but only if the men sleep together in one room," Shilu's mother said, "and the ladies do so too. Is that agreeable?"

"More than agreeable Marius said. It will be my pleasure," he answered while scanning the faces of the soldiers who just smiled.

"Then come with me Shilu so you can help me with getting a Naga dinner going. Let's surprise your friends?"

Shilu smiled and followed her.

"Here we are now," Marius said, thinking of something to say to fill the sudden gap in conversation, "so you will be sleeping with Shilu."

"Yes, and I will ask her about you," she teased, "you slipped away from me and jumped into her arms. If I would have known this was going to happen I would have intervened!"

"You can ask her anything, we have no secrets," Marius smiled, "but why would you have intervened Jeanie?"

"It is finished now, but for a long time I wanted you to make a move and you did not! Now I want to know what it is that you let your professional attitude win from the feelings we share," she explained.

"Because we are in the same profession I do not allow myself to be with you. It is better like this. I can settle for the deep friendship we have. I do not want to jeopardize anything between us. If we get disappointed when we are in love, then how do we get back to normal friendship?"

"Well, that is true and of course is masculine thinking," she laughed.

"Think of it like this," Marius continued, "should there be a problem between the UK and the Netherlands and this is possible, given the different stands on issues in the EU or the allegiance of the UK to the USA, then we may stand opposite each other. What then if we are in love Jeanie?", he asked noticing the two soldiers listening with open ears, but luckily only understanding half of what they were talking about.

Jeanie laughed, "I don't know but if we would have been going for each other and a conflict of interest would occur, I think we would be wise enough to leave that aside. Either you or I would resign from the service?"

"That could be, but I don't think it would happen. When you are trained so much in what you do, you cannot just drop it because you love somebody. Let's just say it did not happen and that we are saved from having to make that choice?"

"I wonder how we would be together if we were not bound this way," she said.

"I have dreamed about you too in that way sometimes," Marius smiled.

"Well, let's forget it," Jeanie said, "you are a happy man now that you found Shilu and she is a fine woman. I just wanted to tell you this, so I can get it off my chest, if I can," Jeanie said, "let's stay friends through thick and thin?"

"That is a deal," Marius smiled, "we are good friends and will stay that way!"

The young Naga soldiers had no idea what they had really decided about their friendship, the driver asked then:

"You are good friends but also love? How can that be?"

Jeanie laughed: "Oh yes that must be rather strange for an outsider."

Marius laughed too and added: "Without knowing or realizing we did like each other and not just as friends, like we were. Only when I met Shilu in Amsterdam and fell in love with her, we realized that we had felt this, but kept it hidden for reasons of our work."

"Oh what do you do then? I thought you were journalists!", the driver said.

"If you do not tell anyone, I will tell you," Jeanie said.

"Hmmm, I cannot promise you that," he said, "if my superiors ask I may have to tell?"

"Shall we agree then that we will tell after we have left Nagaland and even India?", Marius suggested.

"Yes that I can promise," the driver laughed, "for then I am not bound to secrecy."

"We are on holiday and wanted to know all about the Naga cause. Now especially because of your slain leader," Jeanie said.

"And, we are trained commandos, but on holiday indeed," Marius added.

"Oh now I understand you disarmed this K-man," the driver exclaimed in total surprise.

"I am sure you could have done that too," Jeanie reassured him he was as much a soldier as they were, but the driver much more trained for guerilla warfare. They were still talking when Shilu and her mother returned with the food. Shilu set the table while her father and a brother came home. Greetings were exchanged and introductions made then they seated around a big table which could take them all. Marius praised Shilu's mother for the hot meal and steaming rice she had prepared in such a short time when Shilu's father smirked saying:

"I think we may have some rice wine left for the men darling?"

"You could be right," she smiled and fetched a big bottle with the fantastic liquid. Savoring the rice wine they talked about the political effects of the assassination and what it would do to the Nagas, but also on the Indians. They talked till late about what the plotter wanted to achieve and reviewed many possibilities, checked who would benefit from that till Shilu's father bluntly said:

"Did we take this option seriously, the option of our former Chief Minister? He is a Jamir too and I am pretty ashamed of what he has done. He is now in another state as governor, but comes here regularly to meddle. I hear he is still in touch with the K-group."

"You think he deployed assassins for a lot of money father?", Shilu asked, "could the man, our own kind, be so devious."

"If you check his record from the Sixteen Point Agreement of the Sixties onwards, the agreement which made Nagaland State and you know he is supported by the Indian Government, then I think you have quite a few elements in your hands to come to the conclusion this will be most beneficial to him and his yes-men!"

"I did not know Jamir was such an important man, well for the Indians then of course," Marius sighed.

"He was their handyman, their butler; do you know he once as a young boy wanted to be adopted by Nehru?"

"Quite something when you have a whole army fighting against invaders and you have a Naga of your tribe wanting to be Indian and in a high post too?", Jeanie remarked.

"Some Nagas think it is all futile," Shilu came in, "they just want to give up but in a way that they have special status in Indian."

"Do you think you can trust the Indians for that," the driver suddenly contributed, "we have had so many bitter experiences with that. They say one thing and then backtrack. They are also divided. You cannot actually trust them. It depends how their wind blows."

They talked a long time and briefly about what to do the next few days. Shilu suggested a cultural exposure, the remnants and revival of culture. And after they had finished that luminous bottle of fine rice wine and that idea in mind, they finally went to bed.

After the Scorpion had had success in the New York meet, as a high leader of the Baptist community he was due in Washington to do a lecture on Baptist history. This type of lecture he could produce practically while he was sleeping so he did not care to prepare for that. What actually bothered him was that engagements like this were obstructing his plans. Yet, he should not call them off because that would cause suspicion. And, he wanted to determine himself when to come out to let the light shine on what he alone in the USA and beyond was fighting for. It was imperative to his plans that he and he alone would release the info to carefully manage what do so the moments of exposure could be exploited to the fullest. On the flight he thought back on what he had achieved so far and felt rather happy about his discussion in New York with the other

Baptists. He thought some of them had understood and were now open to change as well.

"Yes thank you a glass of wine please," he said to the air hostess half an hour before landing and thought about all the consequences, even about the Baptists association or the USA at large, the assassination and its aftermath would have. He sipped his wine thinking about the idea of giving up he had announced, but now with its full consequences. When the plane landed he knew he had his thoughts in order. With a smile he waited for his turn to get off the plane then went town to meet his people.

"Can I help you," the lady at the reception of the four star hotel booked for him said.

"Yes I am booked here so I would like to check in," he answered.

"Oh I have already a few messages for you," the attractive lady said, "we assigned a room to you this morning and already mail and messages are pouring in Sir," she smiled.

"Aaaahhhh, thank you, can I have them," he smiled back at her..

"You are expected for a prep meeting Sir," the lady announced.

"I am on time then right?", he answered in asking.

"The small conference hall you will find on your right not too far from the elevators," she pointed out and handed him a stack of messages, "some are colleagues waiting for you!"

"Thank you again," he nodded and walked off. In the conference room he saw a few Baptist colleagues he knew well, others primarily young and ambitious fellows he sized up immediately. As soon as he joined them, he was warmly welcome as one of the thinkers in their organization and thus well respected, a Californian Baptist leader asked:

"While waiting for you we were discussing something remarkable. Have you heard about the murder of this Baptists leader of Nagaland?", he asked.

"Yes," he answered, "quite remarkable a development. I don't know quite how to place it. Is it not so the man was murdered in Manila?"

"Yes, the assassins have been traced. Via Bangkok and Amsterdam they are said to have escaped to Brazil! We were talking about the motivation of these assassins, Europeans for that matter, to murder this Baptist. Everyone knows the Indians have occupied Nagaland. We all know too that the Nagas don't want to be part of India and resist this occupation form the beginning, so a very long time. Why would anyone want kill a man like that?"

"Aside from the obvious like money or the Indians behind it, are there no other interests?", one of the younger men asked."

"Hhhmm," the Scorpion answered thoughtfully, dropping a bit of silence to raise interest, "there are indeed. Let's take the assassins, British and Dutch. The peace talks are held in the Netherlands and in Thailand so could there be an interest there? Unless of course," he interrupted himself, "there is a group or an individual who has plotted this to raise some attention for this long term conflict?"

"That is not very likely I think!", the young man reacted, "what can an individual do?"

"Where else can we look but the Indian individuals of course? A tycoon perhaps who sees the advantage of the natural resources of Nagaland and wants this endless war to come to a conclusion so that these resources can be exploited?" the Scorpion answered, "or could it be there are some hawks in the Indian opposition or even the government, who have been plotting to overthrow this government of India through this assassination? If this is so," the Scorpion continued, "this Government would have no knowledge of it whatsoever and the Foreign minister with the Home Minister, are right. It will surely not make the apprehensions under the Nagas disappear, yet they seem to be credible representatives nevertheless."

"Once we know what the motivation for this assassination is, we will know where to look," the younger man agreed.

"And, we are at loss there," the chairman of the discussion said, "we have no idea about their motives!"

"We have a long history with the Nagas. I am sure the younger ones with us do not know much about that, but I feel a responsibility towards these people," said the man from California, "I heard the slain man was here in the USA?"

"Yes," the chairman reacted, "I am told he had a senator interested who was going to do a speech on the matter, Barbara Boxer I believe? Does anyone know about this and why we as Baptists we did not meet him?"

"I heard about it," said the Californian man..

"I was in a meeting and I have met him," a woman from Missouri contributed, "I did not know it was important or that we had a long relationship with the Nagas," she said.

"Well, I am sure not many know. It has been a while since we heard about them, but do you know we had missionaries there from 1830 onwards?", said the man from California.

"That long? How come we do not know they are at war then?", now one of the younger ones asked in surprise.

"I am not really sure, but I heard it had to do with our missions in other parts of India. If we would have raised a lot of attention then we could have endangered them. Perhaps we should look into this more closely," the Californian suggested.

"Should we not try to find out first why we did not look into this unfortunate situation? Someone important to those people has been murdered. These people are Baptists like us and we were there to convert them to our religion. They are still fighting for freedom. I bet we had reasons but why we abandoned them," the scorpion contributed.

The men and two women looked at each other. One of the two women present asked:

"Could this be a dangerous thing? A man was killed we have no idea by who. If we do it right we should have our Government make a stand."

"Oh come on Jean, be a little down to earth. Our Government will not make a stand on the Indo-Naga issue and you know why!" "Honestly," Jean reacted slightly angered, "I don't!"

"Well Jean," the scorpion explained, "India is getting very important a nation. Already because of the difference in wages, you can get an operator on the phone who is actually in India but explains to you what you should do if you have a problem with phone or internet. No, India is growing fast in importance and the USA will strike a deal with it to prevent the nuclear capability from going out of hand. Mind you both Pakistan and India are nuclear powers. India is growing fast, economically too!"

"How to get attention then?", Jean asked.

"Well for once we could take the side of those who need support," the Californian said.

"This will make us collide with our people here, our poor," the other lady said.

"Also the rich who contribute much to our churches, don't like to see their businesses tampered with," one of the younger men said.

"So, we have to try and convince them that real Baptism is what is in the bible too; love your neighbor?", the Californian smiled.

"I second that," said a young enthusiastic man who was followed by another three plus one lady and three older men.

"We seem to have a majority on this topic," the Chairman concluded.

"This means we will move on this as a proposal," Jean concluded, "I recommend myself as the person who is responsible for designing a project proposal and I expect than when it is accepted the budget attached will be approved as well," she suggested.

"Jean, money is scarce so please make it as lean as possible?", the chairman answered.

"Will do," she smiled knowing the ball could be rolling as she winked to the Californian and looked at the Scorpion too trying to assess what this important man was really after. In the discussion he had been quite knowledgeable and decisive but had not actively involved himself. He was planning on keeping tabs on the progress. After the meeting he had time to talk to some of those in the group informally and so he invited them for a drink. In a restaurant of their choice the Scorpion provided them with some background information on the establishments of the missions in Nagaland as he worked himself up to clarify the idea of why the Nagas were so adamant about their freedom from India. So, he talked about the Simon Commission of 1929 and how the Nagas had stated their aspirations when the British would leave and he quoted: 'If you British are going then we are as free as you came. With you away this means that the situation was like it was before. We were free when you colonized us, we will be free again.' The Nagas had followed up and wanted to take the British to their word. When they learned the British were not making provisions that were required, they formed (1946) their own organization; the Naga National Council.

"That organization, for a long time, did represent all Nagas," he said, "with the nine point agreement also known as the Hydari agreement, the Nagas showed their flexibility as it was stipulated therein that Nagaland would be part of India, but that the people after ten years could decide whether they wanted to be separate and sovereign of remain part of India. This led to opposition and the agreement never made it to parliament. It was the first Prime Minister, Jawarhlal Nehru, who changed his mind on this issue and called for war against those secessionists. You have not heard much about the American Baptists, our missionaries, but they received pressure when the Indian Government began to accuse them of initiating rebellion against India. As you have seen that was a rather false accusation but the Indians told them they had to leave the country or they would be forced to leave. Our missionaries decided to leave and did not look back. Of course they kept in touch, but not even the well known evangelist Billy Graham made much mention about the situation the Nagas were in when he, on his India tour, also visited Nagaland."

"Do these people feel bad about us then," the lady asked. "To my surprise they do not," the Scorpion answered and this led to them asking more questions which he playfully began to answer.

"You are a well known Baptist, a scholar," the lady commented, "how do you assess then that these missionaries abandoned them and not made the atrocities known here. Now the Indian Government through its Army could oppress a people like that. They know the right to self determination exists?"

"A little difficult to say," he said ponderingly. Perhaps it was the time, political things were different then? On the other hand it now looks like our forebears blotted out of their minds how they abandoned their own people?", he smiled.

"But we can do something about that," she said.

"I am glad that you have taken it upon yourself to begin this group. I am sure this will bring you some salvation. The Lord after all rewards all who work in His glory," the Scorpion praised her and the group felt encouraged by his words. Accordingly the goodbyes were heartfelt and warm.

The first thing he did when he had returned to the airport for a flight back home, was to pick up the phone to get in touch with Sean:

"Sean here," he heard.

"Hi Sean, I am waiting for the actual latest news from Manila and Delhi. I believe these three suicides in the intelligence agencies will slow the process a little, but will ultimately lead to the plan to be executed in full. So I will turn myself in when it is sure these three people had nothing to do with the plot, but are judged to have designed these plans just in case and to predict what would happen."

"So, what are you going to do then?", Sean asked.

"I will wait till these people are cleared. Then I will make the announcement," he said, "are these Indians closing in already?"

"I hear them breathing," Sean laughed, "The longer it takes the better it is to me!"

"I can imagine. What would you like better Sean, for me to make the announcement and drop your names, or when it happens before that?

"When we get captured there is nothing you can do right?"

"Right!", the scorpion said.

"Well, then it is rather simple. We will just sit it out!"

"And live in bliss till heaven comes down?", the Scorpion said.

"Not idly. We are in love man, so we use every minute of the day to explore all we are, know and feel. But we are in tune about our future," Sean told.

"And what is that?"

"We know we are soul mates and we have thoroughly evaluated our lives and are ready for a new beginning," he explained.

"You may to have wait quite some time to really start anew," the Scorpion cautioned him against too much optimism.

"Oh I know that, we do, but if you are true to your word we will not get too many years we are required to rot in jail. We will be young enough to sit it through it hopefully?"

"You deserve a fresh start, both of you!", the Scorpion said.

"Thank you," Sean answered and blushed.

"Wait for my signal then or get caught. In any case I will do my best to vindicate you," the Scorpion concluded before hanging up. Sean turned and told the good news to Jacky.

"Perhaps we should move house, so they cannot too easily find us?", she suggested smiling broadly. Not that she did mind about getting caught, they had talked and confirmed this was the best way, but to have a prolonged stay would not be bad after all. She wanted to feel him, touch him, and even inhale him. It would be hard to leave him; she knew that, but could not do anything about it.

In Delhi things were hectic. The crack down by the appointed team of investigators on the intelligence agencies bore fruit, but not the fruit envisaged. They operated secretly of course. Only known to each other this team invaded from within and without announcing or showing or paying surprise visits to offices. No, the investigation went on unseen, but was felt. When knowing people are snooping about and their targets cannot foresee what they are looking for, apprehension, nervousness and tension sets in. So soon after the word was out that a team was working to check each and everyone for connections all involved became busy trying to be above any kind of suspicion. Most knew this was impossible, for most were involved in practices either initiated by them or ordered by someone higher in the chain of command. Since all kinds of dealings and wheelings were relatively normal and worked like lubrication to keep the machinery running smoothly, all had something to worry about. Especially because no one actually knew what the investigators were checking. With respect to that no one knew who would be targeted. Consequently the havoc was based on the uncertainty felt by all and it was an uncertainty no one could really talk about, but everyone concerned, felt it. Meanwhile the investigators were closing in. They uncovered some shady dealings, but did not find any evidence of foul play in relation to the assassination.

"Well not yet," stated Glupta, the assigned leader of the team when he presided over one of the rare meetings of the team. To synchronize findings their meetings were arranged every few days, but to avoid being noticed they were held outside any office, even outside town. Glupta had a hard time to just arrange these meetings, because his members had to be able to leave their posts without questions asked. They too had to act concerned and play with the general atmosphere they themselves had created. Only Glupta would report to the relevant authority, was the deal. When together for an hour in a farmhouse in the countryside, rapidly everyone concerned gave their findings and now for the next half hour these were assessed before any new assignments would be distributed.

"Yes not yet, but we are getting warm," Glupta concluded, "this is a fantastic exercise men. We see several alliances being played with. We now know who is behind what dealings and we clearly see that the Government with its different plans also has different supporters for the different plans. We see that the doves, who want to create peace, have their ardent representatives in the bureau and we see the hawks are well represented too. So, the schisms in the Governments policies advocated by well known politicians are being played out here. We knew that of course, but the evidence of what RAW and IB are organizing in Kashmir, Punjab and the North East we can all see now, our team can that is. With RAW and IB fighting each other we see a reflection of that in Government too, hence the talks and many other areas of conflict cannot progress."

"Do you expect someone from our circles who acts on behalf of the hawks could have come up with this plan to assassinate the Naga leader?", a prominent young member of the team asked.

"Since the scheming has been going on for a long time and I do consider the divide and rule game played to segregate the Nagas policy, I can easily imagine the hawks among us have lost confidence. The Naga Army proved not only it can stand its ground against our forces, but it skillfully knows how to negotiate too. So, it is quite possible that a unit has been commanded to design a plain to break this deadlock and the assassination could very well have been hatched from right under our noses," Glupta smiled.

"Well we are intelligence agencies," another operative contributed, "we are trained to design plans, so it is possible."

"Yes indeed," Glupta agreed, "but we have to see what kind of consequences we are talking about. The feasibility may be one thing, the fall out of a plan quite another. Don't you think?"

"I think the idea of hired assassins and Europeans at that may not have been hatched from our circles," the young team member volunteered.

"What do you mean," Glupta asked.

"Well, with the European assassins already identified sooner or later police investigators will find a lead to those who handed out the contract to them. Consequently these people would be discovered and if that came from our circles this revelation would be very embarrassing to our Government?"

"You are right," Glupta said, "so it is your assessment the agencies scheme to set the Nagas up against each other using public funds, but are not involved in contracts to kill a persistent adversary?"

"We can't be sure of course. But it looks too obvious to me. The Indian Army is there to subdue the Nagas, so naturally when these people resists the suspicion is on us. We are the ones with the interest to once and for all get the Nagas into our fold. I am sure many in the Government are quite irritated by the unrelenting resistance of the Nagas. I hear some even find that humiliating. And, humiliation is a fine motivator to design a plan to kill those causing this type of anguish. I am sure the leaders of the Nagas are felt to be thorns in the flesh?"

"Right," Glupta agreed, "but we have to uncover that connection and so far we came up with nothing yet," he said.

"Oh. There were some not too well worked out plans," another team member said, "they seemed to be too immature to be carried out."

"You found some?"

"Yes I did," he said, "but not worth mentioning, "they were regarded as back up plans. Just in case things would really go wrong, like when the Indian Army would be inflicted with numerous losses. Things like that, so as a last resort."

"Emergency plans, but from those someone could have been inspired. So, I want you to look into them and take them seriously," Glupta said.

"Okay Sir," the operative answered.

"And show me those half baked plans," Glupta added.

"Of course Sir," he answered and opened his briefcase and took out some papers, "I copied them Sir, so I have only one. We don't want anyone else to notice what we are doing right?", he smiled.

"Of course," Glupta agreed taking the papers to study them. Then he handed them over to the others, who eagerly looked at them.

"Well, half baked indeed, but of plans which could be hatched, one comes awfully close to what has been done?"

"Only in the sense where and who, Sir, not when or for what purpose yet."

"Well we do not know the purpose yet either. This makes me wonder about something else. Did you all check yet those who are propping up the K-group? I am thinking if anyone of them had access to these plans, the plans alone could have inspired them to take action?", Glupta suggested.

"We have no evidence these plans are in their hands, but we can't be sure of course what they did with them at this stage," the operative answered.

"Make sure yes or no?", Glupta ordered again.

"Sure Sir, but what do you expect when indeed these plans may have reached them?" he asked ponderingly.

"Don't ask the obvious," Glupta lashed out, "of course we will have to check on them thoroughly then. I am sure we have some reliable people among them?"

Shaken by Gupta's sudden outburst, he was not just their superior but one of high command, the only thing the operative could say was a meek:

"Yes Sir, that speaks for itself."

"Well check these direct contacts immediately, who knows they might know something?"

"This is one angle indeed we should look into!", the operative answered.

"Then something else before we depart," Glupta said, "who is in charge of the NNC angle now?"

A member of the team raised his hand.

"Wait, I am thinking this," Glupta said, "there was a British man involved. The Manila Police mentioned a certain Sean. He was running a Bordello called The Bordello in Thailand too and in Amsterdam. Did you check there is British connection? Did you get in touch with those who are on the NNC in London? I want to know if this NNC mounted this plan to get rid of the leaders of the Naga Army. This grudge which was forced upon them years ago, 1975 I believe with the Shillong Accord, caused a lot of hatred among them. Now this NNC is languishing in Britain, while the leaders of the Naga Army are talking to our Government.

"We know the NNC office is supported by us Sir, the RAW," he said

"Can you sense the animosity? I want you to take this angle very seriously. They may have been supplied with money by our agency to do this trick!"

"I have not found anything yet Sir, no movement of significant sums of money," he explained.

"Well, this does not seem to be a simple case. I am sure the original contractor stays in the shadows as long as possible. Would you like to be seen when you designed this kind of devilish plan?", Glupta smirked. Nobody answered but all were getting ready to scoot off. Glupta noticed that and gave them a last thought on the seriousness of the assignment they were working on"

"Men," he said, "this is one of the most important assignments we ever had. Don't fail me. Even if it proves to be one of you, do not hope to remain under cover. I will find you. So, if you are, you better come forward. When you do this now I will be lenient and will think you did this for your nation, our beloved India. If later I find anyone of you to be the plotter, I will see to it you will be severely punished."

A daring operative for a moment forgetting about the stratification of the command was compelled to take up this challenge Glupta had posed:

"Sir, if I may?", he asked.

"Yes, go ahead," Glupta answered, "what is it?'

"Well Sir, if it would be one of us or a few working together I am sure we would not be able to trust what you just said. Telling you we are behind it would compromise the Government anyway and we would have become immediate targets right? So, I think even if we were, I am not, I don't think anyone would consider telling you. And more so for the effects of the assassination are now appearing and may need to be fine tuned."

"So that person or group will have to see through because of the motivation behind this plan, is what you say?"

"Precisely Sir!", the operative confirmed with a straight face.

"Sound thinking," Glupta said, "good answer. I am sure you also know why I did mention that the idea of giving up now is better than later?"

"To check our faces for reactions and so to see if there would be a consideration on any of us perhaps?", he asked.

"Precisely, you are a clever man," Glupta said and looked at him straight for a moment, then to all he said, "we will see each other in three days, same place, same time, dismissed now gentlemen."

In the head offices of the agencies, one of them, it was discovered someone had tampered with papers. The copy machine showed a larger number than the actual copies made in the office that day. One of the lower civil servants had noticed and reported that. The consternation among the operatives working there was great, for immediately it was understood plans had leaked. A meeting of that unit in the department was called and there is was discussed that one of them, now part of the investigative team led by Glupta, was the one who must have done that. The operatives working in that unit felt beaten. They knew these plans were a harmless for they were only commissioned as back up plans for calamities to be reviewed by the Government for immediate implementation, now they knew these plans could be used against them. They could be used and sacrificed as scapegoats, if it was decided that the assassins were suspected to either have been commissioned by another office, or had been deployed by the people of this unit. The one who actually had designed these plans worked in a very small team consisting of just three people. When these three people were found dead in their office, all hell broke loose. Not too long after this news leaked; the newspapers read with extra bold headings:

Three Suicides in Delhi intelligence agencies

Discovered by a cleaner this early morning the bodies of three men were found dead in their office. Since this is the office of a well known intelligence agency and no traces of foul play were found yet, presumably the doctors thought of suicide. An autopsy on the bodies is yet to be performed before anything conclusive can be determined.

A full investigation is under way, but already well informed sources indicated a connection between the assassination of the Naga leader and the suicides. These sources disclosed:

"Since both the Home and Foreign Minister closed ranks and appointed an investigative team to check on its own intelligence agencies, the heat is on in all circles of Delhi. Evidently the first causalities of this purification drive have taken their toll.

"My oh my", the Home Minister sighed when he learned the news, "Goodness, this will give us big trouble," he said to the Foreign minister whom he visited right away.

"Yeah," Patill agreed thinking what it meant and summoning both heads of the agencies and the police. Soon it was found out the men had taken their lives because of the plans now discovered, plans that would lead suspicion to not just them personally but the whole agency. This was not a small thing both realized. It could lead to quite some complications, with the suspicion now on India itself.

"So, there were plans and commissioned by who?", Patill asked, "I know nothing."

"Oh, but I do," the Home Minister said, "some time ago I gave the idea to think through some scenarios, possibilities, of what might happen when either ourselves would have to do things or others could be doing. Just a precaution I thought at the time."

"This seems to have gone out of hand completely," Patill said.

"Risks are everywhere, given the circumstances and the responsible people in them precautions can turn against us, like what is happening now," the Home Minister said.

"I cannot understand why these people committed suicide. What could they have been afraid of if they were commissioned by you?", Patill asked.

"I don't know if they actually knew that that directive came from me. They might have thought it came from someone else. You do know of course that the chain of command cannot be transparent."

"Are you telling me they were afraid to be blamed, that they thought they were scape goated?", Patill asked.

"The investigation has to show that but considering what they actually did, I think it was an act of desperation and on the basis of fear. The point now is fear of what?"

"I think we have to look into our intelligence agencies and check on what is happening there, how they are led. This is shameful, if our people commit suicide over things that they are no even responsible for, where will that lead us?", Patill said.

"Yes we clear this up. It can't be tolerated things are misunderstood and people take blame for what they did not do. Now what do you think we should do to curb this bad publicity? I think this is going affect us terribly. Do you have an idea Patill?", the Home Minister asked.

"Some plan of course I have," Patill smiled, "don't you?"

"It affects us both so we should share on behalf of the nation," the Home Minister said negating Patill's question.

"Are you telling me you have no idea how to deal with this?", Patill asked mounting some pressure on him. The Home Minister laughed:

"I am telling you to close ranks and share information so share the info man!"

"You have your own things you keep to yourself, so please realize that I hesitate and wonder at times," Patill reacted.

"Well, our ministries have a different focus, so there you are," the Home Minister answered, "let's not fight over this now, we are facing a serious situation," he said.

"Okay then," Patill agreed, "what I suggest we do is that we deny any involvement but publish the plans and stress that these were emergency plans, only to be implemented when we would face a real emergency and since we had none, there plans were not commissioned to be executed," Patill said.

"When going public Patill are we not inviting more trouble then? I mean all will know we had such plans in the first place and ordered to be designed by us?"

"There is nothing wrong with plans meant for just in case situations. I fact, rather than playing hide and seek, I think by going public with them it shows we are honestly dealing with situations. It shows we are looking after security and are an honest Government. Only to make sure our nation is secure we do not disclose certain things. But to deflect any suspicion the best thing to do is to go public," Patill argued.

"I would like to think about that," the Home Minister reacted, "but you have a good point there," he agreed.

"You mean you want to confer with some others before saying yes or no?", Patill asked, "I saved your neck with giving you the Manila information in time for you to be able to stand up to a mad crowd, don't you think this idea will at least take the pressure off us regarding suspicion?"

"True," the Home Minister admitted, "yeah indeed I do not see a reason why we should not. I was more thinking about the way to go public and get some media people to advice for maximum effect," he said.

"All right," Patill said, "take this morning to get advised. I am sure the sooner we go public the better it is. Too much damage is done as we speak," Patill stressed.

And with that Patill and the Home Minister parted.

In the intelligence offices things were in complete disarray. Understandably so for now that it was discovered that someone, most probably the appointed investigative team had access to their files, all felt they were being watched, but did not know from where and what the purpose was. Three colleagues had killed themselves, that was certain but other than the highest in command nobody knew exactly why. So, when later the press statement was given out before it reached the press, at least all intelligence personnel was reassured that the discovered plans would have no bearing on the work they were doing. Yet, they understood very well now, that in whatever they did, the danger lured they could be used as scapegoats too and would have to take appropriate action. Many operatives were quite convinced of course that the action the three had taken had been based on fear, a fear they all felt for no one actually knew for certain what the upper echelons were after. They could command them to do the same thing, or now that this had happened, something similar.

When the statement reached the press the reactions were diverse. Some, as predicted by Patill, praised the Government for being open but others commented on the set up of the agencies which had led to so much fear that they felt so much cornered the only way out was to take their own lives. Harping on this angle was something the Home Minister had not taken into account enough, it was assessed. But then in the end that was the only thing he was particularly criticized about and when he had made another statement the next day that all was had been initiated before and would be reviewed to be taken care of, the critique had died down.

Chapter 13

The Cease Fire monitoring Group and Delhi

Marius and Jeanie were talking to the Cease Fire Monitoring Group in Dimapur. There was a meeting and they were invited, not to attend to hear about the cease fire violations and how to deal with them, but to talk to some of the members afterwards. They had returned from their trip into the country side, the mountains, the villages, in short the culture and life of Nagaland. Also they had visited the rehabilitation camp Shilu worked for and had spent some days there too. They had been on a long journey, well only a couple of days, just a week, but it felt that way, for their days had been full of impressions. They had gone from village to village and had met and talked to many people from different tribes. Apart from slight differences in culture, also expressed in language, they had noticed one thing the people had in common, their sense and conviction of wanting to be free. And, many, the older men and women and the young soldiers, men and women too, had many sordid stories shared with them. But when Jeanie and Marius had arrived in the rehabilitation camp for the first time on their journey they had been able to take some rest too. Situated in the middle of the Naga Homeland though near a village, the camp was on a slope where the idea had been planted that, as much as possible, the organization had to be self sufficient. The leaders and trainers who looked after the derailed young men and women had a program in place which was followed with iron hand. Knowing that, when addicted, it was extremely difficult to get physically detoxified it was even more so mentally. By teaching basic skills the underlying idea was to provide perspective, for without perspective in life the addicts would in no time be lured back into the state they had let themselves slide into.

"So, instilling, maintaining and encouraging motivation to grow were the primary goals of the centre next to the physical detoxification program," Shilu had said when they attended a staff meeting. They had also talked about the causes for addiction and the staff had introduced them to the ins and outs of the pulling forces which had lured the youngsters into having this drug habit: constant occupation led to lack of confidence in the future, availability of drugs was another, disappearing culture a good third, then the constant reminder of the terrible stories of traumatized men and women a fourth. But for Marius and Shilu there was also something quite interesting possible. After this talk with Jeanie in the house of Shilu's parents, Shilu had had a talk with Jeanie too when they were sleeping in the room meant for the women. There Jeanie had aired her heart about her friendship with Marius, a friendship that for all the right and perhaps wrong reasons never developed into the closeness Jeanie had hoped for. She told Shilu she had never actively pursued Marius because she thought Marius, in the end, would be hers anyway. "Now that he has fallen in love with you dear Shilu, I am sorry I have acted the way I did. It must have been the idea of me feeling he would sway away and so far even that he would be out of reach."

Shilu in turn had disclosed how she had met Marius and how through some witty communications and his unexpected eagerness to come to her and into the Naga story, she had come to like him much more than she had thought possible. When she noticed he had felt the same if not more for her too, she could hardly resist going and exploring what could be in store for her, for them. Only when in Nagaland Shilu realized that Jeanie had felt more for Marius and it made her feel reluctant to continue, something she felt not quite possible when they were traveling together.

"So," Shilu had concluded during that intimate talk, "I never had the intention to be in your way, but I was delighted when he actually came. Of course he told me you would come along and that the main reason was to get the RAP's needed to get into Nagaland. I saw you felt for him and did not want to pursue, but Marius did and now I feel free to be with him. I am glad you have told me how you feel about him. Let's all be friends?"

Wholeheartedly Jeanie had agreed, though now she knew she had waited too long and played to long with her own as well as Marius' feelings on this matter. It was Jeanie who encouraged Shilu to spend some time with Marius alone. Since they were in rehabilitation centre, set up by the Naga Forces, they did not have to play as if they were a married couple. So, Jeanie and Marius had taken off alone and like the lily which made Shilu and Marius feel on, that special lily of the Naga Highlands, which grows and shows only under very special circumstances, the beauty and the uniqueness' of their feelings were growing too under these indeed peculiar circumstances. So they had gone out for walks and talked, made plans to meet again and had made love there in the fields of Nagaland, on the forest floor. They were delighted with each other and even when Marius had opened up to her and told her about his work as a covert operative, Shilu had felt not that he had withheld important things from her, but that he had showed her what conviction and loyalty could lead to. There in the woods and away from everyone they were nude and wrapped up in each other when Marius had declared his love for her and had said:

"I have this burning feeling and I know I am in love, I know it is the very foundation what I want to build on with you, to come together as one and to stay together."

Shilu's heart had jumped and without a word had met the revelation of Marius with joy and in kind. They came together with tenderness and with force and they merged. When the passion had left them, but their togetherness grown, they sat, nude still, to discuss how they could follow up on these wonderful feelings:

"My darling Shilu we are so far apart from each other and I have no idea yet how we can progress in being together when we have no way yet. You are working here and it is a rewarding and responsible task. For obvious reasons I cannot live here so I can only think of arranging for you to come to me. Perhaps we can find an equally important job for you but in relation to the Naga struggle too," he had said.

"This is something to consider," she had said, "I will talk to the leaders about it and perhaps with the leaders of the Naga Army and government later. Oh, Marius I am excited about the idea alone," she had practically cried of happiness. They flowed into each others arms again and for the next hour or so could not stop touching stroking, sensing, feeling and coupling.

Shilu and Marius were sure now. They had found each other and their main aim was to arrange that their feelings could grow by making it possible to be with each other. When she had informed her superiors about her plan they had suggested her to move away from the rehabilitation centre to focus on international work. That way she could meet Marius in the future too. She could then fortify the international aspects regarding support for the cause. So, both personal and interpersonal issues could go hand in hand. On face value this was excellent proposition and her heart went out to it. On the other hand she felt that very strongly about her rehabilitation work and knew she would miss being with those in dire need; to help those who had fallen between the quay and the ship so were at peril to drown. The argument by both the leaders and Marius was that Shilu had experience and mental skills as she had been abroad and could relate to people from other countries. This was something she should have to value too as one important for the Naga cause too. After long consideration and talking to each other, Shilu and Marius decided together that she would come to Europe, but that for some months in the year she would retreat to work at the centre.

"You will have the best of both worlds, Marius had smiled to her. Thus decided and with Marius and Jeanie to depart Shilu spent a long night with Marius before the jeep would take them back to Dimapur. It was decided too that to prepare for her first trip abroad Shilu would stay behind. So, after the meeting of the Cease Fire Monitoring Group, CFMG, Marius tried to first speak with the Indian chairman and his colleagues, while Jeanie found the spokesperson of the Naga Army. Soon Marius joined them for the Indians were tightlipped and as Lungthing confirmed to him:

"They will not make any public performance or talk to the press unless the higher ones from Delhi want them to make an official announcement. It is not possible for them to say much, because the group, although decided on to really monitor cease fire violations, has no jurisdiction. We do report, we do allege but on both sides we cannot check on the violations properly!", he said.

"Why is that then?", Jeanie asked.

"This is because of the dreadful Armed Forces Special Powers Act, AFSPA, which not just provides the Army with special powers but equally important makes it impossible for us to check on them. Through this act they are above the law. They cannot be heard but voluntarily only. As CFMG we cannot confront them with witnesses or ask those to prove there whereabouts, produce evidence on those who have been part of a violation for questioning. When confronted all they do is to remain aloof. The Act prevents us from holding them accountable. In short they can do as they like. Only their superiors can call them off."

"So this CFMG is a paper tiger?", Jeanie asked Lungthing.

"We cannot force anyone to come clean. This is a problem of course, so the ground rules which have been agreed upon during the talks cannot be enforced and of course when the Indians are not to be questioned on major issues, we will not voluntarily do so either."

"So a deadlock here too," Marius concluded.

"Yes, officially they are not accountable but they of course cannot get away with everything they wish to do either. They know we will retaliate and if need be these violations will be talked about again in the talks themselves," Lungthing said.

"The implications and consequences of this big plan, hatched somewhere we should find out very soon, but are huge," the Prime minister said in the cabinet meeting, "tell me Patill how could this happen. We have three suicides of operatives who as you say most likely do not even have anything to do with it. How do you rhyme this?"

"They had been designing plans and a few looked treacherously close to what actually happened. They felt they could have been picked as the plotters, undermining our policies of course. Also, there is a lot of fear in our secret services. We should stop this, but I cannot if we do not work closely together."

"The opposition has a stake there?", the Home Minister asked?

"Well what do we know Prime Minister," Patill asked.

"To tell you the truth I must say that we are facing infighting. IB and RAW are at loggerheads and this is how they were set up. They operate from a different command centers," the Home Minister said

"Yes it was set up like that for a very good reason, internal end external and one checking the other. But what has crept in is, that they are used by different parties and so have different loyalties too!"

"We will have to figure out what has gone wrong," the Home Minister answered, "we already have a team on the case which does and internal probe. I will not be surprised when the suicides have something to do with that probe. I wonder if these people did that out of loyalty to us, to vindicate us?", he wondered aloud.

"How do their suicides relate to get our Government above suspicion?", Patill asked.

"Well, they took the blame and with that suicide they show that they were the ones planning the disruption in the peace talks. To kill the whole team is to me as good as a confession," the Home Minister explained his thoughts.

"Could it not be too because they killed themselves they are saying we take the blame for those who ordered this? The loyalty is the same, the reference you made is only quite different!", Patill reacted.

"Yeah, you are right, that is why I want us to agree on putting another team on the matter. I want to get to the bottom of this really," the Home Minister said. It did not take the members at the cabinet meeting long to take a decision before other ministers moved on to other issues. The Prime Minister though made one last remark:

"Look gentlemen, I want this issue to be resolved. It is a very difficult one, but by being so stubborn and arrogant and only thinking we have every right to subdue these Nagas we are inviting more trouble again. I am an economist and I know when there is peace the climate for development will be there too. Think of the Northeast as the jumping board of south East Asia through Burma. Already we have better relations with that country and I think to pacify the people of the North East as a whole, peace with the Nagas is crucial. Without a stable agreement with them I do not see how we can get to Bangkok and beyond. Let's not forget that this brokered peace will be beneficial for all?", he asked in conclusion.

"We are to be dependent on a bunch of renegade Nagas?", the defense Minister asked.

"I don't think we can have an alternative now," Patill said, "I do remember that your generals came to us to show that the war could not be won unless we would annihilate all of them," he said. So where does that leave us?"

"That was the reason why we started the talks of course and we hoped we could gently persuade the Nagas, perhaps with some special status some kind of minimal autonomy, to give up the fight and be part of India!"

"For them to accept the constitution?", "Patill asked mockingly.

"That was the idea of the former governments. To be honest with you Patill, I think it was ludicrous to think that way. Okay stalling for time, wearing them out is reason enough, but to think they would yield to something they vehemently went against?"

"You mean the Shillong Accord?", Patill asked.

"Exactly," the Home Minister answered, "the people we are dealing with now went against the implementation of that accord. To go back on that would mean they are betraying their own stand? How can we expect that of anyone? You tell me now Patill, because I think it is quite foolish a think to even think about," he smiled.

"But was that not the unwritten policy then, to wear them out to set some groups up to fight against each other?"

"That is true and the idea was to give them some sort of settlement," the Prime Minister contributed.

"But we do not get anywhere with them," Patill said, "we underestimated them like so many before us."

"We are walking on thin ice yes indeed," the Prime Minister remarked, "when this blows out of proportion the backlash could be something we cannot control. Let's assess what could happen and let's foresee what we could do about it?"

"Perhaps first I should inform you about the three teams we have assigned now," Patill informed and the Prime Minister nodded, "our team of Manila is in Rio de Janeiro and the latest is that they can closely work with the Brazilians there. They are closing in. They nearly have the assassins in custody and it seems the Brazilians don't mind us to interrogate them in their presence. They will also extradite them to their respective countries. Once we have them, and it is a matter of time, we will go after the plotter. That is one. We have a team in full operation which is doing the internal investigations and they found these plans that led to the suicides. Another team is checking on the assigners of these plans and the motivation for the suicides. Then we have a special team in place in Nagaland. This team investigates the connections between the Nagas and either individual Indians or directly the government. Their task is to find out the lines of command between those renegade Nagas who could have implemented this plan. We are currently calculating the execution of the plan and the presumed implications of it."

"Yeah, that I would say is practically standard procedure," the Prime Minister remarked, "of course I expect you to do this and to have plans ready in case of emergencies. I want you to tell me what we can expect when this goes out of hand and I have to defend our stand in the international arena," he said showing some irritation.

"Well let's see," the Home Minister hastily said, "if the Nagas rise this will be known and depending on the severity of our intervention this will attract a lot of attention. We will be questioned. For some time we can push them aside credibly by saying 'we are studying the situation closely' and 'we are there only to save the lives of those at peril because the situation is very volatile', but only for so long Prime Minster."

"Again, that is standard practice I should say," the Prime Minister reacted, "I want some innovative ideas for me to handle this. How about you Justice Minister, or are you already planning how to move in?"

"You are a witty man," the Defense minister laughed a laugh of praise and respect, "I was thinking about the following. You see when the news breaks India in any way is behind this assassination we can really be screwed up. The wrath of the people will be on us and they rise. When we move in with the Army we are going to dig our own graves because this I believe would lead to our demise.

"Really?", the prime Minister shot up and now listening very very carefully.

"This time it will be quite impossible for anyone to keep this domestic. Don't forget the assassination took place in Manila. The Philippines may be a poor nation, it is part of the international community and a man, a leader of an unrecognized nation has been killed on their soil. This alone attracts international attention. Then there is Rio and two European assassins who will be arrested soon hopefully, this makes it more and more international. When these people on top of everything else are going to reveal their ideas internationally on why this man was to be killed, then I can tell you there will be many more listeners than you would have ever thinkable. In fact I think this is what the main aim of this operation was. Those who are responsible for it I am sure will agree," the Defense Minister suggested.

"Do you say we should prepare for that?", The Prime Minister asked.

"I do not say what is obvious," The Defense Minister shrugged, "I explain what could be behind this. Let's hope it is not going into that direction?

"That is not good enough," The Prime Minister reacted, "if you think that there is some people somewhere who have been planning this, the conflict with the Nagas will burst out into the open. Then what?", he asked, "you are to just to inform but to advise me."

"The conclusion is that we should prepare of course. We have to tell the same story!", The Home Minister tried.

"Also not good enough, like that we do not know what to prepare for and stories have to be based or they will fall through. You Patill?", the prime Minister asked.

"When we do not find the plotter and we have no defense for our action surely the international community will be drawn to the conflict. I say we better come clean and talk about the integrity of the state," Patill said but not convincingly either.

"You all know the European countries and even the USA will think twice on the idea of colliding with us," The Prime Minister said in an effort to see things from a different angle. When we look at things from an economic perspective most countries are dancing to appease India because of the trade we provide. We are expanding fast, our economy grows, and now that the West sees us as both a provider of cheap labor, so finished products, and as consumers of their higher end products, the intricacy of the relationships with India is not easily jeopardized by them"

"Are you saying prime Minister that we can tell them to mind their own affairs before judging ours?", Patill asked.

"Precisely," the prime Minister nodded.

"The times have changed Prime Minister," said the Defense Minister, "I think that the talks are on several levels at the same time. And don't forget the freedom of expression. If the press harps on it the governments have to follow. Without referring to the trade pacts or relations we have, they will come on to talk about human rights and democracy."

"That could be a weak point indeed, but what are we really afraid of?", he asked and looked at all of them one by one.

"Well, that is clear to me," said Patill. That we loose power is one, that we are to be accountable is two, that we are questioned is three and there are more points I am sure you are all aware of?" "Okay," the Prime Minister agreed, "if the news breaks and the motivation is clear we may be in for a bumpy ride. It will require statesmanship to steer us out of the quack mire the revelations might be a spin off."

"That is true!", the Defense Minister smiled, "and we are all in it to show ourselves with straight back while we keep composure."

"What is the worst we can expect?", the Prime Minister pushed on. "I think the plotter's main aim was to get the Indo-Naga conflict on the agenda of many countries and also on the agendas of non governmental agencies. Honestly I think, but we will soon see what transpires, that this could be the beginning of a concerted effort to discredit the Indian Government. I don't think those who are responsible for this will stop at the Nagas. I am sure they will have a back up plan, like on the Sikhs and the Kashmiri, to drive their point home and abroad," the Defense Minister said.

"Which is?", Patill asked.

"Well, to destabilize the Indian government?", he answered.

"For what purpose?", Patill now pushed.

"To solve these extremely long lingering conflicts we have for one," he answered thoughtfully feeling cornered, "a destabilized India will work for the West and Pakistan, but I do not think it is possible to hire European assassins to initiate that kind of destabilizations. I think it is to stop the fast rise of India. Some could feel it as a threat that India and China may take over from other world powers."

"So you think the Americans are behind this?", the Prime Minister shot out.

"Not just the Americans will profit, it could have been initiated by some European powers, through its security agencies?", he clarified

"Oh come on, why would they sacrifice a Naga leader for that? If they are caught then of course the fall out of that scenario would be great, for diplomatically we will make minced meat of them!", The Prime Minister laughed trying to crack a joke so the creativity would flow better.

"We do not know how devilish they think, but then we will see when these assassins are caught what will happen," the Home Minister said.

"If it does not stop at the two assassins we have to assume the plotter only deployed them. Are we certain there is a plotter?", The Prime Minister asked.

"Nothing is certain at this point. The assassins could just have been doing it by themselves. What is the relation with this Indian Philippino, the Manila police identified? Has he been caught?", the Home Minister answered.

"They are closing in too," Patill answered, "most likely both parties are caught soon."

"I hoped we could foresee things and take preparatory action," a disappointed Prime Minister concluded.

"The only concrete thing I can think about is that we should anticipate the worst and move on that in preparation. If however this has been ordered from within our own circles, we are in for a worse ride. How will we explain this?," the home Minister sighed.

"I think we have to seriously take that into account too," Patill reacted, "we do know our own animosities in the different circles. Some grudging politicians who are fed up with the Nagas and want to go against us can do that!"

"Enough discussion now," the Prime Minister said sharply, "rather than defining the worst let's project some possibilities on how to come out of this stronger. We cannot be seen as an important emerging economy which cannot keep its house clean. I do not want the bad publicity on this. Let's get to work. We will meet again in two days!"

Chapter14

The chase is on

Bailung was wondering what to do. He had Celia, his wife to be, Celia his woman checking out his house and so he knew it was being watched. This meant of course when he would return to pick up his things, or she in his place, either one would be arrested. Both knew there was no way they could escape the police now.

"Surely when we move publicly," Bai said, "we will be caught. I am sure they check airports and possibly even bus stations and the harbor. They have taken this very seriously now that they know India is heavily involved."

"Well, well, it is only a matter of time then Bai and now that I found you I don't let you go again. No way," Celia smiled.

"What can I do but to stay with you for as long as possible?", Bai smiled, "of course there will be a day they will find me. Staying with you in your place only makes it more difficult for them to catch me, especially when I stay home here."

"What shall we do?", Celia asked as she moved towards him to sit on his lap, broadly smiling.

"You are making it very difficult for me to leave you again and I must, there is no real escape," Bai smiled back at her, "it is best we determine the time and place ourselves for me to be taken in. I am wondering if I should make it coincide with Sean and Jacky."

"Call him and see what developments there are?", she suggested strongly, "use my phone so they cannot check easily!"

"Right," Bai agreed and dialed Sean's number.

"Hey Bai good man," Sean responded, "you are lying low man?"

"Yes for the moment of course. I am now I am very much enjoying my time with Celia. You know we found each other and I am too reluctant to throw the towel man. I do not want to leave her and giving myself up might mean that.

"I have some news," Sean I interrupted him.

"Shoot," an eager Bai reacted.

"I was called by the plotter, the one who gave me the contract through Jeanie, an operative of the UK. He is the one with a purpose for the assassination. He has the interests and motivation. But the idiotic thing is he told me that within a few days he will expose himself. He just wants to wait and see what transpires about the suicides in the Indian agencies. He said when suspicion on India fades with the suicides being confirmed of having nothing to do with the plotting, he will go public. And, what is more he will tell he has coerced us to do the killing."

"That last one is true of course," Bai said, "he knowing our history in Rwanda knew we could hardly say no. He deployed you well for that. I could not say no and you know it!"

"That is right," Sean acknowledged, but we may have a way out now. I am going to move places to make it more difficult for the Indian team to find us. You too wait some two days more and we will get in touch to be caught when the plotter opens up Bai?"

"Not too bad perhaps, two days you say?"

"Yes, let's be free two more days, all right?", he asked and Sean looked at Jacky who nodded while Bai looked at Celia who showed she wanted more days.

"Done," Bai agreed, "two days and I will after your confirmation go to my house. I am sure they will bring me in then."

Eddie was anxious. Much had happened, but now all had gone stagnant. He had gone back to the morgue to check on things for the release of the body but found out something peculiar. When he had a talk with the pathologist, the coroner, something strange had come to him and he had to talk to Bailung about that. But first he had to find him for Eddie was sure Bai had to return one of these days, so though anxious he was not worried about catching him, although? Could it be Bai had posted someone there himself? To get rid of that thought he had instructed his men on the spot to look out for people around the house but had nothing to do there. Some around looked conspicuous, but nothing indicative had materialized. Then, Eddie thinking about the Delhi suicides what this could that mean? Was the plotter was among them? Was it the Indians after all who were behind this? He could not believe it, for then also the Government itself was behind it or had known about it. It was their responsibility and Patill had not made the impression he had a lot to hide.

He had talked openly and had even introduced his colleagues to the Indian team, a team made up of experts on police and investigative work. This team had also direct connections to the intelligence agencies and through them Eddie had better access than the Indian Embassy Of course when a plan was hatched by some individual or a group which wanted to embarrass the Government, only the intelligence agency could possibly know about it. The uncovering of the plans drawn up by some in the agencies, plans on discovery which led to the demise of three agents, led away form the suspicion the government of India was directly involved. It was established no sane Government would have emergency plans to assassinate people available. So, the way it looked Eddie thought, was that through the team of assassins only they could find who the plotter of this turmoil was and with him or her the grand plan behind it. Eddie loved puzzles and was quite certain some crucial pieces were missing. Eager he was about catching Bai, he was sure through him he could get in touch with Sean and the woman who had carried out the assassination with Bai, plus the fact he had to take him to the coroner too. The Indian team meanwhile was hot on the track of Sean and Jacky and with the help of the Brazilian authorities had finally an address. Just about an hour ago Eddie had received a call from them and they had told him they were going to move in to catch them that very day. Stay near the phone, their leader had advised him, for soon you will know we will have them. Eddie had reacted with a: Don't be too sure man, they are as slippery as eels in your hands, I will no be surprised they will elude you again. But the man had laughed and had said:

"We are pretty sure now!", and had hung up.

Now Eddie was thinking about the open ends this case. He was aware this assassination could have tremendous political implications. If not handled well it could have impact on the relationship between the two countries or worse it could put the Philippines in bad light internationally. Very much a patriotic man this was not what Eddie liked to see. No matter how corrupt the Philippines how badly run it is, I don't want any bad impressions born out of this case, he thought. So he put it upon himself to make sure that this case would be led to a satisfactory ending. This case must be solved, he told himself.

Sean and Jacky were moving. They had just left their rented house to move into another place, now near Copacabana beach. It was one that was in a compound and rented in somebody else's name, so it was kind of sub-letted. A friend who had arranged this house for them had gone into action when Sean had asked him to find a more secure place. They were just like holiday makers and would, when outside, behave accordingly.

The problem with this was Jacky, for with her appearance she attracted dozens of Brazilians, well any type of men, to her when she showed up in bikini on the beach. They did not need this type of attention at all right now, so Sean ran some errands at times and they stayed in the compound as much as possible. Luckily the compound had a swimming pool and behind the house a garden. So at least they could taste the tropical atmosphere and catch some rays of sun in the process. The Indian team meanwhile had come in running into the old house they stayed, along with Brazilian police they found the place empty. Sure they had been given the right address, but to their immense disappointment the birds had flown.

"What to do now?", the Brazilian counterpart asked.

"Try to find out where they went," the Indian team leader answered showing surprise.

"We have other things to do," the man said, "this is not that important to us."

"Okay," the team leader said, "we will take it up with our Embassy and so our government. I can understand when you have no order to do anything you can spend your time on this, so I will get you what you need," he stressed.

"Yes do that," The Brazilian policeman said, "we can check around and ask their neighbors then the owner while we are here?", he volunteered.

"That is nice of you for we do not speak the language so we need you," the Indian smiled.

For about an hour they talked to neighbors but they came up with nothing. They just heard the couple had left taking only a few things with them. It did not look like they were gone forever, but when they got in touch with the owner they knew better. The man told them they had left suddenly and only had informed him yesterday. The house rent was paid for the rest of the month and of course no forwarding address was given, but the one of the friend of the couple.

"That could be a lead," the Brazilian said, "let's go find him and put some pressure?"

"We could do that," the team leader said. They jumped in their cars to go there in person.

"We know you organized the house for Sean and Jacky, now they are gone. We believe you are in contact with them?", the policeman asked without further introductions.

"I only get a call and we did not meet in person so I can't help you," Sean's friend said, "I did not even know they had left so suddenly. Normally he calls me when they leave, the rent is paid! What do you want him for?"

"That is not your business. We want to talk to him," the policeman said, "what is his phone number?", he asked.

Sean's friend handed the policeman his mobile. On it of course was the number but not under Sean's or Jacky's name.

"Not on my GSM," he smiled, "I told you the man calls me!"

"Then there will be a number on your phone," came the answer.

"When it is a secret number?", he asked.

"We will see then," the policeman said and checked to find calls indeed on a list but some without numbers.

"We will have to bring this phone to check it," the policeman decided and announced.

"Oh no you don't," the friend smiled, "when you get a warrant you have no jurisdiction to take anything that belongs to me!"

"Then we will check it out here," the team leader said and they began right away. They called all the numbers stored on the phone, including the one of the calls and the missed calls list. This took some time and the friend just waited patiently and decided to brew some coffee. Because he had anticipated his phone could be confiscated, he was reassured by the idea he had instructed Sean and Jacky to check all calls from him before answering,. So, when both of them saw their friend number appearing, they ignored it for right now he had no business with them.

"They are now really hot onto us," Jacky smiled. We will get another number all right?", she asked, "they can trace where we are you know. When we keep on using this number we will be caught in no time."

"Okay we will get several new ones and I need to call Bai. The problem will be that our friends will not be able to reach us. We have enough money to get pre paid cards and loads to call all of them to tell we will be out of communication," Sean had said.

So, the police then in the end had to leave empty handed but with a bunch of phone numbers to be tried out from other phones and different times. Meanwhile Sean and Jacky burned up their Sim cards.

In the offices of the RAW and IB right under their very noses things had happened higher officers had no knowledge of. Apart from the disastrous feeling their agencies were at stake for failing to know their own agents, the idea alone someone, the Indian Government or worse outsiders had access to the plans and ideas, was indigestible. .

"Our work is secretive by nature, we work conspicuously, but now it looks like there are people who have had access to our files. How can this be?", the question rang out and all present, all rank and file felt they had slipped up. No one actually knew how this could have been averted, "this happened under our noses. How can it be nobody knows about this? I will order a deep investigation so no stone will be left unturned, all gory details must surface. Is that understood? I demand full cooperation from everyone in the bureau. This agency will be clean," the director said in a stern, emotional and threatening manner.

"Do you suspect infiltration?", one of the agents dared to ask.

"Can you explain what has been going on we do not but should know about?", the director answered by asking a question again.

"I cannot," the man answered admitting there was a flaw, "but you cannot be sure also it has been brewed up by any one of us either."

"Yeah, yeah, we are being targeted as the culprits so make sure our house is clean. That is foremost important now. Whoever hatched this plan and deployed these Europeans is thought to be from this very office. Prove them wrong is what I am saying, all right?", he said with power in his voice he closed the important meeting.

Meanwhile the Scorpion moved again. This time he had decided to move rapidly for the news he received meant the Indians were getting off the suspicion list. Since they had been able to deflect attention and the possible uprising in Nagaland itself had been averted too, this was the time to open up. The Scorpion knew, only when he delivered the assassins first before opening up to the media himself, could he trigger the attention on real matters, the matters that counted, and the matters he had described in the plot he designed. Back in New York he began to draft a press release:

Assassins of the slain Naga leader fled to Rio de Janeiro arrested, he wrote. This would not catch the attention he needed. Well, not in the USA but in India perhaps. From now on things planned had to be certain. Since Sean had told him where he would move to with Jacky he disclosed the place where they staying. First I want them to be arrested before I will come out myself. Let them try to find out from Sean and Jacky first what the idea behind the assassination was, he thought. So while working on this press release, the first step in the revelations he plotted, he thought ahead, so the impact of the assassination would be in his hands to maneuver with. He was pulling the strings and wanted to be sure there was no stopping; the Indian Government would not be able to turn the tide. So when he had finished with his press statement it read like this:

Assassins of slain American Baptist leader from Nagaland caught in Rio de Janeiro The assassins of the slain Naga leader who fled to Brazil to hide were caught today in Rio de Janeiro. After thoroughly searching for them and following their trail from Manila Philippines, The Indian Police, in full cooperation with the Brazilian Police, apprehended the couple at a beach resort near Copacabana beach. The perpetrators did not resist arrest but upon the question of why they murdered this Naga leader, they just stated it was done on contract. They did not explain further and are being interrogated.

Of course the Scorpion knew the Brazilian Police might not find Jacky and Sean, so he picked up the phone and called the Brazilian embassy in Washington.

"I have an important message for you," he said, "I am going to issue a press release very soon and this is what I would like you to do. So, listen carefully," he announced when he had the right person, the first secretary, on the phone.

"Who are you?", came the expected question.

"That is not important now. I told you to listen carefully. Now the assassins of the Naga leader are in Rio near Copacabana. Both your police and an Indian team are trying to find them. Here is the address where you can catch them," the Scorpion said as he dropped some silence to let the man pick up a pen and catch his breath, "now signal this fast enough so they will be caught indeed. I will give you one hour before I issue the statement that they have been caught. Is this understood?"

"Yes Sir, but who are you and how do you know this? What has Brazil got to do with a murder in the Philippines?", he asked trying to get over his astonishment.

"You will soon find out. I will send a full statement to the press in one hour. In it I will reveal who and where. I suggest you will use your time well," the Scorpion said and then for fear of being traced hung up immediately. He worked a little on some fine-tuning of the statement, and then looked at it again before sending it off to the big news agencies like Associated Press and Reuters. He also phoned a couple of editors of the major newspapers with the words:

"I have some big news and I want you to listen closely. Then he read the statement word for word and said that much would be revealed later:

"This is only the start of a very far reaching impact which will involve the United States of America in an unprecedented manner," the Scorpion concluded.

"How can we verify your words," the editor asked, "we are not at all interested in some sort of hoax," he said condescendingly.

"Check with the police in Rio and with those in Manila and with the Indian agents too with the Indian Embassy. Checking information is your work," the Scorpion curtly answered before he hung up. Now I will wait till Jacky and Sean and perhaps Bailung are caught, he thought.

It was nearly the end of their two days together and no one had bothered Sean and Jacky. They had spent some unforgettable days after they had fled the other house. As much as possible they had stayed indoors but they were well aware, as the Scorpion had pointed out, any time now it would be their turn to be caught. They had just had their lunch and after it, it had become their ritual to engage fully and unabashed into each other. Today for some strange reason they fore felt the inevitable was in the air, so after they had eaten they looked into each other eyes and saw it was near now. Sensing this could be the last time for a very long time to come, they ripped the clothes off their bodies to fully meet each other in the flesh. Feverishly, desperately, they made love, totally engrossed and in awe with each other. Like unleashed furies they had taken possession of each other, fiercely thrusting their flesh. Jacky sucked in Sean as he moved in to her with force while she blissfully accommodated him before like she was made of elastic bounced back on him. They reached a climax and felt their bodies and minds fusing to be whole. They knew they were part of each other. Exhausted now, sweating profusely, they noticed they had lack of drinks in the house and Jacky suggested Sean to go to the super Mercado nearby for some supplies. Smiling after a shower Sean dressed left Jacky in lingerie to run the errands. Jacky put on a house coat just in case anyone would drop but when all hell broke loose. Shouting in Portuguese followed by English people bonked on the door:

"Open up rapido, police here!!"

Jacky though she knew they would get arrested was nevertheless shaken. I am alone what to do, she thought. God knows what this kind of police will do with a woman alone. She decided to wait till Sean returned and to call Sean and asked him to return instantly.

"Open up, police!", she heard again as she locked herself into the bedroom. The police not at all deterred, kept on shouting loud enough for the whole neighborhood to hear:

"Open up now, we know you are there. Open now or we break down the door."

Sean raced back as he promised. Who cares, Jacky thought, when they do break down the door it was to arrest them anyway, so she kept quiet to wait for Sean. She quickly put on jeans then thinking she did not want Sean arrested outside she shouted back::

"Wait, wait, I am not dressed!!!"

"Okay, make it hurry up," the answer came.

Two minutes later to make herself look unattractive, she put on a shirt and a jacket. Then she opened the door and was cuffed right away and ten uniformed police stormed inside.

"Where is the man," the leader of the team demanded. Jacky trying to keep composure in spite of her handcuffed hands reacted:

"Tell me what you are here for and I might answer your question too?"

"You are under arrest for the murder of a Naga leader in Manila," he said.

"You have no jurisdiction here," she said feeling her heart race but calming down fast, "You can arrest me for crimes committed here. On the basis of what authority do you think you can arrest me?"

"We followed the Manila and Indian Police who traced you here! Where is the man?"

"You are looking for me?", Sean asked and smiled. He had arrived all eyes were on the house, not with people passing by..

"Arrest that man," the leader shouted noticing none of the policemen under his command had guarded the approach to the house. Instead they had just watched what was happening inside the house. The unit commander looked very dissatisfied with the behavior of his men. This would not be the end of the matter as he said:

"You are a bunch of amateurs!"

The men quickly cuffed the smiling Sean and after a search of the house, a warrant to that effect was never shown, Jacky and Sean were led away and put into a car. Then the whole team sped off to a police station.

At the head office of the Rio police the Indian team had been anxiously waiting and now that they saw the cars pulling in they felt they should immediately relay the good news to the home front. They had been lying low for two days as they did not know what to do but to check on the phone numbers of this friend of Jacky and Sean, but it did not lead to anything substantial, until that phone call reached this station and a voice had entrusted them with the address of their hide out. They would have liked to find them themselves, for that would have given them much more credit. Still it was quite strange that, as they later learned, a complete stranger had phoned the Brazilian Embassy with the message where the assassins could be found. Instantly the Embassy had relayed the message to the Foreign Ministry, which without, delay had called the head office of the police. And now it happened right in front of them, Jacky and Sean coming out of the car to be led inside.

Celia and Bailung were trying to keep in touch with the developments. Only dependent on the news they could not be fully informed and so they could not take precautions either. Keeping to the house as much as possible, just what Jacky and Sean had decided to do, it was Celia who went out to go to work and to shop for essentials, like food and drinks. Aside from being confined they had the time of their lives catching up on lost time and ultimately loving each other. Though extremely difficult now, they prepared for they time that they had to live without each other.

"Oh Celia," Bai said when he felt time was really short now, "should we not try to leave the country and get to a place where we cannot be extradited?"

"Good idea," she smiled, "if you were alone! Are you serious you want us to be together as much as I want that?"

"With all my heart," he exclaimed and took her in his arms to hug her tight and as they were lost in each other, only something like half an hour later they could talk seriously on the matter again after hectically expressing their loving feelings to each other in the flesh. Fully satisfied and lying on a rug, nude and vulnerable, this was the most intense exchange and they had. Too beautiful and serene to continue that almost hostile conversation they had begun:

"Then repent and hope you will get off with a light sentence when the plotter tells the story behind the assassination? Oh darling I don't want us to be on the run for the rest of our life, my man."

"It is what we really decided already," Bai agreed, "but being here with you and feeling I can do things again, makes it of so difficult to leave you again," he explained.

"Yes of course, I feel the same. I know I will miss you tremendously, but the alternative is worse. We will live a very uncertain life. I do not want that, I want you fully," Celia said as a tear of joy fell from her eye as she softly touched his manhood. To Bai this was a sign to make love again, this time much more gentle and taking longer time. When they were capable prepared themselves something to eat, Bai suddenly announced:

"Look Celia, let's get it over with. Another such day like we have now and it will be impossible to forget you or to turn myself in?"

"Yeah let's enjoy each other as much as we can and then face all the consequences. It is the best thing to do my darling," she said.

They spend the rest of the day like they had no care in the world. But then the next morning after a wonderful night of lovemaking in which the explored all avenues and discovered many untouched and little known places of body and mind, they had coffee and breakfast.

"So, I should take you seriously Celia I should go to my house today?"

"I will take my day off, man of mine," Celia answered laughing, "so not this morning or afternoon, but this evening or even tomorrow morning you will do it," she answered while she went to the door to pick up the newspaper called the Inquirer.

"Okay my love," Bai smirked.

He took a sip from his coffee when he heard Celia shouting:

"Baaaiiiu, Baaaiiiiii," she cried out.

"Oh gosh, what is wrong," Bai reacted immediately worried.

"Oh no, darling, nothing it is what we did not expect. There is a headline in the newspaper that Sean and Jacky, your partner, have been arrested in Rio de Janeiro."

"Come let me see?", he asked. Celia sat his lap so they could both read and read how things had developed, precisely as the Scorpion had orchestrated it. The article ended with the suggestion that only it was the plotter and the man in Manila were still at large and either one would know why they had planned to kill the Naga leader.

"My goodness," Bai exclaimed, they think I am with the plotter or that I have designed this diabolical plan."

"They don't seem to be any wiser from Sean. Did Jacky know anything?", Celia asked.

"I cannot be sure but I have no indication she knew more about it. So no," Bai answered.

"So, it was Sean who took the contract?", Celia asked Bai.

"Well it was more shoved up to us then taking the contract," Bai answered.

"Because of the Rwanda shamble? So, both of you took the contract?", Celia kept on asking now.

"Yes through Sean on both accounts," Bai answered.

"So, you did not do it for the money, all right, that suits me much better," Celia sighed.

"No, no, not for the money at all," Bai said and pondered how his friend Sean and Jacky were faring.

"They know nothing," he said after a while, "well unless my best friend deludes us and is the actual plotter, but I am quite certain it is not him," Bai qualified after his silence.

"You are sure indeed then? Plotters normally do not come out to show themselves. They have reason to stay back to influence. This assassination has many implications for India and the Nagas," Celia said.

"I never knew the Nagas as well as I do now," Bai agreed, "the one pulling the strings knew and decided that by way of this assassination this case would be a catching one. This could be behind it, I think," Bai said.

"So, you have decided to go to your house then?", Celia suddenly asked. Bai looked at her, pain in his eyes as he said.

"I cannot hide forever and we decided against running, so yes I better face the music."

"We better face the music we are a team now darling," Celia murmured in protest.

"Of course we are," Bai smiled, "but this was my doing, not yours. I am responsible and it hurts me that you are involved. I should face the music alone."

"That is good of you and you carry that load like a man, but I am your woman now and we shall face this together," Celia said in a very decisive tone, one Bai could no longer argue with and so he smiled;

"Stand by your man?", he playfully asked as he took her in his arms and did not stop holding her till they were both fully satisfied in spirit and in the flesh.

"It is too difficult to say goodbye," Celia sighed, "I have prepared for the moment but when it is so near, like right now, I cannot do it. It will be the same tomorrow morning. I don't want to be alone tonight, but tomorrow you will gone and you will tear my heart out," Celia said emotionally, her face flushed as she gently touching his'. Overcome by her he held on to her like she was his beacon, his shining light and let his tears freely run over his face whispering:

"Oh darling what we have is unique and we made it ourselves. Let's be strong enough to face all difficulties which are right in front of us? We will suffer and yearn for each other and we will be tempted to give up too. I pledge to you here and now Celia, my woman, that you my soul mate I will never leave ever again!"

"Oh Bai, you are going to be put away for some time. Who knows how long, so don't pledge what you cannot do?", she mockingly said yet very well knowing what Bai had meant, prompting him back to face reality nevertheless.

"I will never leave you again," he said now very seriously, "in spirit we are connected. In body we will be again. No matter how long we have to wait, we will be reunited," he solemnly said.

This time Celia could not quite hold herself either. Her tears flowed freely as she moved her face on Bai's chest. They lay for a long time and communicated without words. Only in the middle of the night they realized they were getting cold and they crept into bed to sleep the sleep of the innocent. That morning after, they day they had decided Bai would go to his house, Celia felt her courage sinking in her shoes and she clung to him pleading to forget what she had said the night before.

"Don't go my darling Bai; life is too difficult without you!"

Bai looked and felt torn apart, but he was determined. Just one thing bothered him, a thing that could give her hope. Something he did and was the only thing he had not revealed to her. As he kissed Celia gently his mind raced on the idea to tell her or not. After taking a shower with her and had dressed he took her in his arms and whispered:

"We decided and we must carry our cross. I pledged to you that I will return. Now you do that too, we will feel both strong and connected?"

Celia felt her blood rushing through her veins as she hopelessly let emotion now rule her reasoning, thinking normally she was in command of. She cried as she spoke:

"Yes I love you Bai you are in me, we are connected, and you are my soul. Now go or I will not be able to let you," she said and turned around. Bai went after her, from behind he embraced her, brushed his lips over the skin of her neck:

"Now my Celia I can go, you should feel we are inseparable in spirit. United we are!", he said very slowly and thinking the surprise which would materialize some time later he would keep for her. Having decided that he let her go and without either one looking back, he walked out of the house into the daylight of busy Manila. He stopped a taxi passing by to get to his house. Bai smiled when he was driven to his house by a jolly taxi driver and thought all was good now. Now there was no turning back, he thought and mentally embraced Celia before he was dropped. In front of his house it shot through him the fridge could have come alive, the fungi growing like wildfire and the remnants of cooked meat would be infested by maggots. He waved to the taxi driver who bowed for him when he saw the handsome tip and went inside. Silence encapsulated him, but not for very long. He opened the fridge and saw the spoiled items had been removed and he realized there must have been people inside. He was just thinking about that and checked what could have been taken, when it dawned on him nothing was and so it must have been the doing of the police. This thought, still on his mind, was confirmed by a sudden voice from the door. It took the Manila Police only a few minutes to come down on him.

Bai turned and saw two policemen in the doorway, revolvers loosely in hand:

"You must be Bailung," the man who obviously was in command said in a friendly tone, "we have been waiting for you."

"You know I am and I have returned so you can take me in," Bai smiled. This unsettled Eddie who by chance had been checking on the two officers assigned to keep an eye on the house, "I know you wanted me, so here I am," he said happily.

"Turn yourself in?", Eddie said, hardly able to conceal his surprise.

"Yes, my friends have been arrested in Rio de Janeiro, I follow their example,' Bai said.

"They have been betrayed by someone who called the Embassy to show where to find them," Eddie said, "and you give yourself up voluntarily?"

"Yes, I am," Bai confirmed, "I will tell you all about it, but don't ask me why we did it or what is behind this assassination, for I do not know, Sean and Jacky don't know either.

"Really now," Eddie smirked in contempt, "so you killed a man for fun?", Eddie mocked as he paced forward ~~to~~ put cuffs around Bai's hands, who smiled still, put his hands in front of Eddie to help him.

"Really!" Bai parroted.

"Well we will see," Eddie smiled now.

"Did you clean up my fridge?", Bai asked,

"Yeah, it was stinking in here man, we opened the doors too for a while," Eddie nodded.

"That is commendable and thoughtful of you, but I instantly knew no robbers had been here but the police," Bai said.

"That is why we were near, so you would not be able to run again," Eddie laughed.

"No running from my side," Bai smirked.

"You are prepared then, you are under arrest for the murder of the Naga leader. You can get yourself a lawyer?", Eddie asked.

"I did not kill him," Bai whispered.

"You did not? Who did?", Eddie, now astounded asked.

"It will soon be known," Bai answered and produced a smile again, "it was Jacky who pulled the trigger. I am an accomplice. I did drive the care from which the shots were fired. I planned and surveyed so we would be in the right spot and at the right time. I am fully responsible, but I did not pull the trigger," Bai stressed but talked slowly.

"Let's talk further in the station," Eddie said and led Bai to the car, the other policeman smiling now too opened for him, as he was relieved things had gone so smoothly.

At the station Bai was received and treated with full regards. He was after all their prime suspect of an international network and the first one they had actually captured. Eddie was a happy man for thanks to his perseverance in pursuing the leads he had dug up himself, the Indian Police could apprehend the culprits in Rio and he, Eddie himself, here in Manila now too. Granted without the help of this unknown person who had also posted a press release on those assassins on the international news wires, the Brazilians could not have taken them into their custody. However now they seemed to have a big problem on their hands Eddie remembered. Those two had different nationalities, but the Indians were pulling strings on the Brazilians, yet they could only be extradited to their own countries. The Brazilians only had some international responsibility with respect to criminality, so they would cooperate with the Indians in interrogating the two, but they could not extradite those people to India, no matter how much they would have liked that. With Bai there was no such problem. Bai was a Philippino national and the Philippine authorities would not mind the Indians interrogating Bai about his motives. Bai would be under Philippine law and would be prosecuted here. There was something bugging him however; why would Bai give himself up? Did he cover for someone else? Was this act meant to delude them? Yes, I will work with the Indian police for this is still an enigmatic story and I want to get to the bottom of it, he said to himself as Bai looked at him and smiled in quite friendly a way.

Chapter 15

Leaving Nagaland

To his great surprise and just after they had left Lungthing's office, suddenly, even from a distance already Marius saw Shilu on the doorstep of their hotel in Dimapur.

"Surprise, surprise," she shouted smiled at Jeanie, "I could not stay away Marius!!!"

"I can see that," Marius gasped as he fell into her arms.

"I think I should leave you two alone," Jeanie said as she turned, "I will go into town for a while, we have some hours left before our bus rides to Guwahati, all right?"

"Of course, but you don't have to run off," Shilu and Marius said like they were speaking through one mouth.

"That does it," Jeanie reacted as she felt the simmering pain in her heart, a pain she was determined to get rid off, but did cut deeper when she had this confrontation.

"You need not go," Marius tried again, but Jeanie resolutely had turned and walked off only saying while leaving:

"See you for dinner man!", and was soon out of sight.

"So here we are alone together, let's use our time man," Shilu smiled, "she will get over it. Jeanie is a strong woman and we did talk about this before."

"Yeah you did and so she did with me," Marius smiled and he lifted her, lifted her all the way up in the room, leaving the people inside the lobby stunned as they saw him pass.

Inside the room he laid her down on the bed, smiled, then thought of something, turned to lock the door, returned, looked at her, taking in a relaxed and smiling Shilu, bowed over to her and like it was extraordinarily normal began to undress her. Shilu did not protest, her smile not fading.

"Off are the shoes, "Marius whispered, no it was more like softly hissing, "off is your blouse," he continued after he had lifted her and unbuttoned it to take it off of her, "your pants now too, he smiled after unzipping the stretch pants she wore elegantly and had pulled the pair off her. "Now for your lingerie," Marius said softly, swallowing some liquid in his throat, as he moved his hands behind her back and their faces touched each other sending shivers through their spines, "off is your brassiere," he said smiling excitedly when their eyes met and he could have sworn they were drowning in each other. "Now for the grand finale," he said hearing his heart beating faster and lifted her buttocks to get her panty off.

"It is my turn now," Shilu giggled and came up fully nude to guide Marius now who willingly took the position Shilu had been in.

"Off are you shoes," she said equally excited and gasping to control her breath after she had unlaced his shoes and looked up to him. "Now my man, off goes the jacket," and she threw it away like it was a nuisance to her. She opened the first buttons off Marius' shirt but then looked at him a moment, scanning his feelings and still looking into his eyes with a quick motion of her wrist tore his shirts to shreds, only making Marius giggle in delight. "Now your trousers my man," she smiled innocently as she unzipped him and studied what came into view, then pulled off his trousers. "Oh I forgot your socks," she fumbled and pulled them off throwing far away from her in the direction of the trousers as she overcome some hindrance, triumphant about that, "hhhmmmm," she laughed, "I see some black underpants here, underpants with a bulge, what could that mean?", she said seriously but could not compose herself and smiled then burst out in laughter. Before Marius could react Shilu buried her face into his chest and began to smooch him, her breasts on his flesh igniting the fire that had been simmering for a long time but now had all the ingredients present to enflame him. He held her head as she, unabashed now, tasted his flesh, his skin. He let her be and felt the intensity of the now ultimately direct contact. Marius sighed, which made Shilu lift her head which he moved to hold and squirmed under her weight. He moved his lips to hers and without any inhibition kissed her passionately. Gone was his intention to be gentle, soft, warm and considerate. She had lighted the fire further as she moved on him and he hauled her in, practically screamed at her to tell her about his burning love and desire for her.

"We will unite here and now," Shilu hissed softly again

"Oh yesssssss," he screamed back at her, "I am yearning to be united!" "Oooooohhhhhhhhh darling, I want you around me, in me, come to me!", Shilu hissed back at him as he picked her up and tossed her on the bed to open her legs. He bent over to kiss her jewel as she shuddered in delight when he ran his tongue over her labia, the lips he had called playfully her doors of his perception. He slowly went up over her belly as she laid there in ecstasy, eagerly anticipating his coming over to her and inside her very being. He felt like penetrating her soul through her body and he slowly slid his tongue over her inner lips, her quivering sensitivity rising. And, as he briefly touched it while she quivered, like her royal wetness opened to him. Awe rose in him and slowly he made his tongue travel up through her pubic hair, back against her faintly tanned skin. Slowly up now, as she lay helpless but in joy and exasperation. Up he went playing with her belly button, making her giggle to move further up and reached in between her breasts to slide his full tongue there and made it rest while his hands now fondled her form ever so softly. He squeezed her nipples and she felt his shaft rising against her knee and he did not know and where to concentrate or feel, anymore, now that all in her was opened and the floodgates of feeling thundered over her. No longer able to lay still she grabbed him by his buttocks to pull him towards her. On her she gasped and took his face in her hands to kiss her man, her man Marius, passionately. He had awaked her lust, her whole being now lifted up to him, as she moved to lead his shaft to into her sanctuary:

"This is out moment darling," she whispered.

"This is our celebration of life," Marius whispered back.

This is our union fro life," she answered.

"This is our unbreakable connection," Marius agreed as his shaft entered her inner being. Both shuddered and lay still savoring the moment of feeling now being physically one too. Quivering as lust took possession of them, Marius brushed his lips over her neck and gentle bit in her earlobe, making her shiver. Unbearable it became and by their command their lips were sealed, all of them. They began to move, slowly but gaining confidence when both felt lust was equally met and they boldly moved and faster.

"Harder," he hissed as she sad nothing but sighed to show they were ready to outdo themselves, "faster," she added as she grabbed his buttocks and began to thrust, both on the verge of loosing control willingly so to let their real inner feelings speak to peak. Unleashed now, Shilu thrust up to Marius and began the eternal dance of up and down. Suddenly with a twist her body they turned both so she could to ride him. Grimacing openly she heaved and arched to dance on the full length of his shaft, eyes closed. Marius thrusts went up high and made her fly in the air, only to come down on him with force as she was impaled by his shaft.

"Oh baby," Shilu moaned.

"Oh darling," he replied as sweat poured out of him now.

She suddenly bent over to him spreading her breasts over his chest, letting her nipples grind his skin there. Marius took her buttocks and buried himself as deeply as he could in her. Faster now they moved, "deeper more," she moaned, "harder darling," he cried out loud, but realizing all in the hotel might hear her she muffled her face into his. Marius encouraged by her wildness unleashed his vigor and thrust so strongly they were being airborne without a soft landing. So tightly their sweated bodies merged which, the pearly perspiration made them slip and slide effortlessly over each other. Marius moaned as their eyes met for the last round, the round that would take them to heaven itself. He sucked in her face as he felt her pulsating flesh around him, swirled around to let her move her legs around his back. She opened herself fully to make him dive deeper into her as she heaved her breasts lustily shuddering before the explosion. Nearly there too now Marius hammered a series of thrusts into her flesh desperately clinging to her buttocks and he rhythmically began to pound her like the earth itself moved. There was no stopping now when Marius he felt Shilu convulsing, her flesh reacting in spasms around him. She sighed in sheer climax and again cried out to muffle herself on his sweated face. The last of the pounding thrusts made him jerk up and cry out for the wave enveloped both of them as he jetted out to release his fertile juices into her being. Pulsating, quivering, jerking, shuddering, pounding, shaking and all that went on between them but escaped them for the feelings could not to be caught in mere words and they collapsed into each other to feel they were floating up to the heavens above.

Still sighing and shuddering on top of her, deeply connected but incapacitated Marius came to rest letting her take possession of him in the aftermath. Marius began to recuperate and heaved his head from her chest to briefly look at her. Then on impulse he showered her with hundreds of little kisses. It felt like he could not stop, making her burst into giggles. No longer in lust but connected in the flesh their togetherness grew and playful now and Shilu reacted with giggles when she felt Marius' shaft leaving her sanctuary as it decreased to normal size.

"Only momentarily it changed form a sanctuary into a cavern of lust," she whispered and held him as she kissed his face. Slowly they returned to the sanity of life, but were merged in mind now though and less in body, yet they touched and felt mentally closer than ever. Now that their unity had been felt and they had touched the core, the bond between them felt like it was forged by a blacksmith, the heat they had whipped up for each other had bound iron and made it into their shape.

"Beautiful," Shilu whispered as they lay close, so close as they casually touched very softly but decisively.

"Beautiful," Marius repeated and let silence sink in for now they communicated without words. No restriction to be felt anymore for them. They were inseparable and felt it in their pores. Shilu said it out loud, not for his confirmation on what they felt but know it was a solemn occasion:

"You are my man Marius," she said and looked at him.

"This is our celebration of life Shilu, my woman," Marius said feeling overwhelmed.

Slowly they landed down on earth again and sensually washed in the shower, hilariously playing with each other.

Finally Marius suggested making a few calls to find out what was happening. Though the uprising had been momentarily subdued, the tension was simmering and could flare up any time should there be an indication for it and many reasons if found to be holding water were laying in waiting.

"Hello Bram, anything you found out?", Marius asked when he had him on the phone.

"Lots;" Bram smirked, "you know the people in Rio have been arrested?"

"They caught them?"

"Yeah, Bram," answered, "an anonymous person gave details where to find them and published an article on the wires!"

"Oh, so the police did not find them then?"

"No, but the Manila Police caught the one who stayed behind there, the man quite happily had himself arrested when he returned to his house," Bram explained.

"Did they reveal anything of what they were after by killing this Naga leader," Marius asked him.

"Nothing yet, they say they were hired assassins, well sort of coerced. They have no idea; they say why the man should have been killed. Although? May be that is not true. They say only after the killing they found out he was a Naga leader and tried to find out what that really meant."

"You mean they had no idea about Nagaland and only found out later the Naga People had been at war with India?", Marius asked further.

"Precisely," Bram said.

"But do they know about who commissioned, coerced them then?", Marius eagerly asked, "do they know the person? Can they point him or her out?"

"Nothing like that Marius," Bram replied.

"How is that possible man?", Marius exclaimed.

"Don't be naïve," Bram laughed, "you know of course anything is possible if a plotter wants to remain in the shadows. Of course the man or woman operated by remote control, nobody knows who he or she is."

"Not even if it is a woman or a man?", Marius asked.

"Where are you with our head," Bram laughed again; "you are an agent. You have come across many plots, dirty dealings and deception, so why are you surprised about this. What have you been doing there in Nagaland man?"

"When in this beautiful countryside with ordinary people, who live directly from the earth all is pure and to an extent simple and down to earth I seem to be out of it. Perhaps the idea that these people deserve to determine their own future has influenced my thinking. That could be it," Marius laughed too.

"Your job as an agent is a thing of the past," Bram mocked him, "but seriously man, it looks like these people do not know the one who handed them the contract. They do not even know what country the person came from."

"How did they communicate then?"

"Through email and with aliases, not the real names," Bram said, "it is quite simple to do that on the internet."

"But how did they get the money delivered to them. Isn't that an act that can be traced?", Marius asked.

"Yes, that is a good one and your mind seems to be working again," Bram could not stop himself from mocking Marius some more, "I did come up with the same question. They received 1 million dollars in cash and the money was brought to them. Up front the first part in Amsterdam, the second part in Manila after the assassination had been carried out and was confirmed."

"The Manila Police is on it?"

"Like the Indian and the Brazilian," Bram confirmed.

"Any leads?", Marius asked.

"Nothing yet, there seems to be a trail which leads to the USA via UPS," Bram said, "though nothing is certain yet man."

"You mean the money has been shipped through UPS?"

"Yes, only later it was found that the box contained money, twice it was sent!"

"From the USA?", Marius asked.

"Yes a label was found with UPS on it, sloppy of the sender don't you think?", Bram laughed.

"Yeah, so they went over to UPS to check on the dealings through that company?", Marius smiled, "so, that could be a lead indeed. Soon you might have the address in front of you then!"

"Let's hope so, but if true this will mean another predicament. If the USA is implicated or even the initiator this could have far reaching repercussions," Bram analyzed.

"It is strange," Marius reacted, "very strange, for what is actually in it for the USA? I can't imagine anything, you?"

"Not yet, but before long we will know. Perhaps it is something to get India disturbed about, the Americans do not like anyone with nuclear weapons!", Bram analyzed.

"True, but they did clinch a deal with India recently, so I do not see why they need to scheme under the table again and over the heads of innocent people, already at war for such a long time? Your analysis exposes a vile attitude to me Bram!", Marius told him.

"It is a hunch man," don't take it too seriously, but I am known to have hunches which came to be true, even after a while, you know that!", Bram laughed.

"Yeah that is true," Marius laughed with him, "anything else?"

"No nothing specific there is now?" Bram answered, "are you doing well?"

I am in heaven, that should tell you enough," Marius smirked.

"You are returning soon then, a week or so?"

"Less than that Bram," Marius answered, "tonight we are off to Guwahati, a day or two there for talks then to Delhi and the same day back to Amsterdam. So in about three to four days from now you can expect me in the office."

"Good, I need help, checking on your interests takes too much time man!", he said in jest.

"I will relieve you soon," Marius replied.

"All right, see you then, only call when you need to," Bram concluded.

Marius disconnected too and briefed Shilu on the other half of the conversation she could not have heard.

"Now I want to check on some things," she said, "but first I want you to flow over me so I can feel you in body, heart and soul," she smiled and came to him and touched him with her skin. Marius responded but since it was an intense but gentle interlude they did not push on to fully engage. On his lap sporting her lingerie Shilu called Lungthing to tell what she heard and to hear if he had something new too since that very morning:

"That is a strange development if proven to be true," Lungthing said.

"Yeah I thought so too," Shilu confirmed as she smiled at Marius and played with his chest and teased his shaft.

"There is s lot going on among the people here too. There are reports of the people wanting to rise again. Considering the suicides, which many do not believe to be true, but judge as a diversion of the Indian Government, they are practically certain they are being deluded and demonstrations are organized to demand the truth," Lungthing told her.

"This will put a lot of pressure on the Indian government Lungthing," Shilu replied.

"Indeed it will and troops here already on alert."

"Something must be done or the bloodbath will take place in couple of days. When the Army goes out to contain and shoots with live ammunition, there will be massacres?", he asked rhetorically.

"Do you think it is possible the Indians deployed Europeans for the assassination, directed by an American company?"

"Ha," Lungthing reacted, "I am not surprised by anything anymore. The Indians are capable of anything if it suits them and the Americans? They are opportunists; they don't care for us whatsoever, but will sacrifice us for their own interests. So, the answer is yes, this could be an Indian plan in collaboration with the USA!"

"Seems to be far fetched though," Shilu judged, "it will be too transparent when it comes out into the open, then the critique will be overwhelming?", she asked.

"You would be surprised how susceptible the international community is to safety precautions; the Americans after all want to keep their own house clean and will say that it is all done to prevent a bigger war from breaking out!"

"I don't know," Shilu replied looking at Marius, "I think it is an organization behind this, or an individual trying to remain obscure as long as possible or forever, just to make still waters ripple with action. I would not surprise me if it is all then to break through the stalemate in the peace talks that do not seem to go anywhere," she explained.

"Well that could be true too," Lungthing laughed, "yes that could be as well! But let's face it we do not know and there will be a lot more speculation before we have come to the bottom of this. Speculation does not help, but to be prepared for all alternatives could a wise thing. This we do here in practice," he said, implicitly calling her back to reality.

"Okay, got your point," she smiled, "I will see you soon brigadier!"

"Is there anything left for us to do," Shilu turned to Marius after the call.

"I can't think of anything from here," Marius answered.

"You have to leave tonight," Shilu said, "we have to arrange to meet again. I have accepted the job for international exposure of the cause!"

"That is an excellent surprise," Marius reacted, "that is so wonderful."

"And I could go and live in Amsterdam. The talks are there and I should find a place to stay and an office, so I can run it," she smiled. "you will loose your freedom Marius, for I will be checking on you constantly, she said joyfully.

"You are welcome to do that and when you are certain I am trustworthy. It is the time I will make my move," Marius laughed.

"You better don't think about that," Shilu grimaced, "you don't know Naga women yet!"

"Oh, oh, you are threatening me?", he asked laughing and picking her up to smooch her face wonderfully.

"Seriously now Marius, this has come as a surprise indeed and you have your work, irregular work. I am sure whatever comes out of this unfortunate happening, which did cost our leader his life, could blow the Naga issue out into the open. I want to be there to capitalize on it, so I feel I have to move fast. They will send me over in a week or so, Shilu explained.

"You are welcome to stay with me. My place can accommodate two people easily. It will be yours and with that base in mind you can go around finding some cheap office space. And, you should connect with this Naga International Support Center. What do you think about that, darling?"

That's simply wonderful, Marius. I will make the arrangements after you have gone. I will stay in Dimapur for a couple of days to do that," she said.

"So, I can expect you in a week or so?"

"Certainly!"

"Then I will adapt my apartment a little, it is a man's house after all, you know." Marius laughed, "I suspect you will take over in no time?"

"Very funny you think you are, but yes, I am sure we will have to make some changes. Living alone is quite different from living together if that is what you meant," Shilu teased him further.

"You will be the first woman to actually live with me Shilu. I have lived alone for quite some time. I come and go and I have not been home that much anyway, so do keep in mind to go easy on me?"

"Well, you are my man. I have hardly lived on my own at all and I might feel that living with you is not very lively. I am used to many people around me," Shilu said.

"Let's not worry about it," Marius smiled, "You have your work and you can start your Naga office from my place. I will be away more than you would like or expect, you know!", Marius stressed but smiled.

"Yes, I should be realistic, it will not be easy and I am sure to need your help and your expertise too," she acknowledged.

"We feel close and get easily irritated too, but we love each other so we should be able to deal with things, don't you think?", Marius asked.

"I agree, we should both adapt, we are both strong personalities though Marius, it is not unthinkable we will clash at times," she teased.

"I would not expect anything else darling," Marius smiled, "but think of this, as long as our base is solid we can weather a storm!"

And with that remark both felt that a possible clash which could occur when moving in with each other blindly was averted. There was not much time left before Jeanie was to return and Shilu and Marius suddenly felt very hungry. But first Shilu helped Marius packing his things and when he had written down and punched phone numbers and addresses, as if by prior arrangement Jeanie walked in on them.

"Hello there," she said, "shall we go and eat now? I have packed my things and just like to take a shower before we go."

"Take your time; we have two hours before the bus leaves from the station Jeanie. Check your case, take your bath and come to the restaurant around the corner, same one," Marius said.

"You did not have enough time yet?", she laughed, "okay go ahead I will see you in half an hour or so. Then I will tell you all about my experiences and my brush with the law."

"What," Marius exclaimed, "you had a run in with the law?"

"It is an interesting story but it meant little to me. It was more significant to how people are treated here. It was no policeman but the military. Can you believe they tried to get into my pants?"

"I can believe many a man is like that, but I did not realize those soldiers actually dared to get to you. Yes tell us all about that over dinner, Jeanie," Shilu said.

Chapter 16

In accordance to the master plan the Scorpion reveals

"We are getting nowhere," Eddie remarked, "whatever we do we cannot find the connection to plotter, the person who assigned these three people. Bailung is willing to cooperate but the only direct connection is that the plotter knows both Bailung and Sean because of their Rwanda misdeeds, but they have no idea who that person is assigned them. They checked all they were with then and came to the conclusion it could be anyone of more than a hundred. And, even then, the story could have been told to the plotter, so without actually knowing Sean or Bai, he could have moved. The money trail through UPS led us not to the man too. We are at a dead end men," he explained during a meeting in which was discussed to drop further investigation as it did take a lot of time needed for other cases, "I can only hope, considering what little impact the assassination had on Nagaland yet, the plotter will move again," he added, "but not here!"

"What makes you think so?" the chief asked.

"This murder only makes sense if it has impact. I was puzzled by that, the real motivation, that is why I call the perpetrator the plotter. He did not assign to assassinate for fun. There is purpose," he said.

"Well, we can't do much now and we need you all for more pressing domestic things," the chief announced.

"I will get into this puzzle," Eddie smiled, "but in my spare time then!"

"I will help you," Efren said.

"Then let's get back to work, the team is dissolved and officially I don't know you are still on this case, all right?", the chief concluded.

"It is odd," said Efren when they were on their own again, "the Brazilian police does not get anywhere either. Sean simply can't figure out who it is. There were too many people involved. I am sure they will not devote much of their time to figure out who it can be!"

“Yeah, we have to drop it. We too don’t have enough time and manpower to check out the people Bailung could come up with,” Eddie agreed, “I think the plotter will move soon. Nothing has changed in Nagaland. I think this change is what the plotter is after.”

“Do you think that because the suicides have taken the suspicion off the Indian Government and things look like returning to normal there the plotter has to move again?”, Efren asked.

“Precisely,” Eddie stated, “let’s see what it will be. I wonder what room he will use to move for he must whip up some attention, of that I am certain.”.

Alone in his hone in New York the Scorpion was deep in thought. Assessing the developments he knew he had not achieved what he envisaged. The impact of the assassination was diverted, deflected. It was time for the back up plan, he thought. The Brazilians could not get to him, neither those in Manila could, he knew. He had covered his tracks wonderfully; it could even be that even when he would reveal the person behind this, he would not be believed. He was convinced now to break the case open once and for all. Displaced shame of what the Baptists had left behind consumed him. To be a real Baptist here, we should not have left the Nagas to rot in their misery of being occupied brutally. Too many people have been killed and that has to stop. However my first attempt failed. Oh God the feeling alone to calculate this assassination was bad enough. The idea to sacrifice one person to make sure the suffering of these people could come to an end, made me decide to do it. But now that it did not have the impact I thought, I should have other measures to follow up on or it will just be an assassination on an innocent victim. I cannot let that happen, he said to himself, quite angrily in fact. He forced himself to think ahead to assess, to choose and effectuate one of his back up plans. He had promised already that, as much as possible, he would spare the assassins Sean, Bailung and Jacky, now he knew he had to be true to his word. Already he had been feeling bad about recruiting Sean and Bailung on coercion. He absolved himself for that with the idea that, to an extent they had deserved that for what they had done in Rwanda, and that this act was for a good purpose, so they could redeem themselves. This was not entirely true of course, because by murdering someone and on command there was little redemption to be gained if at all. But, the good purpose should count too and he had given them up so they were in custody of the police to be brought to court and sentenced. That was real redemption and they could get the death penalty for that if he, the Scorpion, would leave it at that. He smiled about that idea, for he knew he would not let it rest, now that he had come this far. This time I should be conclusive and decisive and the only way I can do just that is when I reveal all, without any reservation. Yeah, he said out loud now, not to convince himself for he knew that already, but to encourage himself to come out into the open. The impact of the revelations would reverberate in every corner on earth he smiled. But he should not reveal all in one go, he should keep the attention raised going by revealing bits and pieces. So, he began to design a publicity plan, a step by step plan that ultimately would lead to him, the Scorpion and he would have himself arrested. Before that he would arrange to be interviewed by renowned journalists, he would reveal the core of the plot. From that point on he would draw attention to the long term problem and would point his fingers to those responsible for it. He began to work on a declaration he intended to send to the press, an enigmatic one which would be the first of series which would lead to him. This first one would be focused on the assassins he had hired and he would focus on the coercion for a purpose, the purpose? The hint to the purpose he would give, but first the vindication of the assassins for he would confess, without revealing his name, who the real culprit was, but a culprit with a mission. Literally and figuratively he had a mission, he laughed to himself, for the missionaries broke off their mission he now picked up. Was he not a missionary too?

The draft of this declaration he had finished within an hour and it went like this:

Assassins of slain Naga leader in Manila coerced for the purpose of dislodging the Indian Government for its occupation and mass oppression of the Naga people

Set the projected assassins of the slain Naga leader free for the real responsible person behind this assassination is running free. With the assassination this person had this single objective in mind, to get the Indian troops out of Nagaland. It is a disgrace to the international community that it let the Indian Forces unabatedly oppress the Naga people who have but one way to uphold their rights and that is to defend themselves against a brutal aggressor. The International Community should call on the Indian Government to speed up negotiations to achieve an honorable and mutually agreeable settlement with the Naga People. The assassins were commissioned to sacrifice the Naga leader so the attention of the sullen International Community and that of the Baptist Community of the USA is drawn to this terribly long term predicament the Nagas are in.

The Baptists you wonder? Yes the Baptists of the USA who have been there for over a hundred years were coerced too, they had to leave when the Indians after they began the war against the Nagas. They were coerced to leave for fear that their other missions in India would be threatened. They left the Nagas to bleed on their own. The American Baptists did forsake them and left them to be overrun by the India. Not even when back in the USA did they raise the alarm on the genocide that was taking place. They disqualified them for the lack of the 'love your neighbor principle' they tacitly displayed.

I call on all concerned, on the International Community and the Baptists in America and the world to intervene in the hopeless peace process between India and Nagaland, to condemn India and to order that country to stop subduing the Naga Peoples. In order to redeem them I ask the Baptists specifically to muster all their resources to support the Nagas. More on the matter I will release in a few days.

This Press release which did not have a sender or address hit the press like a bomb. Though nobody seemed to be able to verify the credibility of the source, so at first it was judged to be a hoax, when it was published the reactions were strong, far and wide. Immediately the Baptist communities were asked for comments, but since not too many people knew about the Baptist legacy it took some time to both find old missionaries, who knew, as well as well versed spokesperson who could shed light on the situation. That was not all, how so these assassins were to be vindicated? Was the author of the press statement the plotter? In Manila Eddie laughed:

"It begins men, the plotter moves!"

When Bai was told what would happen he only smiled and said to Eddie:

"It is what was predicted!"

Bai took another step not so much on this release but because of it. He took Eddie aside and whispered to him he had done something on his own account, not even the plotter could know, but Eddie could. Eddie was all ears; he had come to like Bai and wondered if it had anything to do with the pathologist. When Bai confirmed this, Eddie took Bai by surprise by telling him he knew and as he had thought would leave this alone for the moment, as it could too much intervene in the process that had begun to unfold.

In Brazil Sean and Jacky, separated but both in jail now, were reacting to the Indian investigators with similar words.

In Delhi then things were still unsettled. The news that Bailung had been arrested fell good, but when it was known both Sean and Bailung could not produce the connection to the plotter, this raised more than just apprehension. Still it was possible an Indian was behind this. This was very worrisome, not just to the agencies who were already under severe pressure, but also to the responsible ministers.

"Surely the suspicion will be on India again," Patill remarked, "what the hell this team is doing in Rio de Janeiro," he asked, "they have not accomplished anything on their own there. It was the plotter who revealed their position. Are we being led on here?," he asked in the meeting of ministers.

"Hmmm," the Defense minister mumbled, "we are at loss. How can we prepare for the worst if we don't know where to look?," he asked rhetorically.

"There is a not so remote chance that the culprit or culprits are not Indian," the Home Minister said trying to reduce the tension among them.

"Tell that to the Nagas," Patill burst out, "man the longer it takes to find the real plotter the more chance we have the Nagas will rise and because it is now an international, due to the nationalities of the assassins alone, we can forget about keeping the uprising under the table. Gosh, we can expect hundreds of journalist going into Nagaland when things begin in earnest."

"Right," The Home Minister had to agree.

"You tell me now what we should do when the Nagas will protest. Can we stick to the old plan to send in the troops, do you think Defense Minister?"

"Military speaking I see no problem of course. These will be people who demonstrate. We can as much as possible keep journalists out, but I am sure many will take the risk and come in as tourists. We can only prevent anyone from entering when we declare martial law?", he explained.

"What do you mean militarily no problem, you mean you will order people without weapons to be killed by the hundreds?", Patill asked.

"That is why I said there is no problem; the Naga forces cannot do anything in such a situation. It will be a moral and an exposure problem," he said.

"That's right," the Home minister agreed, "but we have to do something!"

"Let's issue a press release stating it could not have been ordered by the Government of India so if it proves to be an Indian, then he would be fully prosecuted as a terrorist and as a plotter to undermine the peace talks," the Defense Minister thought aloud.

"That's an idea, but I predict it will not get us far but could buy us some time," Patill replied as a civil servant came into the room stating there was an emergency.

"What kind man, speak up," the authoritative voice of the Home Minister sounded.

"There is a press statement by someone in the USA about the assassination of the Naga leader," he said quickly and he handed out copies of it to all of them. They read and already after a few lines it became clear they were off the hook, well as the plotters.

"This is good news," the Home minister said and smiled.

"You better read it again," the defense Minister took a bite at him.

They read again and realized that although full blame would be taken by this unknown Baptist American, something far worse was looming. The man admitted he was behind it and blamed the Baptists for leaving Nagaland on the orders of the then Indian Government because of genocide to be concealed.

"This is going to do us in!", Patill understood and said it aloud. The whole world will come to know what happened here and there will be lots of attention drawn to the case. India is openly held responsible. Oh this means international condemnation if we do not swiftly do something about this."

"Well," the Defense Minister said, "this news means also that the Nagas will band together for an uprising, so that will give us time to counteract any allegation!"

"Yeah," the Home Minister who had practically misjudged the dynamics of the situation which was fast spinning out of control, "that is an advantage, but the longer term effects are devastating."

"Yeah devastating," Patill agreed, "I suggest we will take a positive direction, positive for the peace talks. Let's seriously get them on the road so the Nagas will be a little happier and we show the world we are taking them into account too?"

"That is dangerous too," the Home Minister expressed referring to the potential of the domino effect, "we must keep in mind that this could be the beginning of the disintegration of India. Other people see this as an example India will yield to their demands. Think of the Sikhs and the Punjab or the Kashmiri?"

"It all depends how we show the Indian population what it means for the Nagas to be much freer of India. We should allow more insight into the background of their situation," Patill suggested, "only when it is known the Nagas, considering their history and their colonial background plus the idea that Nehru was a little rash in unleashing that war, have a right to fend for themselves. India did not treat them very nicely at all."

"We could start a publicity campaign which aims at propagating a close working relationship with them. It could serve as an example to others as well. That way we can still use the Northeast as the economic jumping board to South East Asia," the Home Minister contributed, "the Look East Policy might work then?"

"Well, at least we are thinking positively, "Patill said, "that way we may be able to avert war and bad publicity. On the other hand we do not know the outcome of this policy of friendliness either. I may be good for the Nagas, but will it be for India? I am not that convinced the other secessionists will put down their protests and say yes we love you India. Considering what India has done to them, this is not very likely!"

"In the end and long run I will say we will not be able to keep the country together, only by applying force. This proved the assault on the Golden Temple of the Sikhs in Amritsar and what did we actually achieve militarily against the Nagas? Of course we could wipe them out. This is what the generals before me said too; we can only by force keep the Nagas within our border. In fact they advised the government then and I speak about 1995 before the cease fire was agreed upon, that the Indian Army could only win the war by annihilating all Nagas. You know as well as I do that the sitting Government then decided to open talks with the Naga leaders to get to the existing cease fire. I can very well imagine the Nagas are getting restless when nothing much in the peace talks is achieved. And now we have this then?"

"Yes, when you are a Naga I can imagine it must be infuriating," Patill smiled.

"That may be all nice and well," the Defense Minister said, "the empathy for the Nagas and that may be good to show in the talks, but we are facing a crisis here, a deluge of questions may come to us. Can we answer them?"

"We are a nation that is internationally growing fast in importance. Many countries are economically connected to India and so we have something important to deal. Yet, we must realize that, if this is blowing out of proportion, we will not be able to depend on countries backing us up. We have to show a good face in public, or if we are not going to do that we must be prepared to be criticized strongly. Now the choice is ours," he said.

"Yeah, we must talk to the PM and set up a strategy for I fear this plotter may be a magician who will pull something else out of his hat."

"Right let's inform the PM right now," the Home Minister suggested, "this is serious enough for an immediate meeting."

They all agreed and adjourned the meeting to be continued with the Prime Minister.

Overseeing the results of his press statement, the ripples in the international water caused by the stone he threw in the pond, the Scorpion smiled. It is going into the right direction, he concluded. In the USA he had caught attention because of the Baptist involvement he exposed and hordes of journalists had come to the different offices of the large Baptist community, the results were spread out in the papers and were shown on television. Of course the Indo-Naga case gained prominence suddenly too, because after all the Baptists had the people they left, hanging dry. And I will make them feel that this is very unchristian. So, this is round two. Because of me America will be involved, because of Sean the British will pay attention soon. Of course they have a legacy there for them, as the colonizers, should have handled things properly. This is called post colonial responsibility or in lay men's terms caring for those you have ruled and overruled. Perhaps it should be called accountability, the Scorpion wondered. It should not stop with just the USA and Britain, he thought. Now that Manila is involved we can trigger the interest of South East Asia. This could bring some pressure on India. The European commission should come into to it as well and fast. As a bloc the individual countries should not be too afraid of the economic backlash that India could threaten them with. The EU could be in this respect as powerful as India too by just buying less finished products and by reverting to South East Asia and China. This could mean the Indians will be in for a rough ride, he thought. This will only happen when the EU and the United Nations will look into this matter seriously. The United Nations of course had an office that deals with decolonization, but although it should be swamped with claims of people who, against their will, are part of a nation they have never agreed to be part of, the office does not do much in that respect. When I play this well then it will get attention from the UN this deserves. Also the Unrepresented Nations and Peoples Organization, UNPO, should be revived and fortified. The Nagas are members there, he knew, but that organization with its seat in The Hague, the Netherlands, had been through some rough weather and while it was getting back on its feet, it still had quite a long way to go in order to gain the prominence and influence it deserved. So, it was good the assassin, Jacky, was from the Netherlands and only a coincidence that Marius was from there too. The Scorpion had been briefed about the visit of Jeanie, Marius and Shilu for his Naga friends in Nagaland kept tabs on things happening in Nagaland for him. They had reported that the three of them had been going around. Good, I will put that to good use, he decided. Now what was left to do, he asked himself. Things were in motion and progressing, soon it would be timely to issue a follow up press statement, one in which he would announce some former but direct connections between the British and the Nagas and then a summary of how the Indians took Nagaland for granted in spite of the wishes of the people, who already at an early stage had made clear to the British they wanted to be left alone. I will review a few highlights of that long war inflicted on the Nagas and hold India responsible for killing many innocent people. Then at the end of that statement I will announce that only in the next and last statement I will reveal who the Scorpion, or as they say in the press already, the plotter is. The Scorpion smiled and thought of where it would be best to be caught. Hmmm, not in the USA, they might turn against me, he smiled and he had to rely on good exposure to influence public opinion favorably. To be caught in Britain perhaps or even the Netherlands?, he thought. In Britain at least the leaders would be forced to talk to India. And, as the United Kingdom is part of the European Union, all countries would have to have their say about this too, so yes a good option. Or better even in The Hague and near the Peace Palace? That alone would be a good statement, he considered, but not in the USA. There they should bleed without him, disgusting is it is that these Baptists of which I am part could let this happen. He wondered about the notion: The land of the free? Such delusional thinking, he concluded, just comes from a bunch of self centered holy people using religion for their own capitalistic ends and for achieving power, perhaps even more so for holding on to it. This is a very greedy society, he thought. How can it be determined a Christian nation?

People carry weapons, for even small things they pick them up, hurt someone and call it defense. We even have that in our constitution. The weapons lobby is so powerful, but the result is that we have percentage wise the highest homicidal killings in the world. These revelations about weaponry, planned assassination, but also how people defend themselves and take the law into their own hands, have to stop. So, this could have some purifying effects on my own society too, he thought and smiled. This is going to be good. Never mind if I get arrested. In the USA they may serve me with the death sentence and we do know that it is only God who gives and takes life. Man is not good at all but full of greed for him too, weapons should have been outlawed a long time ago. This also might lead to it and to a more humane and considerate society, he thought aloud now. It is time to tap the wires he interrupted himself and started internet on his laptop. Oh, perhaps I should get in touch with the group that was recently formed. I wonder what they have been able to come up with and if not much I will give them something, a scoop. So, he picked up the phone to get in touch with the lady in charge.

"I need to tell you a few things," he began when she identified herself, "but first I like to know what your people have come up with?"

"Nothing much yet, but it seems to be quite obvious that the Nagas have been able to hold their ground against the Indians for a very long time and that the British then knew very well the Nagas had nothing much to do with India."

"So, you did some research. What do you think of the departure of our people when they were evicted by the Indian Government?"

"It is difficult to say, but we think you are right about the missionaries when they returned, did not do everything they could to make this war known to the America. I see that as a failure on our part. I do not see any evidence yet that this was done for political reasons, but just negligence."

"Well I am sure you have seen what allegations were in that press statement," the Scorpion said to her, "what did it do among your people?'

"Such havoc, many are embarrassed about what happened, they hope it will not spread for that would lead them to trouble," she said nervously. "I am sure they have left a few stitches undone and hid that in a cupboard somewhere," the Scorpion said.

"The older missionaries neither know nor recall why they did not blow the whistle on this. They feel even more embarrassed and wonder now if spreading the word of Christianity was done by them out of selflessness or not. They doubt their stand and are being questioned about their role now too," she explained.

"Okay," the Scorpion then said, "I was going to tell you something and now I can. I think you may sense already what I am going to tell you?", he asked.

"No, unless it is that you are the plotter and wanted to show Christianity is more than reeling in souls hoping it will bring you points for entry to heaven?", she smirked.

"We will see about that," the Scorpion laughed, "good joking but I'll tell you now that soon there is more to come, for it is not just the Baptists who abandoned the Nagas."

"Yes, the British too," she agreed.

"And the United Nations as well," the Scorpion added.

"That mean the whole wide world man," she laughed.

"Yes indeed, you know of course that the Nagas are part of this world and should be known by the international community, but the UNO turned down the Naga declaration of Independence in1948 when it was wired to its headquarters a day before India's Independence. So, yes they were let down."

"It is a serious thing indeed," she said, "and I should not have laughed about it."

"We need laughter, or we would go so angry we would become violent," he said, "I will get back to you later and I fear another statement will be issued soon. That is if I read the thinking of this plotter well!"

"Thank you for calling I will try to speed up," she concluded.

The Scorpion sat down again to draft a statement which read like this:

The Baptist Community in the USA and beyond should be ashamed

The British Government should be held accountable for postcolonial negligence

The United Nations are required to decide on the declaration of Independence of the Naga Nation

I invite the Baptist Community of the USA and Baptists elsewhere in the world to stand by their Naga brothers and sisters they abandoned. Make sure the world will know about the rights of the Nagas so brutally squandered by the Indian leaders

It is the British Government which in his post colonial accountability should inform the Indian Nation that the Nagas have every right to be free and to determine their own future.

It is also imperative that the United Nations either declares the Naga independent following the declaration of the Nagas, or motivate before they eyes and ears of the world on what grounds it should deny the Naga People their right.

To make a success of the Peace Talks between the Government of India and the Naga Nation it is nothing short of extremely important for the International Community to not just talk about rights of peoples but to effectuate them. It is not so that big and powerful nations can get away with state terrorism and deny peoples their rights enshrined in the Human Rights Charter.

I, the Scorpion, will show my self through a last press statement. In that I will show how I can be caught so justice can be served, but you will see I will have safeguarded that justice served to me by justice to be dealt for all. This, you guessed right means in practice justice to the Nagas too.

When the Scorpion was finished he corrected some errors, read the text again and then put it out on the net, the addresses of the news agencies, some leading papers, national and international, plus other media like television and radio. Having done that he wondered if agencies like the FBI, CIA were already trying to trace his whereabouts via the service provider he used. The last one I shall send from The Hague, he promised himself. I want to avoid something will interfere with what I have in mind. So, he called a few travel agencies and after he found a confirmed seat, he booked a flight to Amsterdam for that same evening. As he thought to himself, better run now than that they catch me here. I don't like to languish in this type of jail at all, besides I am not at all sure I will get a fair trial. I am sure there is too much politics among the Baptists too and some have their fingers even extended to and in the White House.

Chapter 17

The real motivation spread out reaches all corners

The Scorpion started packing and after having checked all, he left for Newark airport, in heart and mind saying goodbye to the city that never sleeps. On board a plane to Amsterdam and oblivious of what went on on the ground he relaxed, for he escaped prison in the USA where he felt he would be treated badly when the tide would turn against him. The papers still had some remnants of the last release, repercussions he could easily detect and smiled. From nowhere any paper had it at least on page three or the foreign news section. The next one will blow holes in many institutions and Governments. They will be on the look out for me and will try to track me down, he thought. And he was right for after the first statement, the agencies went on red alert. There was a plotter in the USA who was possibly an American national and who had deployed assassins in a foreign country who had killed perhaps the president of an insignificant country, but still it had rippled international agencies. And, now that the plotter was American, some in the CIA who were commissioned to be on this case, believed it was easy to track that person down. Two agents were ordered to get to the offices of the news agencies AP and Reuters with the assignment to check on the reception of that email press statement. John first got the run around at Associated Press while Peter at Reuters was given access after some official prodding:

"It should not be too difficult," Adam said after he was introduced to Peter, "to check on the provider and then follow the trail where to where the email was actually launched from," he explained what Peter already knew to be possible. After all, his agency had experts in tapping the wires and knew how to fish out emails which could potentially be harmful to the USA. But in front of Adam he played kind of ignorant and happily let the man explain what he could do. Patiently Peter waited for him to check and trace. Then after some time Adam shrieked and said:

"It was sent from New York and went through this provider (ISP or International Service provider in computer language)."

"In Manhattan?", Peter asked.

"Yeah, but you have to go there or ask them over the phone or through other means of communication to release the name of the account connected to the person they bill for monthly subscription!", he explained

"Should be easy Adam," Peter smiled.

"Don't be too certain of that Peter," Adam answered, "they might like to protect privacy and you may have to come up with a court order to convince them, you know!"

"We will deal with it," Peter smiled again, "don't you worry about it okay?", he said now with a bit more conviction in his voice.

"Okay Sir, I am just hinting to what you can do when you don't get access," Adam said feeling slightly brushed aside.

"No problem, I must run Adam, be fine and thank you mucho," Peter said.

"At the office of the service provider in Manhattan he was not as lucky as he had thought. The CIA introduction meant nothing to them; in fact it turned them around for they became defiant rather than cooperative. Threatening them with closure on account of national security did not help either, the director became furious and said he would call the police if this kind of harassment without any order would continue. Peter thought of pulling a revolver on them but decided against that for these people could be clever enough to prosecute him and that would perhaps embarrass the bureau. So, under the circumstances he thought it was better to return and ask for advice, rather than getting himself into an avoidable predicament.

At the bureau, though John got his ISP too, both had to get official clearance to get access to personal data. The CIA could only get that through a court and hastily this was applied for, but then unfortunately it was late in the afternoon, offices were closing and they could only get their court orders, signed and sealed, the day after. But since that was a Sunday, this still had to wait till Monday morning first thing. Meanwhile when they were working on getting to the source information, the account and address, the next press statement appeared and they were called by the news agencies to come and see if this concerned the same person. Little did they know but that the bird had flown already?

Indeed, it was sent though the same provider, but they still had to wait till the order was released. When they finally got it and moments later the address, they stormed the house and found the identity of the plotter, but not the person himself. At least the identity of the person who had sent the press statements, they had. Now the next question was where this bird flown to and like the Manila Police in the person of Eddie, or the Brazilians in Rio again the bird had eluded them. Or perhaps he had not?

The men of the CIA, John and Peter were on the spot when the house was searched and what did they find? They found the man was an important person in the Baptist Organization, well known and a scholar, person with enough influence to make a difference. The point was now if it had been this person who had sent the statements or was only his laptop used? They could not figure it out, but soon when they checked the airlines for the name that this person they found out he had flown of to Amsterdam. Flying of to Amsterdam did not ring a bell whatsoever, because when they put the pieces they had together, they could not come up with Amsterdam fitting in somewhere. So, they questioned the Baptist organization he worked for only to learn that no one there had an idea what the person was set out to do in Amsterdam. Perhaps, the suggestion was given to them, he had taken a holiday? Since he was a scholar and rather independent at that, he could have followed up on connections for no one in his organization had anything against him or did suspect him of any kind of deviant or foul play. Again stuck now John and Peter could not do much else but to assign someone to keep an eye on the house as there might be other people using it in the person's absence. They had to sit it out till the plotter would send off a signal again. The person's home, no matter how interesting it had been to comb though, did not lead them any further. However, they were clear enough about potential connection, so they informed the Dutch Police. Though the lady at the headquarters of the Dutch Police took the CIA info quite seriously, they had no leads to follow up on the request of the CIA and no spare time to devote to find someone who could be anywhere in the Netherlands, either in a hotel or in the house of a friend. John and Peter understood that well enough but did also inform the AIVD, the secret agency's counterpart I n the Netherlands. This agency took things quite seriously and the matter was referred to Bram. Hearing from John and Peter what happened in New York Bram promised them check on a few things to see if he could get a lead on the plotter. Marius was on his way home now and could join him anytime Bram knew; in fact Marius was expected to be at the office the next day. Rather than waiting for his return Bram this time phoned Marius.

"Mobiles are nice in emergencies," Bram joked, "but calls can be traced so we have to have our own systems in place. It is not good Marius if the others can follow up on all we say, plan and do man! When are you coming in? I need to share something and it is quite urgent," he said.

"I am already home. I just came from the airport, a long ride man, so come to see me later on and we will talk," Marius suggested.

"Take a shower Marius when you are finished I am on your doorstep. I am in a hurry, all right?", he stressed.

"Okay then," Marius agreed, too sullen to say no.

Half and hour later and refreshed, the doorbell rang announcing the arrival of Bram.

"Okay Marius," Bram began when Marius sat in a chair his bathrobe still on him, "this is what is brewing," he continued and told him what he head heard from the CIA and concerning the case what had transpired elsewhere.

"So, you do think the plotter is going to do something here you reckon?" Marius asked.

"Let's review what has been set in motion and how things were set according to plotters plan and see if we can find a reason for him to be here. Things go haywire man, after that last statement!"

"Yes I saw that when I landed, this one could have far reaching effects," Marius acknowledged.

"Okay Bram said, he mentioned three important things; the Baptist responsibility, the British and the United Nations, so all in all he calls on the International Community's accountability for this Indo-Naga conflict, but what has the Netherlands got to do with that. How come he singled the Netherlands out?", Bram wondered aloud.

"Let's see if we can get into the plotter's thinking," Marius answered, "to me it is clear now all has been set in motion on the basis of a well designed plan with the assassination to make it operational. I think only when a leader would be the target could this plotter rally up so much attention. So, that is one, because the assassination of the leader would have great effect on the Nagas and as we have seen and I reported they are ready to rise against India and for good reasons, I might add!"

"Yeah, okay," Bram agreed, "so that means he wedged in the Indians but what does that say about the rest of the world?", he asked.

"Well Bram, Sean is an Englishman, Jeanie is English too, but Sean he said was coerced to commit the crime. Don't you think that refers to the accountability of the British in this conflict?"

"That is a point I considered too," Bram agreed.

“Then we have Jacky, a Dutch woman, a friend, an intimate friend of Sean. It could mean nothing and it could mean a lot.”

“What do you mean?”, Bram asked again.

“Well if Jacky was deployed because Sean could do that then it may mean nothing, but if the plotter knew about their relationship it could mean it was envisaged and so deliberately in some way would implicate the Dutch. Mind you we do have quite a legacy on post colonial negligence too. I would not be surprised our nation will be met with some aftermath on nations like West Papua and others too. It could mean the plotter wants to make a statement with that too.”

“Possible, okay, but likely?”, Bram asked

“Not immediately likely but we are reviewing possibilities,” Marius reminded Bram, “now the plotter is an American. Americans only from the Baptist circles have an interest in the Nagas. The Netherlands though remotely has an interest too and you know what I mean for the Nagas have their peace talks in the Netherlands at times and so need visa to be here. In short, the Netherlands tacitly provides the venue and makes it possible for the negotiators to be here, right?”

“Right!”, Bram agreed.

“What else can you come up with, other than the United Nations and perhaps the British being frantic about how they would squirm themselves out of this one?”, Marius asked.

“Let me see what we have here,” Bram answered, “perhaps because the Netherlands is a safe haven for the Nagas the plotter may think in the end when he reveals his identity here, he will be caught here?”

“Yeah, that is logical possibility, the plotter will be near some international institutions he could use to highlight the situation and not just his’ too?”, Marius concluded as he looked at Bram to see if he agreed on that rather far fetched idea.

“Not bad a thought,” Bram replied in smiles, “this plotter has things thought out and I do not think it to be as remote a possibility as you suggested.”

“Well then, let’s think some more on it,” Marius, encouraged now, said, “when he releases his final statement, he will be caught and most likely he will be caught by us. Where would he be enabled to be both in custody and to speak freely to the press? I think when we got him the international press will be swarming all over us.”

“Ahhh, so you think it is all planned to get maximum attention?”, Bram sighed..

"Precisely Bram, for I think when he goes to reveal in Britain, the heart of the matter, he would have more trouble to open up. This man can become a kind of celebrity here. He will explain the plot and I am sure he will tell that the world would only intervene in the Indo-Naga conflict when its nose is put on to it and it cannot be avoided. Now in Britain and in the USA they will try to keep him out of the limelight, but here?" "Here we may be ordered to subdue him too, once we have him of course," Bram said.

"True of course, but then I think that last statement will leave too many open ends and questions will be asked from all corners. I am sure that last statement will make the whole world to want to know and here it is perhaps the best place to get arrested. I am sure he will bank on the so-called tolerance here. I am sure the British will do all they can to make the man shut up. So will the Indians, for they will fall flat on their face when things start moving at greater speed than they are doing now already," Marius concluded.

"So, what can we do?", Bram asked.

"To accelerate the process, to seize the moment," Marius suggested.

"How then?", Bram asked laughing at him.

"I think I have an idea what the plotter is after," Marius said thoughtfully, head in his hands thinking.

"Let's have it man," Bram said pounding him.

"Okay, it is a hunch, let's magnify the idea and weigh it for what it might be worth?"

"Right," Bram replied.

"The person is from the USA, a Baptist. That is the connection to Nagaland. The Baptists abandoned the Nagas in the year 1956, a long time ago. As you would expect after forcibly leaving they could, or better said, should have the idea of making the invasion, as it was then known, known to every nook and corner of the world, they would have redeemed themselves as they love thy neighbor people. But, they did not do that. Hardly an American can be found who has ever heard about the Nagas. I think someone in these Baptist circles knows about this very well and feels terribly bad about how his Baptists have treated their brothers and sisters. The person plotted it for the attention the conflict deserves and to hold those responsible."

"Sounds plausible," Bram nodded.

"Then when he did plot he had to make it real and called on some people he knew he had something on which he could cash in. Sean and

Bailung after all said they were coerced and they released some info about Rwanda. This genocide in Rwanda had something to do with it. Now aside from that he was able to deploy them and so the deed was done."

"Right, and cleverly too for it elicited maximum exposure because the assassination took place in Manila, first in obscurity till it was known it was a leader and he had hoped an uprising of the Nagas would follow. Too soon Sean and Bailung were known so the Indians could defuse the situation which was almost ready to explode. I know Bram, I was there and you know that too."

"Yes," Bram confirmed.

"He had back up plans and through these he made sure the assassins would be caught, but he was not out to sacrifice them. He actually had gone through some painful decisions, I estimate, for he as a man of ethics decided on something, he really could not; like order an assassination which would take the life of a man but would most likely save others."

"If that is what he is after then he wants to influence the peace talks, I think," Bram said.

"That is the ultimate goal indeed I think so too!", Marius agreed.

"But how is he going to get there, that's the question?"

"That is the question yes and one we may be able to answer Bram!"

"Okay continue," Bram eagerly said.

"Okay with his second statement he set the tune. I am pretty sure he has quite a few people on the alert. And, he wants to be caught too, but on his terms. Why should he want to be caught in the USA? They could put the case on the shelf, have him in a court of law and treat him as a criminal and put away there. That is not what he is after. In Britain? There they might all sorts of reasons to keep his mouth shut and may try and convict him without allowing him to speak in public. But then here in the Netherlands is his alternative? Here the case may be open and even though many countries will pressure our government, I do not think they will prevent him from making public statements. So, he came here to reveal and he timed his moment! That is my thinking!", Marius concluded.

"Because the peace talks are held here too?", Bram asked.

"A minor reason but I am sure the person will capitalize on it, if he can. His main aim is to go public. Perhaps he will give a press conference in some hotel near the Peace Palace for impact? Being caught there while speaking would be quite an international event don't you think?"

"Remarkable indeed! I am sure there are quite a few on the look out for him Marius; Bram confirmed he understood the path of thinking.

"What he wants is to expose is what goes on in Nagaland and the injustices that are common place and have been for over fifty years. With his high spirited exposure and following that his being caught in public makes sure that person will get maximum attention indeed. I am sure he will take time to explain history and will switch to the peace talks. I am not surprised if that person is a scholar and comprehensively can give a lecture on the matter," Marius smiled.

"If he can explain very well, I think," Bram said..

"This is going to hit like a bomb explosion," Marius laughed, " now tell me Bram, if we are ordered to do so, are we really capable of apprehending this person? Do you think we would even want to do that?"

"Hhhhmmm a question of ethics again," Bram said and thought a moment.

"Really Bram? Apart from being loyal to our nation what does your heart say?"

"My heart is with the unfortunates of course, so when you talk about the Nagas it is with them and not because you have fallen in love there Marius," he laughed now too.

"Seriously now Bram, I must know, for any moment that phone can ring with the order to find this person. Our Government knows already the person has landed here and I am sure the Americans told our agency to look for him or her."

"Yeah, that is true. I saw a communiqué this morning, but it was not specific. After all the Americans also do not know who the man is."

"I think they know more by now and will communicate that to us Bram. I am sure they found his house though the internet communications and there they found the name."

"This house, even when he lived there, could have been used by a friend and the person there may not even know Marius?"

"True you know more about that than I, computer stuff connections," Marius laughed.

"Well, you know how dependable I am Marius when it comes to core issues," Bram laughed enigmatically.

"Hey man, don't tell anyone about this conversation. Even when they put us on it I don't want to intervene in what this person is doing. The Nagas deserve to be free and to get rid of these persistent Indians, it should be good if this case gets to be infused with some fresh input and angles. The whole world should know about the Nagas man."

"Even if I wanted to, Marius, I don't think it is very easy to catch him. He is clever. So far he has not exactly done the expected," Bram said, "but the essence I will keep between you and me only!"

"He is on our home turf man and he is American. If he wants to avoid us he must be extremely clever. Only that will help him," Marius laughed.

"I am sure you too, isn't that right?" Bram asked

"Don't you?", Marius answered with a question.

"Yeah of course," Bram smiled, "you revealed a lot!"

"If it is true of course," Marius laughed again.

"I warn you Marius," Bram smirked.

"And I you," Marius replied when the phone rang and indeed there was talk between Bram and someone of the AIVD to commission a team to try and find this person.

"This is now officially serious man," Bram said after the call, "we are going to have to go after the plotter."

"I am not going to Bram," Marius answered, "I do not feel like it. The person will not escape punishment. He said he was going to turn himself in."

"Yeah, this way we only follow up on a stern request from the USA or Britain to haul the person in before he can deal his last blow. This second one already reverberates throughout the world."

"Even when we catch that man or woman, I don't think we can stop him. I think already plans are in motion to that effect. I am pretty sure the person cannot be stopped anymore. Catching him/her, throwing him/her in jail will not stifle that person. In fact at this stage it could mean that revelations will lead to people in many countries crying out that it is an outrage, both to subdue this person but more so trying muffle what he has poked up. This case blows open Bram, whether we, or they or anyone like it or not. I will not be running in subservience to the Americans or British," Marius concluded.

"We have to show something Marius," Bram said.

"Yeah, but then we have many leads and also those for the opposite direction. I don't think we can be questioned much on what we do now, man."

The Scorpion had arrived and he had checked into a hotel not too far from the Peace Palace. He had a few passports with him and picked one to match with his appearance he had just changed. His checked in under the name John Williamson and he had turned from pepper and color hair to brown/black. He changed his clothes too, from more or less official three piece suit to casual, jeans, belt shirt and jacket. The Scorpion wanted to be arrested on his terms, for he wanted to keep the initiative. The jetlag got to him so after scanning the papers; luckily he could find some English and American ones too besides the ones in Dutch language, he took a nap. An hour or two later and now mid afternoon he rose to think about what he should do. He had planned to go UNPO to introduce himself and to speak to the secretary general there. To him he wanted to reveal all and he thought it should be UNPO which could turn him over to the police after having sent the last statement through their computers. It would be best if he could seduce this Italian secretary general, Barino Musdachin was his name, to a press conference before the police would arrive, so that he would be arrested while the press conference was going on. The Scorpion smiled and thought that such an approach would garner maximum effect. He then wondered if he should move really fast at this stage or slow. First of all I want the effects of the second statement sink in as it should inspire some people around to follow up on the matter. And, he stressed now within himself, I want this matter to get maximum attention. He was sure by now they would have found his identity and although they could not be certain as soon as they had checked his name to the house and the airline they could be pretty sure it would have been him, the Scorpion, who had gone to the Netherlands himself. Hence, once in the terminal he had changed his appearance and his identity with it in one of the toilets. From now on he would use another passport. From Schiphol airport, situated in the tunnel beneath the arrival hall and plaza he left by the twice hourly train to The Hague, after he had changed his dollars for euros. Now tired but on the train, just less than half an hour journey, he had been thinking of the risks involved to be caught before his time. To cut short potential interferences by the authorities on alert, he thought of going to the UNPO right away but decided against it because he needed time to let the last statement take effect. The free newspapers, Metro and Spits, on the train were all in Dutch and he could not read that. In his room however he had brought some and he was told that CNN and BBC station could be received by his television set in the toom. After his nap he briefly watched and there it was confirmed now they were on his trail and had already traced him to the plane taking him to the Netherlands, The Dutch authorities had been informed was the last thing on CNN, but the papers showed much more interest as the enigma as they had called the 'situation", could lead to quite a few repercussion from The USA, the United Kingdom and not in the least in India and of course Nagaland itself. Interest was already raised as to what this Nagaland really was and some journalists who had some notion, because they had had remote interest in the Indo-Naga conflict now could shed what they knew and although it was not very actual or very well researched it did spur others on to dive and dig into it. The conclusion was, things were fast brewing and some editors had given word to the authorities concerned they would like to dispatch some reporters to the region. Suddenly the correspondents in Delhi and elsewhere were working over time and were already on their way to Dimapur. Other newspapers and TV station and radio with strong ties to Indian media hinged upon their knowledge of the situation. In Manila too the situation was followed closely and not just by the police but the Ministry of Foreign Affairs which could not have anticipated the effect of this assassination. Statements by governments were issued to show their concern about the volatility of the situation. The Scorpion smiled and he wondered what would be happening in Nagaland, but for fear of possibly being traced he did not call his friends there.

So, there is two things I can do, he thought, go to UNPO now and talk first about what I have in mind but running the risk the people there will turn me in for fear they might be prosecuted for harboring a the plotter of an assassination. The other thing I could do is to just relax and keep tabs on things to wait for the right moment. Here the risk was of course the commissioned agents would get to him before he could reveal and have himself arrested in a grand and televised event, a press conference on the matter. And, he needed UNPO for getting this press conference arranged, he knew that well enough. Thinking that it would take them some time to get to him, he decided to wait but to lay very low and behave like a tourist who is not interested in anything else but sightseeing.

Shilu in Dimapur meanwhile was confronted with a deluge of news concerning the revelations of the plotter. These revelations had great impact on the Nagas for they were completely taken by surprise that it had been an American Baptist, who had confessed to have given the order to kill their leader. This was quite something to many, for remarkably the Nagas in 1956 had forgiven the American Baptist who had left them behind when the war of invasion and the Nagas defending them had just begun in earnest. So, to know now that, out of shame and a sense of responsibility, this person just to go international sacrificed their leader was felt as a blow from a friend. Yes of course when they found out the reasoning behind it through the press statements they understood, but could not approve. The leaders of the Naga Hobo, most of the civil society, but also the Baptist organization where shocked at first.

“This is quite odd to me Shilu,” said to Lungthing, “they have been lying low for so long. Okay some came to show some interest but more so to show back in the USA how they had been successful in the past. Help for our cause they did not extend. Now someone has woken up, feels some responsibility and creates a hell of lot attention. To me that is good. Not the assassination of course, but the attention will lead us to be free," he told Shilu.

"We have a very strong moral and religious dilemma here, Lungthing," Shilu reacted, "I hope you see that too? Of course it is rather hypocritical to criticize an assassination while you yourself fight some renegade Naga Forces sponsored by the Indians. You do engage and kill your own people. Well of course I do not absolve the other groups, but you will admit when one person dead can prevent thousands from not being put to death that this is a very good move on the chess board? Does it not make the negotiating partners more equal too?"

"I agree with you, the moral dilemma of course is the one we are facing but not through us, by an outsider feeling remorse who thought of this devilishly handsome plan. As an Army Officer, a brigadier, I can think of the results of his efforts rather than thinking of the moral dilemma I know it is based on," Lungthing answered.

"What do you expect now?", Shilu asked.

"I think in Delhi they are working overtime thinking how to deal with the new situation Shilu," he thought aloud.

"That is not what I mean Lungthing," she said getting angry, "you too have to deal with the moral dilemma here. This is not good, you command people and no one is accountable. That Baptist cannot play God. He cannot take a life. The creep put pressure on other people to commit that crime. How low can you go as a Christian?"

"True, but the plan was well thought out," he defended his stand, "he did it to do justice to the Nagas to redeem to and extent what had been omitted by the Baptist/Christian missionaries. He is restoring the Christian connection."

"You like it because all things will sway in our direction now. The British will be pressed, the United Nations have to answer and the Indians will have to change their tune. The man unleashed a tide that can't be stopped. It is all true, but we cannot walk over the assassination as if it is nothing, just a means to achieve an end?", Shilu replied

"We are with our backs against the wall for how long? Most of our youth, you included Shilu, have known nothing but war, their life determined by alien soldiers, our people defending ourselves through our Naga Army. Many, many people have been killed, think of the lives which are lost and of those we can save? Yes it is wrong to kill someone of course. I agree fully, but it is done and now we must capitalize on it,"

Lungthing tried to explain assessing the opportunities which rose from this bad deplorable deed, "like a phoenix rising from the ashes our leader had led us the way to finally come to a conclusion," he said.

"You are truly someone Lunthing," Shilu laughed, "victory is what you are fighting for. Our conviction is strong and you take this assassination as a fact of history and of course to achieve what we all want our freedom."

"Yes of course," Lungthing replied attentive for he felt she was luring him to a trap.

"Nothing condones killing a fellow human being; it does not matter if it concerns a commoner or a leader. That man realizing the mistakes made in the past could have put his full weight behind a revival for attention of the Naga plight for self determination. We revere Gandhi and the stand he made on Nagaland in 1947, right?", she asked.

"Yes of course and that leader was assassinated too but he preached and won against the British non-violently. Yes that is true, but he was killed too and is a martyr now."

"Don't we deplore killing good people Lungthing, any people?", Shilu said.

"We do," Lungthing agreed.

"Okay good, listen carefully, please?" Shilu asked, "I have a suggestion for you not to consider but to plead for, all right?"

"All right," Lungthing smiled.

"Right then, now in his press statements the plotter stated he would be caught but that this will happen on his terms, so time and place. I want this person to be charged here in Nagaland. I think internationally we should insist on bringing him to court here in Nagaland and to be tried by our customary laws."

"That is a shrewd idea and I will take it up with the Naga Government, our leaders," he agreed immediately, "this is very good Shilu.

"Yes let them issue a press statement to that effect, the sooner the better!", she said.

"Yeah, this is a grand idea and can strategically work in our favor," he smiled.

"That is not why I am suggesting it," she reacted and you know that.

"Of course," Lungthing said and kept smiling as he assessed the opportunities that would come from such act.

"What are you thinking Lungthing?", Shilu asked apprehensively.

"That we, in that case, take two birds down but with just one stone," he said.

"Oh really," Shilu said, "name them?"

"All right," Lungthing smirked, "listen! Having the man tried under customary laws would mean that the whole world would follow the trial and would want to know about our village state democracy and judiciary system. This will raise the interest in the Nagas world wide even further, right? And, justice will be done of course. Judging the man and think on why he plotted this out and in the end wants to be caught is that he will get a fair trial from us. He wants to make a statement. But then the other thing will be that in the wake of this even tremendous pressure will be levied on the Indian Government, so strong that pressure will be that I estimate the peace talks will flow again and will pass the rapids fast. This time the whole world will be watching and India can no longer afford to stall for time or to play us out against each other. This is what I see," he concluded.

"Yeah that may be true, but the reason I suggested this is that the Christians in general and the Baptists in particular should feel that we all as brothers and sisters have responsibilities and when the going gets tough as they say in the USA then the tough get going, right Lungthing, you should know you are one of the tough men around here!"

Lungthing laughed: "Yes of course I should be tough but also compassionate and understanding, a balanced person?" he asked.

"But there is no need to be opportunistic, let's grab all angles now so we use everything from the bad to put that to good only. I do not want to see anything happening to the contrary. I will run an office in Amsterdam you know and will hook up with the Naga International Support Center and UNPO. I want to be sure I can count on the Naga Forces to be true and cooperative," she said.

"Are you leaving soon?", Lungthing asked.

"You know it will be a matter of days and I understand that Marius, you know he is the one I will be with, is also busy in tracking down this plotter! I will discuss this with him too, so when the man is caught there, Marius just might have enough influence to persuade the authorities there to send our plotter over to us here."

"Okay understood," Lungthing said, "let's work in close cooperation then. We actually might be able too encourage each other?"

"Might?", Shilu said sharply, but seeing Lunthing's innocent face, smiling ironically she understood he was teasing her, "you rascal," she laughed.

"Of course by talking to each other and openly sharing ideas and assessing the situation, we do encourage each other. I wish you all the best there and between you and me I can say Marius is very much in love with you. I do not quite understand what you see in him though. He is not Naga," he smirked.

"You are an ethno centrist man, you are happily married, so what do you know. You will not explore anymore, well you should not. And, I want to finish exploring. I think I have found my mate, so you better stifle your comments!"

"Okay, okay, I know, but you are such a fine woman to tease," he said and laughed.

"So are you Lungthing, so are you, half the time you do not sense it, but then you are a soldier, so I cannot expect subtlety from you?"

"Oh, oh, that sneer did really hit Shilu, but I should not take offense and should have expected this kind of assault on me. Please be kind to me," he humbly smiled now, for although my limitations may be many my work for my people comes first," he said not looking too firmly serious again.

"Of course I know that, so don't worry, we are teasing over serious business. At the earliest mention it to your leaders and let's get cracking on this. I count on you. If there is any argument against it for the person to be tried under our customary law here and the leaders decide against that, I want to know about that!"

"Okay, you will know in a few hours. Call me when you have to leave, I will take you to the airport, all right?"

"That is a nice gesture man, thank you," Shilu said and left Lungthing's office.

Shilu went over to where she stayed with family and friends to hear from them how they felt about the spiraling situation. But first she bought some local papers to find out the latest. This was not something small indeed. The Baptists of Nagaland called for a convention which adopted a resolution to officially lodge a strong complaint both against the Baptist Organization of the USA and of course the USA Government itself too aiming to make it known the Baptists of the USA had gone astray and were responsible for killing a person. That was one angle which reached the news in the USA. The British were another angle when that country was confronted with its colonial and more so post colonial past. Also by the Nagas who encouraged by several institutions and the UNPO were holding Britain accountable for the mess the Nagas were in. Though known in several circles as colonialists without much responsibility for the people they ruled, the British had been able to keep most of their mistakes in handling the change of the colonies to become independent under the lid. When those colonies were independent and the borders were decided and the British had left all trouble rising from their departure, peoples who did not want to follow the nations designed by them were left to the new nations themselves. The British did not show or feel responsible to repair the mistakes they had made. This time with the full focus on Britain now too, that Government there had to react. Likewise the International Community could not remain idle. Through the Scorpion the United Nations too were on everyone's lip, anyone of importance in international politics. The UN this time like Britain could not escape some accountability as to why no explanation of denial of independence had been sent to Nagaland. Frantically most countries concurred so as to not just get informed about this conflict they never heard of, but to make some sort of united stand. They did realize this stand touched on the attitudes of the nations who had had colonies and their accountability for having turned people over to be left without rights or cultural prospects. The Netherlands in relation to West Papua and the role the United Nations had played, came into the picture again, the French too but on a different note, the Belgians for the mess they had left behind in Africa. In fact it was more than just a thought that the genocide in Burundi and Rwanda between the Hutu's and the Tutsi's had been evoked by neglecting the aftermath of colonialism there.

Thinking about that the same was true for the British; Shilu knew from her own experiences. The relics of the British past were omnipresent. Recollecting what the Nagas had done before India became independent was to convince the British they should not be part of that country for the Nagas had no historical, religious, cultural or ethnical links with it. Yet in the aftermath of the Second World War the British declined to accommodate the Nagas. They had too much to do with themselves and later did not feel they should intervene into the policies of an independent nation. This attitude of course strengthened the Indian leaders for, even though it kept quiet, they felt they were backed by Britain,.

Okay Shilu thought this Baptist did move the thinking on the nations who formerly had colonies. This was food for thought and it could for once change things, most probably for the Nagas but also for other peoples and she thought of UNPO which would be rising in importance because of it.

The Scorpion had only one thought on mind now, to prevent himself from being caught in The Hague before he would have had the press conference. He knew the agencies were trying their best to get him and though they did not quite know what he was up to besides giving himself up, well they had to believe he would do that, they wanted to get him at any cost if only for their pride as secret agencies for the nations they worked for. So, Marius and Bram commissioned to close in on the Scorpion had more than just an idea to find the person, but deliberately looked in another direction first. This was not so for the American and British agents, who had come to The Hague straight away and were now being briefed by their counterparts of the AIVD, yes Marius and Bram. The Americans primarily felt they should be briefed to the fullest because it was their citizen who had done the things reported.

"This is the Netherlands," Marius clarified to them, five men strong, "you will do it the way we deem fit!"

"We will see about that," one of the British said, colleagues of Jeanie, who by the way, as fresh from Nagaland as Marius, had come along with them.

"Hello Jeanie," Marius smiled in between addressing the Americans and British.

"What is the problem?", Bram asked.

"We got to catch him, so brief us on what you know?", the American of the CIA said.

"Yes we read the papers here. I understand your Governments might feel a little embarrassed when this plotter opens up. You have a lot of interest to quiet that person. tell me," Bram felt like challenging them, tease them really, "what is in it for us?"

"What?" Peter asked, looking at John and scanning other colleagues, "what do you mean?"

"Well Peter, you dump your problems on us, you come running in like you own the place. Like Marius said man, this is the Netherlands. You do not order anyone around here, Got it?"

"Okay, okay," Peter laughed, we are eager man. We nearly got this plotter!"

"Nearly is not enough," Marius smiled with him, besides as I was told the message was sent from that house. It could still be someone else deluding all of us. Did you check that from your end Peter?"

"As much as we could in deed Marius, we are pretty sure we are on the right track."

"Okay then, Marius continued as he looked at the puzzled British agents too now and winked at Jeanie, "now listen carefully, "we lost track when he disappeared from the airport. We believe but we are not certain he boarded a train to The Hague."

"How do you know," Jeanie asked.

"Calculated guess, Bram answered.

"Based on what?", Peter asked, not unfriendly now.

"I think you can make that out for yourself, should we spell it out for you," Marius was getting irritated, "come on Jeanie, I am certain you can figure it out?"

"Be nice, Marius," she smiled as an answer, "tell them?"

"Well I am irritated by you people barging in and demanding all sorts of things without racking your own brains on this matter, but okay, here is it: this person choose for the Netherlands and I think if he would be caught in the USA he would be treated like an ordinary criminal without political implications."

"Likely," Peter reacted.

"He ruled that out and he did rule out Britain too, I think, because the British would like to severely punish him and also on criminal content or extradite him when they were sure he would be put away properly."

"Yeah, our government could be embarrassed by this development," Jeanie agreed,

"But here?", "Bram asked, dropping some silence before continuing, "here things are rather different. True we also have a checkered colonial past, but here the peace talks between India and Nagaland are held, so that makes it a good place to get public attention. This is also the land with the Peace Palace and the Criminal Court of justice and on top of all that we have the still quite insignificant UNPO here."

"Are you saying he would be sending his last statement from The Hague and then he will be showing himself to be arrested," Jeanie and Peter said almost at the same time.

"Yes, I am," Marius said, "you tell me what other motivation he could have? Where else would he go to get attention?"

"Yeah," they said one by one.

"I think we do not catch him before he decides to give himself up," Bram said, "and besides it will be a matter of days before we will get the person."

"Really?", Peter asked.

"When the person has come this far, do you actually think he will be caught on other people's terms?", Marius asked, "that would be stupid. No, he is planning something and if I am not mistaken if we really want to catch him, we should be looking at places where the person could be and feel safe."

"Now I think our task could be to figure out where that could be!", Bram added.

"Right, can we have access to mobile phone records?", Peter asked.

"Yes you can, but I doubt if you get anywhere."

"It is worth trying when we screen for certain words?"," he explained.

"I'd rather do something else," Jeanie said to her mate.

"I think we will waste a lot of time like this, but it is up to you," Marius said, " I think I better figure out a few things for myself."

"Anything on your mind?", Jeanie asked.

"Well, think of it. You Americans have the name and possibly a picture. You did not volunteer to share, because you want the credit for catching the person. Well, let me tell you this then. We do not need it, because the person no doubt would have changed both appearance and identity. If this is not done that person has forgotten how powerful we can be and what kind of resources we have. No, he changed. I think he booked a hotel under a different name, he may be staying with friends too and I am sure when you see the person you will not recognize him from the photograph Peter."

"What makes you so sure I carry a picture?", Peter asked.

"O I know quite a few CIA men and women. I should think that is answering enough Peter," Marius smiled.

Peter smiled too and so did Jeanie. They talked about who did what and decided that Bram and Marius would be acting as the nerve center of the small operation in finding the plotter. So now alone again Bram concluded by saying:

"Let's not help them too much!"

Marius nodded.

During the briefing Marius had signaled Jeanie he wanted to see her alone. When the meeting was over he took her to his office and opened up to here on what had bugged him for quite a while now:

"I think I know now what is playing Jeanie," he began,

"Oh, I thought you wanted to give me some extra info so we could catch the person together," Jeanie smiled but surprised she was.

"It is not that Jeanie," he said and looked at her for a while before continuing making her feeling uneasy, "you see my dear Jeanie, after we boarded the flight to Delhi I noticed a few things and put some other pieces together."

"Goodness, what is wrong now Marius. Did you drop Shilu?", she tried to deflect.

"Cut the nonsense now Jeanie, you can tell me now yourself for I remember we pledged friendship, or I will tell you my suspicions. Do you remember why I thought we could not make it together, no matter how high I hold you?"

"Of course Marius and it hurts still," she whispered.

"Then if you actually were serious and want to remain friends, you'd better tell me what you did regarding this assassination," he said looking straight at her.

"So you know?", she asked.

"No I do not, but I have some hunches and one is that you because you have kept things from me deliberately, I suspect you for being involved. I just don't know in what way or how deep Jeanie!"

"I hate you Marius, no, I hate myself more. I will tell you why. I felt infatuated by you and I know you felt the same since we met, years ago now. I had the same professional feelings for you, but those faded and I should have made my move. I did not, I hate myself for that, but I can live with that mistake. The mistake I reveal to you now is much worse and it leads me to Sean, the one getting the assassination team together."

"You were implicated by the plotter?"

"Yes I was," she answered with a tear in her eye.

"So, you knew all along who the plotter was?", Marius asked rising fury he felt.

"No, no, not at all, but the plotter knew something about me. He pressed me to find some reliable people who could do anything. I had something with Sean and knew he had gone astray and I sold him out to escape."

"He pressed you to reveal what he knew about you?"

"Yes," she said, "at the time I was not aware it would lead to an assassination, or I would have refused. When I got caught in it, I felt devastated, especially because I could not get the identity of the plotter."

"But you never confided in me and the easy was you took to get rid of me was not like you. You want your nose in many things. You are a good and curious person, but on this trip I discovered you have secret and you tried to delude me."

"Oh God, you did notice!"

"I think I did, for confessing only now you wanted to be with me actually but still wanted to go on a trip knowing I would be with Shilu is the first thing I felt strange about."

"That was true, I did feel bad I could not be with you anymore, only because I took you for granted," Jeanie reacted.

"You got over it real quick and left us alone, which was nice but raised my suspicion. I am practically sure you used your time well?"

"I had to be alone to be in touch with those who were keeping tabs on things."

"Of course," Marius reacted and smiled, "but you never cared to disclose what you knew and kept me, as a friend, in the dark."

"I am truly sorry for that," she said and it looked like she meant it, "I felt cornered and with what I did, my job was at stake too."

"Was it such a bad thing someone knew about you that you could go from bad to worse?"

"Not so in retrospect, but I feared it could jeopardize my position," Jeanie answered.

"We will talk about this later Jeanie, but I advice you to come clean with me, both on the idea of friendship as well as with the case we have at hand here now. We will catch him, your plotter. I don't want to know what he had on you, but tell you both my country as well as the UK will be nailed. This is what I meant by conflict of interests."

The Scorpion was gathering thoughts as he walked through The Hague like a regular tourist. He spent the day visiting the old parliament house on the Spui and went over to the modern city hall. He got attracted by the narrow shopping streets and spent some time there looking and comparing prices before exploring the route to the Peace Palace. He walked through the Arcade and went around the old church before returning the other side of the Parliament buildings and the pond in front of them with the little tower office at the far end, the office of the Prime Minister . He passed that to turn into the street where the tram followed him to the Mauritskade then after having crossed that he moved towards the Javastraat, turned left there and then still following the tram track to the right to find the Peace Palace to the left of him. He stood there for a while watching this majestic building which to him was the embodiment of peace indeed. This is where he wanted to be tried, but little did he know that Shilu was already on it to get him tried in his beloved Nagaland. After some contemplation he walked back and did some shopping, primarily he bought things to change appearance again. He then went back to the hotel after he had taken a meal from, mind you, the American take away

Burger King. Back into the hotel he promised himself he would check out the next day and get into another hotel, under a different name again, somewhere in between the UNPO Office and the Peace Palace. Later that evening he passed by the comparatively small UNPO office on the Paviljoensgracht, his target to arrange a press conference. It was dark, the lights of the windows with the ladies in them, on of the bordello streets of The Hague made an odd impression on him for the entrance of the street faced the UNPO office.

Chapter 18

World wide impact

The Scorpion, back in the hotel, began to draft his latest and last press statement. When he was finished he watched the evening news and noticed \ all corners of the world, governments, had become worried about possible escalations. There was also news flash from Nagaland. For a fair trial the Nagas through the Naga Army demanded the plotter should be handed over to them, this on the basis of their customary laws in turn based on the village state democracy. Aha, he thought, that is not a bad idea. This way all nations would be focused on Nagaland and he decided to go along with it instantly. The United Nations meanwhile had called for an emergency session and the Security Council. So, he thought now, the ball is rolling and the impact is going world wide. There is no stopping now he smiled. My last revelation would just drop some more oil on the fire. Already some countries were venting it would be wise for India to resume the peace talks but now in higher gear. The British too should show some responsibility by revealing the position of the Government on the Nagas, before India became independent. The Government of United Kingdom felt pressure was mounting, but had not yielded to any commitment yet. This obviously was due to the ruling party and the opposition being hopelessly divided and that the ruling Labor party expected a rough ride on this matter. Consequently the British Government commissioned researchers to provide background on what had been neglected for so long. They came up with papers showing the British in the field then already foresaw a devastating war could take place. The British administrators then knew the Nagas would react if they were not set free like they wanted. They had expressed their wish on many occasions. But this team of history researchers needed time to come up with a sound report with recommendation of course, yet one thing was quite certain: already from 1929 onwards when the Simon Commission had visited Nagaland it was to the British the Nagas wanted to be free. Consequently Britain had a few things to answer for. The United Nations too, because so many nations were involved, had to pay attention to what evolved. Most post colonial nations however immediately sensed that, when Britain would yield and so would be held accountable for post colonial neglect then the others could follow Nagaland. The implication of yielding to the call for post colonial accountability could raise a new standard, the newsreader cum analyst concluded on television. Because it was harmless to put some pressure on the Indian Government to achieve what it wanted to do anyway namely to get some peace in the land and on a superficial level a consensus to encourage to resume peace talks was found. Yeah, the Scorpion smiled, you find it difficult now for though large countries have more power, but what did you see? A small people could hold you, a non aggressive people could fight your aggression. Normally the big nations minimally discouraged steps which could tock the boat and when they felt their balance of power was to be disturbed, maximally vetoed these initiatives. But not this time!

Having been informed about the participation of some fighters of the then UN Forces in Rwanda and Burundi did raise questions at the grand meeting and it was mentioned that lack of post colonial accountability was the underlying cause of many conflicts in the world. Although not much attention was given to it the UN had a bureau for this simmering predicament. Because of the status quo in fact it was not taken seriously at all. But now the question was pushed and fast enough it surfaced on the table again, where in the past it had been conveniently shoved under. The countries known to have been colonizers, countries which had imprinted their ethnocentric notions on the peoples concerned, were now gradually held accountable for what they did. Specifically the focus was on how they arranged the then emerging nations to become independent. Thus, when they spoke the Rwandans made an impact on the UN, so did the other nations which were plagued by wars within their borders, wars by disgruntled peoples who were restricted. And there were many wars raging; in Africa, South East Asia and Latin America, with primarily little understood indigenous peoples who aspired to live freely on their own land in their nations. In the UN they demanded time to voice out and when they spoke their sound reverberated throughout the world. For the time the countries of the first world, read post colonial countries here, could not do much more than listening to what was expressed. All this, the Scorpion smiled is fantastic. Unfortunately this sequence of events had tō be set off by the murder on the Naga leader. Yeah, he had to admit it, this was perhaps the only stain on his plot. Granted, he thought, an important one, a very important one even, but insignificant in itself. It was the moral dilemma he wanted to find a way out for, for himself at least and now it was high time now to take the blame. This way he knew the knife would cut both ways. 'I don't mind to go to jail or to get the death penalty', he murmured to himself. It is interesting though the Nagas want to judge me. That is good and given the chance, I will do it, he smiled. For now let's see what follow up I can arrange. First of all I have to convince this Musdachin that my giving up in the office of UNPO will lead to something of greater importance for all concerned and the members of UNPO, he decided before sleeping the sleep of the innocent.

Anxious to begin this crucial day he woke early the next morning,. Te first thing he did was gathering his things again and to switch hotels. While walking around he had found one near the office of UNPO. When settled in he realized he most probably would never actually return here. He know of course that, in cooperation with the British the Americans had been trying to trace him. They were hot on his trail because when they did a search on all hotel rooms they were, via the local police, provided with relevant names of people staying in The Hague! They singled out in the centre hotels first and scanned for names remotely American and with some resemblance on the plotters name the Americans and who had arrived that day. There were around thirty hotels fitting that description and attendance, so they had begun calling. After checking 20 of them they had come up with nothing. The next day was a hit but they were told the potential person had already left that morning. When they had arrived at the hotel, the description of the fellow that had been there did not resemble theirs. Not quite deterred for they knew a clever man would change appearance, they were practically certain it was the person they were after. But, like what Marius had said to them, they could not hope to find him. The bird had flown again, no trace!

The Scorpion was getting ready to go to the UNPO office. The adrenaline shot through his veins. Now it is going to happen. This is the day, he thought. He trembled with excitement. For the last time looked around but knowing from now on there was no way back, he resolutely turned and walked off and crossed the street, passed some shops then turned left to get into the Paviljoensgracht. In sunlight he walked for about five minutes; it was a bright day and he felt excitedly pleased to find himself in front the door of the UNPO office. The window next to the door had no curtains and he saw some young men and women working at their desks. Then he rang the bell

"Good morning who is there," a voice rang out through the door speaker.

"I like to speak to Barino Musdachin, it is important," the Scorpion answered.

"Just a moment please," the voice continued. Moments later the door was electrically opened and a young woman, perhaps 26 years of age showed herself:

"Mr. Musdachin is rather busy, could you make an appointment?", she asked.

"No," he answered and smiled, "please tell it is important?"

"Who can I tell you are?", she asked again.

"The plotter, the Scorpion, the assigner of the Naga assassination," he said. The young lady startled visibly and stuttered:

"You mean you are the person behind this killing?"

"Don't worry this is bigger than anyone of us and I need to discuss this with your secretary general," the Scorpion said.

"Okay," she answered and ran inside all mixed up and overwhelmed. She returned a minute later and asked him to come in. She led him to a desk at the far end of the room and behind a pantry but close to a garden Musdachin had his desk. There the Italian Musdachin sat behind a small and a thin notebook and looked up to him:

"Sit down please," he said.

"I am sure this is as much a surprise to you as it is to me," the Scorpion began as they shook hands.

"It is stunning is you are what Kim said, so be kind and explain yourself. After all you have plotted an assassination and I should turn you in, in no time," he smiled,

"You are right of course" the Scorpion smiled too, "and it is what I have come for. Well to tell you the full truth, not only that but you can turn me over to the police from here," the Scorpion said and smiled.

"Then who are you. Why are you doing this," Musdachin asked in his typical Italian accent.

"I am Uhllrich, a Baptist scholar from the USA and if you like not only can you turn me in but I like the UNPO to capitalize on this. So, let me explain what I have in mind?"

"Please do," Musdachin reacted cautiously.

"Well then," Uhllrich the Scorpion said, "what I have in mind is this. You know of course I announced a last statement. I like to send it from your office, even your computer. But, before that I like you to phone the press for a press conference here, international press preferably. The reason for this is that this way we, your organization and I as a person, will receive maximum publicity."

"Yes I understand what you are after and it is good you turn yourself in. You realize that if we will do it we will have to call the police too? I suggest you better send the statement while the conference is going on, so nobody can say we were in this plan with you."

"Okay, no problem," Uhllrich said.

"Then do you have the statement ready?", Musdachin asked.

"Yes, I have," Uhllrich said and handed it to him.

Press statement conclusion

Today from the Unrepresented Nations and Peoples Organization I disclose that I am J.J.M. Uhllrich, the plotter of the assassination on the Naga leader. The assassins or those with a hand in it Bailung, Jacky and Sean, languishing in jail in Manila and Rio de Janeiro respectfully, were coerced by me. They are not to blame. I blackmailed them to do as they were told and I threatened to murder them. Take this into consideration when you do them justice. More importantly is why I did what I did. What was I motivated by. The Baptists of the USA of which I am part, have done nothing for the Nagas when their troubles began. They let them languish while in dire straits. For fifty years the American Baptists did not act like they loved the neighbor they converted and convinced them to become Christians of the Baptist faith. This I am convinced is an act of bad Christian behavior and should be changed. The war of defense forced upon the Nagas because they rightfully want to determine their own future has two formidable and dominant players against them: the British who left the Nagas unprotected and the Indians who attacked them so that the Naga Homeland could be part of India. Both nations have conducted acts of state terrorism and I invite all investigative media to check on all data concerning this. **As for my motivation?**

This is rather simple but also complex. It is simple because of the tremendous neglect of first the American Baptist. In that wake the British kept quiet. Because I am convinced Christians cannot be righteous when they abandon their fellow men, I felt a responsibility to show what Christians profess could be realized in practice,. It is complex because after ample thought I came to the conclusion it was practically impossible to get to where we are now by just talking and trying to convince peoples, religious organizations and governments to do what is right. I have tried that. To think out this plot I only did after assessing how many lives could be saved when the peace process would come to an end with a solution favorable to the Nagas, one that serves as an example for other peoples.

To order someone to be killed is not right. And so, I do not hesitate to stand before you and to be judged. I am sure many will be eager to take me into custody and up to a point are ready to sentence me to the death penalty. I am very much aware of that but command myself to be in the hands of the Dutch authorities.

When Musdachin finished reading at first an expression of disbelief appeared on his face as he exclaimed: "Goodness man, are you serious?" "Yes, I am," Uhllrich smiled, "I want your organization to take the credit for my arrest. I am sure when we have the press conference here, UNPO will benefit and as a pleading organization for those nations without self determination I think you can use all the attention you can get. That way you can have much more influence on the UN too!", Uhllrich said.

"Let me think Uhllrich, I am overwhelmed. Yes, you are right even though unofficially and officially I am not quite certain that you should be absolved from the assassination. Yes, I am certain you did this with good intentions. Okay then, let's inform the staff and transform this into a nerve center. Let's get the press here on the double and then you read that press statement out loud, after this send it to the authorities' world wide too. I am sure within a few minutes they are here to arrest you," Musdachin smiled.

"Alright," Uhllrich simply said.

Musdachin walked over to the front where most of the staff had their desks and asked attention. He briefly explained what had transpired and requested them to get to their press files so the relevant news organizations could be reached.

"Ask them to come here and right away, for news will break here," he said. Stunned like Musdachin had been at first now the staff sat there a minute but then the young woman who had received Uhllrich stood up and said quite solemnly"

"Let's get to work; we are going to write history here!"

This broke the spell and minutes later the phones were ringing, the young men and women talking about a scoop and wetting the appetites of journalists and reporters. Fifteen minutes later the young woman said:

"So far we have three camera crews, five radio teams and ten journalists. Most are from international agencies. Will that do? We said to be here at 11 am sharp. That is just over an hour from now!"

"That will do nicely," Musdachin smiled.

"Shall we go out and get some drinks and snacks," the young lady asked.

"I will come with you," Uhllrich volunteered and I will pay for the damage!"

No one objected and so they went to return not much later with a young man who carried a box with soft drinks, wine and beer while the young lady and Uhllrich carried the snacks; nuts, some different sliced meats, crackers and something like Dutch leverworst.. The others had been busy arranging the elongated room which in itself was large enough but for some desks which were put against the wall. Then the chairs in a few rows made the idea of a press conference complete.

So eager some of the pressmen, some women too, that they arrived early. Since they did not know who the person was Uhllrich among the staff arranging the chairs and the table was not noticed. When they asked Musdachin he only answered them with a very pleasant but also short:

"The person will be here at exactly eleven!"

"The reason why some had come early was primarily because they had to get ready for action and that meant to mount cameras on tripods and doing some sound checks. The rest of the staff now having nothing to do just watched the proceedings or were occupied receiving the eager press.

Just before eleven Musdachin took Uhllrich to the garden with him to talk for a moment.

"We have been following what you set in motion of course. We hoped that through the fall out of what you did, UNPO, our member nations, could profit from that. The pity we felt was that we had no connection with you, so we could not supply you with ideas and suggestions either. So, what made you think of the UNPO to come to terms with the situation you created? You know of course that our members pledge to be non violent, so no terrorism is condoned. Hence, we cannot condone any assassination!"

"I understand that well Musdachin. It is why I kept UNPO out of it. I ordered the assassination only because there was no other way to get the attention required to get some real and significant changes going, vested interests are too strong and you know that. It is wrong what I did and it cannot be condoned, under normal circumstances. I judged a people under siege for over 50 years as not normal. I judged Baptists and Englishmen not taking any responsibility for what they set in motion as not normal. So, Musdachin let God be my judge in heaven and let the Dutch authorities on the doorstep of the Peace Palace be my judge on earth?"

"I can't add much to that," Musdachin smiled, "it is time Uhllrich, shall I introduce you to the lions so they can devour you?", he said with his Italian sense of humor.

"Do you actually mean you see me as a gladiator now," Uhllrich retorted, "you throw me before the lions and I will survive like Spartacus?"

"Precisely," Musdachin laughed and he walked back in, Uhllrich following suit.

"Ladies and Gentlemen," Musdachin began at eleven sharp, "thank you for coming. UNPO has been able to identify the plotter of the assassination and you are the first to know him. Yes, a him it is," Musdachin said in earnest. This is a very serious press conference so I would like you to pay attention. The plotter will present himself to read the press statement he announced as his last one. So, I present to you:

To the great surprise of the present press Uhllrich stepped forward and said:

"I am J.J.M. Uhllrich, Baptist of the United States of America. I am responsible for all this and I shall be held accountable after your reports have been sent out to the public and will reach all corners of the earth."

Cameras were being pointed as Uhllrich spoke and a pin could be heard to drop when he resumed by reading his prepared press statement. When he had finished phones began ringing while obvious questions were asked. Uhllrich took his time answering them and because hardly anyone of these international journalist had any knowledge of the Indo-Naga conflict he could tell stories. Then suddenly a voice rang out:

"When are the next talks then and where are they going to be held?", an Indian looking journalist asked.

"I do not know," Uhllrich answered honestly.

"Ahhhh, but I do," Musdachin answered in his place, "the next round of talks will take place in Amsterdam and within a fortnight I am told."

"Can we get there?", the man asked.

"Normally these talks are held without anyone knowing where, yet I think when this news goes out this might change," Musdachin said.

He had hardly finished the sentence when the expected happened. The police bonked on the door and faces looked through the window. Uhllrich knew it was going to happen soon and signaled Musdachin to let them in. One of the staff opened the door for them and as they barged in and went straight to the table the journalists were watching or had their cameras pointed at.

"Who is Uhllrich?" the commander of the bunch asked.

"News travels fast," Uhllrich chuckled, "I only gave my name something like half an hour ago and already it is the first thing on your lips!"

"So you are Uhllrich?", the officer asked again.

"Yes I am," he said.

"I am afraid we have to read you your rights and arrest you," the officer said.

"Please do," Uhllrich smirked.

Without further ado and with rolling cameras Uhllrich was cuffed and taken away. Things happened so quickly that most of the journalists were stunned, but not all for when they were almost at the door three from the crowd ran after the police and shouted:

"What is the charge against this man? Where are you talking him and under what law are you charging him. One journalist, an American, said then:

"Hey is American and should be prosecuted under our laws."

The police did not react but just did what they were ordered to do, so the moment they were about to drive off they were stopped by the operatives Marius and Bram, the British, led by Jeanie and the Americans John and Peter:

"We will take it from here," Marius said to them in Dutch.

"What are you saying?", the startles police officer replied, "who do you think you are to order us around man. Out of my way, or I will have you arrested."

"Call your superiors now," Bram took a verbal bite at the man, "this is an order. Don't make the mistake of meddling in international affairs," he said. The man could hardly refuse what Bram and Marius ordered, but he was not sure and asked for some identification first. Both of them flashed him their AIVD cards and now kind of satisfied picked up a mobile and called his boss:

"You told me to go there on the double to arrest this man and now I have some AIVD people here who want to take over," the man explained in complaining fashion. He listened to what he was told to do said yes a couple of times, grinded his teeth, looked at the people in front of him now with journalists trying to catch a word and cameramen directing their video cameras too and put down the phone. The police officer showed anger and was nervous, but he had to obey the order and said:

"Okay you are cleared to bring him in instead of us," and bit on his lip.

"Thank you, as I said," Marius repeated, "we will take it from here."

The police on orders of the officer guided Uhllrich out of the van and handed him over to Marius and Bram.

"We will talk," Bram said to Uhllrich, "for an interesting proposition has reached us, let's go to our office shall we?"

"Right," Uhllrich smiled," I do hope you people are knowledgeable about the issue?"

"I have just returned from Nagaland and Jeanie here," Marius introduced Jeanie, "was with me when the news broke of the assassination of the Naga leader you planned," Marius explained to him.

"That is marvelous, so yes we can talk," he answered. They wrestled themselves out of the news people's grip and moved into the vehicles which were parked nearby. Not too long after that they reached the AIVD headquarters but not before Marius had introduced himself to Musdachin and told him to come see him later that day. Leaving the exasperated press people behind and a UNPO staff too, now they were in a room at the headquarters of the AIVD.

"So Uhllrich," Peter began, for he could neither control his curiosity nor his sense of responsibility for working on behalf the nation anymore, "tell me where would you like to be tried for your crimes man and, why the hell did you do it?"

Uhllrich smiled a moment as he saw Marius fuming with the impertinence of the American for interrogating Uhllrich like he was in charge here, so Bram cut in and said:

"This is our jurisdiction Peter. I am sure your time will come, for now though you will leave it to us until we know how to handle this politically too, all right?"

It was Peter and John's time to fume, but they could do very little so had to abide:

"Yes, of course," Peter smiled through his anger.

"Okay then Uhllrich, we are facing a difficulty here. You are under arrest for plotting an assassination in Manila. So, that country I am practically sure would like to have you tried in their courts. Since the USA is close to the Philippines, it was a colony of the USA for some 50 years," Marius said and looked at the Americans, "so politically speaking I don't think the Philippines have any trouble extraditing you. So, that means that Peter may be right, you will be tried in the USA. Then again, you were arrested here in the Netherlands and you murdered, through somebody else's hand, a Dutch woman, by the name of Jacky by the way, a man who is considered to be an Indian citizen. You could be brought to India too for being held accountable for what you did," Marius explained.

"Why not here in the Netherlands?", Uhllrich smiled.

"Yeah, true, why not," Marius smiled and looked around if there was anyone opposing.

"I do not see any claims of the British," Bram contributed and smiled as well..

"That is because we are lucky Uhllrich was not found on our soil Bram," Jeanie smirked at him, but John now could not control himself saying:

"What is there against bringing this man to justice in his homeland?"

"Good question," Marius answered, but with Peter let's first ask Uhllrich what his preference is, shall we?"

"The Netherlands would be a fair place for me," Uhllrich answered, "the Peace Palace is near and I trust things will be handled well here."

"Does that mean you do not trust the American justice system?", Peter asked.

"No, it is not that, I will tell you why. First only some and not too many care to recall the Naga Peoples, so how can Americans judge or get enough information to ensure my trial will be fair? That is the first thing. The second is; this assassination has nothing to do with the USA, only in reference to the Baptists it is, or a reference to our Government which also did not care about the human rights abuses. So, thirdly the crime is committed in the Philippines but directed by me. I could indeed be put on trial there, but I prefer a more impartial environment," Uhllrich explained gently.

"The British are involved in this but took a back seat right after India's independence. How about going before the Old Bailey in London," Bram asked, "that way you are getting near the core of the matter. Don't you think with a trial there the Naga story would become more prominent?

"That is right," Uhllrich agreed, "I am afraid though that the British will do everything to downplay their role and will treat my case as a murder plot only. They will reason that, after all, it comes down to me having successfully plotted to have someone killed. To them that is the crime I committed, nothing else. Here we have the international atmosphere and we can focus on all aspects, like motivation too?"

Marius was called away from the interrogation to attend to an important call. In fact there were three; the Prime Minister of the Netherlands, the secretary general of the United Nations and Shilu were calling him. He attended to Shilu first who told him she would be on her way to the Netherlands the next day and asked him to pick her up from the airport. When Marius confirmed he would, she told him about her idea she launched while talking to Lungthing:

"I like you to look Uhllrich being put to trial here, Marius, seriously. Apart from the publicity it might generate, it will certainly be not only a fair trial but also one that shows the background of our customary laws," she explained.

"That is a good one," Marius answered, "a coincidence Shilu for the latest is that Uhllrich has turned himself in at the UNPO office during a press conference and he is in our custody now. We shall discuss that idea right away."

"This is good news Marius. This man is clever enough to orchestrate the media. Yes, put it to him and let's see what countries will be for or against the idea."

"Right, I will be there tomorrow. I must run now, love you," Marius said and tended to the other calls. He reassured the Prime Minister that all was under control and the secretary general that this would be a golden chance to stand by those peoples who have the right to self determination, but found it too hard to actually get it. Then he returned and off hand launched Shilu's idea to Uhllrich:

"There is this idea of the Nagas to get you to Nagaland to stand trial. How do you feel about that?", Marius asked, sensing the answer already, but now he wanted him to explain his stand to the other agents.

"Excellent idea," Uhllrich happily answered, "it concerns them and I know the Nagas can be fair. So, I would not see a problem with that!"

"Most like under their customary laws Uhllrich they will do you justice!", Marius warned.

"Yes I know, but why should I be afraid of that, I do deserve it, don't you think?"

"It is not up to me or to us here to decide on that," Bram interfered.

"Well," Peter and the British were quick to add, "we will report this to the authorities and I am sure there will be some negotiations, possibly under the leadership of the UN first before this idea can be materialized."

"Yeah, I am sure the Indians want a stake in it too!", Jeanie contributed.

"Okay then," Marius concluded, "there is nothing much more to discuss. Let's frame a press statement for our respective customers on the matter and brief them on the possibilities and preferences. We have got a lot of work to do so let's put Uhllrich in to protective custody," Marius suggested winking one of the guardsmen always omnipresent in the AIVD building.

When Bailung in Manila, likewise in custody Sean and Jacky in Brazil came to know that same day that Uhllrich had turned himself in during a big and well published press conference, they felt elated. The man had kept his word and now that the coercion factor had become realistic too, their trials may not end in death penalties or better even they would possibly only face reduced sentences.

"Not bad for you Bai," Eddie said when he brought him the news, "this has been quite a scheme. I hear the man wants to be tried by the Nagas himself. How do you feel about that for you?", he asked teasing him, but happy he was for at least Bai was not the kind of perpetrator he had once thought. And knowing the secret they shared he was sure of that.

"I do not know the Nagas; I do know the justice system of the Philippines Eddie. You know I love our nation, but the corruption in all places, the judicial system too, does not guarantee a fair trial. And, it could take years too and a lot of money. So, I rather be at the jurisdiction of the United Nations. I am sure Sean and Jacky would feel the same Eddie," Bai explained.

"Perhaps we can do better than that man. When the UN agrees put you under their care it could take years still. I have seen you with Celia and I think it would be a shame if you are to be separated for too long."

"This is good news indeed," Bai smiled, "I am not afraid to take responsibility for what I did, now that I am with Celia for good. I am a happy man even tough I will face the consequences Eddie."

"Yes, we will do our best," Eddied concluded.

In Rio Jacky was in tears. For days now she was separated from Sean and though they had known it was impossible to stay together when caught, the fantastic feelings which had developed between them, made them forget about all they had done in the past. They knew now they were destined for each other. This strong feeling made it practically impossible for her to be in that God forsaken jail without Sean. But then there was hope again, when she was informed what Uhllrich had done, she was thankful the man had followed up on his word and that also that suggestions were made to go to trial in a third country, one that could be impartial. So, informed she was too that possibly soon, she would be taken out of Brazil to be delivered, with Sean, into the hands of those who would prepare the aftermath for them. Possible she would be reunited with Bai and who knows Sean and Bai with Uhllrich too team up, this time in the open.

The Indian team meanwhile had been on guard in Brazil, for knowing all about corruption it was their task now to prevent Sean and Jacky from buying their way out of jail to disappear once again. When the news of

Uhllrich had spread, the Indians were recalled for it looked like it was completely useless to stay in Rio. Also, Jacky and Sean had no reason to flee anymore. In Delhi things were erratic; hardly a soul in high places could come up with an idea to explain the current situation. Another round of talks was coming up and it was certain the Nagas at the table would want to know the Indian Government's stand on this. Though the agencies were happy no finger regarding plotting could be directed at them; they also felt they had failed to find this Uhllrich in time. That man now held all the cards. And, although in jail he still could call the shots.

"Like that idea about having him brought to justice before a Nagas court. This is preposterous," the prime Minister said in one of his very rare emotional outbursts, "why would that man want that?"

"It is not to our advantage indeed, but his' it is," the Home Minister agreed.

"I don't think he opts for that because of an advantage," Patill reacted.

"Well what then, talk to me," the Prime Minister eagerly asked.

"Don't you see that this has been designed to get publicity?", Patill exclaimed, "where and how he would be tried is not important to us, or should not be. How we can minimize the devastating effects of what he is planning to do should be," Patill explained.

"That man makes us look like fools and we will be questioned all over the place, don't you see that Patill?", the Prime Minister reacted.

"Well now you are talking and we should do something about that, but not in the old fashioned way. We should be a little more creative now!"

"Any suggestions?", the Home Minister asked.

"Of course," Patill answered thoughtfully, "but you should have them too, heck we all should be more creative now!"

"Don't beat around the bush Patill," the Prime Minister said, "this is a crisis and we need to act. The prestige of India is at stake here and we are the custodians of that!"

"Well you don't have to lecture me on that Prime Minister. I am well aware of all the elements which could lead us straight down the drain and this was not even of our own making, a bit sour of course but the only deception with that is that we were taken by surprise, we were off guard. Now we should be able to restore the situation and gracefully show the world what a great nation India is."

"That sounds nice," the Prime Minister smiled, "but how do we go about that? I have not heard a suggestion yet!"

"It is not too difficult, Prime Minister, we should make a gesture at the peace talks and we should issue a few successive statements too. This will appease many a nation, our people and the Nagas."

"Are you suggesting we are giving in to the Nagas?", the Home Minister thundered. Patill laughed about that remark making the Prime Minister frown, but then Patill answered:

"Of course not, but what you two do not seem to catch on with is that when you have a fish on the hook, in order to haul it in you will give some leeway when it fights back strongly. And, may I remind you that this is now a political fight? We better show the international community we are well mannered and we have the interest of all our citizens at heart?"

"Fantastic," the Prime Minister said, "let us draw a plan and let's inform the negotiators about to what extent we shall give them leeway."

"You will brief them then?", Patill asked.

"Certainly, I will grant them to have the trial in Nagaland and we will make a stand at the UN to make that possible," the Prime Minister said.

"Should we not give them an incentive at the talks too," Patill asked, as he saw the Home Minister frowning over that.

"We could tell them we are taking both constitutions seriously and are studying the possibilities of a federation based on two constitutions, the Prime Minister said.

"That will do nicely," Patill agreed, "this will show the greatness of India,".

Chapter 19

The peace talks resume as the world watches

The Naga team had arrived and so had Shilu, who had briefed Marius about the upcoming talks. Shilu had taken a flight from Calcutta straight and had touched down a day ahead of the Naga team with its leader. Of course one leader was missing and this was not a small thing, the leader explained to the press in an exclusive interview before the talks. This was something of a novelty because normally only afterwards some comments or explanations on the topics were extended. Now it looked like a fresh wind was blowing and when asked the Naga leader had said:

"The Indians want to keep things secretly, since we are not in the position to ask the governments of the countries for us to go public when the Indians have good relations with them, we have to abide. We are dependent on these countries for visas too and I am sure you have an idea what has to be done to secure ordinary visas and so just to be here is no sinecure!"

"So, it is the Indians who restrict publicity on this long term matter?", the BBC journalist asked him.

"Precisely, we have nothing to hide really. We have sent our proposals years ago already and we have not been met with counter proposals from the Indians."

"Are you glad the Indians have nothing to do with the assassination of your Chairman?"

"Very glad, but sad too because some of them took their own life. It shows to me only how strangely organized the Indians are. Why should three men commit suicide over something they have not done?"

"That is an interesting observation," the BBC man agreed, "but tell me how do you think the talks can progress? Are you not afraid of your own life will be at peril now?"

"No, not at all, thinking like that would only lead me to prejudice and defensive talk in the peace talks. My mind is open to suggestions from the Indian side but they have come to know after all these years that Nagas are not their toy to play with. We stand firm and we mean what we say. We have our history and we have our rights!", the leader said.

"Britain came up too during the press statements of the plotter Uhllrich," the BBC man continued, "do you think the British are to blame for what the Indians do?"

"You know your own history. Britain, your nation, colonized us and we did resist. Only after 60 years an unwritten agreement was reached, accounting to a small part of our homeland. So, your country could not have possibly turned over my land to the Indians, yet it did. Even when there is no proof it did not, Britain did not object to India when it invaded. It did not clarify and it did not reproach India or even as much as question. So, yes to answer your question the British are to blame. Uhllrich was right about that. I still cannot quite belief how strong you were when you came to rule us and stayed till you left and how cowardly you became after decolonization."

"That is a very strong statement indeed, so you blame the British for not defending your rights, if I understand you well enough?", he asked. "Precisely, "the leader said, "but the Indians are to blame for not following up on the words of Gandhi who said he would give his life for the Nagas as 'we have every right to be independent'. The Indians invaded but what right did they have? Did the British give that right to them?"

"I do not know about that Sir," the BBC man answered and was a little embarrassed by that question and asked, "if the Indians are so pertinent of their rights to have Nagaland within their nation, then shouldn't Britain acknowledge this?"

"It does so by keeping its mouth shut, but I can assure you the Nagas have nothing much but humanity, as we are all human beings, in common; no shared history we have, no culture or religion, nothing, so what they claim is not based on anything. Nagaland was handed over by Britain and as long as Britain keeps quiet, the Indians think they are in the clear."

"The situation may have changed after the revelations of Uhllrich, do you feel you can tell them now clearly what you are after, knowing the world will be watching!"

"I am sure this can be a tremendous advantage," the leader agreed and smiled.

"Okay gentlemen," the Indian interlocutor, chief negotiator began after both teams were seated, "I bid you all a warm welcome and I offer you all our deepest sympathy and condolences for the loss of your Chairman and President of Nagaland, I deeply grief with you and with the Naga People. I am sorry the suspicion went out to us first, but I am grateful that it has been proven India was not implicated in this crime."

"Thank you," the leader said eyeing his three companions, the Internal Bureau Chief and the Minister of Defense, "though our loss is great and we do suffer, I can assure you we do have things under control. I think an uprising of our people would not be welcomed by you and I am glad our people behaved gently enough to on the spot listen to the explanation your Home Minister."

"Thank you," the interlocutor said, "and I have something to tell you too. I understand that the plotter, the Baptist Uhllrich has stated a preference for being tried in a Naga court under your customary laws. I can tell you our Government has no objection to that."

"That would imply you will let journalists and lawyers and students and university professors watch the proceedings right?", the leaders asked with an approving smile.

"Certainly," the interlocutor answered, not exactly knowing if he was allowed to do so but given the situation he could hardly say no even with a frowning Defense Minister and IB Chief looking on. The interlocutor feeling uneasy about that quickly moved on:

"I suggest our agenda for today is to discuss a federation on the basis of two constitutions, the Indian one and the Naga constitution."

"We have been waiting for that and we welcome that we can talk about it now," the leader agreed.

"This is a break through," a minister from the Nagaland Government whispered to a member of the steering committee in his own language so that the Indian counterparts could not understand. Feeling the gaze of the leader on them, they stopped short. Though obviously both parties felt there was a difference now in how they treated each other, it was not clear yet how to find a common ground on which progress could be made. Surely the Indians knew they could not concede too much yet but gradually should for the Nagas knew that, on the basis of the international attention alone. they were gaining the upper hand in the talks. So, the leader played this out as best he could. The Indians felt they were in no position to grant anything but to open possibilities, yet felt were on the verge of being outmaneuvered and requested a time out. This request came from the IB Chief for as the representative of the Hawks this watchdog had to look after the interests of the Indian Nation. The IB responsibilities extended further than just serving a sitting government alone. The Nagas felt in winning mood, but were cautious as they feared cornered Indians could shoot back unexpectedly. Their team returned to their hotel where went into conclave with. After analyzing a little what had happened the Information and Publicity Minister of the Nagaland Government came up with an interesting suggestion:

"What I see is that we are very eager to cash in on our good fortune," Aklam said. What transpired is enormous but I can assure you the Indians are thinking fast and are working hard on how to get out of this for them difficult and unusual situation. They were the ones with the trump cards and now we have one or more too. This unsettles them. I don't think we should cash in on them already, for if we pressure them some more, they may soon feel cornered. Already they don't say no but will be recalled by their superiors. Even when we agree one something here at negotiating table here, they can be overruled. Let's face it, they have done so many times, they betrayed us, over smaller things, right?"

"Right," practically all answered him or nodded, but the leader asked:

"Let us hear your suggestions Aklam?"

"What is happening now works in our favor and it does not end here. You may not realize it, but their concession of having Uhllrich tried in Nagaland is very important. As you said it will attract journalist from many countries. They will to follow this up and this alone will put Nagaland on the map as an entity of its own. When we play it well, this will be the beginning of the end of the war. They will not be able to stop the deluge of information about us from spreading like wildfire. Then, step by step, we cash in on what is to be irreversible. In the end they cannot do much else but to set the is free. Certainly when Britain is compelled to join the chorus and advises the Government of India to correct what has been abusively taken for granted. Now, with the USA in the firing zone too, the Baptists at their convention will have to make this a political topic too. They too will encourage the British to take at least some post colonial responsibility. Then the Indians cannot really refuse to set the Nagas free and we can be on our own. I am sure we will be praised if we do not overplay our bid, but make sure we can exercise our right to self determination. This is what I suggest," he concluded, "to go step by step and to surely play on the growing interest in our people."

The leader reacted in agreement with Akalm's suggestions, but stressed the Nagas should not just be reliant of what others could contribute to the cause. One could stimulate the other and all progress was progress from the idea and political will to be free. So, he emphasized that when the Nagas kept in mind they are the masters of their destiny then neither the Indians nor the International Community could positively of negatively influence that stand. Aklam reacted:

"To capitalize on something that happened beyond our control, something sad, but has far reaching but positive effects does not rule out what we stand for and have stood for all these years. I just think that next to our conviction and our Army, which keeps these convictions alive, we were provided with some extra tools. I suggest only we should use these tools carefully and, politically speaking, timely too! That way these tools will create maximum effect and will influence the peace talks. If we overplay now we may make the Indians furious and they might do something the international community may condemn, but they will do anyway."

"I think Aklam is right indeed," Galasa said. "the Kashmir case is the example where international attention had ample international exposure, but do we see a solution looming? Let us indeed use our growing international influence to slowly but surely ready the Indians for the solution we envisage?"

A lively discussion erupted then with the result that when they were to meet the Indians again the next day, not only would they meet an amicable Naga team, but also one which had compassion for the troubles India was facing. So they assured their counterparts that, should there be an agreement acceptable to the Naga People and thus honorable, then all would be forgiven. An enlightened Indian team left a day later in upbeat mood to tell their Government that now the road to indeed have two separate constitutions merged together into one constitution was possible and the framework to achieve this would be discussed during the next session of the talks.

Outside the Indians were stopped by a crowd of journalists who through a leak knew where the talks had been held. Besieged by men and women with clicking and rolling cameras, to their astonishment microphones were put in their faces. The IB chief especially had a hard time for he was used to speak in public.. But the journalists did not know that and an American, followed by a Swiss and Dutch journalist eagerly asked:

"Are you two any closer now? Are you going to withdraw the troops from Nagaland?"

Stunned at first the team was professional enough to regain its composure and so the interlocutor took it upon himself to answer:

"We are getting much closer now. The talks are moving in the right direction. We have decided the trial of Uhllrich can take place in Nagaland," he said and left it at that for the focus had shifted and the question on withdrawing the troops was forgotten.

"Is it to be a public trial? One that would show democracy is alive in Nagaland and India?", a British journalist asked:

"Of course," the interlocutor smiled but feverishly thought on how to get out of this, for him too, unusual situation. He was rescued by the Nagas who came out after them and more than half of the bunch of journalists ran over to them to ask similar questions. A British journalist pushed on and asked:

"Then you will open Nagaland for journalists to attend?"

"We have to designate the details, but yes journalist will be allowed to cover the entire proceedings of the trial," the interlocutor clarified feeling the heat and so in an effort to get rid of them he added quickly, "we will draft a mutual communiqué through which you will know where we are in the talks. All looks hopeful, we make progress and we show mutual respect," he said.

"Okay that is diplomatic rhetoric. The main news event then is," and the Dutch journalist asking this looked at the IB chief and the Defense Minister now, "you grant journalists to be at the trial of the American plotter of the assassination held in Nagaland and conducted by Nagas but your troops remain in place, so Nagaland remains occupied. Is that correct?"

"That is correct," the Defense Minister answered feeling uneasy, "we are working on further measures but we will have to wait for further instructions from our government," he hastily added.

"We have to ensure peace prevails," the IB chief said thinking of making a good point but it backfired for both the Dutch, the American and British journalist frowned, then asked through the Swiss one:

"Are you actually saying there is peace because there is an Army there?"

"Right now there is, for there is a lot of infighting going on," he answered realizing he had made a mistake.

"I understand this infighting, fratricide as the local press calls it, is because certain parties are being paid or are provided with arms to fight against the main Naga Organization, the one you are talking to and meant to destabilize the Naga Society and the Naga Army?"

The interlocutor gave the IB chief a menacing look and took control again:

"We are on much better footing now and we are arranging to curb the influence of these disturbing factors. Also the arrest and consequently the motivation of the plotter Uhllrich provided us with insight," he said.

To the delight of the Indian team most of the journalists due to the official but practically empty talk were drawn towards the Naga team and were swarming around them.

"Did you get anywhere this time?", one of the journalist shouted. It was a very broad question but the good natured Naga team put on a smile and the information minister Aklam answered:

"Oh yes, most importantly is that the trial of Uhllrich will be held in Nagaland if it is up to us and India. It depends of course on the Dutch authorities to release him. However the man himself stated he would cooperate. This trial will be held in all openness and on the basis of the customary laws of the Nagas. So, you are in for a treat gentlemen," smiled.

"Oh, how so?", the British journalist asked.

"Well, not only can you come to Nagaland, previously impossible, but you will be able to see the village state democracy in operation. You will see democracy in action and you will be able to see Nagaland."

"When is it going to be held?", came the follow up question.

"It is a matter of the authorities and I think the Netherlands will consult the United Nations, perhaps UNPO will be involved, but most importantly a debate on how to deal with internationally induced events having devastating effects on nations may be possible. This may trigger such debate."

"The Americans want to bring Uhllrich to justice in the USA," an Americans journalist contributed.

"Yes, but it has nothing to do with the USA as such but with the Baptist community there. The USA, knowing what happens here, could have used its influence though, so I do not think the claim of the Americans will be honored, certainly not by us anyway," Aklam explained, "if they want to pursue this, they will find us in their way."

"Which will again bring you more publicity?", the Dutch journalist smirked.

"Precisely, of course we are overwhelmed by the attention we are receiving now. We have been ignored for many, many years," Aklam reciprocated, but smiled too.

"You need all the publicity you can get," the man enthusiastically added, "but aside from that it looks like things are moving right? What stumbling blocks do you see?"

"Well, when this blows over the Indians will try to return to their old style for they feel they should incorporate us. They cannot allow themselves to bow down to a people of mere tribal nature. That is a loss of face to them!"

"So, only when the pressure is kept on them, international attention and questioning too, will lead them to a settlement they may not like, but will be honorable to both?", the British journalist asked.

"Certainly," Aklam agreed, "and if you British take your responsibility and speak up about our history, then we will greatly be supported in what is our right. I think the British should not remain laid back on this matter. If you rightfully and humanitarianly cry out about human rights then you also should have eye for your own failures and be gracious enough to correct what was wrong."

"You blame the British?"

In our case I can freely say to you that we have been wronged by the former colonial power. It would be very good for Britain too to admit mistakes were made and to put that to the Indian Government to encourage it to make amends. That way the Indians feel backed up and can take steps to come to the solution we all have in mind. Through all nations we do have too, primarily to defend the right to self determination," Aklam explained.

The unplanned and unorganized press conference went on for much longer than anyone anticipated and some of the journalists present, led by the idea that the Indians were caught by surprise and were ill equipped to talk to the press, did try to catch the Indians on quotable promises. Though slightly embarrassed the interlocutor, minister and IB chief as much as they could held the pressmen and women off by stating the negotiations are on the right track and positive, but also referred to the real decision makers were in Delhi and were led by the Prime Minister.

Consequently, after a while of futile questioning them one by one the journalists, reporters and cameramen gave up. They did swarm around both parties as though they wanted to squeeze them from all that was in them, but did not get anywhere near the core issue. There were a few who persistently went on, but unfortunately were not hindered by too much knowledge or insight in the long term conflict. This played in the hands of the Indians who practically, with restrained contempt, brushed them off, but the Nagas, sensing that this was the exposure they needed revealed as much as they could, but without giving away what they had agreed not to. One knowledgeable from the Indian point of view asked with other journalist keenly listening:

"There is a discrepancy between what Indian papers write about the people which have died in this long conflict. I read 25.000 and your people say as much as 300.000. Can you explain that?", The Brit asked.

"Easily," Aklam explained, "there are no official figures, neither for the soldiers who sacrificed their lives in combat not for the Nagas who were, due to burned and bombed villages, had to live in the forests and died of starvation or disease, mostly civilians. Based on eyewitness accounts we estimate in between 250.000 to 300.000 Nagas alone have died since the war began. As the Indian Government does not disclose the fatal causalities on their side, we have no clue about their losses. But we do say, these soldiers had to pay the price of their government's mistakes."

"So there are no figures at all? Is that what you are saying?", he asked.

"Not reliable ones," Aklam responded.

"Then this is something to follow up on," he concluded and with that last question and answer the impromptu press conference had ended and all disappeared.

Chapter 20

All falls into place

Musdachin called his staff to evaluate what had happened and the kind of prospects they could fathom.

"First of all let's do a communiqué to all members, not just to inform them about what they know already through the press, but how we could bank on this tremendous advantage which has been created. We should also call for a steering committee meeting to prepare for an assembly. I am pretty sure we will get access to much more money now as well. This will give us more perspective in organizing things. On the agenda I would like to see two things which are related to each other; post colonial responsibility (if voluntarily taken) or post colonial accountability if we require nations to be accountable) and the right to self determination as a result of decolonization. Let's get to work?"

Musdachin's right hand, Kim, was the young woman who had opened the door for Uhllrich. She had worked for UNPO for more than five years now and had seen it going down the drain due to mismanagement before. With her help it was getting back on its feet. With Musdachin in the driver's seat now after the departure of interim secretary general Baptekin, and Uigur, who had inherited the shambles and done as best to get UNPO our of the doldrums, things now slowly seemed to be moving again. Like no other in the office she knew that this press conference by Uhllrich meant a boost for UNPO and when Uhllrich and Kim talked privately he had revealed to her that why deliberately had chosen for UNPO:

"Because the United Nations has nations as its members who primarily are interested in their own perspectives, it is the large nations which dominate it. Since domestic affairs were not to be interfered with, unless they posed a threat to other nations, it was those powerful nations which led. This of course became painfully clear when the USA decided to invade Iraq and bypassed the UN and so it practically made the UN defunct when there was, due to the not fully proven weapons of mass destruction Iraq, no total consensus among the members to begin this war. UNPO is an organization of Peoples and Nations which are not represented and have no status as a nation. They are voiceless and I want to have a voice to, I want to contribute to that. So, the UNPO must gain prominence and prestige. The Nagas are just one example of peoples paying the price for being neglected and for not being able to get the rights they are entitled to, also adopted and acknowledged by the United Nations. So, this is the reason why I thought it a good idea to have this press conference here, it will set things in motion. Don't you think?", he had said and smiled.

And Kim understood but was till torn between the idea of going as far as having to kill someone to achieve these goals to rally up support enough to get there through peaceful means and she had put that to him:

"Yes of course that has been playing through my mind many a time too, but you see Kim fifty years now and there is little to no change. These countries are so blatantly arrogant and are accepted to be so in the international community that I see the UNPO as the only viable alternative to the United Nations. The nations good and bad determine the domestic problems, no matter if they entail independent peoples. They are not to be tampered with, not even when the right tot self determination is concerned. So, the bad nations control and the peoples are dependent on them. You cannot depend on those politicians who are only out to make sure their power is perpetuated. I feel bad about how India treats the Nagas and other peoples. And, when we are successful in creating a situation in which the Indians have to bow, then this is as an example for other countries to revise their policies, for it will not stop there and UNPO will grow in importance too."

"You have really thought this out indeed," Kim agreed, "but to kill someone how did you come to terms with that? You are a man of religion, a Baptist, why should you have to resort to that? You are not only going to be judged by the people, the international community, perhaps the Nagas themselves, but by God himself, the God you believe in!", she said and was all heated up.

"I have struggled a long time dear Kim. I have seen how callous my friends are about abandoning the Nagas. When asking about it and I am influential in the Baptist community, I was led astray or in other word advised to let it rest. Yet, we are servants of God and we did not intervene in matters of great importance because people were being killed, our brothers. It is easy for me to say of course that now only one man died because of me and because of me many lives are saved. That is a question of numbers 'Thou shall not kill!' is my kind of solution too. I may burn in hell if I have taken the wrong decision. Once I had taken it I knew there was no way back and I had to execute the plan so that it could emerge. This war has to come to an end that was on my mind. It is because as Baptists we are also responsible for what we have done. To make people feel responsible and to make them act on that is what my motivation was. But also to follow up and make sure that the people who feel it and are responsible will correct what they or their forebears had done wrong. I hope I can contribute to that process. I hope too that the Nagas can forgive us all!"

"So, you want to appear before a customary court, a tribal one then!", Kim asked.

"But of course," he said," I have wronged them. They can weigh what should be done. I will deliver myself into their hands and I will gladly do so!"

"What if they sentence you to death," she asked.

"Then so be it," he answered calmly.

In Manila things were monitored with rising Interest. Learning about the arrest of Uhllrich Eddie and Efren were flabbergasted:

"A Christian, how can this be man?", Efren exclaimed.

"Well, well, a high class prostitute committing the crime of murder, ex soldiers setting her up and a Baptist planning the whole thing, this is quite something man," Eddie answered, "let's visit Bailung in jail?"

"Yeah, let's see how he reacts!", Efren smiled. From their office to the municipal jail where Bailung was locked up till it was known what to do with him, was not very far. Efren and Eddie traveled by jeep through the dense traffic Manila is known for and got nearly knocked over by a bus on Epificio de los Santos. Since Efren knew the traffic on this route well, he could anticipate the sudden moves of bus drivers looking for passengers. They would be stopping even in the middle of the road. At the jail Bailung came out to meet them with a smile on his face.

"You must have reconciled with your destiny," Eddie laughed.

"We may have some good news dear Bailung," Efren added.

"Yes, I am at ease. I am in love too and hopefully after having paid for my sins and my dues to society too I can start my life with Celia. I know I may be naïve, but now that I am in the process of redeeming myself, I feel relieved of the burden which weighed on me for so long," he said.

"It is good to feel remorse indeed Bai," Eddie smiled, "you know that the person contracting you for the assassination, the man named Uhllrich, has been arrested and he has publicly said that you and Sean have been coerced by him to do this job?"

"Yes I heard," Bai reacted.

"I don't think you will get off, but a reduced sentence could be quite possible. You better talk to your lawyer at the earliest," Efren said.

"Has there been a date set for the trial?", Bai asked.

"Not that we know of, but with the prominence of the case, now an international affair, I think the judiciary likes to go ahead as soon as possible. Since you are a Philippino you will appear before a Philippino court, even though it is an international case."

"Right, well the Naga leader was murdered here indeed," Bai agreed.

"But there is a development with this too," Efren continued, "you see this Uhllrich the plotter wants to be brought before of customary law court in Nagaland, the homeland of the leader you murdered."

"Will that be possible?", Bai asked.

"I suppose it depends on the Netherlands and the USA, Uhllrich is an American Baptist but caught in the Netherlands, so I suppose it is those two countries who decide where the man should be charged. Also I think the Indian Government has to allow that too. It is not a simple thing yet, but for you it is important that he will take all the blame. Tell me Bai, how could he have coerced you into doing such atrocious act?"

"The Rwanda UN military assignment changed us terribly. What we have done there I cannot begin to tell you. Uhllrich knew about it, either heard or was there, I do not know, but he did implicate Sean and me. We could not refuse and he also said it was for a good cause," Bai explained.

"Do you think it is?", Eddie asked.

"I have had time to study the background of the man we killed and of course it is not a good thing to kill anyone. I can't condone that, so also not from myself, but 50 years of defensive war against brutal Indian soldiers and no perspective?"

"He is a Baptist Bai and he felt guilt about the missionaries who left the Nagas alone, not a very Christian thing to do right. He wanted to put the record straight and do what his predecessors shied away from," Efren analyzed.

"But the man should not have implicated people like you, who already had experienced so much in Rwanda and he preyed on that. That is not nice at all," Eddie added.

"We did deserve to be punished severely," Bai answered.

"We will see how it turns out Bai, but we think you may escape the death penalty and perhaps only do a few years in this filthy joint," Eddie smiled as he concluded and announced they would be back to see him some time later. Bai though rather happy about that development had felt guilty indeed even more so, now that he had some perspective in life. When later that day Celia came to visit him, he broke down and cried about not deserving to be treated so nicely. Celia was astounded about Bai's emotions. She thought he would have been very happy, yet his feelings of remorse and guilt appeared to be stronger. He felt he should pay for his sins, but thought he was getting rewarded instead.

"Don't be too hard on yourself Bai," Celia tried to calm him, "take responsibility but for what you are accountable for, not more than that?"

"I cannot do that anymore. I have been very wrong in Rwanda and out of fear I did not say no to Sean and, at a distance, to the plotter Uhllrich. The excuse of me being in total shakedown at the time is not valid when you really think about it. I should not be absolved and I should stand to be judged."

"And you will be, you will be judged and you will have to repent. It has already begun and I am glad, so very glad, that you know and accept this. Yet, you should not take more on your shoulders than what you are responsible for. There are other ways to purify yourself too!", Celia stressed.

"I know this, but the idea will not absolve me. The rest of my life I will work to stand by people who are in dire straits and I will begin with the Nagas," Bai said.

"What do you have in mind darling," Celia asked as she saw some spirit returning.

"I will marry you," Bai laughed, "and I will start a human rights organization which will firstly support the Nagas but will later, when the Nagas are free, become an organization for all deprived people. What do you think about that?"

"Only when we do this together Bai I will let you!", Celia smiled.

"There is something else," he whispered to her.

"Do not keep it from me," Celia said astonished when he saw his face, like he was conspiring, "there are secrets and you did not share with me?"

"Just one," he said faintly smiling, "I was about to tell you when we decided I should go and give myself up," he explained.

"Well then tell me now," Celia eagerly demanded.

In the USA the Baptist group which was commissioned to look into the past of the missionaries concerning their behavior with the Nagas around 1956 convened. And the lady who was chairperson spoke:

"This is quite a development! Who could have foreseen it was Uhllrich himself behind all this? What are we going to do now? Any suggestions?", she asked nervously.

"This is going to be a big blow to our credibility," the older Missouri man said. Also the Baterson man from Texas was present, the one who had visited Nagaland once and who had been celebrating then with some pomp and splendor the more than 100 years successful presence in Nagaland. He conveniently had omitted to mention the predicament the Nagas were in when there. So the lady asked him:

"When I look at you and your missionary training centre I wonder if you should not have known what our brothers and sisters there were going through. I wonder how you could be so self-contained about our achievements. Did you not notice anything when there?"

"I just did as had been done before," he answered innocently, "we did not intervene in politics but in religion!"

"This is not quite true for in 1964 through some intervention of reverend Scott the first cease was agreed on. And, what makes us think that religion is not connected to politics when people are being killed because they defend their rights. I believe we should stand by them. I wonder why Baptists do not do that, or did not do that?, she asked out loud.

"Love your neighbor is a strong principle indeed; stand by your neighbor in need is what it means of course," the Missouri man said, "I am surprised we have not followed up on it where the Nagas are concerned. Uhllrich, the Baptist scholar, a learned man, with a big heart had a bad conscience. On that conscience he tried to act but failed and came up with this darned plot. Despicable and admirable at the same time," he said with emotion in his voice, "how could this man we all know well and admired come to this kind of act. Does he think he is God? One who can take a life whenever he deems that befitting?", he added all worked up now. The lady looked at both of them and shook her head:

"I think it would be wise to assess what he did. He is a respectable man in our Baptist society and as a large Baptist community we have failed. He points that out to us. Did he not try his best though other means to make us feel responsible? He failed because we failed him. It is true he should not have resorted to killing anyone. You are all quite right about that of course, but it is too simple to conclude to stay on that. There is much more to this. How do you feel about being tried by a customary law court in Nagaland?", she asked in challenging manner.

"Well, I think that is ridiculous," a middle aged skinny reverend responded to that, "they may still have the menacing headhunter mentality. I would not allow it. The man gave the order to commit a murder. He is an American and should be brought to be judged here."

"Do not be so short sighted," the Missouri man reacted, "he plotted from here, he had some people deployed he now absolves, but coerced them, he was caught in the Netherlands under the smoke of the Peace Palace. When we go against that we are in for a strange fight and I think we will loose it for it has become much more an international matter rather than a domestic American one. I am more concerned about the reactions of our Government and our own Baptists. I suggest we should encourage a national debate on this matter. This is way too serious for us to just talk about this important matter. The murder was committed in Manila, should the Philippines not have their first say in the decision on where Uhllrich should be brought to justice?"

The talked and talked and gradually agreed the matter was a big one and had an undisclosed number of implications.

"This will damage us as American Baptists," the skinny reverend remarked so I opt for distancing us from Uhllrich and condemn his plotting acts."

"Oh come on, the man did not go to UNPO to surrender himself for nothing. Even when you distance yourself in any way we still are going to get it and worse then, because we will be seen as cowards. Instead I think we should be compassionate and disclose our mistakes, condemn the method Uhllrich used to seek attention by, but stand by the Nagas now," the Missouri man said and had Baterson nodding and the lady thinking.

"We must prepare for a national convention for I am afraid our conservatives will try to hide the mistakes we made and we will be judged. I mean not just by our fellow Americans but much worse by God himself. We should elaborately show the motivation of Uhllrich," can we agree on that?", she asked and there was no one then who objected.

In London the cabinet was meeting. One of the points on the agenda was the situation of Uhllrich having exposed the lack of post colonial responsibility of the British then and now they were facing a minor crisis as Tony Blair put it. Strong at one time Blair looked like he could not take another potshot at his labor reign government after his failure of convincing his own people the UK should be part of the war against Iraq. But, aside from that, this minor problem should be well in his capacity to solve as the statesman he had once proved to be. So, after the Foreign Minister had briefed the cabinet Tony spoke:

"This man Uhllrich is an American Baptist right, a man who out of spite of his Baptist religion felt the necessity to expose what the Indians have been doing with the Nagas."

"Our legacy," the Foreign Minister interrupted.

"Yes, our legacy but we are done with our British Empire. India is independent so what can we do about it? Any suggestions?", he asked.

"I think the best thing to do is to call for a thorough investigation on how our people planted the hand over, on what is was based, to have it done like we did and if we had the right, morally or legally, to do as we did then. That will take time and so it will provide us time to draw up a plan. Fact is, whether we like it or not, that we are held to take the right to self determination seriously. This is a predicament we are in, one that may lead to publications that we made mistakes in the decolonization process and when so decided we should inform India about this," the Home Minister explained.

"If it comes to that it will not be a simple thing to do," Tony reacted, "not only do we get criticized but we might be held accountable. How do we deal with that?"

"It is not too difficult Tony; we blame it on the postwar experience and the zest for all our colonies for their desire to be independent. They decided the wanted to, we just followed their wishes," the Foreign Minister volunteered.

"But that means of course we did neglect those peoples who at the time had no or little say in things and I am sure when we investigate this we will come across evidence of peoples who wanted to be independent," Tony brought in.

"That is true and in the case of the Nagas this was known from the beginning and certainly this was made clear in 1929 when the Simon Commission seriously heard most peoples in the northeast of India. So, when it was known why did we not do anything about it I wonder," the Foreign Minister mentioned.

"We have to do something or the United Kingdom will be blemished," Tony remarked.

"What we could do is to make it known that during the decolonization days all, both the colonizing countries as well as the colonized ones were very eager to become independent and so the decolonization process took relatively little time and all seemed to be happy with it," the Home Minister said.

"Not so when you consider the peoples who felt they were taken for a ride," the Defense Minister intervened, "most wars that are fought now, have their roots in colonial times. Let's not forget that countries like ours made nations where before we came and colonized the peoples had no nations or borders before? The peoples lived in their own realms and free, now quite a number of them are part of a dominant majority and are to be part of that without questioning. This is what the Nagas are going through. Need I remind you that colonial powers drew borders and sometimes straight though tribal territories? The aftermath of the Palestine Israel conflict is also because Israel was carved out of British designated Palestine areas. This is not a simple thing and now that it is out into the open the United Kingdom should perhaps stimulate a greater debate on the matter namely how to correct the mistakes made in the past by the former colonial powers?"

"Are we going too far doing that?", Tony said, "will we not loose prestige in the world when we admit to that? We would be declaring ourselves guilty of gross negligence!"

"Only if we go about it the wrong way, we would," the Defense Minister continued, "we should get the other former colonial powers on our side. I believe it is high time to do something about these unfortunate wars, the seeds of which have been sewn long ago. Perhaps out of ignorance, perhaps out of laziness, perhaps out of lack of responsibility then but we are capable of advising the present independent states, once our colonies, to do the people justice, those who are longing for their right to self determination,"

"So we take the initiative to organize an international debate on the matter with the Nagas as the prime example right," Tony summarized, "shall we plant this at the United Nations? The post colonial kind of unit there seems to be quite defunct at the moment."

"Well to revive that would be a good idea," the Foreign Minister cut in.

"Then I suggest we will bring that up on the agenda we have with the United Nations," Tony concluded.

In Geneva the secretary general of the United Nations was talking to the heads of departments about the developments around the world concerning the Indo Naga talks which had just been held in Amsterdam with regard to the recent development."

"This could be going out of hand," Kofi began, "I think this assassination could have great consequences for our thinking on post colonial life and the rights a number of people have been denied over the years. Most of these wars in Africa are a result of that. Needless to say the Dutch and us at the time have been failing to do justice to the West

Papuans who is now considered to be part of Indonesia. On the other hand, and that is what most post colonial nations are afraid of, it is the fear that many nations will be broken up and disintegration will set in, a very unstable future will be ahead of us."

"So?", the both the UNHCR and the UNDP, the High commission for Refugees and Development simultaneously answered. They smiled as the UNDP Commissioner carried on, "what has been wronged in the past can be corrected with the right attitude. Under the Human Rights Commission for years we had a multitude of indigenous peoples working on a Human Rights declaration concerning collective rights, an expansion of rights of individuals. So, on the consequences of this assassination and the impact it had, why not see the Nagas as the people who could be granted their right to self determination once India will see it should let the Nagas go free. Certainly if we can convince Britain to show what they meant in the past, but neglected at the time of handing over the Nagas to India, then India may feel compelled to talk about that."

"I am not so sure Britain is inclined to do so. Not one of the colonial countries likes to be reminded of the bloody mistakes they made and the crimes their people have committed," the UNHCR commissioner said, "but if they are susceptible let's try to open a debate on the matter and perhaps that way we can solve these wars once and for all. This will also prepare the road for the UNDP to encourage development and care for the environment, for increasingly our planet is in danger. The Kyoto agreement after all was just a beginning; we actually need more drastic measures to save our planet for posterity."

"I will take the initiative for it if you like," the UNHCR Commissioner said, "just on the idea we can repatriate many refugees when this is solved encourages me greatly," he said.

"I hope we can get Great Britain to take the lead. In that case the Dutch will follow I think. That way we can clear a lot of situations," Kofi said as the phone rang and a secretary answered. The man kept on talking as they were trying to find ways and means to get the postcolonial affairs on the agenda of the United Nations. knowing most countries had to agree on that before it could even be debated:

"The Prime Minister of the United Kingdom, Tony Blair, for you Sir," the secretary said, "I said you are in a meeting but he asked me to tell you it is important. He says he needs a few minutes!"

"Okay," Kofi said to her.

"Yes Kofi," Tony Blair began, "we are facing this predicament with the American Baptist plotter. So much attention is drawn to the Nagas that we need to talk on some postcolonial things. I would like to make it a debate among the nations. Can we put it on the agenda, so we can take some wind out of our sail?"

"I will see what I can do Tony," Kofi answered rejoicing inside but playing it cool.

"Please do that. I know colonial nations should show some responsibility, but I don't think we should feel the heat alone," Tony said and concluded, "thank you Kofi!"

Kofi in turn thanked him and turned to the others in the meeting to tell about the coincidence of Tony Blair talking about the Naga case and coming up with the idea of a debate on post colonial behavior."

"That is set then," the refugee commissioner said, "and it is good news too. Let's get ahead with it. To make it serious let's get a commission going and publicize its mandate, meaning and scope. That way any country remotely connected to this long standing problem could be involved and it will be a broad specter debate."

"True," the UNDP commissioner mentioned, "but it could dilute the issue too. I suggest we first study the legitimacy of the claims put forward by the nations who want to be independent. How many members does the UNPO have?"

"Oh that is indeed true too," the UNHCR Commissioner said, "all members of UNPO want to be free. Perhaps it is wise to let the UNPO organize this debate or at least the UN should be working much more closely on the issue?"

"I will instruct my people to do the needful," Kofi concluded.

In Washington and at the UN headquarters the Baptist group has made its presence felt. The lady had requested an audience with the President and she wanted to address the meeting at the United Nations too. When President Bush was briefed on the matter he first had exclaimed that this Uhllrich was an unpatriotic man. He had reasoned the man had jeopardized the good name and standing of the USA in the world.

"He tarnished our good name," Bush had cried out and the good name of the Baptists, "and we must act for if we don't stamp this out the credibility of the USA could be at stake here. In my addresses to the nation I often call on God and now that the Baptists show themselves to be unreliable I will be in trouble doing that. We must get this man and get him convicted for plotting an assassination, a criminal act punishable by death."

"Wait, wait Mr. President, Condoleezza Rice the foreign secretary said, "the man is in custody in the Netherlands. He has been clever enough to surrender to the UNPO, in The Hague and near the Peace Palace. He will use all his might to show what has been done wrong by the Baptists here, the British there and the Indians who are doing it now. If the Dutch will extradite the man, they will be severely criticized. Besides, the man he plotted against if not American, but Indian, well so far for that is what this is all about, the Nagas want to be free of India Mr. President."

"Why did we not know about this," Bush asked.

"We have a good relationship with India, a nuclear power. We need them as friends so we can check on China properly. Do we meddle in domestic affairs," Rice asked.

"If I am not mistaken some Indians murdered nuns there in India? Is it domestic when Americans are killed there and the Baptists have planted Christianity there long before it became India? So, how can it domestic only this conflict?", Bush rhetorically asked.

"I don't think we are actively concerned with religious affairs Mr. President, but in this case perhaps we should look into the background of things. This American Baptist after all plotted the murder of this Indian Naga. He will be held responsible no doubt, but he turned himself in for a purpose."

"Yes to show American, Britain and the UN that all of us have neglected these people. Can't we do anything so India will bring this war to a quick end?"

"Of course we can talk and get to know why either party is persistent. Call in this Baptist woman now Mr. President?"

Bush nodded and the lady was called in:

"How can this happen?", Bush asked her right away.

"We are as stunned as you Mr. President," she answered, "but when we actively see why he did this, his motivation, we believe he has a point. The Baptists did leave the Nagas to fend for themselves!"

"Yeah, yeah, but the Baptists are not the United Stated lady, now the man created a situation. What will happen if the man is not brought to court here, but has he agreed on to be tried in Nagaland?"

"Don't we have a responsibility Mr. president?", she asked, "I think the Baptist community of the USA has!", she firmly said.

"So, you want us to wait and see," he asked.

"I think it would be a good gesture if you show the Indian authorities that the USA has no objection for him to be brought to justice under a customary law court of the Nagas. You will show to the rest of the word that the man is being tried by their own people and of course we could make sure we have some experts there so a fair trial is guaranteed?"

"Well may be that is not such a bad idea," Bush smiled, "thank you for elaborating. We will continue the meeting without you."

The lady left and Bush decided some time later and after some more deepening talk about alternatives to follow the advice of the lady.

On her way to New York now she prepared too for a meeting with some key UN officials, one being Indian. She flew into Kennedy Airport and made her way to the UN headquarters by taxi. There she had herself announced from the reception in the large lobby. Once in the meeting room and very strong in her attitude and appearance she began immediately:

"I had a talk with our president and I think Uhllrich could be produced before a Naga court. What I like to discuss with you is what we can do about this declaration of independence which was received but never replied on by the UN. I think the Naga People have the right to know what the international community decides on their fate. Also I like you to find out if the British then have been determining that non decision. I think it is high time we get this conflict solved?"

"This is strong talk," the Indian smiled as the first in the group to react, "I suspect this will lead to your appeal for the secession of the Nagas and their land?", he asked.

"I would like to see that the war ends and on a mutually agreeable solution.. I do not see the need to prologue this senseless war of occupation. Perhaps when the British speak up it will be easier for you to know what the right way is," the lady retorted.

"You know what is better for India then I see," the Indian UN man said sardonically.

"I know what we, the Baptists of the USA, have not done. I know we should have stood by our brothers and sisters. I cannot say anything about the Indian motivation on occupying the Naga lands," the lady answered him.

"Yes, it is a complicated affair," a representative of the European Union cut in.

"One with colonial roots, like many others?", a woman from Latin America smiled.

"Yes the colonial powers should show some concern to say the least," a woman from Uganda said, "I am sure that with that concern many a war could have been avoided."

"That is rather difficult for the nations which became independent and are sovereign. They inherited all that made up their borders," the Indian said provocatively.

"We can argue like this a long time," the lady said as she was determined to take the lead, "but that war is tragic and we should all feel responsibility to end this ever so long conflict and if need be I will feel compelled to drag Britain into it. I like to see what the United Nations can do too. I am afraid, though it cannot be condoned what Uhllrich did and I mean the plotting of the assassination. Yet we cannot turn back the clock now, for he has also proven that talking alone will not solve that conflict. Something has to be done by all of us," the lady said with vigor in her voice.

Chapter 21

Nagaland part of the International Community

In the United Nations things were not upbeat that was certain now. The pressure was felt and meetings were held both in Geneva and New York, also in the large UNHCR office in Bangkok, Thailand. Painfully clear it was made that the UN had shown many flaws. It is all nice and well and a very important achievement to have a Universal Declaration of Human rights and a written statement on the rights to self determination of peoples, it was another to get these rights. And this is where the United Nations had no clout. For years nations had been watching NGO's pointing out these flaws and the emergence, decline and rebirth of the UNPO was seen as insignificant with respect to the greater picture, but interesting enough to keep it going if only for the flaws of the larger body, the UN. So, some nations paid heed to that thought and gave some money to keep it going, some subsidies. But the organization could hardly be managed to keep itself going if not for the volunteers, who as much as possible worked without salaries. This Uhllrich confession had done wonders though. Journalists flocked and politicians came to enquire. Both wanted back ground information:

"Who are these Nagas?", was a recurrent question and tirelessly answered by the UNPO till one of the staff came up with the idea of making a sheet of facts on the Indo-Naga conflict, so that most on request would have access to the basics. After the talks which were held in Amsterdam, the Naga team spent some time in the Hague to catch up with UNPO and this was an occasion for many, because now many Europeans of all delineation and background eagerly besieged the men who normally would go around quite inconspicuously.

"Your days as ordinary people are over," Musdachin laughed, "you will become celebrities. Just show that you are only defending your right to self determination and tell your land has been invaded and you should get lots of admiration."

"Our goal is to be known in the international community and to safeguard our rights," a Naga leader said.

"You will have lots of opposition but now that Uhllrich has catapulted your case into the limelight, things will take a different turn. I am glad for your people as this will serve as an example for others too. I would like you to work with us on a stand which solely concerns the aftermath of colonialism. We will focus on post colonial responsibility. We could hold the former colonial powers accountable for the conflicts they turned a blind eye to. And, when your people are successful this will be quite a jumpstart for the others," Musdachin explained.

"Of course, it goes without saying that we will stand by you. UNPO has been a great asset to us. It is just natural we can do something in return," the Naga leader spoke, but they were interrupted by journalists from Italy this time, who were requesting an interview with both Musdachin and the Naga leader.

Meanwhile Uhllrich was in jail worked on an explanatory paper, but was interrupted by Marius for an informal talk:

"We are working on something," Marius said, "we would like you to get as much as possible out of here, but you will not escape from plotting a serious crime!"

"Of course," Uhllrich agreed, "no problem for I planned that too. I just hope that it will lead to a trial in Nagaland," Uhllrich shrewdly smiled.

"You may become a celebrity, you know," Marius chuckled, "we have to fend off the journalists as we speak!"

"Let me talk to them?", Uhllrich pleaded.

"Only when the authorities here will agree to it," Marius smiled, "but, I think they cannot keep you from going public!", he said encouragingly. And, he was right, the call to get Uhllrich's background became louder and so the Dutch Ministry of Justice as well as Foreign Affairs through the Prime Minister were compelled to let him talk and Uhllrich did. His motivation for the murder he spelled out widely and did confront the press by stating it looked like it had been the only way to catch attention. This was reported widely and so when the television crews had come and had gone and the programs had been on the screens in quite a few countries in Europe, Asia, Australasia the USA and where not, the politicians could hardly refrain from ignoring it. The long time war against the Nagas was meted out and crews were commissioned to go and shoot documentaries:

"If only to check on the validity of what this man Uhllrich is saying," a producer of NBC, USA, and of the BBC World service commented in choir.

"I am going to see what these Baptists have to say and will you do Britain?" the NBC man asked his colleague, "then when we have done that let's team up and go to Nagaland. It is on the map now," he said.

"I am told you do not get in there very easily, only tourists in groups," the BBC man answered.

"Well we should get our politicians involved then. The Indians should not hide anything anymore; this is now serious business," he laughed, "what does your government think about this fast developing situation?'

"Informally I know something," he answered, "it involves the idea of doing some research on what has been done at the time of the hand over," the BBC man said, "it is like buying some time to get a well founded decision. I also heard our government considers a debate on the matter, an international debate, not just this actual matter but the matter of post colonial responsibility."

"Really the labor government is willing to do that?", the American asked.

"Well, I can't be certain but I heard from a reliable source, an agent," he said.

"This is a tremendous breakthrough you know, if true," the American said in earnest.

They made some arrangements then and applied first at the embassy for visas to get into Nagaland. They were turned down but after the interventions of their respective governments could organize a trip into the heart of Nagaland. The BBC man meanwhile was looking for his resource persons, one of them was Jeanie.

Jeanie in turn had taken a deep interest in the people of Nagaland; her journey into the hills had made her fall in love with both the people and the land. So, being elated by what had happened, she had witnessed the near uprising too and had been quite impressed, she had looked at the role of her own country. Of course she was loyal, only not loyal to negligent decisions which only comforted the then leaders of the land, but had had a devastating effect on the Naga People. She was quite convinced that these people had paid the price for that negligence, so when she had learned about what was being brewed up by the present Government headed by Tony Blair; she had leaked that information to the BBC journalist. This news through that journalist who had the scoop had spread like wildfire. Now it had become fodder for the United Nations too.

Although the United States had had a colony, the Philippines where the murder was committed, essentially that government had little to do with that. Some senators however, Democrats, saw in this initiative a chance to raise some pressure against the present government of the United States, so Bush did feel some heat over that. However it was much more the colonial powers that were being scrutinized and the former colonies were heading the pack where the demand for openness in the post colonial affairs was concerned. A debate was initiated and according to Great Britain it should be organized by the United Nations. Now UNPO came into the picture too and was by way of Musdachin opening an avenue to do more than cover the debate as an organization with observant status, No, it demanded to fully talk on behalf and with the representatives of the respective peoples concerned, to participate. Musdachin had argued that, when the decolonization process had begun then the peoples who were now dependent on the big nations they did not want to be part of, had had no say in things. Consequently this was the first major breakthrough in the debate, for now the peoples themselves on the basis of their past could come forward and talk about their right to self determination. One can imagine that this created a lot of disturbance, for more than breeching rusted thinking, which was protective of the then colonial powers, they had to come forward and tell how it was and in which way the peoples voluntarily were part of colonies, who were now independent nations. The Nagas of course were the first people to show their background and the debate put Great Britain on the defensive. It was obvious that Nagaland had arrived and was respected for the endurance it had shown in order to stand for their rights. But, not only Great Britain had to show its accountability and was sternly asked to repair what damage had been done. Also the Dutch Government in relation to West Papua par example, the French with its francophone nations in Africa, Latin America and so on and of course the Spanish and the Portuguese were questioned and here it concerned the rights of the Indigenous peoples. The United States of America meanwhile was terribly afraid it would be held accountable for the atrocities it had inflicted on the original peoples of the land now called the Native Americans, many of which were banned into special reservations where they were said they could live as they liked. The Philippines, its indigenous peoples too, saw a chance for redemption when their land was taken during the 50 year colonial tenure of the Americans on islands like Mindanao. Everywhere there were debates held and the results were published in a way it had never been done before.

In the Philippines Bai was happy too. Not only would he get a lesser sentence but he was allowed to see Celia more often. The Philippine judiciary would take Bai to court but the charge would not be murder, t would be coerced conspiracy. Celia had come to learn about the good news as it was published in the papers for the international news was directly linked to one of their countrymen. The journalist here had shaped an atmosphere now which made him look more like a hero than an assassin. This was not good he knew, so in every interview he gave he stressed that although he had been coerced he still could have said no. he should not have taken a life.

Also in Rio de Janeiro, Brazil, the debate had begun. In jail Jacky was talking to Sean about it and knowing that both of them could escape with a lighter sentence now that Uhllrich had confessed at least Sean had been pressed by him to prepare for the assassination but she wondered about her own status in this now:

"You committed me to do the actual killing. Bai prepared this but I pulled the trigger. I did this to help you and so I think I will have to bear the consequences in full as I cannot expect leniency," she said when they were allowed to meet and prepare for their defense. In the presence of their lawyers they knew they were to be brought to courts in Brazil:

"Unless of course both your countries will ask for extradition, but I don't think they will in your case," their Brazilian lawyer said.

"I think so too," a sad Jacky agreed with him.

"Don't be too sad!", the lawyer smiled, "I do see some advantages. Let's see; first of all you have the high publicity world wide which will work in your favor, then if Sean here tells he committed you so you could be together a story of love will work in your favor too. I would not be too disappointed yet. I am sure we can get a lot out of this. Right now however I would like to know from both of you f you want to be tried here or if we should approach your own countries so extradition procedures can be started?"

"Considering the debate of the rights of indigenous peoples, something brought about by Uhllrich on the basis of the assassination, I think it may be more advantageous if we go to court here in Rio de Janeiro," Jacky thought aloud, "do you agree Sean?", she asked.

"It's difficult to say but it looks good, the debate is gaining momentum and the politicians refer to what we did in Manila. They know we are not quite responsible for the debate; surely that is what Uhllrich arranged cleverly, but without us the debate would not have been possible, so we might get some leverage from that yes. Let's have it here," Sean said to his lawyer.

In Delhi there was a lot of uncertainty still. Many felt the attention India received regarding the Indo-Naga conflict was not at all favorable. Slowly but gradually public opinion world wide turned against India and the call to solve this conflict fast now became louder by the day. Debates in different countries and regions were on and more an more representatives of India were called to explain what exactly was the matter with these Nagas and why India had occupied the Naga lands with so many soldiers. What was their policy on the matter was the question repeatedly asked? But the leaders of India could not easily come up with to the point answers. This in turn made journalists, politicians and ambassadors uneasy for it felt like this greatest democracy on earth, a title India liked to adorn itself with, was not that democratic after ll. In fact hardly a relevant figure on cost and losses was published so the leaders were not showing any sign of accountability. Lack of policy also meant that the leaders could do as they pleased. When journalist by the hundreds then wanted to go into Nagaland they cause jitters in the flesh of the Government and it put them on the defensive. They came back with the old and worn out statements like; for your own safety we will not allow anyone to enter Nagaland or this is purely a domestic affair. No other nation should interfere with our domestic problems. To the chagrin of the Government of India this did not deter many a journalist who, under the guise of being tourists, sneaked in. When this was discovered and some of them were arrested, the reactions were strong. India felt it had managed to move itself into a predicament of international importance, a situation so to speak.

Chapter 22
Beyond Twilight

In Manila things were much quiet. Bai was talking to Eddie. Eddie had not been able to find Bai, though he knew Bai was part of the assassination team, was only due to the fact he had moved in with Celia. Bai had returned to his house when he decided to give himself up. But now they were talking on Bai's idea, Eddie had shared with the pathologist who had screened the body after the actual assassination.

"When do you think it is time to reveal all?", Eddie asked, "the plot is to be unraveled and I believe the time is near now Bai," he said.

"Yes, things are in motion and seem to be irreversible. How is the family of the Naga leader doing?", Bai asked in return.

"Oh I was there yesterday," he answered, "they are tightlipped, "just like I am, but my conscience is not clear Bai. Give the word man and we will go public. Not even the other Naga families know about it." Eddie said

"Good, good, nobody actually knows but you and me," Bai smiled, "okay brief me on the latest and we will assess how we are going to move from there?", Bai said to Eddie.

"Okay, I will, I am anxious too, this is too much for me to keep inside. The international impact is overwhelming. Does Uhllrich know about this," Eddie asked.

"No, just you and me," Bai smiled.

"I am flabbergasted man, we will make headlines you know?", Eddie exclaimed and talked about what was happening around the world including the mounting pressure on India and the pack of journalists who were marching into Nagaland, in spite being held back by the Indian authorities. The debate on where to produce Uhllrich was on now too and while India at first had shown it would allow now it had reluctance but the latest was that they would seriously consider it.

"Provided the Nagas allow both Indians and international experts of law to be present and that customary law is enough and procedures fair, we will not oppose," the Justice Minister of India had made public," Eddie quoted the man from a paper.

"Okay that is good enough, things move fast now," Bai said, "the world could be ready for another blow now. Let's prepare a statement and publish from here, but be sure Eddie it will reach all corners of the world?"

"You are a naughty man Bai," Eddie laughed, "you may even get out of here soon!"

Marius and Shilu were at home when Shilu announced she was ready able and willing:

"What do you mean darling?", a startled Marius laughed.

"I am ready, able and willing to see our negotiators. They are here and I want to be sure they have put forward my idea of having Uhllrich tried before a court in Nagaland," she laughed, "but of course I am also ready, able and willing to elope with you," she laughed even harder now, much harder. Marius laughed too but did more; he smooched her and while doing so he asked her in whisper:

"When are you going to see your men?"

"This evening I will, you want to come with me? The talks have been concluded here and as I understand it they went well, but I like to hear from them what actually transpired. You can meet them, they already know about you."

"Oh that is not good," Marius smiled.

"Why not?", Shilu asked looking surprised.

"I am a covert agent darling, so being known is not good at all. However in this case it might not matter much."

"You are right, but then you are not known in your capacity as an agent, but as my man, you know," she smirked.

"That is all right then, Marius laughed, "you speak to your people and I will go to prison for I want to talk to Uhllrich. I feel he has a card left still," he said.

In between all these rapid developments there was one important thing to be done and this would attract a lot of attention too, Swu's homecoming! The Home people had been planning he funeral and it was near now. Shilu wanted to talk to the leaders about this In Manila the organization commissioned to embalm him stumbled on some irregularity; the body had not yet been released by the Philippine authorities. In Nagaland all had been arranged to receive him but the authorities officially declared they wanted to check his body again. It would be just a matter of days, the Nagas were assured, for Swu to be flown back home. With the funeral igniting anti India feelings the Indians were afraid the Nagas might rise again,. Not so much because they thought the Indians were behind the assassination plot, everyone knew it had been Uhllrich; it was because with all the attention they had received through Uhllrich's plot, the Nagas could show to the world they did not demand anything but wanted to rule themselves in their own land. Beginning with the expected uprising followed by Uhllrich's trial the whole world was drawn to the plight of the Nagas India feared it was answerable to that. The world through the international press would be witnessing both events. The Indians knew and were afraid of that. They realized they had to put and end to the conflict, the leaders having the conflict to explain to their own people in casu why the Nagas had every right to be free. Shilu was thinking about this when with Marius she arrived at the house where the Nagas were staying. In the presence of respected elders it was customary to call them uncle so affectionally she said:

"Good day to you uncle, it is good to see you!"

"Oh yes and you too Shilu," he answered. After the ritual of extending hospitality she came to the point:

"Uncle, I do not know if you have heard about the idea yet from Uhllrich himself, but I know that he has no objection to be brought before a Naga customary court, so a traditional one. I suggested this, because that way there will be ample coverage from all corners and it will give us a fine opportunity to expose Naga culture too. The Indians might not be able to stop this for when they do they would be heavily criticized and questioned too. What do you think about this?"

"Oh Shilu it was on the news, so I know. I don't think any other Government should claim this man to be tried for the murder he plotted. So, your idea is good, it also shows Baptists are nor above their own laws and preaching. But Shilu, I think the USA does not like its own people tried before an alien court. I think the USA has to agree with us on this. I will go for it, but not for the exposure only. I agree with you because of the sincerity we display in doing justice. I am sure the Naga Government will not object too this either," he reacted.

"I wonder if Nagaland is equipped enough for such a big event. Though i am sure your traditional judiciary system will not fail you, you will have many people present and from all over the world. I don't think a trial like that has ever attracted this many people?"

Marius remarked.

"We will manage," the leader smiled, "yes when I trust the news reports there will be many people attending. This will be a big event and we realize, to organize it without flaws there are many things to think about. We will be judged on respect for our laws, those of the international community, but to me it is also important to be fair to Uhllrich, the person who confessed for plotting the assassination!"

"The verdict may not be appreciated by outsiders?", Marius said.

"That is possible of course," Shilu answered, "and it would mean our sense of justice would become part of the international community too. So, uncle I ask you, would you dare to leave the overall international organization concerning the exposure to me? It would be a tremendous boost to our newly founded organization we base here in the Netherlands," she said

"You could be right Shilu. Please put these ideas on paper and work them out so I can present them to the Government."

"Thank you uncle, I will do that," Shilu respectfully said and with the official business over, the aids of the leader cooked a Naga meal, before returning. Enjoying a good Naga meal, they took time for small talk; family talk and Marius talk as they joked with her:

"Are you sure you want to marry a foreigner, a man without Naga roots. He may not understand your ways. Does he behave himself?", uncle asked sporting cheeky eyes..

"You are worried about that?" Shilu laughed.

"Your point is taken," Marius laughed too, "be sure uncle that O do not fear the ways of the Nagas. Shilu, a knowledgeable woman, a woman too open to talk about anything, should not either."

"I have seen him among our people uncle and you are right he is not a tribesman. I thank you for cautioning me, but, like you, I do take risks too, calculated ones?", she smiled a radiant at him, an ironic smile. Not long after this they returned. Back at Marius' place they had some rather astonishing news waiting for them.

Composing his press release, Bai smiled. He knew it would send shockwaves through the world, Eddie looking over his shoulder, beamed. He had known the content of what Bai's release from the very first day he stumbled on Bai's secret, but had kept his mouth shut and so had the pathologist with him. Of course the body of Swu was brought to the morgue. Since there was no hurry, the man was obviously shot to death; he had been put on ice. But then the pathologist had received an anonymous phone call and summoned Eddie before he checked Swu to officially establish the cause of death. This anonymous caller revealed to them and warned them that they would find something stunning but had to be kept secret. He had pointed out what it was and said the Manila police would not believe it unless they showed the proof. He warned them that if they would reveal the secret before they were told to do so, the consequences could be devastating for then they would never be able to find the culprits. With this in mind the pathologist and Eddie decided to keep their secret with them.

But the anonymous called left the pathologist and Eddie dumbfounded when they found out. So, later when Bai in Eddie's custody revealed he was the anonymous caller Eddie could not believe him, but had to. First, how would he know there had been an anonymous caller at all? Then when Bai had gave him details on the call only the caller could know, Eddie agreed with Bai to reveal the truth at an appropriate time. This had put Eddie under severe strain because for Nagaland and the Indian Government requested the police authorities to have the body sent to Kohima. Officially Swu's family made this request too and Eddie had to find all sorts of reasons to stall for time. Swu's family however, the pathologist and Eddie were the only people who actually knew what Bai now wrote in his press release.

"You know Bai?", Eddie smirked, "all is well that ends well!"

"Did not know you liked Hemingway," Bai laughed, "but dear Eddie I am ever so glad you did trust me enough to go through with this. I thank you and my thanks are more than I can express to you. Not even Celia, my wife to be, knew about this. Can you believe that? We were making plans for being together after my long term in jail. Can you call Celia to come over Eddie? I like her to see this before it goes out for. She must know.. Oh, I think I still deserve punishment, but not what was in store for me," Bai smiled.

"Yes I will do that," Eddie answered, "but tell me, how did you get the idea? Not even the assassin herself, Jacky the high class prostitute of your friend Sean, knew about it?"

"That is right Eddie. She never knew. She killed Swu and that is all there is to it. It will be a big and pleasant surprise for her too, I am sure."

"Yes, of course, I am sure about," Eddie sported a big laugh now too.

Bai and Eddie had been waiting for this grand moment and now that Celia had arrived Bai's press release was finished. Since her home was in Quezon City and considering the famous traffic jams of Manila and as it was quite out of town it took Celia a while to get to Bicutan jail. Still faster than they had imagined they could welcome her. After sharing the joy of seeing each other again, Bai handed her the press release saying softly:

"This might shock you for I did not even tell you. Eddie was bound to discover and only the direct family knows about it. I am sorry darling for fear of loosing the momentum and so there would be lesser impact, I could not tell you."

Celia hardly listened to him for already the headline he showed her baffled her completely. Bai and Eddie did not say anything but led her read as she gasped and looked. It astounded here, rocked her off her socks. She screamed as she read the release:

Two weeks after his assassination Naga leader resurrects from the dead

Assassin's assistant prevented the high profile murder on the president Swu of the forbidden Nagaland

In Manila Bailung, a Philippino of Indian descent and assistant to assassin Jacky of the Netherlands, who fled to Brazil, says president Swu of Nagaland is alive and well. Both Jacky and her British lover Sean flew to Rio de Janeiro but were caught and locked up as the three of them formed a team deployed by the now known American. Uhllrich assigned them to assassinate Swu. It is now official all are being held for a murder they thought they committed. They did not. Bailung prevented that.

The murdered Naga leader was shot by the now known team of arrested British, Dutch and Philippino assailants, but Swu is alive and well and recovering from minor injuries. Jacky fired the shots but did not know they were blanks but for one which contained a strong tranquilizer Bailung disclosed today from his prison cell. Why only now I disclose this? Why this charade? Sean and I were seriously threatened by the person we only now know as Uhllrich. We did not know who he was then. On the basis of things in our past he could coerce us to commit ourselves to this high profiled crime. Uhllrich had motivation to do this, a motivation we all know now. Concerned and frightened to commit another crime, one for which no redemption is possible, I deliberately decided to change the ammunition. Jacky and Sean never knew, neither did Uhllrich. Now that I know about Uhllrich's motivation and what he hoped to achieve I can only thank God I prevented this killing from happening. Mr. Swu is very much alive and he suffered only some minor injuries. I asked him and his family to be quiet about this until an appropriate moment would arrive. Now that I see the effects of the assassination, I make public Mr. Swu is indeed alive and journalists can interview him in his house in Manila today. A press conference to verify his well being will be held at 5 pm in the afternoon.

The Bicutan jail number was mentioned, a number many Philippino journalists knew by heart. Bailung did not say anything about the police in this press release which was both emailed to the international news agencies as well as distributed to all correspondents as hard copies. An hour later Swu was informed about the disclosure of the press release and press conference and should expect journalists to come to his house. Bai and Eddie had prepared him for that and had given him some prefabricated texts. Here in Bicutan prison Celia gasped aloud and said to Bai"

"God man, how could you do this? I mean how could you not do this and not tell me? Did you not trust me? Eddie here knew!"

"Oh, oh, oh," Bai smiled feigning he lamented, "no darling, I wanted to protect you from any kind of senseless guilt feelings on your conscience. If you had known this our state of bliss would have ended too. And then, I did not know Uhllrich would come out, motivated by something much more profound. He used this assassination for a better purpose and in the process showed us all the dilemmas we live in. I am overjoyed now that for defying them by taking the decision not to kill Swu after all."

"Yes, of course, that was a very good intervention, but you should have told me. I cannot grasp you kept it from me. Don't get me wrong, I do understand your motivation but feeling so close and knowing you schemed this while you were in my arms it feels like there are two person housed in your body."

"I schemed this before I met you again Celia, remember that! And not likely it will happen again. This had to be done Celia!"

"You were hiding from the police and you knew Eddie was implicated, he knew what you did. Did you not Eddie?"

"Yes I did, but through an anonymous call Mrs. Celia," Eddie smiled.

"So you confide in a complete stranger and not in me?", she asked.

"Not intentionally," Bai answered seeing Celia was serious, "I could not prevent Eddie from finding out anyway. You had nothing to do with it and it all happened before we met again to find each other as soul mates. This was the end of the old chapter in my life. Please Celia do forgive me," Bai asked humbly

"Of course Bai," Celia smiled, "and yes it happened before we met again."

"With the chill out of the air now Eddie, Celia and Bai began planning the aftermath. The press release would detonate like a bomb and so they briefed Swu for a second time. This was needed because the recognized

Bicutan number attracted Philippino journalists to be at the gate of this well known jail complex which housed political prisoners. Since he had prevented the murder Bai possibly would be set free by the court and the journalists already swarming at the gate were anxious to question him on the matter.

"Why did you not make this public immediately," a Philippino reporter asked.

"Sean, Jacky and I, were held to secrecy by the one whom we now know as Uhllrich. When Uhllrich came out and I could see the effects of his planned plot, I thought it was time to have us all vindicated. Nobody actually got hurt but Uhllrich did manage to get world attention for the plight of the Nagas to be free. I understand his predicament and the dilemma he faced. I am overjoyed I made that decision to swap the bullets for blanks," Bailung said with a serious tone in his voice.

"The Manila police must have known this, how did you delude them?"

"I phoned the pathologist anonymously with threats after Swu was whisked Swu off to proclaim him dead,", Bailung answered

"So that is how you made it look like a real assassination?", another journalist asked, "because you implicated your fellow men in this!"

"Precisely, it was too tricky to reveal this right away. I had to be sure about the motivation of the plotter Uhllrich. I am glad Swu understood and because I used a compound which knocked him off his feet, he needed time to recuperate anyway. The police will lead you to his home," Bailung patiently explained.

"You were afraid to be killed once the plotter Uhllrich knew the assassins had failed?", another reporter squirmed himself in.

"Not exactly that only, but true too I think," Bailung said, "I wanted to know why this man had to die and when I found out, just like you, that it had been done for an important purpose, I was glad that I did not report this immediately. It would have taken out the exposure the Nagas deserve."

Later that day the journalist stormed the place where Swu was to hold the announced press conference. This was televised, the images and words shown throughout the world..

"Look at this darling," Marius said to Shilu showing extreme excitement as he handed her a newspaper. Startled she took it from him and saw the headline:

Two weeks after his assassination Naga leader resurrects from the dead. Assassin's assistant prevented high profiled murder on the president Swu of the Forbidden Nagaland

"Oh my goodness," Shilu exclaimed, "Swu is alive, hallelujah."

"Yeah, this is quite a turn of events my sweet," Marius smirked, all this plotting of Uhllrich but he could not control the Philippino he thought he had deployed. This is fascinating. Food for psychologists too," he smiled.

"I wonder what will happen now," Shilu thought aloud.

"I think Bai will be set free, I am not sure about the other two"

"Yeah, Jacky and Sean did think they had hit on Swu, but were coerced and now that there is no one killed, they will be let off with something small," Shilu said.

"How about Uhllrich then, what will happen to him?", Marius asked.

"Hhhmmm, yes indeed. Can we not still get him to Nagaland before a court? It was only his luck through Bailung he did not actually assassinate Swu."

"If not for Bailung Swu had been dead and buried," Marius said, "but now that Swu is alive I am sure his sentence too will be less severe. Let's try and convince him to get to Nagaland anyway. He might become more of a hero Shilu. That is the risk we run!"

"Yeah let's go and see him to hear what he has to say about this?", Shilu answered.

"Good idea," Marius smiled, "I was going anyway, but now that this news is out, I think we could go together, it puts all in a different light!"

"Right," Shilu acknowledged and got ready to leave, anxious as she was, Marius no less.

Another surprise awaited them for they not expect Bram or Jeanie in prison too. They had been there for an hour or so already talking to Uhllrich. They shook hands and embraced. Marius and Shilu looked at Uhllrich and Shilu said

"Good heavens man do we have news for you. Do you know what happened after the Manila assassination?", Shilu asked.

"Lots happened," Uhllrich smiled, "what news are you referring to?"

Shilu pulled the newspaper from her handbag and showed it to the three of them.

"Oh it can't be true," Jeanie exclaimed with Bram leaning over her to read the headline Bram gasped as he showed to Uhllrich Swu had been resurrected and was living with his family in the town he was shot in.. Astounded but very controlled, Uhllrich and read on. A few minutes later he lifted his head and all could see him smile.

"This is good news indeed. I am glad the man is alive and I thought I could only do justice to the Nagas by attracting world wide attention through a murder. I tried many ways but only by plotting a killing, not through negotiations, we achieved so much. For doing your own thing I thank you Bailung. It will not absolve me, but I rejoice knowing Mr. Swu is alive and well," he said quite solemnly.

Stunned about Uhllrich's confession to take the consequences Marius asked:

"So what now?"

Shilu jumped on this and asked Uhllrich: "Do you still want to be tried in Nagaland?"

"Of course," he smiled, "it will add fuel to the fire. We must not loose the momentum. Upon learning Swu is alive so no assassination took place, post colonial nations will retract their commitments. They will feel they were deceived by a devious plotter and will seek some vengeance. Their leaders may even think they have been fooled and the consequences of lost face could come in," he said with strong conviction, "if I back out now from being brought to justice by the Nagas it will be their advantage."

"You may have deserved this," Jeanie smiled thinking she could come home with some result after all but was taken off that thought instantly when Uhllrich continued, "oh yes," he agreed, "that is very true. I certainly do, but I won't be tried by them. This I want to refuse vehemently. The Nagas have the right to try me Jeanie!"

"What about deploying and coercing the others like Sean and Bail? Jacky was put forward by Sean, or did you have anything to do with this too," Marius asked Uhllrich.

"Indirectly only, but then you are right. It was my plan. I plotted it. I did coerce Sean and Bailung as I knew from the Rwanda tour what they and many others did there. I also knew how much they suffered from that terrible disaster and especially Bai was seeking redemption from what he did during that experience. He blamed himself and true enough he should, but I initiated this too to provide him with a chance to seek vindication."

"Oh really you gave them the chance by way of coercing them? That is an interesting one," Jeanie laughed, "I am not too sure the British courts will go along with that interpretation," she said.

"When they know all my motivations and they know what the two did there, you will change your attitude young lady," Uhllrich smiled, "but I need not discuss this with you. I can leave that to the courts."

"She has a point though," Bram said, "you know that the coercion part has nothing to do with the actual assassination. This means there is no roadblock on getting you to court on that charge in the USA, Netherlands or even Britain or Nagaland."

"I don't mind," Uhllrich laughed louder now, "as long as the Nagas get the attention they need. The word Naga should be a household name, I will rest when that has been achieved," he stressed.

"You are a persistent fellow," Shilu remarked, "but okay our leader has agreed for you to come to Nagaland. We will leave it to the authorities here to get you there. They can get you on coercion charges when they want, but for the assassination plot we want you to come to Nagaland, okay?"

"Sure," Uhllrich smiled, "I am a happy man today, Shilu"

"Let's forget about where the man is to be tried," Marius said and laughed too now, "look I want to see the reaction of this. I think many will try to frame Uhllrich now for having plotted this too. I think some scape-goating will be done, Uhllrich?"

"Anything Marius?"

"Yes, will you expose your relationship with Sean and Bailung?"

"Of course, it would mean they will go free, certainly now that the assassination took on this unexpected turn. I will testify in their case and I will plead for them," Uhllrich said.

This Bailung might become a hero you know, Uhllrich, at your expense even perhaps!"

"No, I don't think so. I know Bailung as a man of integrity who has made a terrible mistake he is still paying for and I made him pay some more," Uhllrich answered, "and where there is any doubt about him. I will take it up for him."

"The Good Samaritan you are playing now Uhllrich," Bram chuckled.

"Not intentionally Bram," Uhllrich answered sternly, "but I tell you those two men could not say not to me and Bailung did disobey. Of course he did not know then it was me behind it, but his fear was great enough for me to use him. This is my responsibility and as a man I should take it, not just playing a Good Samaritan but to do justice."

"Because others failed to do justice to the Nagas?", Jeanie asked.

"Is that not reason enough Jeanie?" Uhllrich asked in return with an ironic smile.

"It could be," Jeanie smiled..

According to Bram the Dutch authorities had no objection against Uhllrich to be tried before a Naga court. The Indians, convinced refusing such trial on Naga soil would make them loose prestige in the international community, had requested UN and UNPO to be present. Jeanie however, sent by the British Government, argued the United Kingdom would loose face with Uhllrich speaking up on the basis of the stalemate between India and Nagaland. This infuriated Marius for Bram had not informed him and Jeanie apparently had come to persuade Uhllrich not to go to Nagaland. The British Government could be blamed for badly arranging the decolonization process and initiating a debate on post colonial accountability should put the British in place and so she had asked Uhllrich not to pursue the matter. Marius knew how Jeanie was implicated as the go between for Uhllrich, but Bram did not, so she had used him. This is the conflict of interests I feared, Marius thought and he took Jeanie away from the others:

"Now Jeanie," Marius said, "you were his right hand for a while. You got the others on his trail. What do you want to achieve with this?"

"Britain fears it will be implicated far worse than anticipated. I was asked to try and get Uhllrich of Britain's back. You were right Marius, we have our loyalties and you know of course they are conflicting now. This time it is us, next time the Dutch. Things like this would cause our relationship to fail," she agreed.

"I see you have taken Bram into your protective custody? Don't you think the same applies to him Jeanie?"

"No, no," Jeanie smiled, "it is Bram who did that. Considering how we fared I think I should not let him? What do you think," she asked.

"I know we could have had something under different circumstances," Marius said, "who knows the circumstances for you and Bram are more favorable? I wonder though why you don't get yourself a man whom you know to be on your side."

"It is not that, I saw it only as a complication, but I do like Bram," she said.

"Well, like you, I am here to know what Uhllrich wants to do. If I asses him right, he wants to go to Nagaland for his trial, Swu alive or dead, it does not matter to him."

"Yeah, I can't persuade him otherwise," she said as they joined the others again.

"Look," Uhllrich said to them, "I am very happy with the events and that Bai had the courage to prevent the assassination. What we see is a torn and unequal world; rights, resources, labor. In my world, less social than you might think for a leading nation, people rather than standing by their neighbors, act spoiled. They think how to acquire money, prestige and power. The essence of Baptism is not charity but sharing, a social concept, uplifting rather than downgrading. So Jeanie, to make a long story short, I have to repent for what I did. I did something terribly wrong and no matter how many lives may have been saved by that act of plotting, the means do not justify the ends. Of course the ends will be spectacular and your Government dear Jeanie should bow down too."

Jeanie knew she could not make headway. Emotional now for she knew Marius as a trusted friend and hearing Bram talking sense and Uhllrich to them, she was convinced Uhllrich should do as he pleased. In conclusion she said to Uhllrich:

"I am afraid our Government has to bite some dust. In all fairness I agree the UK should stand up to be counted for, but will you do me one favor?", she asked.

"By all means if I can," Uhllrich answered.

"I have been sent to try and win you over. For that purpose I even have money with me, big money," and she mentioned a figure, "take that money and hand it to the Human Rights organization there, NPMHR? I know many people have suffered through our negligence. When interviewed then tell you agreed not to go to Nagaland."

"But I want to go and won't be bribed," he said, looking surprised.

"Yes I know that. Please at first say you agreed for it was useless as nobody died. Then later say you changed your mind because the plan was executed and you are accountable. This way it will be money well spent. If you like you can even expose you have been bribed by the UK, all right?"

"It is against my conviction, even against my nature, but I agree with you, the money put to good use by the Nagas, is more important now. Okay I will do as you instructed."

"Let's go and find out what the implications are of this news?", Marius suggested.

"Yes, you do just that," Uhllrich was quick to answer, "and then return to tell me?"

Bailung's confession, followed by Swu's resurrection speech, was both screened on television. It was done just to prove the man, the president of the Nagas, was alive and well, for all to see. This news hit Sean and Jacky, still in separately confined, like an explosion. Jacky could not stop talking to herself saying: 'It is impossible. I know I shot him, how can he be alive still. He was proclaimed dead too. Oh God, I must speak to him right away. I will ask permission from the guards.'

She had the heavily guarded prison cell all to herself; an exception. In Rio it was possible to buy some comfort. This was good for her but it also made her public enemy for all women looked green with envy at her. So, since money was not the option to make them happy she did distribute some of it to them and she bought herself the privilege to see Sean personally too. With this fresh news on her mind and hour later she was marched off to her cell into the men's cellblock. She was left alone but for a guard to eaves drop as she had been instructed to do till Sean arrived:

"Sean man my love, have you heard?", she asked but from his face already she could read he had not.

"What news," Sean asked in return, a stupefied grin on his lips.

"Bailung switched bullets with blanks and a tranquilizer. Our target, the man called Swu, the leader of the Nagas is not dead. I saw him on TV just now."

"You did? I want to see too Jacky," he said now also anxious.

"Are you allowed to see it here?"

"No not really indeed," Sean answered.

"Then I tell you the main points. Swu is alive. Bailung has said that on television here and I saw Swu stating he was injured but already back in shape. What will happen Sean? Could it be we are going to benefit from this?"

"That is quite possible," Sean smiled, "knowing Bai he will come forward and explain everything. He did not mention anything about us?"

"Yes he did, he said in front of journalists we should go free as nobody was hurt or killed and we were coerced to assassinate. Uhllrich will confirm this," he added.

"I am sure the authorities here will take this into consideration," Sean smiled.

"When we are free, you might still run the chance to be charged with political conspiracy in your home country, like I could be in mine. We should be witnesses of each other, for each other and get ourselves out of this humble and god forsaken place."

Man I want to go to Nagaland to see things for myself," Jacky suddenly said, "now that it looks chances are we may still have a future my dear Sean I want you to come with me to explore. Oh my head spins with excitement and possibilities. This could be our chance Sean. Don't you think so too?"

"Possibly so," the reserved Sean smiled in a typically English fashion, "and yes we could go and visit Nagaland. Perhaps we will open a travel agency too, that way both adventurers and culture lovers can see what people the Nagas are and how they have been able to withstand the Indians for so long. This is going to be great my love. No more bordellos for me, but exploring each other and then some of the world, but together," Sean said ravishing her till the guard intervened.

Delhi was getting politically insane. The leaders had just adjusted, were getting used to the new situation, and had taken precautions to Uhllrich's disclosures when Bailung came out with his news. This put all and everything in a new light again. How to react now? It would be internationally damaging to retract from the court case of Uhllrich in Nagaland. That was clear! Although, now that there had not been an assassination? Now that it was apparent the Indian secret services were not involved whatsoever, the Naga uprising was off. On the other hand the damage to the Indian stand on subduing the Nagas was done and gained momentum. It could soon lead to more exposure on the conflict, the cabinet of ministers presided over by the Prime Minister feared. Still, it was too late to withdraw the permission to have the court case in Nagaland for the whole world to see.

"We may have to ease down on the Nagas and review our policies on the Northeast as a whole," the Prime Minister began the emergency meeting.

"Do you think we should come up with a compromise so we show we are not ill willed and the international community will be satisfied," Patill asked.

"I do not think it would harm India, not when we explain their unique history to the Indian populace and make that a known fact. I don't think most Indians know or care about the conflict anyway," the Prime Minister smiled, "perhaps we can lead India out of this conflict. It is costly anyway, right," he said and looked at the Defense Minister who reacted immediately.

"It is tremendously costly," he answered, "I am sure that money could be spent well elsewhere indeed. Just to keep 200.000 soldiers equipped, fed, housed and salaried, not to mention our losses, a figure we never disclosed, but it comes to a staggering amount."

"Yes," the Minister for development cut in. The thought alone what I could do with this money to turn the Northeast into a jump off board and economic power house for South East Asia, is enlightening. This would contribute greatly to our fast growing economy anyway," he smiled.

"We could finally implement the Look East policy," the Home Minister contributed.

"So, what will we do with all these other peoples in the Northeast who want to be independent," the Home Minister asked.

"Let's make a gesture and talk to all of them. Not all want to be independent. The Boro of Assam for instance favor autonomy but within the Indian Constitution. And, let's face it; we did not treat the Nagas very well. If I were a Naga I would trust the India very much either," the Prime Minister laughed.

"We might be in trouble with all our opponents, the hawks in our own party plus the opposition will question us for selling out India to some tribal people. They will accuse us of selling out the legacy of Jawarhlal Nehru, our predecessor," Patill remarked.

"True but we could explain and defend our stand and given the international pressure I am sure we could convince them," the Prime Minister retorted.

"You could try," the Home Minister said, "but I assure you, you won't get far and you know it."

"Yeah, but then we can show our people too that Nehru made some minor mistakes which led to this war nobody really wants. He said crushing the Nagas is a matter of days and that he would never let the Nagas go free," The Prime Minister remarked.

"He was angry and haughty for he said even 'when the rivers will run red with blood and India falls to pieces, I will never let the Nagas be independent', or words to that effect," Patill added, "and here we are, the Nagas are still not subdued. Yes, it should come to an end. It has taken long enough; why not form of a federation? We know the Nagas are not ill willed; they just want to rule themselves. They don't want to be under India, for they fear they will be dominated by us and we all know their fear is justified," Patill concluded, but for the Prime Minister who came with a line to be remembered

"I think we have been too long in the twilight with the Nagas," he said, "it is time to go beyond that."

"Beyond twilight?", Patill asked.

"Sixty years of twilight," the Prime Minister smiled, "let's take a few giant steps and go beyond it. Let's speed through the night and start afresh at daybreak, agreed?"

"Beyond twilight," the Home Minister repeated, "yeah I like it we must try and communicate this with all our might. A new era now beyond twilight has begun."

Now that decided the trial could take place in Nagaland, the international community closely watching, finally real talks for peace could commence.

Sean and Jacky were informed after they heard the news they were summoned to appear at the trial as witnesses. It was not decided if and where they were to be taken to court but it appeared both were going to be extradited to their respective countries. Jacky in jail alone had time to think; her life in shambles but with a glimpse of hope she considered how she had fallen for Sean's call to assassinate this unknown man. Foolish she had been for though fallen for this man and because of it able to come close to him she had also decided to do it because of the adventure. She had been a nut, she realized. Her life had been promising, not only was she an educated woman but attractive too. Why then did she decide to be part of this high class bordello? Well, for sensational experiences of course and she had had them. Impressed with the high rollers and being in command while giving and sharing in style had this had kept her going till she met Sean. The reserved Sean who like so many men, was not exactly after her, had captivated her attention. She knew he was in command. He did not boast, but was dependable. Jacky was attracted to because of this mentality. He was also open yet enigmatic, demanding yet courteous, convincing yet understanding and had kept his distance. Though he never mentioned it, she felt he found her too shallow to relate to. Unconsciously she wanted to prove herself to him and so when he had come up with the idea, at first she thought he wanted to test her. When he had asked her how far she would go in trying to achieve what she was really after, she answered him: 'for the right purpose and with the right motivation I would go all out.' He had looked at her, thinking. Days afterwards he had produced this proposition and she had not been able to refuse. But she could not blindly murder a man without knowing its purpose. So, he had explained the background. Perhaps it was only the third time they had talked to each other in depth but she realized new relationship was forming. Though for her not a point Jack knew Sean was now indebted.. The point was Sean's reservations were melting. They could talk and relate knowing they had things in common. When they could come together in mind then they could express themselves in body too. Their simmering love, had taken flight and from then on they were a team, inseparable. In this prison in Rio she had come to the conclusion both Sean and she had been extremely lucky for Bailung had saved them from a terrible mistake. Though Jacky understood how mentally cornered Sean had felt when coerced by the Uhllrich. 'From bad to worse', Sean had said before she left for Manila, 'but now only our love will keep us sane' and that had strengthened her. Then it happened, on the recommendations of the UN and YNPO Jacky and Sean were released taken to be taken India so they could appear at the trial to testify against Uhllrich.

In Nagaland and with Sean by her side, Bai had joined them. Bai too was released to face possible charges later and she felt elated with the turn of events initiated by him, By disobeying he provided them with a possible future.

And Jeanie? How did Jeanie fare after Marius found out she was deployed by Uhllrich to get to Sean? Well, in the presence of Uhllrich who did not disclose how he had been able to persuade her, he said it was too personal, Marius absolved her. Nobody but Marius knew about her involvement anyway, so after ample consideration and talking to both of them he decided to let her off the hook.

Epilogue

Musdachin with some representatives of UNPO was traveling to Nagaland. While changing planes in Delhi they met with Marius and Shilu, who with some security people had been assigned to guide Uhllrich to Nagaland. In Dimapur thousands of Nagas had flocked to the airport to welcome the group. From Manila Bailung had been given permission to travel with Eddie to Nagaland and even Sean and Jacky, though not free yet, were accompanied to Nagaland too, both as observers and as defendants. In their wake all sorts of journalist had followed and the planes to Dimapur had been fully booked. Extra planes had be to added to the normal frequencies and it was on one of those packed ones Shilu had smiled while poking Marius:

"You know a 60 year old twilight has gone through darkness, the dark soul now in the light, I think Marius to take Sean, Bailung and Jacky to Nagaland as witnesses was a golden idea. Now the eyes of the world will be on Nagaland and I am sure the Indian leaders are biting their tongues wondering how this could have happened!"

Marius smiled and let her rave on about her twilight she was going beyond and answered:

"You know, the Indians when they have swallowed their pride may just come to know how gentle and cooperative the Nagas can be. They will be much better off being close to them, but with them independent than with the Nagas in India and holding grudges against them. In the event the Nagas would agree to be within the union, there will always be resurrections, don't you think?"

"There will always be Nagas who oppose to be part of India and will not consent, just like the leaders did when they opposed the Shillong Accord," she agreed.

"So, the bygones can be bygones and a new Indian Naga relationship can begin when we have all this behind us?", Marius looked ahead.

"I think it could be, but we are not there yet Marius," Shilu said thoughtfully, "we do not know if the Indians have something in their back pockets. In the past they have always had some surprise coming to us."

"With the eyes of the world on them now do you actually think they would dare to pull some tricks again Shilu?", Marius asked.

"Yes things are different, you could be right Marius," Shilu said squeezing his hand.

An hour later they landed in the to Marius now familiar Dimapur airport and were taken to Kohima by friends, then to village beyond town. When they arrived there the village had been taken over occupied by the press, people of academic standard, politicians and yes tourists now too. The atmosphere was gay, the police only present unobtrusively, the Armed Forces far away and the Assam Rifles laid low too.

"Marvelous how this was organized, a while village cooperating!", Marius exclaimed. I am curious to know how the council will go about it. I am sure you know Shilu, but with the whole wide world watching and done in the open this could be quite a pressure on the council members?"

"Yeah, I think undeterred they will go to the bottom of the case and judge it then pass verdict on what is prescribed by our customary laws. There will be no revenge in the sense that it has been a leader who was supposed to be slain."

"The press can be a powerful force. What about the Indians are they not going meddle by pressuring council members, either with threats or bags full of money?"

"It is all possible but now not very likely, darling. They too have the eyes of the world on them. I think they understood the message that a faux pas will land them into much more trouble this time, trouble they cannot anticipate how big that will be," Shilu said.

They went about the grounds greeting the villagers, visited the makeshift places for people and visitors to stay in and went over to Shilu's friends who arranged their sleeping quarters too. When Bailung arrived with Swu the chairman of the Naga forces a roar went through the crowd. They were welcomed like genuine celebrities.

"This is remarkable," Marius said as he saw Celia on Bai's arm, visibly touched she was by the warm welcome, "have they forgotten he idea was to assassinate your leader Swu?"

"You may be right, but they do admire him for having had the courage not to do it of course," she laughed.

Then they saw Jacky walking in, more attractive than ever, radiating with Sean by her. There were also greeted but when the crowd saw Jacky, the woman who actually had pulled the trigger on a defenseless man the boooooo's sounded too. Not too seriously though for all had come to a good ending. It was only that Jacky, Sean and Uhllrich had known nothing about it and the crowd sensed it was those three would had gone through with it. Knowing too that Sean and Jacky had been coerced as they had read about the Rwanda massacre with Bailung and Sean and Jacky had done it out of love, the admiration for doing something significant gained the upper hand. Lots of people poured in: Indian ministers, scholars, and of course scores of journalists. It looked like Nagaland was taken over by stranger. This was all too much for Marius and Shilu and they decided to retreat to enjoy the fresh mountain air. They climbed up to face the light of day and while looking down and around and now, a fair distance below them, they saw the gathering crowd. From all corners people had come, also Nagas from the different tribes, looking proud in their traditional attires, colorful and respectful. And they smiled as they looked over the hills far and beyond. The light of day was clear. Marius zoomed in coming closer to Shilu, looking into her dark brown eyes and whispered:

"Your Nagaland here, now, overlooking Shilu, it is that I feel we join forever."

"I am at home our hearts are joined," Shilu whispered as twilight had broken, their personal twilight too. Marius felt his blood surging feeling one:

"Nothing can separate us now, not anymore, he said."

"Yeah," she reacted, "we are beyond twilight, no more word my Marius, and a new era has begun!"

